Advance Praise for *The Deadly Scrolls*

"In this thriller, Ellen Frankel has created a fine cast of Jerusalem types—corrupt antiquities hawkers, end-of-days preachers, scholars of the obscure past, and lost innocents abroad—but the true star is her detective, daring intelligence agent and conflicted single mom Maya Rimon. You won't stop turning the page."

—Gershom Gorenberg, author of *War of Shadows: Codebreakers, Spies, and the Secret Struggle to Drive the Nazis from the Middle East*

"An exciting thriller from which one can learn a tremendous amount about the world of the Dead Sea Scrolls and the academic community that researches them."

—Lawrence Schiffman, Judge Abraham Lieberman Professor of Hebrew and Judaic Studies at New York University and author of *Reclaiming the Dead Sea Scrolls*

THE
DEADLY
SCROLLS

The Jerusalem Mysteries, Book One

ELLEN FRANKEL

WICKED SON

A WICKED SON BOOK
An Imprint of Post Hill Press
ISBN: 978-1-63758-934-2

The Deadly Scrolls
© 2022 by Ellen Frankel
All Rights Reserved

First Wicked Son Hardcover Edition: May 2022

Cover Design by Tiffani Shea

Post Hill Press
New York • Nashville
posthillpress.com

Published in the United States of America
1 2 3 4 5 6 7 8 9 10

To Larry Schiffman who introduced me to the Dead Sea Scrolls

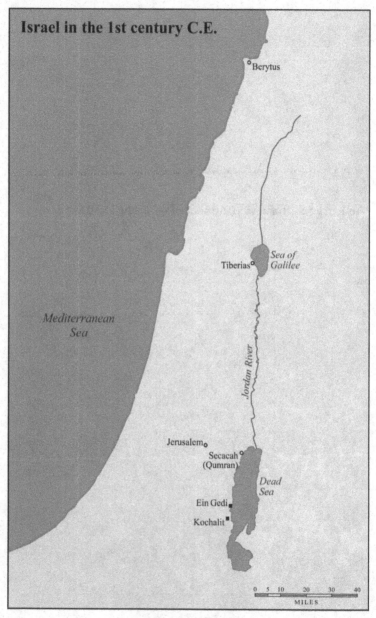

Israel in the 1st century C.E.

Berytus

Mediterranean
Sea

Sea of
Galilee

Tiberias

Jordan River

Jerusalem

Secacah
(Qumran)

Dead
Sea

Ein Gedi

Kochalit

0 5 10   20   30   40
MILES

Credit: Mapping Specialists Ltd.

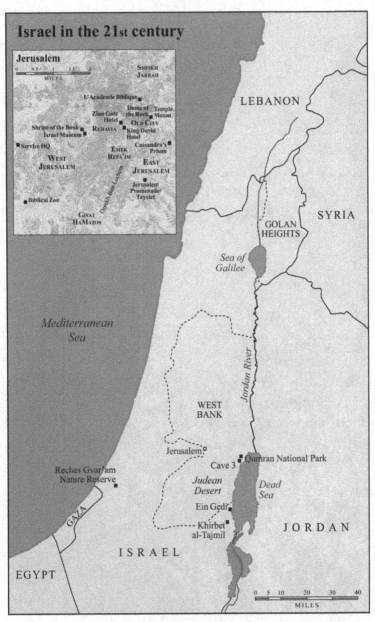

Israel in the 21st century

Jerusalem

0   0.5   1   1.5   2
MILES

SHEIKH
JARRAH

L'Academie Biblique

Zion Gate   Dome of   Temple
Hotel   the Rock   Mount
                   OLD CITY
Shrine of the Book   REHAVIA   King David
Israel Museum   Hotel

Service HQ   Cassandra's
                                 Prison
            EMEK   EAST
WEST   REFA'IM   JERUSALEM
JERUSALEM
                             Jerusalem
                             Promenade/
                             Tayelet
Biblical Zoo

        GIVAT
        HaMATOS

LEBANON

SYRIA

GOLAN
HEIGHTS

*Sea of
Galilee*

*Mediterranean
Sea*

Jordan River

WEST
BANK

Jerusalem

Cave 3   Qumran National Park

Reches Gvar'am
Nature Reserve

*Judean
Desert*   *Dead
                 Sea*

Ein Gedi

Khirbet   JORDAN
al-Tajmil

ISRAEL

EGYPT

0 5 10   20   30   40
MILES

GAZA

Timeline of Ancient Jewish History

1000 BCE	David unifies the Twelve Tribes, making Jerusalem his capital; his son Solomon builds the First Temple
975 BCE	The Kingdom splits under David's grandson into Israel (in the north) and Judah (in the south)
722 BCE	Assyria conquers the Northern Kingdom and exiles Ten Tribes
586 BCE	Babylonia conquers the Southern Kingdom and exiles most of the Jews to Babylon
538 BCE	Cyrus the Great of Persia permits the Jewish exiles to return to Israel
515 BCE	Second Temple built in Jerusalem
332 BCE	Alexander defeats the Persian Empire; Israel comes under Greek rule
164 BCE	The Maccabees drive out the Greeks; Israel ruled by their Hellenized descendants, the Hasmoneans
134-104 BCE	Qumran (Secacah) established in Judean Desert; Dead Sea Scrolls written
63 BCE	Rome conquers the Greek Empire and imposes Roman rule over Israel

66 CE	Jews in the Galilee rebel against Roman rule; the Jewish wars begin
68 CE	Vespasian becomes Caesar; his son Titus finishes the war; Qumran is destroyed
69 CE	Siege of Jerusalem begins
70 CE	Jerusalem falls to Rome; Second Temple destroyed; Jews exiled
73 CE	Masada, the last Jewish stronghold, falls to Roman army
135 CE	Jews rebel against Rome, led by Bar Kochba; Rome puts down revolt

DAY 1

Monday

DAY 1

_____

philosophy

1

FOUR DAYS AFTER SHE BEGAN working at the Zion Gate Hotel in West Jerusalem, a nineteen-year-old Palestinian chambermaid named A'isha Jamal discovered the lifeless body of Professor Boaz Goldmayer lying on the bathroom floor of room 527. It was the beginning of her early morning shift. She and her friend Maryam had been assigned to clean and make up the rooms on the fifth and sixth floors of the hotel. Their boss, a humorless, middle-aged Jewish woman with enormous teeth named Sarah Shtern, had instructed them to be extra careful not to disturb anything placed on the desks or bureaus in these particular rooms. The scholars attending the conference at the hotel would complain if any of their important papers or electronic devices were tampered with.

As soon as A'isha opened the door to room 527, she sensed that something was wrong. There were papers scattered all over the carpeted floor. A few thin white computer cables lay on the desk, unattached to any electronic device, but the smooth black surface of the desk was otherwise empty. On the floor to the right of the queen-sized bed lay a thick white electrical cord, stretched out like a dead snake. The purple and gold lamé bedspread had not been disturbed. Gold-wrapped chocolate squares still lay on the smooth pillow shams.

Then, the smell hit her: an unpleasant odor, reminding her of the fetid stink of mouse droppings that hung around her father's goat pens. It got stronger when she neared the bathroom. That's when she saw the room's occupant sprawled on the white tiled floor. A wet stain darkened the old man's pants between his legs and pooled on the white tiles. His glasses lay broken beside him on the floor. She was glad there was no blood.

Perhaps he had died of a stroke or a heart attack? But the scattered papers suggested foul play.

She dropped the tall pile of freshly laundered towels and sheets onto the bed. Then, she lifted the receiver of the black telephone on the night table and pushed zero. Koby picked up right away.

"Front desk. How can I help you?"

"This A'isha. Guest...."

She paused. Her mind drew a blank. What was the Hebrew word for "died?" Or "got sick?" Though A'isha had been born in Israel, her Hebrew was patchy. The shock of seeing the dead man in the bathroom had rattled her so much that she couldn't summon up the words she needed.

"*Nu?*"

"Guest," A'isha repeated. Her voice quavered. "Please. Security. *Beetakhon.*"

Like most Palestinians working in Israel, A'isha knew that Hebrew word only too well.

2

FIVE MINUTES LATER, YOEL GINSBERG, head of the hotel's security staff, arrived accompanied by two of his men. He questioned A'isha in Arabic, then dismissed her to continue her work. She fled the room, leaving the towels and bed linens strewn on the bed.

Careful not to disturb anything, Yoel quickly examined the body, declaring the man "as dead as a shoe." He walked through the large bedroom, stepping gingerly over the scattered papers and the detached power cord on the floor. Then, he speed-dialed the Jerusalem District Police on his mobile.

"Tell Levine we got a suspicious death at the Zion Gate. An American professor. Room 527. I'll stay with the body 'til she gets here."

As soon as he disconnected, Ziggy Dweck was in his ear.

"Mind if I go downstairs for a minute? I'd rather not take a crap in front of the dead guy."

Yoel looked at his new hire with undisguised irritation. Although Ziggy had come to him highly recommended, Yoel had his doubts about the young man. He disappeared too often while on duty, citing "irritable bowel issues." He'd give the guy a few more weeks to settle in. If he couldn't measure up to the job by then, Yoel would have no problem firing him. In the upscale hotel business, professional security was as important as fresh linen and premium cable.

"Make it quick, Dweck!"

Ziggy left the room and headed down the corridor. He took the elevator to the floor below, then ducked into an empty guest room.

Closing the door behind him, he pulled out his mobile phone.

"Roni? It's Ziggy. You were right to send me over here to snoop around. For once, the chatter we intercepted was legit. Got a dead body here. An American scholar. Laptop's gone. Room trashed. Might be worth looking into."

"Okay, nose around," said Roni. "But be discreet. Steer clear of the police. This is their turf. Who caught the case?"

"Chief Inspector Sarit Levine."

Roni chuckled.

"Then be extra careful, *motek*. She bites." Smoke from his cigarette hissed in Ziggy's ear. "Maybe I'll unleash Maya Rimon on her. Let the two harpies claw each other's eyes out."

The two women were like Siamese twins, he thought to himself, *competing for a single blood supply.*

Ziggy hung up, pocketed his phone, and hurried back to room 527. He reached the door just moments before Sarit Levine and her team barged into the room. Yoel's scowl barely had time to twist into a forced smile before the diminutive police detective barked at him to get out of her way and let the experts take over.

Ziggy spun on his heels and joined the rest of his team in their hasty retreat.

3

IT WAS ALMOST ELEVEN WHEN Maya Rimon arrived at Service Headquarters. Today was supposed to be her day off, but Roni had called, saying they had a "situation." She needed to report in ASAP.

Maya's parents had offered to take her three-year-old daughter Vered for the day, but they'd balked at letting her bring her new kitten to their fancy apartment. Vered had thrown a tantrum.

Maya's mother, Camille, had sniffed and wriggled her large nose. "What a stupid idea to give that child a *bezoona* for her birthday! And a black one, no less! But that's Rafi for you! My Jeddah used to say that witches and djinns can turn themselves into black cats—"

"Oh, cut it out, Camille!" Maya's father, Moti, had sliced the air with the side of his hand. "We're living in the 21st century, for God's sake! Enough with the Moroccan fairy tales!"

In the end, they'd capitulated. But only this once, because it was Vered's birthday. After that, the kitten stayed home.

Maya's office at the Service, a shadowy branch of Israeli Intelligence that conducted special investigations with potentially serious political ramifications, was located in a three-story apartment house in the middle of a residential section of West Jerusalem. Like many buildings in this neighborhood, the architecture was a blend of European and Ottoman styles, with massive iron gates, a spacious first floor front hall, wrought-iron balconies, painted shutters, and a domed roof. Behind the building was a fenced-in garden. Like many similar 19th century structures, this one had suffered neglect over the years. And it would remain in this state of partial disrepair; the Service specialized in avoiding notice.

Maya walked up to the building's wrought-iron front gates and stood there for a moment, her strong hands grasping the sinuous vertical bars, hesitating.

She closed her eyes and visualized her little daughter at her parents' apartment, spending yet another birthday without her mother. She thought of her own birthdays as a child. Being the center of all that adult attention, the presents, the candy, the special Meskouta sponge cake with chocolate icing that her Moroccan mother baked for each of their birthdays, and the fun she'd had with all her cousins. But now, all Maya could think about was how stressful Vered's birthday party would be, her mother smothering Vered with presents and food, then sniping at her husband, who would sit on the couch smoldering in morose silence. Her stomach twisted into a knot.

She opened her eyes and looked up at the building's stone façade, wondering if anyone was watching her. As usual, the tall, thick windows were dark.

If someone had been looking down at that moment, they would have seen a petite young woman, with a dense mane of curly red hair the color of sun-drenched rust. As she peered up at the building's top floor, her auburn eyebrows arched delicately over green eyes flecked with gold; eyes that turned an unsettled color, like disturbed silt on the ocean floor, in dim light. When her features were smooth as they were now, she seemed younger than her thirty-two years, but when she gazed at someone, especially a rival or a foe, with an intense stare or with hostility, her age was indeterminate. At those moments she assumed an air of mystery, even of menace.

Maya broke free of her reverie and leaned forward to push the gate open. But before the gate gave way, she was startled by the shrill whine of a siren speeding in her direction.

The yellow ambulance, marked with the characteristic red stripe of Magen David Adom, Israel's Red Cross, screeched to a halt directly across the street from where Maya stood. Two male medics in white uniforms sprang out of the back of the ambulance. One carried a small medical kit.

The two men raced into the two-story building. Moments later, they emerged, holding an agitated young man between them. The youth was thin to the point of emaciation. His dark hair was tangled in long dreadlocks, and a black beard reached down to the middle of his chest. He wore a long gray robe, which hung loosely on him like a collapsed parachute.

Grunting, swinging his shaggy head from side to side, he struggled to free himself. But his movements were futile; the medics held him firmly in their grip. Giving up his struggle, he started to scream.

"You can't hold me! I am the resurrected Christ! I've come back to redeem the world! Tell your corrupt leaders that their earthly powers are at an end! Release me before the Lord strikes you down!"

A window suddenly shot open on the building's second floor. A middle-aged woman wearing a flowered housedress, her blonde hair festooned in curlers, thrust out her head. Her heavy accent betrayed her origins in the American south.

"I'm so sorry, Kyle! But I don't got no choice. You done become a danger to yourself!"

The young man swiveled his head to stare up at the speaker. His jaw fell slack. His eyes bulged out of their sockets.

It was only then that Maya noticed Kyle's bare feet. Both were covered in blood. Jutting out of the top of his left foot was a large metal spike.

"Whore of Babylon!" he shouted up at the woman in the window. "Judas!"

A third medic now emerged from inside the ambulance. In one hand, she held a hypodermic syringe, which she proceeded to jab into Kyle's arm. Within seconds, he slumped forward. The two medics caught him before he fell.

They dragged him over to the ambulance, his bleeding feet leaving a thin red line on the white pavement. With the help of their female colleague, the two men lifted him up into the back of the vehicle, then slammed shut the double doors.

The woman in the window wailed, "Don't you worry none, Kyle! Those Jew doctors will fix you right up. Then, I'll take you on home."

The ambulance sped away, lights flashing but its siren mute.

Shaking her fist at the retreating ambulance, the woman in the window shouted, "Damn that crazy preacher! He done poisoned your mind!"

The woman pulled her head back inside and slammed down the window with a loud thunk.

On her side of the street, Maya stood watching until the yellow and red vehicle disappeared around the corner. Then, she turned around and slowly pushed open the iron gate to Service Headquarters.

4

Roni Qattawi caught sight of Maya as she came in.

He was a small man, thin and wiry but unusually muscular, especially in his upper arms. His dark eyes, stony like burnt olive pits, were set too close together in his bullet-shaped head. He had a thin, sharp wedge of a nose. He was dark-complexioned, and his small teeth were stained by too much black tea. But his most prominent feature was the large diamond-shaped port-wine stain on his left cheek. His mother always blamed herself for this blemish, persuaded by the Egyptian superstition that a pregnant woman who doesn't appease her cravings would bear a child with such a hideous birthmark. Even now, Mrs. Qattawi overindulged in *basbusa* at the end of festival meals.

Roni was sitting at his large wooden desk in his office at the far end of the giant room, looking out over the central section of the floor, which was bordered on both sides by glassed-in offices. She was too far away for him to see her face clearly, but he knew she was staring back at him. He could almost hear her mind clicking like an abacus.

Maya strode confidently across the floor toward Roni, hiking up her shoulders, clenching her jaw. She stopped in his open doorway.

"*Nu*, what's so important that it couldn't wait 'til tomorrow?"

"A homicide at the Zion Gate Hotel," said Roni. "An American professor. Attending some kind of conference there."

"Not our problem. The Jerusalem District Police will handle it."

Roni shook his head. "The Israel Antiquities Authority has asked us to step in. The crime might involve the theft of Jewish antiquities. Possibly a newly discovered Dead Sea Scroll. Don't know all the details yet."

Maya felt her heart racing, her pulse speeding up. Here was her chance to make up for the mess she'd made of her last case! What did the Americans call it? A "do-over."

But Roni immediately put the kibosh on such fantasies.

"Arik Ophir thinks the whole thing's complete bullshit. If it were really that important, IAA wouldn't be giving away the case so quickly. He thinks they just want to stick it to the Jerusalem Police for interfering in that ossuary *balagan* last year. What a fiasco!"

"Or it could be just the tip of the iceberg."

Roni grabbed Maya's shoulders, squeezing so hard she yelped and broke free. She stared at him with undisguised irritation.

"Hey, cool it, Roni!"

"No, you cool it, Rimon! Didn't you learn anything from your last screw-up?"

Maya drew in a deep breath and blew it out. Would that bungled case haunt her for the rest of her career?

Maya shook out her shoulders, then crossed her arms. She thought about sitting down in the wooden chair across from Roni but decided to remain standing. Being a short man, Roni was especially sensitive about the angle of a person's gaze.

"I still say we missed something when we were at the LTM Center the last time," she said. "My gut tells me we shut down that investigation too soon. If you hadn't nixed my interview with—"

Roni balled his right hand into a fist and smacked it into the opposite palm.

"That's enough, Maya! You're just like your father. Always gunning to land the Big One. You just don't know when to quit, do you?"

She hated to admit it, but Roni had a point. On that last case, she'd almost ended her career before it had even started. Although Maya had only recently been promoted to field agent, Roni had assigned her to a high-profile case involving Christian extremists, who called themselves the LTM, Liberators of the Temple Mount.

She knew that he'd expected her to botch the investigation. And thereby hasten her exit from the Service.

Which she did. True to form, she blew off protocol.

When her confidential informant had told her powdered explosives were being manufactured at the LTM Center in East Jerusalem, she'd immediately suspected a terrorist conspiracy. Before obtaining hard evidence, she'd pressured Roni into engaging their whole team in a complicated sting. But it had turned out that the suspected "explosives" were just reproductions of ancient temple incense. The Service was lucky that Arik Ophir, the newly appointed Minister of Internal Security, had convinced the director of the LTM Center not to sue them. And it was also lucky that they'd managed to keep it out of the papers.

Maya stomped her foot on the concrete floor, raising a plume of dust.

"Just lay off me, Roni! I've got a lot on my plate at the moment."

Maya took a deep breath. *Better learn to control your temper, girl. You can't afford to lose this job.* Not when her ex was threatening to sue for sole custody. She had to hold onto Vered. Her daughter and her work, that was all that mattered. If she were to lose them both...

Maya looked down at her boss, who was now lighting a cigarette. He tossed the spent match to the floor. He drew in a lungful of smoke, held it briefly, then blew out several perfect smoke rings, which rose slowly into the air and dissipated.

Maya's gaze settled on Roni's ears, which were unusually small, their dark rims wrinkled like dried apricots. Dark bristles sprouted out of his ears like chia grass. She closed her eyes, took a deep breath, then opened her eyes and smiled.

"Sorry. I'm just upset 'cause I had a nasty run-in with my ex this morning. Over my daughter's birthday party."

Roni blew another perfect smoke ring toward the ceiling.

She wasn't surprised that he ignored her appeal for sympathy. Her boss was singularly indifferent to his agents' personal affairs, especially their domestic troubles.

"The Jerusalem Police are already on the scene," Roni said. "The ME's doing a preliminary post. Go see what you can find out."

"Who's the lead on the case?"

"An old friend of yours." Roni grinned. "Sarit Levine."

Maya conjured up the face of her old army buddy. They'd been stationed together at the beginning of their military service. Bored to tears in their remote Negev outpost, they'd passed the time playing chess and Go, or stumping each other with abstruse brain-teasers. They'd strongly bonded over their shared ambition to pursue a career in Israeli military intelligence, following in their fathers' footsteps. But afterwards, they'd drifted apart. Maya had attended Hebrew University in Jerusalem; Sarit, the Technion, Israel's MIT. When they'd met up after graduation to take the qualifying exams for the Service, they'd quickly recognized that their friendship wasn't as strong as their rivalry for the single position the spy bureau had open at that time.

Once Maya had landed the job, they'd cut off all ties. She hoped they could behave professionally on this case, but she was ready to play hardball if she had to.

"You okay with this assignment?" asked Roni.

"Sure, why not? I'll get over there now."

"No heroics, okay? Just get the evidence. Arik's probably right that it's all bullshit."

5

THE CROWD THAT GATHERED AT the high school basketball court in East Jerusalem was small. Less than a hundred men, women, and children. But then this was only a rehearsal, not the real thing. The authentic sacrifice would take place, God willing, soon after the blood moon. The time and place of the rehearsal had not been made public. Yet a hundred people had still shown up, alerted by word of mouth. They now strained against the chain-link fence surrounding the black-topped ball court. Eager, nervous, expectant.

The run-through began with a lecture delivered by a noted authority on ancient sacrificial practices during the Second Temple period. Then came a short video, projected on the white outside wall of the high school. The video dramatized the ancient pilgrimage of a Jewish family traveling to Jerusalem to offer an animal for sacrifice on the Temple altar.

By now, many of the children had become restless. Quietly, they snuck away from their parents to seek out perches on balconies and in trees, where they could get a good view of what they'd come to see. An animal giving its life in the service of God. The spilling of real blood.

The crowd hushed. Even the children, looking down upon the scene, fell dumb, sensing the awesomeness of the moment.

A priest-in-training, wearing a white robe and a puffy white cap, now appeared on the blacktop. He led a small, frightened lamb on a rope leash into the center of the basketball court. Then, a second man stepped forward. He wore a white medical coat and dark pants. Carefully, he inspected the animal for blemishes. When he nodded his head to indicate that the lamb was acceptable for sacrifice, the crowd cheered. Smiling, he nodded toward the crowd and walked off the court.

The priest then drew from inside his robe a sharp knife, whose blade glinted in the bright sun. Quickly, he drew it across the lamb's throat, releasing a stream of bright red blood, which spurted like a garden hose. A second priest-in-training now ran toward the dying lamb, carrying a gold cup with a long handle. Grasping the handle with both hands, he skillfully angled the cup to catch the gushing blood.

Because it was only a rehearsal, the organizers hadn't felt it necessary to erect an authentic facsimile of the Temple altar. Instead, they'd hastily assembled a large square wooden structure mounted on cinder blocks, with a long wooden ramp, painted white, leading up to it. The first priest now walked slowly up the ramp, carrying the gold cup by its handle. When he reached the top, he walked the perimeter of the makeshift stone altar, sprinkling the lamb's blood on all four of its corners.

He then descended the ramp and walked over to the slaughtered lamb. With expert precision and speed, he skinned the animal, removing the organs and body parts that in former times had been designated to be consumed on the altar. Holding these bloody pieces of meat between both hands, he walked around the inside perimeter of the fence. The enraptured crowd looked on in wonder.

When he'd finished the circuit, he laid the organs down at one edge of the macadam court and returned to the eviscerated lamb. He gently lifted it up in his arms. Solemnly, he carried the small body up the ramp and placed it on the flaming altar. The smell of roasting meat wafted over the crowd.

Using special tongs, he then lifted the blackened carcass from the fire and carried it back down the ramp. Two more white-robed priests came forward and quickly cut the charred body into tiny pieces, each about the size of an olive. The roasted morsels were distributed to the waiting crowd, who shoved and jostled to grab a piece of the holy offering. The children, who had been watching the ceremony from their high perches, now scrambled down to the ground and ran over to the fence, but they were too late. The scrawny lamb had not been able to feed the entire multitude.

As the spectators licked their lips and guzzled water from plastic bottles, the lead priest held up his hands for silence. In a few moments, nothing could be heard except for a few birds chirping in the nearby cypress trees.

"In four days, the blood moon will appear. That is the moment that the Anointed One will make himself known. The End is near. Prepare yourselves!"

In the continuing silence, he and the other white-robed men walked over to a white stretch limousine parked just outside the chain-link fence. For a few moments, they spoke with someone inside the vehicle. During this time, the spectators remained frozen in place. Even the birds ceased to sing. Then, the window glided shut, and the limousine drove off.

The crowd slowly dispersed, speaking in whispers.

Moments later, the bloody sinews, organs, and head of the lamb disappeared under a murder of crows, which descended upon them to feast. When they flew off, all that remained on the black macadam was a bright red stain.

6

THE MAN KNEW HE WAS paying too much for this cramped studio apartment in an unsavory section of East Jerusalem, but it met his needs. He needed privacy, as little foot traffic as possible, and an air conditioner. But no access to the internet. He would download whatever the girl needed in his own apartment and bring it to her on a flash drive.

As the girl set up her workspace, he watched her carefully.

Cassandra Sucher, the oddest young American he'd ever encountered. With her short, spiked lavender hair, pierced eyebrows, lips, and nasal septum, purple eye makeup, and lipstick, he'd worried that she would be loud and insolent. But it turned out to be just the opposite. She refused to make eye contact. Her high-pitched voice barely rose above a whisper. She was like a robot: indefatigable, single-minded, with the focus of a ninja. Her watery hazel eyes focused on the screen like twin highbeams, her wide brow furrowed like a shar pei.

She wore ragged jean cut-offs and a tee shirt declaring war on non-geeks. She wore unusual sandals, more fitting for a Roman centurion than a twenty-first century American girl, her thin ankles and calves crisscrossed tightly by long leather thongs. He noted that her toenails were painted glittery purple.

If she removed all the metal piercings and purple makeup masking her face, he thought, *she would probably be a pretty girl.* He wondered how old she was. Probably not even twenty-five.

First, she positioned Goldmayer's MacBook Pro precisely in the center of the wide wooden desk. She then inserted a cable into one of the USB ports, which connected the laptop to an external backup drive. She attached a second cable to a port on the other side, which hooked into a removable storage access utility. He'd thought a thumb drive would have been adequate for storing a copy of the decrypted files, but she'd insisted on a detachable drive.

She knelt on the floor and plugged the laptop's power cord into the six-outlet power strip. Seated back at the desk, she bent over the keyboard and began to type. Her thin fingers flew over the white letters. It reminded the man of his mother at her loom; how deftly she pitched the shuttle across the warp threads. As she worked, the girl swiveled back and forth in the overpriced ergonomic chair she'd made him buy for her. Perched atop her spiky purple hair were expensive Bose wireless headphones that she claimed she needed in order to "focus." *These spoiled Americans!* He prayed she wasn't just joyriding, imagining his pockets as bottomless wells.

A sleek halogen desk lamp cast a halo of light on her work surface. From its elbowed arm dangled a Native American dreamcatcher. In one corner of the desk sat a round blue ceramic incense holder, with a white lotus flower in its center.

What a strange young woman, traveling the world in search of enlightenment. He simply couldn't figure her out. Not that he needed to. As long as she decrypted the professor's files, he didn't care if she believed in shaytan and djinns.

Threading her fingers through her short-cropped hair, the girl took a sip of her tea, brewed in the Keurig machine she'd also made him buy, together with an assortment of green and herbal teas and fair trade coffees. She had insisted on drinking from her own mug. "Handcrafted in Nepal and shlepped across half a continent."

When she finished her tea, she slipped off the headphones and set them down on the desk. Out of the cushioned earpieces came female voices droning in a singsong hum.

"I eat the same thing every day for breakfast," she had informed him. "Asparagus, carrots, and sprouts. Organic. Chia seeds would be nice, but I can do without them for a few days. I make my own dressings. Lemon juice, Dijon mustard, raw honey, and extra-virgin olive oil. Fresh fruit salad for lunch. But go light on the citrus. Not great for my stomach. For dinner, miso soup with extra-firm tofu and ginger root. And brown rice. For a beverage, I'd prefer fresh carrot juice, but any kind of vegetable juice is fine. No additives."

Allah laenatan laha! Where was he going to find such things in East Jerusalem? She would eat what he brought her.

He took another long look at the girl. How could he have hired someone like her for such an important assignment? A flowerchild. A poor lost soul. She was probably mentally unstable. Despite what she'd told him, he didn't trust her. Well, she'd better live up to her vaunted reputation as a decrypting genius. Because his fortune was now inextricably entangled with hers.

Once again, he called to mind the single unencrypted file he had found on Goldmayer's computer. A brief entry from the professor's journal:

> *February 24: Borrowed B.R.'s jeep for a few days. Decided not to ask permission from IAA. Need to maintain maximum secrecy. Will spend 2–3 days looking for the cave. I hope De Vaux's instincts pan out. Need to check his unpublished field notes. So much is riding on this! Probably my last chance to leave my mark on the field. I'm glad Marjorie stayed home. She's too old to traipse around desert caves. David called again to urge me to encrypt all my files. If I find anything worth concealing, I'll take his advice.*

Nothing in the entry about the precise location of the cave. Nothing about the scroll. And what was this cryptic comment about "De Vaux's instincts"? He'd have to ask the monk about that.

A terrible thought suddenly seized him. What if Goldmayer hadn't succeeded in finding the scroll? What if he'd only been guessing at the cave's location? What if they'd murdered the man in vain?

But why then were all the rest of the professor's files encrypted? He must have found something worth concealing. What else could that be but the location of the scroll? Boaz Goldmayer was reputed to have the best nose in the business for sniffing out such things. The information he sought had to be in his encrypted files.

The girl looked up at him from the screen. Her eyes darted from side to side, never quite meeting his.

"I will stop by every morning and evening to bring you food. And to check on your progress." He turned to leave, then paused. "I will need to take your cell phone. For security."

She swiveled around in her chair, addressing one of the bare white walls. Her purple-lidded eyes blazed with anger.

"You can't take my phone! My whole life's on there! My apps, music, photos, contacts, passwords, Instagram, Snapchat. It's, like, my whole identity!"

He turned around slowly. His face was calm, but his voice was clipped and stern.

"I have already explained to you. We cannot risk exposure. While you are working on these files, you will not have access to the internet or to your phone. I will download anything you need and bring it to you. I am sure you can appreciate my need for caution."

"But what if I need something right away, like an upgrade of the decryption software? How am I going to reach you without phone service or Wi-Fi? It'll really slow me down!"

"Sorry. The risk is too great."

His lower lip curled over his upper in a half-hearted expression of sympathy. Turning, he walked to the apartment door, opened it, and pivoted around to face her. The girl was leaning forward in her chair, as if ready to leap at him. Her high brow furrowed. Both hands gripped the chair's padded arms.

"Oh, one more thing. In the interests of security, you will not be allowed to leave these premises until the job is done. But you need not worry. You will have everything you need. And I promise you that you will be more than amply compensated for your time and effort. See you this evening, my dear."

He stepped over the threshold and pulled the heavy wooden door shut behind him.

From his pocket, he took out a small metal padlock. He rotated the four disks to their unlocked positions and pulled open the shackle. Then, he threaded it through the hasp-and-staple assembly he'd affixed outside the door. He snapped the shackle back into the lock and spun all four disks. He tested the door. It didn't budge.

From inside, he heard her panicked footsteps running toward the door. Saw the knob turn, heard it rattle, then heard her fists pounding on the wood. Her steps receded. He heard grunts as she tried to lift each of the locked windows, which were secured on the outside by iron bars. A few moments of silence. Then, she moved on to the bathroom, testing the single window there. He heard loud sobs. Choking gulps of air. Shrieks and cursing. Then silence again. He prayed she would soon get over the theatrics and get down to work.

He needed the information in four days. At the latest.

7

LOCATED IN THE HEART OF West Jerusalem, the Zion Gate Hotel was built to resemble a fortress. But nothing about this building constructed of sparkling Jerusalem stone inspired terror in the heart of its guests. Each of its terraced roofs featured a lush subtropical landscape, with flowered vines dangling down like the famed hanging gardens of Babylon. Like its sister hotels in this Israeli chain, the Zion Gate prided itself on its elegance, contemporary décor, and exceptional cuisine. Especially its sumptuous breakfasts, which were what most guests raved about when they returned home.

One of the Zion Gate's most attractive features was its location, cradled between the historic Yemin Moshe neighborhood—with its famous Montefiore Windmill—and the walled Old City, with its bustling shuk and venerated holy places. The Zion Gate had long been a favorite of tourists, especially Americans, not only because of its comfortable accommodations, reliable security, and central location, but also because of its personalized service, which catered to the special needs of its diverse clientele. The hotel made available a Sabbath elevator and special Sabbath room keys for Orthodox Jews not wishing to use electricity on the Sabbath and holy days. For vegetarians and vegans, it offered daily options on its restaurant and room service menus. And most recently, it had made available gluten-free and sugarless snacks in the mini-mart off the main lobby. Guests were encouraged to consult with the two concierges always on duty at the reception desk, both fluent in Hebrew, English, French, and Russian. The concierges could recommend restaurants to suit every palate; suggest the best tours for families, young couples, Christian pilgrims, first time visitors, and disabled people and arrange for a rabbi's services at a moment's notice.

When Maya arrived at the Zion Gate just after 11:15 a.m., the hotel was a hive of activity. She was dressed casually in a white button-down shirt, tan slacks, and sandals. A worn brown purse hung from her shoulder. Just outside the lobby's glass doors, Arab and Jewish beggars competed with each other for handouts. Inside the lobby, tour groups clustered and dispersed. Fashionistas and souvenir merchants hawked their wares. Cell phone ringtones chimed and jangled.

Maya pushed her way through the crowd. She stretched her slender neck to give herself more height and thrust her arms forward, swimming against the tide.

She reached the bank of three elevators just off the main lobby. Her green eyes fixed on the digital displays above the closed steel doors. One of her sandaled feet tapped restlessly on the tiled floor. The numbers rose and fell, but never seemed to arrive at the ground floor.

At last, an elevator came and opened its doors.

As soon as Maya stepped into the car, the two ultra-Orthodox men inside, wearing wide-brimmed black hats, long black coats, and black pants, pressed themselves against the rear, as if fleeing contagion. Ignoring them, she jabbed the button for the fifth floor with her forefinger several times. The three of them rode up in silence. Behind her, the Orthodox men swayed back and forth and muttered under their breath. She was glad her stop came first.

Maya followed the arrows down two right-angled corridors until she came to room 527. A young Israeli policeman stood at attention outside the open door. He held a Jericho semi-automatic across his chest. He glared at her as she marched down the corridor toward him. Red crime scene tape made a large X over the open doorway. When Maya approached the door, the policeman thrust his weapon toward her, blocking her path.

"This is a crime scene," he barked in perfect, heavily accented English. "No one can enter without proper ID."

It was not surprising that the cop had mistaken her for a guest. She was dressed like a casual tourist, and she wasn't carrying her service weapon.

"Maya Rimon. With the Service. Assigned to the Goldmayer case."

The policeman seemed more surprised that she spoke Hebrew than by her disclosure that she was an Israeli intelligence agent.

"ID. Please." His tone was much softer this time. His smile, coy.

She retrieved her credentials from her purse and presented them. He examined them carefully, then detached one end of the red tape and lifted it up. She ducked under and stepped into the hotel room of Professor Boaz Goldmayer, recently deceased.

From behind her, the young policeman shouted over her head.

"Hey, Golyat! Somebody here from the Service. Tell Levine!"

Moments later, a petite woman in her mid-thirties stepped out of the bathroom and walked up to Maya. The woman was dressed in plainclothes—white button-down blouse with a Peter Pan collar, knee-length Navy blue twill skirt, and dark blue flats, which were sheathed in blue paper booties. A pair of sunglasses perched atop her sandy hair, which was pulled back in a ponytail bound by a blue scrunchie. On her hip hung a SIG Sauer handgun and a pair of carbon steel handcuffs.

She pulled off her latex gloves, planted her hands on her hips, and looked Maya up and down, as if appraising merchandise. Then, she smiled, her pale lips revealing small, perfect teeth.

"*Nu*, Maya. How long's it been? Two years?"

"Three. But who's counting?"

Maya stared at Sarit, trying to neutralize the other's penetrating glare with feigned indifference. Sometimes, Maya wasn't even sure if the woman ever blinked. In spite of her small stature, not quite five feet tall, the Chief Inspector undeniably radiated power and irrefutable authority. Maya was always on her guard when the two of them crossed paths. Or swords.

The other six members of the Jerusalem homicide team—a police photographer, two crime scene evidence experts, two uniforms, and another detective in plainclothes—who had until this moment been keenly preoccupied with their crime scene analysis—suddenly became aware of a chill in the air. They stopped what they were doing and leaned in toward the two women.

"So, what brings you to *my* crime scene?"

Maya stiffened her back, adding a few centimeters to her height. She smiled at the other woman and nodded, almost imperceptibly.

"IAA has asked us to step in. They suspect antiquities theft. Possibly linked to the Dead Sea Scrolls."

The diminutive police detective laughed. She reached into the small black leather bag draped over her left shoulder and withdrew a small notebook and a ballpoint pen. She flipped back the cardboard cover and poised her pen over the blank white page.

"Fine. Whatever you'd like to share with the Jerusalem Police...."

Maya snorted.

"You know damn well that I'm not here to share information. My assignment is to investigate what the American professor was after."

Sarit swept her right arm around the room. A gold link chain, flashing in the bright sun that filled the room, jangled on her wrist.

"As you can see, the case is already being investigated." She paused, then thrust her notebook and pen back into her shoulder bag. "Thanks for checking in, but we're doing perfectly fine without your help."

She recalled what Roni had once said about Sarit soon after he'd hired Maya: "I chose you over her because you have a talent for 'thinking outside the box.' Sarit sticks too close to the book." She'd have to remind him of these words next time he criticized her for not following protocol.

The two women were close to the same height, although Maya's wild bramble of red curls made her seem a bit taller. She wished she'd brought her pistol with her. *My God, I'm beginning to sound like Jason Bourne!*

She grinned at Sarit, hoping to warm up their exchange. Sarit's dark brown eyes narrowed in response.

"Look," Maya said, "I'm not trying to horn in on your case. Just helping out IAA. I leave it to you and your team to solve the murder."

Sarit was not fooled. Maya hadn't expected her to be. They'd be in each other's way at every turn.

"I suppose you want to take a look?"

"I promise not to contaminate your crime scene."

Sarit pointed toward a cardboard box near the door, filled with purple latex gloves and blue shoe coverings. Maya pulled on the tight gloves, which stuck to her sweaty skin. Then, she slipped blue booties over her sandals and walked into the large bedroom.

"Be careful, Maya. I'll be watching."

8

AT FIRST GLANCE, THE ROOM didn't look like the usual crime scene. It was too neat. The thick quilted bedspread, plum-colored with gold trim, was undisturbed on the queen-sized bed. On each pillow, precisely centered, lay a chocolate square wrapped in gold foil. The surface of the broad black desk was empty, except for some loose computer cables and a sleek desk lamp equipped with Ethernet and USB ports. The black swivel chair, its back contoured for maximum comfort, was tucked under the desk.

But a few things struck Maya as curious. There were no electronic devices visible and no complimentary official conference bag draped over the chair. A handful of computer printouts lay scattered on the floor. Mindful that the crime scene investigators were watching her, Maya walked over to the papers, each tagged with a number, and leaned over a page that was lying face-up. It displayed an array of color photos, accompanied by a description of recent excavations in the City of David. Probably downloaded by the professor from a tourist website, someplace he planned to visit in his spare time.

On a slim black ledge cantilevered out from one of the walls sat an automatic coffee machine. Beside it lay unopened packets of regular and decaf coffee. No tea bags. Maya looked down and saw in the small plastic wastebasket several used Wissotzky tea bags and crumpled paper wrappers.

Then, she noticed a dark brown backpack lying on the floor alongside the bed. As with many of the other items in the room, the backpack was marked with a plastic tag bearing a number. CS #27.

She drew closer, aware that one of the crime scene techs was following close behind her, watching.

The pack lay on its back. Its coarse, heavy fabric was well worn, stained and frayed in several places, patched on one side. All of its compartments were zipped, presumably the way Goldmayer—or the murderer—had left them. She thrust her hands into the pockets of her pants, fighting the urge to peek inside. Glancing over her shoulder, she nodded to her minder. She would not give Sarit an excuse to complain to Roni.

Then, she noticed a blue smudge on the bottom of the backpack. She leaned down for a closer look. The substance was grainy, as if scraped off a rock containing some kind of blue mineral. Parts of the smudge were smeared, indicating that the mineral was easily crumbled.

An image flashed into her mind: the secret laboratory she had uncovered while investigating the LTM Center several months ago. The lab, a long, narrow room furnished with two rows of stainless steel tables, had been hidden behind a false wall off the lobby. Running down the lengths of these tables had been an array of hammered copper pans, each filled with crystals of a single color—amber, white, green, cobalt, blue, black, and gray. These crystallized minerals were what her confidential informant had mistaken for granular explosives. Unfortunately for Maya, the minerals had turned out to be nothing more sinister than reproductions of ancient Temple incense. Maya's imprudent actions—her calling for a full-scale government investigation of the Center and making several high-profile arrests—had almost ended her career. She wouldn't let that happen again.

She glanced around the spacious hotel room. Her minder's eyes remained fixed on her like a sniper's laser. How could she lift a sample of the blue powder under his unwavering gaze? She resorted to one of the oldest tricks in the spy's playbook: diversion.

"Look! Up there!" She stabbed her finger up at the swirled white plaster above her head. "Is that smoke residue?"

All six members of the police investigating team cast their gaze upward, scanning the ceiling for a blackened stain. While they were distracted, Maya bent down and with her fingernail scraped a few grains of the blue mineral from the edge of the dust smear. The small nick left by her nail could only be detected under a microscope. Quickly, she thrust her hand into a pocket of her pants, using her thumbnail to flake the dust into an unzipped plastic baggie she'd brought to collect evidence.

"Just a dead spider," said one of the crime techs. He lowered his head and rubbed the back of his neck. "Not a carbon stain. Anyway, the alarms would have picked up smoke."

Maya was about to straighten up from her crouch when she saw something white on the floor, poking out from under the hem of the bedspread. A paper cocktail napkin. She quickly covered it with her hand. Pinching the napkin between two fingers, she straightened up, slipping it into her folded palm. When her minder's attention was momentarily snagged by a bark from the boss, she glanced down at her find.

The napkin was small and square, folded over twice. One side was darkly stained. Maya brought it to her nose. Red wine and some kind of spicy dipping sauce. Why hadn't Goldmayer discarded the dirty napkin in the dining hall?

She unfolded the square into a rectangle. On the cleaner of the two white squares there were a few scrawled lines in ballpoint pen. Maya couldn't make out the words. Quickly, she jammed the napkin into her pocket. She would have to wait until she was alone to study it more closely.

What are you doing? Are you seriously thinking about stealing evidence from a crime scene?

To do so went against all her training. Never compromise the chain of evidence.

She had felt no guilt about taking the mineral scraping. There was plenty of the stuff left on the backpack for a police analysis. But the same couldn't be said about the paper napkin they'd overlooked.

If I'm caught....

A shudder convulsed Maya's shoulders. She waited until her body stilled, then yelled: "Hey, Levine!"

Her shout grabbed the attention of everyone in the room. They froze.

"I'm busy, Rimon!" The detective's voice came from the bathroom. "I warned you not to get in my way!"

Sarit's peevish tone left no doubt as to how things stood between them. If Maya showed Sarit what she'd found, the police detective would immediately snatch it away. And Maya would never see it again. What if this piece of evidence turned out to be the key to cracking the case? Why should Sarit get all the glory?

The truth was that Maya did not easily mete out trust. Whether by temperament, upbringing, or experience, she tended to hold a rather ungenerous opinion of her fellow human beings, especially those in positions of power. Her therapist Isabel had tried to convince her that her suspiciousness was a defense against being hurt. If Maya would only be more forgiving of herself, she might discover that other people were not so unreliable. Maya always told Isabel that a therapist knows nothing about the real world.

"Never mind," Maya shouted back. "I'll handle it."

She gently curled her fingers around the soft paper in her pocket. These were probably the professor's last written words. She'd turn it over to the police later, explain that it had stuck to her sweaty skin when she'd looked under the bed. If Sarit chose not to believe her story, that was her problem.

Her nose was suddenly assaulted by a vile odor. She sniffed the air. The smell was coming from the bathroom. The stench of urine and something else she couldn't identify. Taking a deep breath, she made a beeline for it.

9

WHEN MAYA REACHED THE OPEN door, she heard a voice she recognized, speaking Hebrew with a heavy Spanish accent. Dr. Avraham Selgundo, the Chief Medical Examiner of the Jerusalem District Police, was dictating his preliminary findings.

She stepped into the large bathroom. Sarit was leaning over Goldmayer's body, listening intently as Dr. Selgundo spoke into a silver digital recorder about the size of a fountain pen.

"...appears to have been in reasonably good health, except for being somewhat overweight.

"Based on lividity, body temperature, and the state of rigor mortis, I estimate the time of death between 8:00 p.m. and midnight last night. Initial forensic analysis reveals petechial hemorrhaging, suggesting asphyxia. This cannot be conclusively determined until after a more thorough examination of the lungs and trachea. At this time, I cannot rule out stroke, heart failure, or respiratory arrest. If the death was a homicide, the victim could have been killed by smothering, strangulation, or poisoning. I will need to consult with the victim's doctors and do a more in-depth examination of the pulmonary system.

"Although I cannot establish the cause of death definitively until the autopsy, I am hypothesizing that the most likely cause was poisoning, probably through ingesting the seeds or leaves of *Conium maculatum*. I base my hypothesis on the mousy odor I detect on the victim's breath as well as in the urine found on the floor near the victim's body, which usually indicates the presence of coniine."

"*Conium maculatum*? What's that?"

Sarit looked up from the body and glowered at Maya.

"You're here solely as a professional courtesy!" Sarit's dark brown eyes drilled into Maya's. "If you can't keep your mouth shut, you need to leave."

Dr. Selgundo leaned back on his haunches and waved indifferently with one hand.

"It's okay, Detective Levine. I don't mind."

The doctor tilted further back on his heels and wriggled his shoulders back and forth. He twisted his head to look up at Maya.

"*Conium maculatum* is the scientific name for poison hemlock. Grows wild all over Israel. The poison blocks the central nervous system. Paralysis progresses up the body. The victim dies when the toxin reaches the respiratory muscles and cuts off oxygen to the heart and brain."

"Hemlock! Like what killed Socrates?"

"Precisely. Not the worst way to die. It's a clever murder weapon. Leaves no post-mortem signs except evidence of asphyxia. Hemorrhages in the whites of the eyes."

"How long would it take for the victim to die?"

"Two hours at most."

"If it's all right with you, Agent Rimon...." Sarit made Maya's formal title sound like an insult. "We'd like to finish before lunch."

Dr. Selgundo looked at the hardened faces of the two women. He turned his thoughts to his dear wife, Matilda, who was waiting for him at home, warming up his bean soup.

"I'm done here," he said.

He leaned back and straightened up, grasping the white toilet bowl to help him rise to his feet. He lowered the top of the toilet seat and sat down, glad not to be kneeling any longer on the hard tile floor.

Sarit picked up the digital recorder from the floor, where Selgundo had carefully placed it. She lifted the device to her lips— *sans* lipstick, Maya noted with surprise—and pressed the "on" button with her thumb. She cleared her throat.

"This is Jerusalem District Police Detective Sarit Levine. I will now dictate my preliminary findings before we remove the body and clear the room. No interruptions, please."

Although she didn't direct her eyes toward Maya, it was clear whom she meant. Dr. Selgundo shrugged his shoulders and looked down at the corpse. Maya stared at Goldmayer's pallid face, imagining his panic as the air bled out of his lungs.

"The victim, Boaz Goldmayer, was discovered early this morning by an Arab chambermaid...." She glanced down at her notes. "A'isha Jamal. The body was found on the bathroom floor of room five-twenty-seven. There are no signs that the body has been moved, which suggests that the victim died where he was found.

"An examination of the room indicates that the victim's laptop and possibly other portable electronic devices were taken. No cell phone was located. On the floor were scattered papers, which will be examined for forensic significance. Nothing else in the room has been touched. The victim's wallet, passport, and other valuables were locked in the hotel safe. Our initial examination has revealed no fingerprints, fibers, hairs, or DNA other than those belonging to the victim and hotel staff, which we have on record.

"There was no forced entry into the room. Whoever killed and robbed the victim must have had a key or was let in by the victim. Further investigation is necessary to find out exactly what happened in the hours prior to the victim's death."

The detective clicked off the recorder. She looked over at Maya, who stood listening intently near the doorway.

"*Nu*, something else you want from me?"

"The hotel security tapes. As soon as possible. And any other evidence your team turns up. I'll do the same on my end."

The police detective snorted. She looked down at her manicured nails, examining them closely. Their pearly surface glistened in the sunlight pouring in from the high bathroom window.

"You have no jurisdiction here."

"We'll get more done if we cooperate, Sarit."

Sarit looked down at the floor, then focused her eyes on Goldmayer's stiffening corpse. She made no effort to disguise her rancor.

"I'll make sure you're kept apprised."

10

FOUR HOURS!

It had never taken Cassandra this long to decrypt a text file. Should have been a piece of cake.

She rocked back in her chair and stretched her thin arms over her head. She'd been working on this file non-stop, not even taking a bathroom break. When in a groove like this, Cassandra became a robot, obedient only to her internal programming. Unrelenting and single-minded. Time unfurled and expanded like a Moebius strip.

Cassandra stood up and walked away from the desk. She needed to clear her head. To remember that she had a body to attend to. She walked to the center of the room and began a Sun Salutation. Spine straight, hands together, breathing mindfully. Raising her arms, bending her spine backwards. Exhaling slowly, she reversed direction, bringing her head to her knees, then dropped into a lunge. Folding over into Mountain Pose. Then sinking down to the floor, arching her back, and stretching her prone body into Cobra. Then, she did it all in reverse, ending up back where she started, spine erect, hands together, her breaths even and relaxed. She performed two more Sun Salutations. Then, she walked over to the mini-fridge, grabbed a plastic bottle, and gulped down some cold water.

Feeling refreshed, she sat back down in her chair and hunched over Goldmayer's laptop. Calmly, she placed her purple-nailed fingers on the keyboard and began clicking keys. Messages popped up all over the screen, warning her to stay out of these files. But she paid them no heed. With the focus of a Jedi, she attacked and parried, intent on prying open Goldmayer's secrets.

And then she was in. A Word document magically materialized on her screen. She shot her arms triumphantly into the air, her small hands balled into fists. She closed her eyes. Her purple lips pursed as though sucking on a lemon.

"Gotcha!" she said aloud. "You used a symmetric encryption algorithm instead of an asymmetric key cipher. Stored the file encryption key in an alternate data stream. Pretty clever, Professor." She arched her back until she felt the bones crack. "But not as clever as me!"

Before reading the file, she stood up and walked over to the kitchen area. With her index finger, she spun around the three-tiered aluminum carousel of K-Cups on the counter and selected Tazo Zen Green Tea. She flipped open the dispenser, popped in the small cup, and lowered the lid. Then, she flicked on the machine and waited for the "Brew" light to turn blue. When her mug was full, she blew softly on the hot liquid and took a sip. Carrying the tea back to the desk, she sank into her chair and looked over the decrypted file.

The text was short, only two pages. The half-dozen paragraphs, double-spaced and formatted into evenly justified columns, were separated from each other by blocks of white space. The document was titled: *Protokollon*. She didn't know what the word meant. Probably Greek or Latin. She assumed she wouldn't understand half of what the professor was talking about.

Sucking in a deep breath, she began to read:

> *My name is Mariamne, daughter of Jonathan and Livia, both of blessed memory. I was born when Claudius still sat upon the throne of Rome. I spent my youth in Tiberias, a beautiful city on the harp-shaped Sea of Kinneret. Our family was once one of the great houses in Lower Galilee, selling precious minerals extracted and refined in our family's mining works near the Salt Sea.*

*But those days of glory are long past. Calamity
has befallen my family as it has our nation. The Holy
Temple lies in ruins, victim to Rome's greed and lust
for dominion. Thousands of our people lie on the
ground, rotting fruit for the birds. Thousands more,
bound by iron chains, have been carried off to foreign lands. The few of us who remain scratch mea-
ger sustenance from unyielding soil. All that I have
left is my story, which I now bequeath to those who
come after me.*

What was this? She'd expected something scholarly and arcane,
littered with tiny footnotes. But this sounded like a page from someone's private journal. Some ancient woman named Mariamne. Was
this her diary? A memoir? A confession?

If only she had access to the internet, she could look things up
in Wikipedia, find out what a "protokollon" was, figure out when
this Mariamne lived. She had no idea when Claudius was the Roman
emperor, or when the Romans destroyed Jerusalem and sent the Jews
into exile.

Truth to tell, Cassandra had only an approximate grasp of Jewish
history. Like her friends in the small Jewish community of Memphis,
Tennessee, she'd gone to Hebrew School from fourth to seventh
grade. But she remembered almost nothing she'd learned there: a
couple of Bible stories; some customs and ceremonies; a few letters
of the Hebrew alphabet; snatches of the Friday night service, which
she'd memorized for her bat mitzvah performance. But she couldn't
recall a single fact about ancient Jewish history. What she knew about
Jewish history since Bible times was strictly limited to the 20th century. The Holocaust and the birth of Israel. As for the thousands of
years in between, they were a huge, black hole.

She took a few sips of her tea, which had cooled. She drew in
several cleansing breaths. Then, she resumed her reading.

Although I am but a woman, I am by no means ignorant. My father saw fit to educate me like my five brothers. Our Greek slave Glyptus schooled me in pagan arts and letters—Greek, music, poetry, philosophy, and history. My father took it upon himself to school me in our own people's holy teachings, not only the Torah, but also the prophets, the wisdom scrolls, the histories, and the sayings of our wise rabbis.

Although I have never heard of a woman writing about armies and wars and affairs of state, I feel duty-bound to render my own account of what has occurred over these ten terrible years. I would argue that men alone cannot tell the whole story. Women experience calamity differently from men.

My story is long and not for the faint of heart. But I entreat you to give heed, for the story I tell contains wisdom won at great cost. I hope it will serve as a parable and warning for future generations.

Cassandra felt a flush of shame suffuse her face and upper chest. Growing up female in a patriarchal culture had made Mariamne appreciate the rare privilege she'd been granted to develop her mind. Cassandra, on the other hand, had thrown away her many opportunities to study. She'd dropped out of college after only one year to hitch-hike through Asia. "Looking for God in all the wrong places," her mother had accused her of. Well, maybe she'd find God here in Jerusalem.

Or maybe in this dead woman's story. Taking another cleansing breath, she resumed her reading:

So it is that in my twenty-fifth year, I now take up my reed to write my history. It has been almost five years since I returned from Berytus, where I journeyed

> *to ransom my brother from King Agrippa's prison in*
> *exchange for the Treasure Scroll.*

A treasure scroll! So that's why these files were encrypted. What the professor had discovered was worth a lot of money. And that's why she was being kept prisoner. This man wanted to make sure that no one else got to the Treasure Scroll before he did.

Cassandra bit her lip in frustration. Being cut off from the internet was going to drive her crazy! Maybe she should have paid more attention in Hebrew school.

There was so much she didn't know!

Cassandra fell back against her chair and exhaled a *whoosh* of exasperation. She realized that she was the first person in thousands of years to read Mariamne's story. No, that wasn't true. She was the second. Someone else—a professor named Boaz Goldmayer—had discovered Mariamne's story first and translated it into English. And then he'd encrypted his files to keep her amazing story secret.

What had she gotten herself into? She'd only agreed to take on this gig because she'd run out of money. The man had promised to pay her enough so she could fly back to the States; maybe live for a year or more without needing to get a job. But maybe she'd been scammed. Maybe the man had no intention of letting her go. What would happen to her once she finished decoding the files?

Because once she completed the job, she'd only be a liability.

She had just four days to figure a way out.

11

THE MAN RETURNED TO THE apartment shortly before five o'clock.

When he learned that Cassandra had still not cracked the second file, he threw the string-net bag of groceries at her. Fruits and vegetables scattered all over the floor. Some of them were now too bruised to eat. Then, he stood there, staring at her, not saying a word. She saw his strong hands pumping inside his pockets like bellows. He was not a patient man.

She hated the way he stared at her with those unflinching black eyes. Like a lizard. She was rattled by all the pressure he was putting on her.

"What is taking so long?"

His voice was mean, like a ravenous dog.

"I'm almost there! A couple more hours at most."

When he raised his hand, Cassandra recoiled, waiting for the slap. But he was only reaching up to stroke his bushy black eyebrow with the soft pad of his thumb. He then ran four dark fingers through his thick, wavy hair, distinguished by a streak of gray on each side. For the first time, she noticed that his otherwise handsome face, the color of worn saddle leather, was pocked with shallow depressions, maybe from acne or some childhood disease. His dark eyes were framed by unusually long lashes.

"I expect answers by tomorrow morning. No excuses." He turned to go, then twisted back to look at her. "There will be consequences if you fail."

He slammed the door behind him, not saying goodbye. She heard the rattle of the shackle and hasp. The lock clicking into place.

She had to crack the next file before he returned with her breakfast. Obviously he was not accustomed to having his will thwarted.

And then, suddenly, she was in.

Mariamne's words filled the screen.

This file was even shorter than the last. Only two paragraphs, formatted in a column like the last document.

Cassandra punched the print key and held out one hand toward the tray to catch the page spilling out. She gathered the single sheet of paper and slapped it down on the desk. Then, she stood up and walked over to the counter to make herself a fresh cup of green tea. Steaming cup in hand, she returned to the desk to continue reading:

> *At the beginning of my eighteenth summer, my parents decided to send my youngest brother Alexander to Jerusalem to train as a priestly scribe. They thought he would be safer there than in Tiberias. Oh, how little we then understood about what Rome intended for us! The war in Galilee had laid waste many of our cities and slaughtered thousands of our young men, including my four older brothers.*
>
> *One day, I went to the Tiberias market to assist my parents at our family's stall. Although we sold all manner of imported goods—spices, Egyptian glass, sheets of papyrus, bronze and copper cookware, and fine pottery—we made most of our money selling semi-precious gems and cosmetics refined in our manufactory at Kochalit, located west of the Salt Sea near Herodium.*

Cassandra paused, then drew in a sharp breath. *Kochalit.* Was this where the Treasure Scroll was hidden? The answers no doubt lay in the other files.

Her watchdog would be pleased. Maybe now he would ease up on her. And maybe let her go.

12

When Maya got home from the hotel, she treated herself to a long shower. Her head throbbed. She washed her face and neck, scrubbing hard until her skin hurt. But not even scalding water could cauterize the toxic conversation she'd had with her ex this morning. Would she never be free of him? The muscles in her shoulders and lower back were coiled in knots. She'd have to schedule a one-hour massage with Shoshana, even though such extravagances were no longer in her budget.

She dried off, wrapped a thin towel around her body, and padded over to the bedroom. Inside, she heard her daughter giggling at cartoons. When she cracked open the door, she saw the black kitten lying on the bed next to Vered, pouncing every so often on some loose threads that stuck up from the thin cotton bedspread. She was glad that her parents had agreed to drop Vered off so Maya could spend more time with her. Not that they'd done so without grumbling.

Closing the door, she padded over to the small Formica table with aluminum legs that she used as a desk and sat down. The table was jammed up against the wall between the refrigerator and the orange loveseat, doing double duty as a kitchen table.

No matter how hard she tried, she couldn't stop seeing her apartment through her mother's critical eyes: the leaky faucet; the dingy linoleum curling up at both ends of the narrow kitchen area; smoke and grime staining the wall behind the stove; the chrome strips on the ancient refrigerator, striated with rust; the kitchen chairs that didn't match. Her mother's cast-off Passover dishes, stacked on an open wooden shelf, most of the glass plates chipped or cracked. Well, what else could she afford on a junior intelligence agent's salary? She'd given up trying to squeeze a few more shekels out of Rafi's tight fist. And she wouldn't accept any more hand-outs from her parents, which always came with strings attached.

She sighed and pushed back a stray lock of hair from her forehead. Then, she lifted up the lid of her laptop. There was a new message from Ziggy Dweck, with several attached video files.

Eagerly, she clicked open his email.

"Hi, Maya! Managed to copy the hotel security tapes without getting nailed by Levine's guard dogs. Police found an extra-large waiter's uniform and black shoes, size fifty, in the basement utility closet near the main hotel kitchen. Also, you might want to check the conference website for leads. See link below. Will keep you posted. And will keep watching my back. Z."

Maya clicked open the first video file. The image was grainy and dark. She could make out a dim corridor, a figure walking rapidly away from the camera. He seemed unusually tall, needing to stoop under exposed pipes. At one point, he turned to the side, revealing the brim of a dark baseball cap. The clip was short, only eighteen seconds.

She clicked on the next file. The tall figure entered a utility closet off a corridor. This time, the camera zoomed closer. No hair peeked out from under his cap. Either he was bald or had a close-cropped cut. Still no shot of his face.

The third clip showed the tall figure entering the basement entrance to the kitchen. Just as the video was ending, the camera caught a close-up of the man's right hand grasping the metal knob. The light wasn't good, but she could make out two large silver rings on the large hand.

Not much to go on, but it was a start.

So much for locking me out of your investigation, Sarit. As my mother would say: Klu shaykh walah tariqa. *Every sheikh has his way.*

13

MAYA RETURNED TO ZIGGY'S EMAIL and clicked on the link to the conference website. The homepage was quite different from what she'd expected. It looked like something straight out of Hollywood. The top of the page displayed an animated banner in rainbow colors, flashing the words: "The First Annual International Matthew Bullock Conference on the Dead Sea Scrolls." As she stared at the heading, the letters dissolved, changing shape and design. A few seconds later, they dissolved and changed again.

Below the banner, the center of the screen displayed a headshot of the eponymous conference sponsor, Matthew Bullock. A beefy, red-faced man, sporting a black Stetson and silver-tipped bolo tie. The caption identified him as a retired periodontist from Bluebonnet, Texas, and an "avid amateur scholar" of the Dead Sea Scrolls.

Circling his photograph like a Ferris wheel was an array of videos running in endless loops: a virtual tour of the recently opened Matthew Bullock Center for Qumran Studies at Holy Baptist University in Bluebonnet; an interview with Dr. Bullock on his 2,300-acre ranch; a scrolling montage of ancient scrolls owned by Bullock, now housed in the Bullock Center's climate-controlled archives; and pictures of Bullock's sponsored archaeological expeditions at various sites in the Middle East. Under the last video was a link to a Texas travel agency.

Chuckling to herself, Maya rapidly clicked through to the program brochure. She was relieved to find this section limited to unadorned black text. The brochure listed the plenary lectures, breakout sessions, and cultural programs that were scheduled over the four days of the conference. Following these pages was an alphabetical list of conference presenters and attendees.

Glancing over yesterday's schedule, she discovered that the conference's opening banquet had taken place the night before, between six and eight o'clock. If Goldmayer's killer, disguised as a waiter, had slipped poison hemlock into the professor's food during that meal, Goldmayer would have sickened and returned to his room well within the ME's proposed time frame for the murder. No doubt Sarit had already come to the same conclusion.

But the more pressing question in Maya's mind was the killer's motive. Why would someone want to murder a professor, who studied ancient scrolls?

If it was a matter of professional jealousy, why not just steal the man's research and publish it under your own name, upstaging your rival? Certainly, scholars could be petty—but would they stoop to murder?

No, it was more likely that the motive was greed. How much was this ancient scroll worth? She'd never heard of a homicide connected to Jewish antiquities. Blackmail and extortion, yes. Even kidnapping. But there was always a first time.

Maya returned to the conference program. Today's activities had been scheduled to begin with a public lecture at 9:00 a.m. delivered by the murder victim: "'The Copper Scroll Deciphered: A Radical New Theory about the Protokollon.' Keynote Address by Boaz Goldmayer, Lawrence and Trudy Goodkind Professor of Qumran Studies. New York University. Ballroom A."

But now that Goldmayer was dead, nobody would ever learn about his radical new theory. Was that why he had been murdered? To silence him? If so, what had the professor discovered that was so threatening to his killer? What secrets did that scroll possess? And why had its ancient author chosen to conceal its contents with some kind of code?

Answering these questions would undoubtedly lead her to Goldmayer's killer.

Maya scrolled through the rest of the schedule until she reached the list of conference attendees. She immediately recognized two names from her previous work with the IAA.

Father Antoine de Plessy was a French Dominican monk and a noted Qumran scholar, who worked at L'Académie biblique in the Old City. She recalled that he was an unusually tall man. He had long been on the Service's radar. In his interactions with Israeli authorities, he'd never been shy about expressing his anti-Zionist and anti-Semitic sentiments. He was known to have ties to Islamic terrorists. Maybe he was after the scroll to help fund his extremist agenda.

She also red-flagged Habib Salameh, a Lebanese antiquities dealer, who carried a French passport. Like De Plessy, Salameh was well known to the Service. He was suspected of all sorts of shady dealings, particularly black-market trade, forgeries, smuggling of Middle East antiquities, and possibly dealing in illegal arms. Maya had interviewed him as a "person of interest" during her investigation into the LTM Center a few months ago.

She'd been so close to cracking that case! She had felt it in her bones. But she hadn't been able to convince Roni to let her keep digging. In the end, no formal charges had been filed against the LTM Center or Salameh. When the Center had threatened a major lawsuit, the investigation had been immediately suspended and buried.

Move on, Maya! Case closed. You've got a new puzzle to solve.

14

After eating an early dinner with her daughter, then driving Vered back to her parents' apartment, Maya headed back to the Zion Gate Hotel. A major academic publisher was sponsoring a reception that evening for conference attendees and guests. It would be a good place to troll for information and single out possible suspects.

Tonight Maya was dressed very differently than she'd been that morning. Now she wore her standard Service outfit: short, dark-blue pencil skirt, white button-down blouse, dark-blue tailored jacket, and navy flats. Under her left armpit she carried her holstered SIG Sauer.

There was still plenty of light. The late afternoon sun ricocheted off the sparkling white stone of the hotel's façade. In the circular driveway in front of the hotel, taxis lined up waiting for fares. A few of the cabbies leaned against their cars, smoking and chatting with each other. Most of the men were dark. Arabs and Mizrachi Jews.

Maya strode briskly through the double glass doors, which parted silently to admit her. She stopped to look around the lobby. She'd been in too much of a rush this morning to take it all in. The large, high-ceilinged room reminded her of a half dozen other upscale tourist hotels she'd been in over the years. Posh and well-appointed. Bellhops pushed wheeled carts piled high with luggage and swaying garment bags. Several children ran wild through the large space, screaming or laughing. Tired American tourists hugged each another in tearful reunions or farewells.

Maya noticed a pair of ultra-orthodox men, dressed head-to-toe in black suits, roaming the crowd. Their black hats floated on their heads like dark cherubim.

At the reception desk, a heavy-set woman and her equally stout husband argued loudly with a clerk about their bill. A second clerk shouted into his mobile phone in Hebrew. Prominently displayed on the wall behind the clerks hung the kashrut certificate for the hotel, framed in gold. A third clerk sat on a stool, reading a newspaper. The hotel manager, sporting a stylish coiffure and subdued necktie, screamed over his shoulder into an open door behind him. He then swiveled forward to smile at the impatient guests. He turned his palms upward in a gesture of earnest sympathy.

Maya remained standing near the front doors, watching. A pair of Jerusalem District policemen now entered the lobby from outside, dressed in light blue and black uniforms. They pushed their way through the crowd, then headed down a hall to the left. Eyeing them nervously, Yoel Ginsberg, head of hotel security, dashed out from behind the reception desk and trailed after them.

Maya was about to follow when she noticed another police officer striding through the automatic doors. It was Sarit Levine. The petite police detective caught sight of Maya and headed straight toward her. She stopped, eyed her from head to toe, and grinned.

"I see your Ima made you dress more appropriately this time."

Maya forced a grin, not bothering to temper her blistering gaze. Her gold-flecked green eyes smoked under their lids, cloudy as sea glass.

"We have to stop locking horns like this, Sarit. People might think we're running rival investigations, instead of cooperating."

The police detective nodded, then raised her eyebrows, saluting her adversary.

"You stay out of my way, and I'll stay out of yours."

"No can do, I'm afraid," said Maya. "I need certain things from you."

"You don't have jurisdiction, dammit! I told you I'd hand over anything that might be useful to the IAA. But the homicide is out of bounds."

Both women were breathing rapidly, their fists clenched at their sides. Sensing trouble, the other guests in the lobby moved away, leaving the two surrounded by an invisible forcefield of mutual hostility.

Maya was the first to yield. Pivoting on her heels, she turned her back to the police detective and headed toward the oscillating hum of conversation emerging from Ballroom B.

Moments later, Sarit turned in the opposite direction. Her eyes scanned for the hotel manager. When she finally spotted him behind the reception desk, she straightened her spine, tugged sharply on the brim of her cap, and marched toward him, her fists balled up like grenades.

15

MAYA HURRIED DOWN THE WIDE corridor to Ballroom B, where the book exhibits were set up. She stood for a moment in front of the open double doors and surveyed the scene.

The large room was filled with long aisles of exhibit booths, separated from each other by white particleboard walls. Most of the cloth-draped tables displayed towers of newly published books as well as individual volumes, placed face-out on white wire stands. On some tables stood laptops or computer monitors, now dark. On the particleboard walls behind the tables hung brightly colored posters, advertising new titles. Maya was surprised that she recognized so few of the publishers' names. Most seemed to be university presses from America. Some names were transliterated from Latin or Greek.

A few booths sold items other than books: Jewish handicrafts and religious articles, music CDs, DVDs of lectures and documentaries, Ahava cosmetics from the Dead Sea, glossy brochures promoting day trips to Qumran and other nearby archaeological sites.

The book exhibits were closed during this evening's reception. No salespeople stood behind the tables, hawking their wares, taking credit cards, or dodging unsolicited manuscripts. Circulating waiters in white jackets and black pants carried trays of hors d'oeuvres and glasses of wine. Conference participants mobbed the wide aisles, conversing in loud, excited voices. In the middle of one aisle stood the pair of Jerusalem District policemen, gobbling down miniature knishes.

When Maya tried to enter the ballroom, she was stopped by a short, balding man wearing a nametag encased in plastic, which dangled at the end of a blue elastic lanyard. The nametag read: "Gregory

R. Ellington. Bullock Conference Staff." The young man smiled at her apologetically.

"May I see your conference badge? This is a private reception."

Maya flashed her Service credentials at him. When he saw who she was, he recoiled, his pale blue eyes wide in astonishment. Not waiting for him to recover his composure, she brushed past him.

She soon discovered that this reception was unlike any party she'd ever attended. The crowd was divided between drinkers and eaters. The former guzzled the free wine with abandon, many of them already loud and sloppy. The eaters gorged on finger foods: tuna hummus crostini, falafel, roasted eggplant matbucha, stuffed figs with goat cheese, spicy deviled eggs, marinated vegetable skewers, baba ghanoush, ful mudammas, borekas.

She was surprised by the wide variation in the scholars' clothing, ranging from smart business attire to "college casual" to downright *shlumpy*. A few wore religious garb—white collars, robes of different colors and patterns, head coverings of many shapes and heights. She'd envisioned a starchier wardrobe at an academic conference.

She caught sight of someone from the hotel staff, wearing a shiny brass nametag above his shirt pocket. He wove nimbly among the scholars, apologizing in impeccable English for "any inconvenience caused by the tragic death of Professor Goldmayer." He promised to make their stay as pleasant as possible, "despite the unfortunate circumstances."

As she continued to meander, she discovered that Goldmayer's death was the topic of most conversations. She caught snippets of dialogue:

"After his scathing review in *The Journal of Classical Biblical*...."

"Murder? Don't be ridiculous! Probably a heart attack like the one that killed...."

"Rumors of a lover's quarrel. Did you hear that...."

"Done in by one of his disgruntled graduate students...."

As the gossip circulated, individual clusters of conversation became momentarily animated, then subsided, like waves cresting and falling on a restive sea.

One of the waves plumed into a swell of contention; edging closer, Maya saw the two Jerusalem policemen trying to usher a distinguished white-haired gentleman out of the room. They were having difficulty extricating him from the lively dispute he was engaged in with two elderly colleagues.

Determined not to disclose her identity until she'd completed her initial surveillance, Maya mingled among the academic partyers. She was pleased to see that her simple outfit allowed her to pass as someone who fit in here. She wasn't especially worried about being made. Few of the local policemen knew her, and she wouldn't be recognized by any of the scholars. They belonged to a different species.

As she made her way down one of the side aisles, her eye was caught by a bright gold banner: "Third Temple Artifacts." The words were printed in heavy black lettering resembling ancient Hebrew calligraphy. A poster hanging underneath the banner advertised "genuine reproductions of sacred Temple implements, priestly vestments, and sacrificial cult items." Like the other booths, this one, too, was dark and unattended.

She walked over to get a closer look. For security reasons, most of the items listed on the poster had been put away while the booth was unstaffed. All that remained on the two white cloth-covered tables were a few coffee table books propped open on wooden stands. All of the books had some connection to the Jerusalem Temple.

Maya picked up one of the oversized volumes and leafed through its glossy pages. It featured architectural drawings of Solomon's Temple and its Herodian successor, detailing all the changes that the Second Temple had undergone until its final destruction in the first century of the Common Era. Another volume focused on items once used in the Temple by the priests, Levites, and Israelite worshippers—vessels and knives for the sacrifices, cleaning tools, and ritual items for public ceremonies. There were also colorful drawings of the priestly garments—the high priest's turban, the breastplate with its twelve semi-precious stones, the pouch for the oracular *Urim* and *Tumim*, even priestly underwear. A third volume presented its author's vision of the future Third Temple, which would be erected at the End of Days on the Temple Mount. Maya found the volumes dense and excessively detailed, something only scholars would have the patience to plow through.

Then, she picked up a book entitled, *Gemstones, Minerals, and Plants Used in the Jerusalem Temple*. Instantly, she felt a frisson rake across her skin. She quickly flipped through the volume's colored photographs, searching for information about the blue powder she'd scraped off Goldmayer's backpack. She found it on page sixty-seven.

On one side of the page were two photographs. The first displayed an assortment of small ancient cosmetic jars, some made of translucent Egyptian glass; others, of painted high-gloss ceramic. The other picture showed a small clear glass bottle lying on its side, with dark purplish-blue grains spilling out of its narrow neck. Next to the small bottle lay a few rocks, stippled with blue and green specks. The caption read: "Kohl powder. Natural cosmetic used in ancient Israel."

The text positioned next to the photograph elaborated:

"Women in the ancient world often adorned their eyes with colored pigment. Such practice was also medicinal. Covering sensitive eyelids with tinted ointments protected against eye diseases and prevented dryness. Eye-paint also repelled flies, thought to transmit inflammations of the eye. The Temple priests distinguished between eye-paint used for healing, which entailed the embellishment of one eye, and kohl and other minerals used for makeup, which entailed the embellishment of both eyes."

A memory suddenly floated up:

> She was interviewing Habib Salameh at the LTM Center. They sat across from each other at a small

wooden table. She peered intently into his wary eyes.
How shocked she was to see that he was wearing eye
makeup! His dark eyes and unusually long lashes were
heavily shaded with blue-black mascara, making him
look like a drag queen or a misanthropic rapper.

Maya filed the memory away in a corner of her mind.

She skimmed rapidly over the next few paragraphs on the page. Something to do with an arcane rabbinic dispute about medical treatment.

The final paragraph made her catch her breath:

"The colors used in kohl were fabricated from various minerals and mineral compounds: black was usually made from lead sulfate; greens and blues from copper oxide, and reds from iron oxide. The materials were crushed into powder and mixed in a preservative oil base, often with the addition of fragrance."

So the blue substance on the bottom of Goldmayer's backpack might be derived from copper oxide. She would need the lab to confirm this, but she felt reasonably certain that's what it was. If so, Goldmayer's scroll might be located near an ancient copper mine. The area around the Dead Sea had long been a source of valuable mineral deposits. It still was today.

Maya looked again at the two photographs, staring intently at the delicate glass vials and the purplish-blue powder. It then hit her that "kohl" must be related to *kachol*, the Hebrew word for blue. And maybe to a place called Kochalit.

She filed away this information, too, in a corner of her mind.

16

_____

AFTER DRIVING ALMOST FOUR HOURS from his home in Efrat, Dov Baer Gittelson, known to his friends as Dubi, exited Route 1 and headed toward Kibbutz Almog. A kilometer beyond the kibbutz, he turned onto a dirt road. He drove past fields of cucumbers and an orange grove before he reached a metal barrier gate.

Dubi got out of his car and walked over to the phone box but then changed his mind. He would park his car outside the gate and walk in. It was late afternoon, and the air had begun to cool. The exercise would do him good, but the primary reason he wanted to walk into the farm was to smell the plants. Even this far away from the fields and gardens, he caught a whiff of the enchanting fragrances. Frankincense, myrrh, and balsam. A dozen varieties of sage. Cinnamon, cassia, and spikenard. By the time he reached the Frankincense Farm Tourist Center, he was smiling from ear to ear.

He was relieved to find only two large tourist buses parked in the large lot in front of the tourist center. The last time he'd come, there had been six, filled with Christian pilgrims from Japan, South Korea, Holland, and Texas. He'd almost been trampled by the mob rushing past him to buy souvenirs before they returned to their Jerusalem hotels.

He picked up his pace. He soon arrived at a dilapidated wooden shack that stood next to a large modern gardening shed, partially covered with plastic sheeting. Unpainted shutters covered two of the shack's windows, blocking out all light.

Dubi knocked twice, then once, then twice more. The door creaked open, and he slipped inside.

Nothing about the shack's exterior hinted at what lay within: a modern scientific laboratory filled with gleaming silver machines and instruments, floor-to-ceiling steel shelves, and an assortment of glass containers. From a steel grid suspended under the shack's wooden roof hung clusters of drying plants.

A woman in her late seventies with long white braids and thick glasses greeted Dubi with a bracing hug. She wore a heavy brown apron and rubber gloves.

"I'm close," she said, "very close."

She pointed to a large white porcelain mortar and pestle sitting on an aluminum table. Dubi peered into the porcelain bowl. At the bottom sat a paste of dark green plant material. He brought his long, thin nose closer. There was no smell.

"It's Leptadenia pyrotechnica. I'm convinced it's what we've been looking for. The source of the *ma'aleh ashan* that made the Temple incense rise up to Heaven in a straight column. It contains nitric acid, which somehow catalyzed the effect."

"So you now have the complete recipe," said Dubi, "all eleven ingredients of the Temple incense?"

"Not everyone will agree with my conclusions. I doubt that LTM and the others will concede that we got it first. But I'm sure this is it."

"When will it be ready? We're running out of time."

"No, we're not!" The shriveled skin hanging down from the old woman's upper arms quivered as she lifted up her hands toward the shack's sloped wooden roof. "The world may indeed be coming to an end, but it won't happen this week, despite what that lunatic American preacher says. You'll have your incense in plenty of time. I promise."

Dubi shuffled his sandaled feet nervously on the tiled floor. The rabbi had been quite clear about the urgency of nailing down the sacred incense formula. He didn't want to be upstaged by the Christians.

"I have something for you, Dubi."

The old woman walked over to another aluminum table. Dubi stared at the array of small brown glass bottles topped with white plastic twist-off caps. She picked one up and handed it to Dubi.

"Just finished a batch of Third Temple anointing oil."

Dubi handed the bottle back to her.

"What am I going to do with this?" He wiped a layer of sweat off his forehead with the back of his hand. It was hot and stuffy in the shack, especially with the windows sealed. "Save it for when it's really needed."

The old woman laughed. Dubi saw that she was missing several molars. Her clear blue eyes sparkled in the bright light of the overhead halogen lights.

"Don't worry. There's plenty more where that came from. This formula only requires five ingredients, all of them grown here."

Dubi slipped the small bottle into a pocket of his shorts. He embraced the old woman, then gave her a quick peck on the cheek. Her ghostly skin turned bright pink.

"Give me a call as soon as it's ready," Dubi said. "With all the military checkpoints, it takes me half a day to get here. And it's only a distance of fifty kilometers. Ridiculous!"

He left the shack and retraced his footsteps until he reached his dented Kia, parked outside the main gate. His earlier good mood was gone. Maybe it was the autumn chill in the air.

Pulling onto the rutted dirt road, he raised the electric windows so that he couldn't smell a thing as he headed home.

17

CASSANDRA'S EYELIDS WERE BEGINNING TO droop, blurring her vision. She was getting tired. But she pushed herself to stay awake. She needed to finish this file and move on to the next one before she went to bed. Her keeper did not tolerate excuses.

By late afternoon, Cassandra could no longer fight off sleep. She'd been up for twenty-six hours straight. As if felled by a blow, her upper body keeled over. Her purple-crowned head crash-landed on the laptop's keyboard. Her thin arms hung down on either side of the chair, drooping like lead sinkers, motionless. Her dark lashes, heavy with black mascara, quivered a few times, then fused together in a thick, gloppy line. In the unsteady breeze created by the window air conditioner, a stack of papers fluttered in a corner of the desk. It was the only sign of life.

Suddenly, Cassandra jerked awake and sat up. She jabbed at the keyboard to bring the computer out of sleep mode. She noted the time. 7:50 p.m. She'd been asleep for over an hour. She quickly shook the kinks out of her neck and slumped back against the sculpted contours of the chair. Then, she focused her attention on the next encrypted file.

She was wearing the same clothes she'd had on since yesterday. Or was it the day before? She'd lost track of time. Her white tee shirt, showing a picture of a spindly alien, saying: "It's All Geek to Me," clung to her back like wet spandex. Her thread-bare cut-offs stuck to her thighs. She could smell the reek of her own body odor.

For a few moments, she stared at the list of filenames in the Finder window. She could no longer focus. Cursing, she pushed back from the desk and unfolded her body into a standing position. She swung her arms and legs vigorously back and forth to restore circulation.

Eyes half-closed, she stumbled toward the two-burner stovetop perched on the wooden counter. She bent down. Under the counter, she found a small aluminum pot. She filled the pot half-full from the tap. Then, from the three-tiered silver carousel, she plucked out all the K-Cups containing coffee, sliced the paper tops open with a paring knife, and emptied the fragrant grounds into the pot, stirring the dark brown mixture with a large spoon. With a wooden match, she lit the burner and watched the muddy brew come to a boil. Then, she lowered the flame and watched it bubble.

A memory arose from early childhood.

Her ninety-year-old Bubbe was making coffee in her tiny kitchen in Memphis. It was the only time Cassandra had stayed overnight with her grandmother. Her mother was scheduled to have minor surgery the next day, and her father was out of town, so Cassandra had been dropped off to spend the night in Bubbe's steamy two-room apartment.

As the acrid aroma of boiled coffee began to perfume the stale air, Cassandra pictured the tiny, old woman, not even five feet tall, standing in front of her compact four-burner stove, stirring the small, red-rimmed white saucepan. She visualized Bubbe's soft dome of short-cropped hair, which was as white as the sweet oleander that grew in her front yard. How fiercely the two of them had loved each other!

With a folded dishtowel, Cassandra grabbed the handle of the small aluminum pot and poured the steaming coffee into her mug. She took a sip. The coffee was almost too bitter to drink. And she had no milk or sugar to dilute it. Well, the stronger, the better. She needed to wake up and stay awake. She needed to get her mojo back.

Cassandra set to work. Within an hour, she had the next file decrypted and printed out.

She skimmed through a few paragraphs, recounting Mariamne's difficult trip on foot from Tiberias to Jerusalem, where she joined her brother, Alexander, now an apprentice scribe in the Temple. How she admired this young woman's courage, risking encounters with cutthroat bandits and Roman patrols on the roads! During the many months Cassandra had hitchhiked through China, Nepal, Bhutan, and India, she'd gotten herself into a few close scrapes. But she'd never feared for her life as Mariamne had on her journey south to Qumran.

Getting caught up in Mariamne's story was foolish; she was only being paid to decrypt the files. Reading the texts wasted valuable time. But she couldn't help being drawn in. Mariamne was a compelling storyteller. And her story touched something deep inside Cassandra.

Her eyes suddenly locked on a passage. The words were Alexander's:

> *"Why preserve the Temple treasures if the Jewish People will soon cease to exist? That is why Eleazar and I have devised a plan to save them both."*

There it was again—another reference to treasure! Cassandra backed up a few paragraphs to re-read the section more carefully.

> *"Our plan is bold and ingenious. The Temple treasury is one of the greatest in the Empire. Not only does every Jew in Israel contribute tithes each year, but donations also continuously pour in from Jewish communities around the world—Alexandria, Rome, Parthia, Babylonia, even faraway Adiabene. The Temple itself contains many sacred vessels of gold, silver, bronze, and copper. Clearly, the Romans covet these riches for themselves. What will happen if Jerusalem falls? They will plunder it all and take it back to Rome. There, they will melt it all down for coin and weapons or will show it off to the world to put us to shame.*
>
> *"To keep them safe, the Sadducean priests have hidden these treasures in secret places all around*

Jerusalem as well as in the Judean Desert. They have recorded these locations in a parchment scroll, which they call the Treasure Scroll.

"Eleazar and I have been chosen by our fellow Pharisees to steal this scroll. Our own scribes will then make a copy of it, but not on parchment as the Sadducees have done. Rather, our duplicate copy will be inscribed on pure copper in the same manner that Rome preserves its official records."

Cassandra lay down the papers in her hands. Her right foot had fallen asleep. She stamped hard on the cement floor, feeling pinpricks in her skin as the blood resumed flowing. She stood up, stretched, and headed toward the small refrigerator. Her mouth was dry. Gulping down half a bottle of cold water, she eyed the halvah that the man had brought her, though it hadn't been on her list. Her tongue craved something sweet, but she knew that the sticky sesame paste would only make her thirstier. Reluctantly, Cassandra shut the refrigerator door.

She headed back to her desk. Sitting down and breathing in and out several times, drawing in the air with her diaphragm. Arching backward to loosen her cramped vertebrae. Then, she straightened her spine, feeling an invisible string at the top of her head drawing her upwards.

Then, she returned to Mariamne's account:

"And what will you do with this copper scroll?" I asked my brother.

"We will offer it to the Romans in exchange for leaving us in peace. No amount of gold and silver is worth the loss of our Holy Temple and our ability to live freely as Jews."

Cassandra looked up from the computer screen. So the scroll was a kind of treasure map that led to the lost riches of the Jerusalem Temple. Two different Jewish groups, Sadducees and Pharisees—whoever they were, yet another embarrassing gap in her Hebrew school education—had disagreed about what to do with these treasures. The Sadducees had opted to hide the Temple treasures to keep them out of Roman hands. The Pharisees, on the other hand, had decided to steal the Sadducees' treasure map and copy it, not in order to protect the treasures but to barter them in exchange for a truce with Rome. Even back then, Jews couldn't agree with each other!

But the Pharisees' clever scheme hadn't worked out, had it? Rome had destroyed the Temple and exiled the Jews for two thousand years.

So what had gone wrong?

By now, Mariamne's story had Cassandra totally in its grip. She was eager to move on to the next file. She wanted to find out what had happened to Mariamne and her brother. And to the treasure scrolls.

And all that treasure.

18

MAYA SNAGGED A GLASS OF white wine from a passing tray and continued to make her way through the crowded ballroom. Now that the day's academic sessions were over, the exhibit hall was packed. Many of the scholars' spouses had joined them after a day of sightseeing or shopping. Despite the steady influx of new guests, the supply of wine and hors d'oeuvres seemed inexhaustible. As did the scholars' tongues.

Turning into the last aisle of exhibit booths, Maya found herself drawn toward a spirited conversation among three men. She guessed that the youngest man, dark-bearded and slim, was about her age. The second man was middle-aged, the third elderly. Only the young man held a wine glass, almost empty. What drew her to these men was the passion in their voices. It was a tone all too familiar to Israelis. In their tone and gestures, Maya recognized fanatic zeal. Each of these men was claiming an exclusive lock on the truth. But she knew it was a flawed comparison. How could such ivory-tower debates rival the life-and-death issues that she and her fellow Israelis dealt with every day?

"I can prove to you, Hillel," said the oldest of the three men, "that the numbering units and weights used in the Copper Scroll are of ancient Egyptian origin, not Canaanite or Judean! In fact, this numbering system is typical of that in use in Egypt around 1300 BCE. I'll have more to say about all this in my paper tomorrow. I assume you're planning to attend the session?"

Maya judged the speaker to be in his mid-eighties, though his erect bearing and piercing blue eyes belied his advanced age. He reminded Maya of her old European history professor at the Hebrew University, Professor Piness. Like Piness, this man had a full head of white hair, untidy like wild marsh grass. His face was craggy, especially the straight-edged nose, which supported on its narrow bridge old-fashioned horn-rimmed glasses. And as with so many elderly people, his ears had drooped with age so that their lobes were now almost level with his square chin. But his teeth remained strong and bright white. She was amused to see that he dressed like a much younger man. His close-fitting pants and snug paisley vest showed off his trim figure.

Then, she noticed the two silver rings on his right hand. Even from a distance, she could identify the designs: scarabs. Beetles sacred to the ancient Egyptians.

The middle-aged man standing next to him bore a strong family resemblance. The intensity with which he listened to everything the old man said convinced Maya that he was the old man's son. Maya found it peculiar the way the younger man stared so intently into his father's face. It was perhaps a sign of a mental disorder. Maybe an autistic spectrum disorder. He shared with the old man the same slender physique, although the son was at least a head taller than his father. He had similar sharp features—the straight-edged nose, bony cheeks, and square chin. But unlike his father's pearly teeth, the son's were stained, probably from drinking too much black tea. His hair was close-cropped, with streaks of white running along the sides.

Compared to his father's stylish taste in clothes, the son seemed indifferent to fashion. He wore a plain dark suit, with a white shirt and a thin yellow tie. Maya noticed that the tie was smeared in a few spots with blue smudges. The color of kohl. The son's only sartorial flourish was a brown fedora, which, combined with the cheap suit, made him look like an anemic Columbo.

"Look, Stanley," said the young man, whom his older companion had addressed as Hillel. He jabbed his index finger toward the old professor's nose. "I know you believe that the Temple treasures date back to Akhenaten's Egypt. But you have to admit that your theory defies all the evidence. At the moment, you're a minority of one."

The professor's son bristled at these remarks but said nothing. He shifted his stare from his father's face to the young interlocutor, gazing at him unblinkingly. Like a lizard pinioned by the sun.

"Everything suggests that the treasures listed in the Copper Scroll," continued Hillel, "date to the Second Temple, not to a much earlier period as you claim. Granted, the pairs and triplets of Greek letters in this scroll have stumped us for decades, but it appears that Boaz Goldmayer may have finally cracked the code."

"How do you know what Boaz was about to disclose?"

The old man's hands attacked the air vigorously, waging an unrelenting war against his critics. Karate chops and butcher's slices. He ended his pugilistic display by stabbing the air decisively with his forefinger, which finally came to rest right in front of Hillel's nose.

The old man's son now took up the baton. He waved his large, bony-fingered hands, then planted them emphatically on his slender hips.

"Has it not occurred to you, Stone, that Boaz Goldmayer was killed precisely because he was about to corroborate my father's theory of the Copper Scroll? Some jealous scholar simply could not bear the thought that Stanley Lowenthal has been right all along. So he had to destroy the messenger along with the message."

Brusquely ending his tirade, the younger Lowenthal drew his long, thin arms to his chest, then crisscrossed them as if protecting himself from assault.

"Oh, give me a break, Adam! No scholar would kill a colleague just because they advance a rival theory."

Hillel Stone began to chuckle. But he stopped when he saw that Adam Lowenthal had balled his bony hands into fists. Adam's father gently placed a wrinkled hand on his son's shoulder. The younger Lowenthal immediately slowed down his breathing and relaxed his hands. Maya noticed that there was something strange about

Adam's left eye, which seemed to wander off as though it had a mind of its own.

Hillel took a sip of wine and made a feeble attempt to smile. The other two men did not echo his conciliatory gesture.

"You know, the whole point of this reception," Hillel said, "is to give us a chance to socialize, not to talk shop or score points. Why don't we save this debate for tomorrow's session on the Copper Scroll? For now, let's just agree to disagree."

Without another word, Lowenthal, father and son, turned and walked away. With their arms linked together, it was hard to tell who was supporting whom.

"Tough opponents, eh?" said Maya, approaching. Her smile was broad and warm. "But you seemed to hold your own."

Hillel grinned, showing only his upper teeth, as if he were holding back his full smile. Maya thought him shy, but puckish. She was unexpectedly charmed.

Hillel's black knit *kippah* pegged him as modern Orthodox. His bushy black beard, which fanned out from his cheeks like a pair of wings, was flecked with gray. His cornflower-blue eyes were framed by thick-lensed wire-rimmed glasses. He wore a simple black suit and white shirt, which made his red French silk tie and matching pocket handkerchief all the more striking. He was obviously not your typical *yeshivah bachur*. Definitely not a religious schoolboy.

"I've faced worse."

Hillel laughed. Maya joined in.

She wondered why she found this man so attractive. His physical form was certainly unremarkable. He was of medium height and somewhat stoop-shouldered. His limbs were long and thin, lacking discernible muscle. And yet there was an intensity about him that she found appealing. He stood close to her, so close that she was tempted to take a few steps back, so she could focus her eyes on his face. His clear blue eyes seemed to zoom in on her.

"I couldn't help overhearing your...conversation." She looked quizzically at him, her head tilted to one side. She brushed a copper curl from her forehead and looped it around one ear.

"Hard to avoid, given how loudly we were talking." Hillel chuckled softly. "That was Professor Stanley Lowenthal and his son, Adam. Stanley's quite an iconoclast in the field."

"And which field is that?"

"Qumran Studies. Dead Sea Scrolls."

"Which I'm guessing is your field, too?"

She smiled, raising her ginger eyebrows. My God, she was flirting with him!

Hillel's thin eyebrows arched up mischievously. He nodded.

Maya was not too certain about the protocols observed by Orthodox men, all the subtle gradations of modesty and aversion they adhered to. But she knew enough not to reach out her own hand first. She was delighted when Hillel set down his empty wine glass on a nearby table and stretched out his right hand toward her. She was even more delighted to see that he wore no ring.

"Hillel Stone. I teach in the Bible Department at Bar Ilan University." Then, his expression darkened, as if a cloud had suddenly eclipsed his sunny mood. "Boaz Goldmayer was my dissertation advisor. And my mentor ever since I finished grad school. I'm still trying to take in his death."

"Maya Rimon."

His hand was strong, the flesh soft. A scholar's hands.

"So what brings you here, Maya? I see you're not wearing a conference badge."

She began reaching for her Service credentials in her pocket, then let her hand drop to her side.

"I'm not attending the conference." She grinned, then immediately became serious. "I work for the Service. Israeli Intelligence. I'm here about the Goldmayer murder."

She had hoped that keeping her ID in her pocket might allow them to keep on chatting informally. But as soon as the words were out of her mouth, the air between them chilled. Hillel cleared his throat, then cleared it again. Was it her imagination, or had the man edged back, widening the distance between them?

19

HILLEL STONE HAD NEVER BEEN very comfortable around women, especially not women as beautiful as Maya Rimon. It was not that he was a prude or didn't have normal sexual urges or enjoy feminine coquetry. It was just that he was frightened of such desires. Even now, he was struggling against them as they stirred within him.

The familiar nattering began in his head. *You're thirty-five years old, Hillel, and still struggling with your yetzer!* Since early adolescence, he'd been tormented by sexual fantasies. He often awoke from vividly erotic dreams, covered in sweat. He'd read everything he could on Jewish remedies for this affliction. He'd even gone to therapists—but he'd found these conversations too embarrassing to sustain for more than a few sessions. He'd considered asking his rabbi at the Kollel, but he was too ashamed. So he did his best to fight off such urges. Every time he pleasured himself, he went right afterwards to the mikveh, vowing never to succumb again. Until the next time.

How strange, he thought to himself, *to find myself sexually aroused at an academic conference. It should be the safest place in the world for someone like me.*

But here he was, flirting with a lovely Israeli spy. He felt a sudden stirring in his groin.

Don't be a fool, Hillel! You'll never see this woman again. The police will quickly solve Goldmayer's murder. And then Secret Agent Maya Rimon will go back to hunting terrorists.

Sensing his discomfort, Maya deftly swung the conversation back to Hillel's turf.

"I heard you talking about a copper scroll. One of the famous Dead Sea Scrolls?"

Hillel nodded. "But the Copper Scroll is unlike any of the others!"

As he warmed to his subject, Hillel's voice rose in volume and speed. His initial awkwardness rapidly gave way to a self-confidence bordering on pedantry.

"This scroll is full of mysteries. That's why so much ink and vitriol's been spilled over it for the past sixty-five years. And why there are so many competing theories about it. Boaz Goldmayer spent most of his career studying it. He knew the Copper Scroll better than any of us. That's probably what got him killed."

Maya's sandy eyebrows spiked sharply.

"Go on."

"The Copper Scroll is an inventory, the only one found among the scrolls. It lists sixty-four places where priceless artifacts from the Second Temple are buried—sacred vessels, tithe coins, lots of gold and silver. So it's kind of a treasure map."

"And have they been found—these treasures?"

"That's just it!" Hillel's voice rose higher in pitch. "Not a single one of them has ever been found. That's because the hiding places described in this scroll are impossible to locate: 'in the salt pit, which is under the steps,' 'in the canal that goes to the pool,' 'in the water tank of the Valley of Job.' How could anyone identify these places? But that hasn't stopped archaeologists and treasure-hunters from trying. They've used everything from radar to bulldozers. Nobody knows how much this treasure's worth in today's dollars. Some say as much as sixty-five billion."

"I'd say that's a pretty good motive for murder."

Hillel raised one slender finger and wagged it at Maya.

"*If* the treasure still exists. Most of us, including me, think it was looted ages ago."

"What about Goldmayer?"

Hillel noticed that Maya's gaze had settled on his hands, which were buried in his pockets. Too bad he'd inherited his father's Yankee reserve. He withdrew his hands from his pockets and began to wave them around to punctuate his words. The movement felt so unnatural that he soon shoved them back into his pants.

"Boaz didn't agree. He thought some of the treasures might still be hidden somewhere in Israel. He spent forty years trying to puzzle out the Copper Scroll's secrets."

Maya made a circle with her hand, urging Hillel to continue. As soon as he resumed speaking, her hand floated up toward her forehead, snagging a curl of auburn hair and twirling it a few times. Then, the hand floated back down to her side.

"He was especially intrigued by the final line of the Copper Scroll. Line sixty. It mentions a 'duplicate of this document' that contains additional information. Boaz thought this duplicate scroll might help him decipher the Copper Scroll's cryptic clues."

"And did he ever find this duplicate scroll?"

Maya's voice had grown in intensity, its volume and rhythm oscillating, as if someone were spinning a radio dial. Unlike Hillel's becalmed hands, hers now took on a life of their own. They whirled in the air, caught in the eddy of her excitement.

"Most of us think he did. Some of my colleagues were sure he'd announce his breakthrough during this morning's keynote. My money was on his making that announcement at the end of the conference at the closing banquet scheduled at Qumran. That's what I'd do if I were going to drop a bombshell like this. What a grand finale to his career!"

"And now?"

Hillel shrugged his shoulders.

"He was too paranoid to back up his research on a flash drive or in the cloud. He was funny that way. He trusted no one."

"With good reason, it turns out."

"Afraid so."

"So no one knows whether Goldmayer actually did locate the duplicate scroll or the treasures?"

"Only his killer."

Hillel sighed. His eyes drifted up to the ceiling of the ballroom, which shimmered with rows of LED lights.

"Any idea who might have killed him?"

"I prefer not to gossip about my colleagues." Hillel paused. Then, he threaded two slender fingers through his beard. "Anyway, detective work is really outside my expertise. I generally confine my investigations to dusty and rusty old scrolls."

They both laughed. Maya's eyes, green with gold flecks floating in their irises, sparkled under the bright lights. They reminded Hillel of the waters of the Kinneret just before sunset. Closing his eyes, he breathed in her Ahava skin cream, redolent with fragrant minerals from the Dead Sea.

He held up his empty wine glass between two fingers and wiggled it in the air, looking around for a waiter. Another glass of wine would help calm him down. But there was no waiter in sight.

The two of them stood alone in the broad aisle. The noise in the cavernous ballroom was ebbing. Then, a bell began to chime, its silvery ring echoing through the high-ceilinged room.

Hillel glanced down at his watch.

"Look, there's a dinner scheduled now for conference participants. And afterwards, a speech by someone from the Israel Museum. Rumor has it that the mayor of Jerusalem is planning to stop by to welcome us."

"Then, I'd better be on my way," said Maya. "I have to check in at the office before I head home."

When Maya glanced down at her watch, Hillel gasped in astonishment. She was wearing an old Soviet Poljot, dating back to the days of Stalin. It must be over seventy-five-years old. The crystal face was so scuffed that it was hard to read the numbers. Hillel had seen watches like this on the wrists of some of his elderly Russian colleagues. Too manly, he thought, for a woman's delicate arm.

"Maybe we could get together later tonight? I have so much more to tell you." Hillel hesitated, then grinned. "About the Copper Scroll."

Beads of sweat had begun pearling under Hillel's armpits.

"Can't tonight. I have...family obligations."

"How about tomorrow?"

Hillel's eyes refused to meet Maya's. Pink seeped into his cheeks.

"Unfortunately, I'm busy all day tomorrow. But we could meet after dinner. Say, eight o'clock?"

"There's a nice bar here. The Twelve Tribes. Corny name, huh?" Hillel winked, his thin eyebrows curving like scythes.

This time, it was Maya who reached out her hand first. Hillel took it, holding on to it a bit longer than he should have.

"Eight o'clock then. At the hotel bar."

Maya turned and headed toward the double doors leading out of the ballroom.

She moves like a cat, he thought to himself. *All that wiry energy, but she glides softly on silken paws.*

He kept his eyes on her until she was gone.

20

By the time Maya exited through the whispering glass doors of the Zion Gate Hotel, it was after eight o'clock. The sun had just set, leaving a rose and purple smear on the western horizon. As she rushed along the broad path leading up to the main sidewalk, she stopped to admire the sky.

Like the sunsets Rafi and I would see when we went camping at Mitzpe Ramon or in the north. What happened to us?

She shook her head vigorously to banish the intrusive memory.

And then she became aware of a loud male voice, off to her left, shouting in English. She turned. In the middle of the elegantly landscaped garden skirting the hotel, a bearded man, clad in disheveled clothes and leaning on a rubber-tipped metal cane, harangued hotel guests as they entered and exited. Occasionally, he stabbed the air with his cane. His eyes were bloodshot and runny. Maya noticed a few grimy toes peeking out of his tattered shoes.

"Repent, ye sinners, before it's too late! The End is almost upon us!"

Most people rushed past the man without looking at him. But Maya drew closer. She could now see that he carried a dog-eared Bible in his left hand. Bright colored Post-its poked out from many of its pages.

The man turned his face up toward the purpling sky.

"'And the sun shall be turned into darkness, and the moon into blood, before the great and terrible day of the Lord come.'"

Normally, Maya ignored such crazies. Jerusalem was full of them. But this was the second time today she'd run into one of these

End-of-the-World types. She shuddered when she recalled the sight of the young American outside Service Headquarters, being dragged into an ambulance with that bloody spike through his feet. Was it her imagination, or were there now more of them in the city? Or were they just taking to the streets more often?

She tried to snag the man's attention.

"Hey!"

He froze in mid-rant and stared at her. His eyes widened. His mouth dropped open, exposing bad teeth.

"Can you tell me precisely when the world's going to end? I'd like to be ready."

Maya had not meant to mock the man, but her voice betrayed her. The singsong way she'd said "precisely" conveyed unmistakable ridicule. A couple of women who were waiting for a taxi in front of the hotel laughed.

Suddenly the man lunged toward her, brandishing his cane like a lance.

"Beware the blood moon! Then, shall ye meet your doom!"

He would have bashed in Maya's head had Sarit Levine not tackled him at that moment.

Maya hadn't noticed Sarit emerging from of the hotel. The diminutive police detective now sat astride Maya's attacker, holding his arms behind his back. Deftly, she clapped his hands in twist-ties, then stood up. She barked a few words into a walkie-talkie strapped to her belt. Within seconds, her two police colleagues exited the hotel, yanked Sarit's prisoner to his feet, and escorted him to a police car parked on the street.

"Thanks," Maya said. "Wasn't expecting that from him."

"He one of your suspects? Doesn't strike me as the type to steal antiquities. But then I don't have your special intelligence training."

Without waiting for a reply, Sarit turned and walked up to a Ford Escort parked at the curb. With a screech of tires, she sped off.

Maya headed toward the bus stop a block away. She needed to check something out at her office before she picked up her daughter. Vered would already be fast asleep, so it didn't much matter how late she arrived at her parents' apartment. Her mother would simply add yet another failing grade to Maya's disappointing maternal report card.

21

It was dark when Maya arrived at Service Headquarters. The streetlight outside the building's entrance was out, as it had been for the past three months. As Maya turned to enter the building, she glimpsed a shadowy figure disappearing around the corner at one end of the block. In the indistinct light, she couldn't clearly distinguish his features—except for the figure's unusual height, which she gauged at over two meters. No point trying to follow him at night. From now on, she would need to be more vigilant.

She walked past the long series of cubicles leading to Roni's office at the end of the floor. He was sitting at his large wooden desk, squeezing a blue stressball. He didn't look up when she came in.

"*Nu*, so how's the case going?"

He reached into his shirt pocket, fished out a cigarette, and lit up. On the wall behind him hung a sign: "No Smoking." Maya's nose wrinkled up when the acrid smoke wafted over to her. Roni glowered at her, his dark pupils hard and glittery.

She forced herself not to stare at the diamond-shaped wine stain marring the Egyptian man's left cheek. Instead, she fixed her gaze on a spidery crack running vertically down one of the green walls of Roni's office.

"No definite leads yet. I'm interviewing some possible suspects over the next few days. But first, I need to turn over a few more rocks."

Tilting his bullet-shaped head off to one side, Roni narrowed his eyes.

"Not too many rocks, Rimon. I don't want you wasting precious resources chasing down another of your cockamamie theories."

Maya refused to take the bait.

She spun on her heels and marched off toward a back corner of the long room. She was so angry that she didn't notice her friend Masha's hand waving at her as she stomped past her friend's desk and slammed her office door behind her.

22

BEFORE SITTING DOWN AT HER desk, Maya grasped the clear plastic rod that controlled the mini-blinds hanging down over the glass window of her office door. She twisted the rod, louvering the white blinds shut. Then, she stepped back, measuring the blinds with her eyes. She pulled up on the double cord until she was satisfied that the bottom slat was straight. Then, she walked over to her massive steel desk and sat down.

She fished out of her pocket the stained napkin she'd found that morning under Goldmayer's hotel bed. She unfolded it, and, with the heel of her hand, flattened it out. She gazed down at the three lines of text, written in a cramped, hurried hand:

> *Without the physical evidence of the duplicate scroll, Wolters' hypothesis about the* prōtokollon *has remained moot. But now, thanks to De Vaux's field notes, I will be able to verify Wolters' theory!*

The note made no more sense now than it had when she'd quickly skimmed it this morning after leaving the hotel.

But at least the note confirmed one thing: Goldmayer had succeeded in pinpointing the location of the lost scroll he'd been seeking. As for the precise coordinates of that location, only his killer knew. The details were stored on the stolen laptop.

She typed "protokollon" into her browser. Only a few links popped up. From an online classics dictionary, she learned that the ancient Greek term referred to "the first sheet of a papyrus scroll, which listed when and where the scroll was composed. Sometimes, the *protokollon* consisted of a leaf of parchment glued to the outside of a manuscript's protective case, describing the text inside."

So it was something like a table of contents. The entry went on to explain that the Greek term was made up of two other Greek words: *prōto*, meaning "first," and *kolla*, meaning "glue." The dictionary speculated that this word might be the source of the modern English word, "protocol."

Maya grunted. So much for the usefulness of Greek etymology.

She Googled the names, "De Vaux" and "Wolters." It turned out that Father Roland De Vaux and Albert Wolters were both Qumran scholars; one French, the other American. She didn't bother to click through to their list of publications.

Maya filed these enigmatic pieces of information away with the others stashed in a corner of her mind. She'd have to ask Hillel Stone about these two scholars and the protokollon.

She was beginning to feel the first tremors of a sugar low. Shaky hands, wobbly legs. But she decided to push on. Better not to appear too uninformed when she met with Hillel tomorrow night. Not if she wanted him to take her seriously.

The first articles she clicked on provided only general background about the Dead Sea Scrolls, some of which she'd already picked up from TV documentaries and mass media. Stories about the scrolls seemed to pop up in the news as frequently as suicide bombings.

She already knew, for instance, that the first seven scrolls were discovered by accident in 1947 when a couple of young Bedouin shepherds, looking for a lost goat, stumbled upon some giant clay jars in a cave near the Dead Sea. Experts soon verified that these scrolls dated back at least two thousand years. For Jews and Christians, this serendipitous find was hailed as the most important archaeological discovery of the twentieth century. These scrolls were the first Hebrew texts ever found that dated all the way back to the Second Temple and the beginning of Christianity. Since that initial discovery, more scrolls had been discovered in other caves. The total number of full or partial Dead Sea Scrolls found to date now stood near a thousand.

She took a few deep breaths and Googled "Copper Scroll." When she clicked on the first link, she was immediately inundated by a flood of academic minutiae.

"In 1952, French archaeologist Henri de Contenson stumbled upon two small metallic lumps in a corner of Cave 3 in Qumran. He knew immediately that he'd found something quite unusual. Because the metal was two thousand years old, the copper had completely oxidized. The original metal cylinder had broken into two pieces.

"De Contenson deduced that these two small dark lumps of oxidized copper were scrolls. He knew not to pry them open, which of course would have completely destroyed them. After three years of scholarly debate, the two pieces were sent to the Manchester College of Science and Technology, where an expert metallurgist coated the copper with a special adhesive and sliced it into twenty-three separate sections, using a special saw that could cut slices one hundredth of a millimeter thick."

A sharp pain stabbed Maya in her left temple. She sat back in her chair and gently rubbed the spot with two fingers. Then, she slid open the center desk drawer and retrieved the large plastic bottle of ibuprofen she kept there. She took four at once, expertly swallowing down the pills without water. She had been in motion since early morning—first, getting things ready for Vered's birthday party, then a stop at her office, two trips to the hotel and then back here again. She needed to come up for air, or she'd crash.

She powered off her computer and stood up.

When she exited the building, she looked down at her watch and laughed. She'd forgotten that it had recently stopped working. She'd have to squeeze in some time over the next few days to tinker with it.

She looked up at the sky. A few ashy clouds shrouded the moon.

23

I⊤ ⊤OOK CASSANDRA AN HOUR and a half to decode the next file. It was the longest one yet. She printed out the pages and began to read.

> *My brother told me that the Treasure Scroll was kept with other Temple scrolls in a small, windowless room in the Court of Priests. Alexander and Eleazar made their way there in the dead of night, stole the scroll, and fled with it to the home of Nahum of Gamala, the leader of the Pharisee conspiracy, who lived in the Lower City. Nahum....*[text corrupted]

Exasperated, Cassandra threw the sheaf of print-outs to the stone floor. She hated when Mariamne's story suddenly broke off like that: "text corrupted." It was like watching a movie when the DVD suddenly froze, forcing you to skip over the scratched part. She prayed that the scroll's hiding place wasn't buried in one of these corrupted parts. Because if it was, she was screwed! Her keeper would put the blame on her. And punish her.

She bent down, gathered up the bundle of pages, and resumed her reading.

> *Writing with a stylus on pure copper proved extremely difficult. The metal surface was rolled very thin. Each letter had to be incised carefully so as not to puncture the metal. After the scribes finished copying the twelve columns of the Treasure Scroll, they riveted the copper sheets together with tiny nails. Then, they carefully*

rolled up the copper sheet into a loose coil so as not to flatten the raised letters.

The Pharisean scribes constantly argued among themselves: What kind of treasure map was this? What did the pairs and triplets of Greek letters mean? Where were these hiding places? The Sadducees had cleverly disguised the locations, offering only cryptic clues.

Cassandra was fascinated that these ancient conspirators had resorted to cryptography to safeguard their treasure. She'd always loved reading about ancient puzzles and codes: Linear A, the Rosetta Stone, the Voynich Manuscript. Goldmayer's encrypted files posed comparable riddles. Despite the danger she now found herself in, she was excited at the thought of cracking this age-old puzzle.

But it wasn't a game for these ancient Jews. Too much was at stake.

When the copper scroll was finished, it was not an exact copy of the original. The Pharisees' duplicate scroll lacked the protokollon found in the first scroll. This was Nahum's idea—to exclude the Sadducees' first leaf from the copy that was to be offered to the Romans. He feared that some of the fanciful notions contained in the priests' protokollon—visions of chariots rimmed with eyes, soothsaying angels, and giant nephilim—would make the Romans dismiss the copper scroll as an elaborate hoax. And then all would be lost.

Some of the other Pharisees argued that the pro-tokollon might contain vital clues to the Treasures' locations. Or it might be part of their secret code. But Nahum would not alter his decision.

He decided to send Alexander into the desert with the two scrolls until Nahum could arrange a meeting with the Romans. I persuaded my brother to let me accompany him. The Pharisees knew that the Temple priests would turn Jerusalem upside down looking for their missing scroll. But they would never think to search for it in Secacah, a remote desert outpost near the Salt Sea, where a handful of Jewish ascetics lived. Nor would the Roman legions bother to attack such an insignificant backwater.

So Mariamne and her brother had escaped the destruction of Jerusalem!

Cassandra stood up and walked over to the sink. She let the cold water run for a few seconds, then held the crusted dish towel under the tap. How good the cool, damp fabric felt pressed against her sweaty forehead! She filled a glass with icy water from a bottle in the refrigerator and returned to the desk.

What sacrifices these Jews had been willing to make to save their people and their way of life! Cassandra had never had to sacrifice anything to be Jewish. She had never experienced anti-Semitism. She'd never had to defend her tradition against those who would deny its legitimacy. A year ago, she had gladly turned her back on Judaism to seek spiritual enlightenment elsewhere. The Buddhism she'd embraced didn't require allegiance to any god or the performance of meaningless rituals. At least not the kind of American Buddhism she practiced—a mash-up of chants, meditation, vegetarianism, and yoga. But the truth was she'd never given her own tradition much of a chance.

And now, here she was, a prisoner in an airless East Jerusalem apartment. Bars on the windows. A padlock on the door. An unknown fate awaiting her once she finished decrypting these files.

Why had she spent all of her time decoding these files instead of trying to escape? Why had she let Mariamne play Scheherezade to her, keeping her captive rather than keeping her alive?

DAY 2

Tuesday

24

A LITTLE AFTER 6:00 A.M., Rafi Miller pounded on the front door of Maya's apartment. The sound echoed in the dark stairwell.

"C'mon, Maya! I don't have all day!"

Curled up in a fetal position on the sagging orange loveseat, Maya struggled out of a deep sleep. She pulled a striped cotton robe over her shorty pajamas.

In bare feet, she shuffled into Vered's room. Her three-year-old daughter lay sprawled on her small bed, uncovered, the pink top sheet crumpled as usual on the floor. Vered's new doll, whom she'd named Merida after the princess in *Brave*, her favorite movie, lay on the floor at the foot of the bed.

Maya sat down on the mattress and placed her hand lightly on Vered's shoulder. Gently, she rocked the thin wing of bone back and forth until Vered opened her willow-green eyes.

"Too sleepy, Ima," she mumbled and shut her eyes. She immediately slid back into sleep.

Maya shook her daughter's shoulders more vigorously.

"You have to get up, sweetheart. Abba's here. He's taking you to the zoo today. Remember? You do want to go, don't you?"

Maya bit down on her lower lip. How she longed to wrap Vered in her arms and keep her safe at home, not release her to her irresponsible father. It was only a matter of time before that *mamzer* put her in harm's way. Maya fought back tears, as she always did on the days her daughter went off with Rafi. It wasn't fair to burden a three-year-old with grown-up worries.

Vered continued to lie still on the narrow mattress, her eyes closed. Then, she suddenly leapt out of bed.

"I 'ready picked out what I wanna wear. My pink party dress! And my princess crown! Won't the a'mals be surprised to see me so dressed up! That's how they'll know yesterday was my birfday."

Before Maya could object, Vered ran over to her dresser, jerked open the bottom drawer, grabbed a pair of panties, and wiggled into them. Using both hands, she wriggled out of her Little Miss Kitty nightgown. Then, she raced over to her closet and yanked a frilly pink dress off its hanger. Grunting, she pulled down the dress, still zipped, over her head. Next, she plucked the pink plastic tiara from the recessed window sill and shoved it into her unruly curls. Finally, she slid her tiny feet into the pink plastic sandals adorned with sequins that lay under the bed, each shoe on the wrong foot, and dashed out the bedroom door.

Maya sighed and followed her daughter into the living room, which also served as Maya's bedroom and office.

She's so much like me. As Ima used to say to me when I was little, especially when she was mad at me, "May you be blessed with a daughter just like yourself."

Catching sight of her father, Vered ran up to him and circled his knees with her freckled arms.

"Abba!"

Even at a distance, Maya could smell Rafi's heavy cologne, so strong it almost made her gag. His dark hair, slicked down with too much pomade, gave off a pungent odor. She noticed a diamond stud in his left ear. When had he had that done? Why had he chosen to wear all black for a trip to the zoo: black silk shirt and black pants, the Rolex coiling around his hairy wrist, and a heavy gold chain around his neck? On his feet, he wore expensive black Italian shoes with no socks. As if he was still a high roller with money to burn.

"We goin' to the zoo! We goin' to the zoo!" Vered sang in a high tuneless voice. "Can we see every a'mal, Abba? And I want ice cream!

Chocolate, with sprinkles! And can I get a stuffie in the gift shop? Merida needs a friend!"

Rafi laughed, his broad chest expanding to fill his sleek dark shirt. Because he was wearing sunglasses, Maya couldn't tell if his amusement was genuine. He always put on such an act for their daughter. He was her storybook knight. And Maya was the wicked stepmother, who wanted to cut out her heart.

"Come on, *ziskeit*." Rafi held out a manicured hand toward Vered. With the forefinger of his other hand, he twirled a dark curl that dangled down in the middle of his forehead. "Let's go have fun!"

"Don't load her up with sugar, Rafi! You know how she gets. I'll meet you at the snack bar at eleven-thirty. Don't be late."

Then, they were gone. The heavy wooden door slammed behind them. The house fell silent. Even the cranky refrigerator shuddered to a stop.

Maya hated these moments. Every Tuesday and Friday, Rafi picked up Vered for a few hours and took her away. As much as Rafi complained about not seeing his daughter enough, Maya knew he was glad to be doing so little "babysitting," as he called the time he spent with his daughter. Since their separation, he had been happy to have Maya shoulder most of the parenting burden, leaving him to play short-order prince.

With sharp bitterness, Maya recalled the last phone conversation she'd had with Penina Yarom, the community social worker assigned to their case. That damn woman was like a cold sore she couldn't get rid of.

"It's all about setting priorities, Maya. If you keep choosing your work over your family, you know how things will turn out. You'll lose Vered."

A swarm of angry bees whirred inside Maya's chest. Blood pulsed in her temples.

"No!"

Maya immediately berated herself for shouting at the case worker. *Calm down. Take a few deep breaths. Listen and think before reacting.* But she just couldn't hold back the desperate cry that had escaped her throat. She would not lose Vered!

"I'm sorry, Penina. I've been extremely busy." Maya's voice was now soft, almost a whisper. "Working on a very important case."

Silence on the other end. The rasp of a match. A sharp intake of breath. A slow, phlegmy outbreath, then a cough as the smoke exited the older woman's ruined lungs.

"As I said, Maya, it's a matter of setting priorities. If you can't find an hour to meet with Rafi and me at my office...."

"Of course I can find an hour, Penina." She was trying hard to keep the pleading out of her voice. "Nothing is more important to me than Vered!"

Penina wasn't buying it. Her tone was brittle. Without a hint of sympathy.

"It's not good for your daughter's mental and emotional health that you're in constant danger."

"I'm not! Is that what Rafi's been telling you? That's bullshit! I spend plenty of time behind a desk."

"And what about your nights away from home? Your distractedness. The stress you're under all the time." A long pause. The rasp of another match. A breath in. Cough. Exhale. "Can you really be present for Vered? I understand that Rafi has a new lady friend, who loves children. He tells me she adores Maya."

That snake! Using his new squeeze as a weapon. Just for spite. The truth was that Rafi didn't really like children. He'd been more of an absentee parent than Maya. Barely paying attention to the baby until she learned to talk, and then losing patience with her over the smallest things. But Maya was not surprised that her handsome ex-husband had managed to fool their caseworker. The man was both snake and snake-charmer.

"Listen, Penina. I expect my case to wrap up in a few days. After that, I can come in whenever you want. Whatever works for you. And for Rafi. I'll work around your schedules."

In truth, no time was convenient for Maya. Her schedule was unpredictable. But she always had her parents for back-up. She would do whatever it took to keep her daughter.

Maya ran to the window and looked down. Rafi was bent over, buckling Vered into the backseat of his leased red Audi. Maya thought she saw someone sitting in the front passenger seat. A woman with long dark hair.

She stood at the window, watching. She felt a sudden tightness in her chest.

After the red Audi drove away, she padded barefoot into the kitchen to make herself a cup of tea. As she lifted the chipped mug from its brass hook, she noticed that one of the wooden cabinet doors was ajar. Reaching up on tiptoe, she slammed it shut, then pushed on the wooden panel firmly until she heard the latch click. Then, she saw that two of the black plastic knobs on the small gas stove were out of alignment. No matter how many times Maya reminded her mother, Camille always left the knobs cockeyed. Carefully, Maya lined them up properly.

Then, she filled up the kettle and set it on the stove to boil.

25

SITTING STIFF AS A SENTRY at the large black oak desk in his office, Father Antoine de Plessy pored over the richly illustrated children's book he'd just received from his nephew Clément. It was entitled *Tales of the Knights Templar*. He was sure that Clément had found it in some musty London bookshop on one of his business trips. Clément was always on the lookout for such curiosities for his favorite uncle.

In his mid-sixties, Father Antoine was a tall, long-boned man, whose angular face was dominated by a scraggly beard, streaked unevenly with gray. He was dressed in the simple habit of a Dominican monk: a white robe extending from his neck down to the floor, with a white yoke over the top of the robe and sleeves down to his wrist, ending in extra-wide cuffs. From the corners of his eyes forked a series of dark lines, not the usual crows'-feet caused by a lifetime of laughter but more like scratches from a raptor's talon. They suggested a temperament beset by bitterness and mistrust.

As the Dominican monk now leafed through the pages of the oversized volume, he marveled at the fine detail—the articulated joints of the greaves and gauntlets, the colored emblems marking each knight's rank on his shield. To a child these were just costumes, such as one might wear for Mardi Gras. But for Father Antoine, they were symbols of the erstwhile splendor of Christendom. Father Antoine had tried to convince all his nieces and nephews that Christianity had lost its way in the centuries following the Crusades. And that it was in danger of losing much more ground to the Muslim hordes currently invading Italy, France, Germany, and other parts of Western Europe. They were now facing a disaster even greater than the excesses of Luther.

That's why Father Antoine had dedicated his life to studying the early Christians. The martyred saints, the noble Crusaders. He believed that it was not too late to restore Christianity to its former glory. To summon Christ back into a fallen world.

For the past fifteen years, he had focused his attention on the mysterious Copper Scroll as the instrument of this deliverance.

One day, he would marshal the resources necessary to restore the Temple treasures to their proper place in Jerusalem: a special chapel in the Church of the Holy Sepulchre. In so doing, he would fulfill the Crusaders' unfinished mission: to win back the Holy Land for Christ. Others might laugh at him, calling his theory about the Copper Scroll "unscientific" and "preposterous." But he would show them all.

A knock on the door interrupted his ruminations.

"What is it, Brother Vincent?"

"Someone to see you, Father Antoine."

The younger monk kept his eyes fixed on the dark floorboards under his black shoes. His spindly figure was almost completely swallowed up by his billowing white robe.

"Who is it?"

"An Israeli Intelligence officer. Maya Rimon. I told her you had no time this morning."

"First the Jerusalem police, and now Israeli Intelligence! Will they never stop harassing me? Send her away!"

Thrusting open the door, Maya strode into Father Antoine's office. Brother Vincent scurried away and disappeared down a dark corridor.

"What is it now?"

Without waiting to be invited, Maya sat down in one of the three straight-backed chairs facing Father Antoine's broad desk.

No doubt the Israeli agent had come here to deliver some new trumped-up charge. Last time, it had been the claim that the Académie was not paying proper fees to the Jerusalem municipal authorities. But Father Antoine knew what this was really about: the

Académie's close relationship with its sister institutions in Lebanon, Iraq, and Egypt. The Israelis had long suspected the Académie of spying for Muslim extremists. They would never admit that their intelligence services were tapping the phone lines, looking for terrorist connections. Intercepting mail. Hacking into the Catholic school's computers with impunity. Of course, they'd found nothing. But they would never stop trying.

"I'm investigating a murder that took place at the Zion Gate Hotel two days ago," Maya said. "The victim was Professor Boaz Goldmayer. Since you're registered for the conference at the hotel, I'd like to ask you a few questions."

"You're wasting your time. I know nothing about this."

"Can you tell me where you were this past Sunday night between eight and midnight?"

Father Antoine bristled. "Sunday night? I was here."

"Can anyone vouch for your whereabouts at that time?"

"I am afraid not. I retired early and spent the evening in my room, reading. Then, I went to bed. Am I a suspect?"

Maya wrote a few notes in her black notebook. Her placid face betrayed nothing.

"I understand you're an expert on the Copper Scroll, Father De Plessy. You must have heard rumors that Goldmayer had succeeded in locating a lost duplicate mentioned at the end of that scroll. Unfortunately, he was killed before he could announce his findings."

"I don't pay attention to conference gossip. Besides, Goldmayer's theories—"

The Dominican monk suddenly clutched his chest and began wheezing. His liver-spotted right hand groped the surface of his desk, knocking over a glass of water and a narrow wooden box, scattering pens and pencils all over the damp blotter. The monk's eyes, wide with panic, stared at his trembling hand. At last, his fingers found what they were searching for. Father De Plessy frantically pressed the inhaler to his bloodless lips, which clamped around the device. For several seconds, he sucked eagerly on the plastic mouthpiece, then collapsed back into his chair.

"Asthma. It's these ancient manuscripts. Saturated with dust and mold."

Maya nodded but said nothing.

When De Plessy finally spoke, his voice was labored and reedy.

"Have you not wondered, Agent Rimon, why nobody has ever found a single one of the treasures listed in the Copper Scroll after decades of excavation? Could the reason be that the Temple treasures no longer remain where they were originally hidden? My research, much of which is still unpublished, has led me to conclude that this is indeed the case. The truth is that the treasures are no longer located in Israel. They were removed long ago and hidden elsewhere."

No reaction from the Israeli agent. She gazed blankly at the bleached white skull sitting at the corner of the monk's desk.

"I can now prove incontrovertibly," the monk continued, "that after defeating Saladin's army in the decisive Battle of Montgisard in 1177, the Knights Templar came into possession of a secret map— uncannily similar to the Copper Scroll—that led them to the buried treasures of the Second Temple. They dug all of them up and brought them to Scotland. Among the treasures was the legendary Stone of Destiny, referred to in line forty-seven of the Copper Scroll as *even shehorah. Le pierre noir. The black stone.* For the past eight centuries, this Stone of Scone has been used in Scottish and English corona-tions. The rest of the Temple treasures are buried somewhere near Rosslyn Chapel on the Scottish borders."

Still no reaction from the Israeli agent. Was she even listen-ing to him?

"So you see," said Father Antoine, "I am not the least interested in whatever your Professor Goldmayer was planning to reveal about the whereabouts of the Copper Scroll. Whatever he was boasting about was obviously wrong."

"Sounds like you and Goldmayer had issues, as the Americans say."

Father Antoine placed both his hands, palms down, on his desk, rose up out of his chair, and leaned forward. Because of the thickness of his glasses, perching uneasily upon his large scythe of a nose, his pupils appeared black and hard like rosary beads.

"Forgive my candor, Agent Rimon, but most of what your Jewish scholars have to say about the scrolls is nothing but parochialism and propaganda, based on a self-interested Zionist agenda. Is it not enough that you seized control of the scrolls after the Six-Day War? Do you also want to monopolize their interpretation?"

Maya sat rigid in her chair, staring at the Dominican monk with undisguised hostility. Her folded hands lay immobile on her dark skirt.

"I'll be in touch if I have any more questions."

Maya stood up, reached into her shoulder bag, and withdrew a business card.

"If you think of anything relevant, please call me."

As she reached forward to give De Plessy her card, Maya's eyes fell upon another business card lying face up on the desk: "Habib Salameh. Dealer in Rare Antiquities." The words—in Hebrew, Arabic, and English—were engraved in raised antique script on top of the image of a parchment scroll.

She lifted up Salameh's card and held it out to De Plessy.

"What's your relationship with this man?"

"Why should that be any concern of yours?"

"He's a person of interest in this case."

"I have purchased antiquities on occasion from Monsieur Salameh. And we share a scholarly interest in the Dead Sea Scrolls. Particularly the Copper Scroll."

With a bony hand, De Plessy reached up and adjusted the black beret perched atop his bald head. Many of his fellow monks at the Académie considered his beret an affectation, but it reminded him of his student days in Paris.

"When was the last time you saw Salameh?"

"It so happens that he came to see me just a few days ago. He wanted to discuss Boaz Goldmayer's most recently published article on the Copper Scroll, a new theory about the *protokollon*. We both assumed that Goldmayer would be expanding upon these ideas in his keynote address. Alas, we'll never know what the poor man was planning to reveal."

Father Antoine could see by the quizzical look on the Israeli agent's face that she was completely out of her depth. How could she hope to get to the bottom of Goldmayer's murder when she was so woefully ignorant of what was at stake?

"Did Salameh mention De Vaux?"

Father Antoine was so surprised by the Israeli agent's question that he was unable to stifle his gasp. His thick eyebrows shot up, then jackknifed to the bridge of his nose, forming a pair of dark wings.

"As a matter of fact, he did. Father De Vaux was one of us, you know. A French Dominican. Monsieur Salameh asked me about De Vaux's unpublished papers. I told him they were no longer housed here at the Académie. They've been moved to the Shrine of the Book."

The Israeli agent nodded but asked no more questions. Why was she so interested in Roland De Vaux? The man had been dead for almost fifty years! Most of his findings had been published decades ago. Why this sudden interest in his scholarship? What did it have to do with the American professor's murder? What had Boaz Goldmayer discovered that interested both Israeli Intelligence and an Arab antiquities merchant?

They did not shake hands when their meeting ended. Through the thick panes of his mullioned window, Father Antoine watched the Israeli agent walk quickly down the stone walk toward the main road. Near the end of the walk, she stopped briefly to admire his herb and wildflower garden planted alongside the path. She bent down to read several of the botanical labels, scribbling in her black notebook. He hoped she was duly impressed by his collection of Biblical poisons: gall, wormwood, and hemlock.

26

BEFORE PICKING UP HER DAUGHTER at the zoo, Maya decided to make a brief stop at headquarters to probe deeper into Habib Salameh's background. His file in the Service database didn't reveal much new information. She already knew he was an authority on ancient Near Eastern scrolls and manuscripts. And that he was connected to a worldwide network of customers, legitimate as well as black market. And that he was rumored to have eyes and ears everywhere.

Given his connections to Qumran scholars, Salameh would certainly have known about Goldmayer's widely publicized claims that he'd finally pinned down the location of the Treasure Scroll. He would also have known that Goldmayer was expected to reveal the scroll's location at the conference in Jerusalem. It was not hard to connect the dots.

Maya scrolled back to the beginning of the file to learn more about Salameh's early years. He'd been born to a French mother and Maronite Christian father and raised in Beirut. The Lebanese Civil War had forced him to abandon his graduate archaeological studies and join his father's banking firm in Paris. When the war had ended, he'd returned to the Middle East and bought a small antiquities shop in Beirut. Fifteen years ago, he'd relocated to East Jerusalem, gaining entrance to Israel on his French passport. He'd built his East Jerusalem antiquities shop into a successful international business, catering to some of the wealthiest collectors in the Middle East, Europe, South Africa, and the Americas.

Salameh's motive for getting involved in this Goldmayer business had to be the lure of fabulous wealth. Sixty-five billion dollars.

But why would he want to murder Goldmayer? Had the American professor discovered Salameh's black market connections and threatened to expose him? Or had the murder been an accident? Until now, Salameh had never been convicted of any violent crime. But if it wasn't Salameh, who else would have benefited from Goldmayer's death?

The sound of nearby church bells startled Maya. She glanced down at the old Poljot watch, which she'd managed to fix late last night. Eleven o'clock! She was supposed to meet Rafi and Vered at the zoo in thirty minutes. At this time of day, she'd have to hustle to get there in time, find parking, and meet them in the snack bar as they'd agreed.

She logged out of the secure site and shut down her computer. Masha waved to her as she dashed toward the front doors. Without slowing down, she flashed an open palm toward her friend, then pushed open the heavy door.

27

By the time Maya parked her 1996 silver Corolla in the sprawling parking lot of the Jerusalem Biblical Zoo, she was already ten minutes late for her meet-up with Rafi. Even on the perimeter of the city, traffic was becoming impossible.

She made her way at a steady trot to the park entrance, paid for her ticket, and headed for the snack bar next to the gift shop. It took only a few moments to see that Rafi and Vered were not there. They weren't in the gift shop, either. She walked rapidly down the winding path leading to the big cats, Vered's favorites. No sign of them at the lions. Or at the cheetahs.

She headed toward the leopard enclosure. As she passed by the howler monkeys, she came upon a large crowd. A shrill voice boomed over the huddle of packed bodies.

"In all of human history, has there ever been a time when the world was worse off than it is now? Cry out to your fellow sinners: 'Cease your sinning! Return to God!'"

"Halleluyah, Jesus!" came a cry from someone in the crowd.

"Praise the Lord!"

Maya moved closer. She raised herself on tiptoe, trying to catch a glimpse of the speaker. No luck. She tried to elbow her way forward. A young woman, gripping a stroller with one hand and a young boy with the other, glared sullenly at her. Maya backed away and found another way in, past a group of schoolchildren jostling one other while their young teacher texted on her phone. Rising up again on tiptoe, she caught sight of a tangle of wild blond curls and the pink tips of the speaker's ears.

"When the Rapture occurs, it will come in the twinkle of an eye. Those who have died in the Lord will be resurrected. They will be caught up in the air to meet the Lord, together with believers, who are still among the living. The Rapture will be altogether unexpected—except by those who have been reading the signs. The remainder of the world will not know that He has been here. They will not know what has become of the missing ones. Then, things will settle back into their old condition. The world will continue on its way, as Sodom did after Lot departed from it."

Maya continued to push toward the front of the crowd, driven by curiosity, but also by irritation. Yet another sidewalk prophet! The city was being overrun. Whether it was ultra-Orthodox Jews exhorting their errant brothers and sisters to return to the right path, or born-again Christians urging sinners toward salvation, or Sharia Muslims haranguing bare-headed women to cover their shame, they were making it increasingly difficult for normal people to go about their business.

And here was yet another lost soul stricken with the city's renowned malady. A kind of religious delirium. Psychologists called it "Jerusalem Syndrome." *La fièvre Jerusalemienne*. Some bore this affliction even before they set foot on holy ground. Others caught the fever once they arrived. They became obsessed with being ritually pure, taking endless baths and constantly clipping their nails. Or they staked out a place at the Western Wall or some other holy site, refusing to decamp. Some believed they were holy emissaries—Jesus Christ or the Messiah. Most of them returned to their senses after a few sessions with a psychiatrist or a brief stay in an Israeli clinic. But for some, the spiritual transformation was permanent. A true metamorphosis. Judging by the fevered pitch and rush of this man's voice, Maya would place him in the latter group.

Maya felt a particular antipathy toward these religious types, those who swore off this world and embraced the fantasy of a better world to come. If someone were to ask her about her own faith, she'd

probably say she was agnostic. Not quite ready to cross off God altogether but not a loyal fan, either. *So different from Hillel Stone.* She
did believe, however, that messianism was a lie. A dangerous lie. In
their rush to secure their special place in the next world, these religious extremists didn't mind trampling underfoot any and all those
living in this one.

Only a few rows of onlookers now separated Maya from the
speaker, whose voice was rising in fervor as he came to the end of his
jeremiad. Riled by the man's strident tone, the howler monkeys began
to screech. Some swung themselves wildly from branch to branch.
The speaker's voice rose to drown them out. Stretching her neck,
Maya finally caught sight of the speaker. An emaciated young man,
dressed in a simple, white robe reaching down to his sandaled feet. In
one hand, he held a crooked wooden staff. A corded rope circled his
slight waist. Clear blue eyes blazed out of a pallid face.

"And then the Antichrist will arrive, an incarnation of the devil,
just as Jesus was an incarnation of God. He will come to Jerusalem
and perform great signs and wonders here. The Antichrist will so
delude the Chosen People that they will accept him as their Messiah
and pay him divine honors in the Temple. And it will be at this very
moment that Jesus will return to Earth and destroy him."

Hearing this man's fervid words summoned up in Maya's mind a
not-too-distant memory:

> She was in Tel Aviv at a left-wing rally that she'd
> been assigned to cover as part of the security detail.
> The rally had been called to protest the latest
> parliamentary outrage enacted by Israel's right-wing
> politicians. At one point, Carmi Gillon, former Head
> of the Shin Bet, Israel's FBI, had declared that Israel
> was being run by "a bunch of pyromaniacs led by an
> egomaniac to its ultimate destruction." Gillon had
> warned his liberal audience that "continuing the

extreme Messianic activity on the Temple Mount will lead to Armageddon." He had urged progressive Israelis to side with the realists, not the zealots, if they wanted the Jewish state to survive.

It was only later that Maya realized how prescient Gillon had been. The truth was that the ancient Jewish Zealots had never really died out. They'd simply updated their wardrobe and weapons.

She now stood face to face with the robed preacher.

His eyes, coals of blue fire, burned into hers like dry ice on raw flesh. Fear rippled through her skin. She shook her arms to shake it off. The man's wild eyes drifted skyward, trained on some ghostly vision in the heavens. Maya followed his gaze. She saw only white cumulus clouds suspended in a blue sky.

When she lowered her eyes, she saw a howler monkey mooning her with his hairless buttocks, his enormous testicles dangling down like ripe fruit. She laughed. Enough with this lunacy. Time to get on with today's mission. To rescue her daughter from Rafi's undependable clutches.

28

SHE FOUND THEM AT THE leopard exhibit. Or rather, she found Rafi.

Her ex-husband was sitting slouched back on a wooden bench, his long legs stretched out in front of him on the white pavement. He was so absorbed in texting on his phone that he didn't hear Maya call out his name. Only when she stood directly in front of him, arms akimbo, glaring down at him, did he look up, startled.

"Maya! I didn't expect you to come inside. Weren't we supposed to do our hand-off at the snack bar?"

"It's way past the time we agreed on." She looked around. "Where's Vered?"

"Dunno," he said. He glanced back down at his screen. "She was here just a minute ago."

Maya scanned the area, feeling the familiar prickle of anxiety in the center of her chest. Vered was nowhere in sight. Two leopards prowled restlessly on the other side of the high glass walls that separated them from visitors, many of whom were pressed up against the glass. A class from an elementary school crowded together at one corner of the giant glass window. Several children tapped repeatedly on the glass to get the big cats' attention. The leopards quickened their nervous pacing, baring their sharp teeth, hissing at the children.

Then she saw Vered.

Her three-year-old daughter was balanced precariously near the top of a low-branching tree, not far from the upper edge of one of the glass walls. Leaning her body forward, Vered curled and uncurled a chubby index finger, beckoning to a pair of young leopard cubs, who were wrestling with each other in the dirt near the front of the enclosure.

The cubs paid no attention to her.

But the mother leopard was moving toward them. Her sleek body slouched close to the ground, her muscled shoulders rippling as she assumed an attack position. Her pointed ears slanted back. Her sharp teeth were clenched in a menacing grin.

Vered climbed up to a higher branch, inching closer to the glass wall's top edge. With both hands she reached out and grabbed hold of the shiny aluminum molding. Then, she stretched out a stubby leg toward the silver strip, hooking one bare ankle over it.

Maya screamed: "Vered! No!"

Surprised to hear her name, the little girl twisted around. The sharp movement made her lose her balance. She wobbled for a moment, then fell backwards.

Maya ran toward her daughter, roughly pushing aside several children in her way. When she reached the base of the tree, she found Vered lying on the ground, looking up, miraculously unhurt. A dense cluster of bushes had broken her fall. On her daughter's face was a gleeful smile. She pointed at the cubs, who were now batting at each other with their floppy paws.

Maya grabbed Vered by the arm and hugged her close. Tears instantly welled up in her eyes, then spilled over, wetting her daughter's cheek. With the side of her hand, Maya wiped them away, then kissed Vered's soft, damp flesh.

"Why are you crying, Ima? I not got hurted."

Breathing raggedly, Maya glanced into the glass enclosure.

On the other side of the glass, the mother leopard's glistening yellow eyes were fixed on Vered. All over her sinewed body, her muscles tensed. Her brindled tail whipped back and forth like an angry serpent.

"Let's move away from here, *motek*. We're making the leopards nervous."

Holding Vered firmly by the hand, Maya walked over to Rafi. He stood watching them, his mouth pinched shut. Blue mirrored sunglasses masked his eyes. The ground in front of the bench where he'd been sitting was littered with blackened butts.

For the first time in months, Maya craved a cigarette. She'd given up smoking almost four years ago, as soon as she'd learned she was pregnant. But she desperately wanted a cigarette now.

She squatted down and stared intently into her daughter's moss-green eyes.

"Abba didn't do such a good job watching you, did he?"

"It wasn't my fault what happened! I had eyes on her every minute 'til you showed up and distracted me."

Maya's mouth dropped open. She gasped, then clamped her jaw shut.

"You know what, Rafi? I don't need to listen to your shit anymore!"

Rafi stamped his foot on the packed ground in front of the bench. "Don't lecture me about being a parent, Maya! The truth is that you'd rather play spy than take care of your own kid. Selfish bitch!"

Maya bit down on her lower lip until she could taste blood. She shook her head, breathed in, then stood up. Her thighs and knees ached. Her mouth felt dry. She grabbed hold of her daughter's wrist.

"Let's go, Vered."

Vered's lower lip began to tremble. She broke free of Maya's grasp and ran over to the far end of the bench. She grabbed the large white plastic bag lying there, reached in, and pulled out a brown plush horse.

"Look what Abba got me! And he bought me chocolate ice cream wi'f sprinkles and hot fudge sauce!"

"Your Abba can do no wrong, can he?"

Rafi threw down his cigarette and smashed it with his heel. "Drop it, Maya! No harm done. Just move on."

Maya sucked in a deep breath. She squeezed her eyes shut, then opened them and glared at Rafi until he looked away. She inhaled deeply, slowing her breathing until she felt calmer.

Rafi shook another cigarette out of the cellophane-wrapped pack, pinched it between his lips, then crumpled the empty pack and threw it to the sidewalk. He lit up and swallowed a mouthful of smoke. Then, he turned his face away, addressing his next remarks to the leopards pacing behind the glass walls.

"There's something I've been meaning to tell you, Maya." He paused, then blew out the smoke in a long, black thread. "I'm suing for sole custody. I think it's best that I assume primary responsibility for raising Vered. You're away from home too much. And your job puts you in constant danger."

Maya's heart dropped into the pit of her stomach. She couldn't breathe. Blood drained from her hands and feet, leaving them numb and cold.

What lousy timing! She didn't need this extra pressure. Now, she'd have to hire a lawyer. Come up with a clever strategy to fight Rafi. Where the hell would she find the time? And the money.

Maya reached out and grabbed her daughter by the hand, pulling her down the zigzag path toward the exit. Vered clutched her new plush horse close to her small body and stumbled along after her mother. She didn't even ask for another chocoloate ice cream as they passed the snack bar on their way out.

29

DRIVING BACK TO THE CENTER of Jerusalem, Maya had second thoughts about her plan to spend a few more hours with Vered before going into work. She just wasn't in the mood to deal with her daughter's incessant demands for attention. She'd ask her father to pick her up as usual at *gan* and bring her home with him to Rivkah.

And she decided not to tell Vered's teacher about what had happened at the zoo. No matter how she spun it, Maya would come off looking as neglectful as Rafi. It was crucial that Rivkah keep trusting Maya as a mother. She was hoping to call her as a character witness at the custody hearing.

When she reached the community center that housed Vered's pre-school, Maya double-parked and dropped her daughter off in the classroom on the first floor. Vered quickly pulled free of her mother's embrace and ran off to join her friends, chattering happily about the leopard cubs and showing off her new stuffed horse. She didn't look back when Maya left the room.

A few blocks from the day care center, Maya turned onto a quiet residential street and parked her silver Corolla at the curb. She dug her cell phone out of her shoulder bag and called Sarit Levine. The police detective picked up after the third ring.

"What now, Maya? I've got nothing new for you. I told you I'd let you know."

"You promised to send over the hotel security tapes."

A long pause at the other end.

"I'll have to get back to you."

"Never mind. They probably weren't useful anyway."

Maya didn't want Sarit to know that she'd already viewed the tapes, thanks to Ziggy. That she already knew about the murderer's unusual height, his silver rings, the oversized waiter's uniform and shoes left behind. If Sarit believed she still held the upper hand, maybe she'd stay out of Maya's way.

"What about your interviews with possible suspects?" asked Maya.

"We questioned a few professors. Goldmayer's rivals. Most of their alibis checked out."

"Whose didn't?"

"Father Antoine De Plessy and Stanley Lowenthal. De Plessy claims he was at the Biblical Academy all night. In his room, reading."

Maya had already crossed De Plessy off her suspect list. Whatever Goldmayer was selling, the Dominican monk wasn't buying. She couldn't understand how any of the other Qumran scholars could possibly take De Plessy's outrageous theories seriously. Medieval knights carting off the Temple treasures to Scotland?

Sarit broke into her thoughts.

"My money's on one of the Lowenthals. Old Stanley didn't show up at the opening banquet. Neither did his son. He claims that he was in his hotel room with Adam when Goldmayer was killed. Hotel confirms he ordered room service for two that night. But that doesn't let them off the hook. One of them could have slipped out, murdered Goldmayer, and slipped back into their room during our time frame. I've asked around about Stanley. It seems like he's had a run-in with just about everyone at the conference."

"So what's the motive?"

"It appears that Goldmayer might have discovered something that these scholars have been after for decades. A lost Dead Sea Scroll. Just the kind of thing that could turn an obscure professor into an international celebrity overnight. And turn all his rivals green with envy. Fits Stanley Lowenthal's profile perfectly."

Maya wasn't so sure. A narcissist like Lowenthal wouldn't be satisfied bringing down a rival by stealth. He would want to humiliate him publicly.

"Did you also interview Lowenthal's son, Adam?"

"What an odd duck! Never looks you in the eye." She snorted. "He confirms that he was with his father all night. Claims they ate together, then rented a movie. The hotel confirms that the movie ended close to midnight. Still gives them plenty of time to commit the murder. So the two of them are staying on my short list."

"What about Habib Salameh?"

"The Lebanese antiquities dealer?" Sarit's gruff laugh was predictably mean-spirited. "Claims he was at a party Sunday night. At the home of that pretentious Arab socialite, Lena al-Sayegh."

"Does his alibi check out?"

"I didn't even bother to follow up. That man always has an ironclad alibi. Paid for in cash. Everyone at that party will swear they saw him there. If he *is* the killer, we'll need hard evidence."

"Keep me posted."

Maya hung up. Then, she speed-dialed Ziggy Dweck.

"Check out the hotel's phone logs for Sunday night. Calls made from the Lowenthals' room between eight and midnight. Cross-check the numbers against Bezeq's records. And do a cell tower dump on Habib Salameh's mobile. Call me as soon as you have that information."

"What about you?"

"I'm going to Sheikh Jarrah to check out Salameh's alibi. I'm betting it's bogus."

"Let me come with. It's not such a good idea for you to go to Sheikh Jarrah by yourself. That neighborhood's always dicey."

"You're such a Jewish mother, Ziggy!" Maya chuckled. "I'll be fine. Save your escort services for when I'm in real danger."

As soon as she hung up, Maya felt a sharp stab of hunger. She'd stop and grab a falafel and lemonade right after her conversation with Madame al-Sayegh.

30

As she made her way into the mixed Arab-Jewish neighborhood of Sheikh Jarrah, Maya's mobile jangled in her shoulder bag. It was Ziggy.

"*Nu?*"

"You were right. Habib Salameh made a number of calls Sunday night. All calls made before ten-thirty came from a cell tower near the Zion Gate Hotel."

"Thanks, Zig. I owe you."

Maya turned the corner. At the end of the block, set well back from the street, stood a three-story villa constructed of glittering pink Jerusalem stone. It was the home of Madame Lena al-Sayegh, the most celebrated hostess in Arab Jerusalem.

As Maya had anticipated, Lena was hospitable and charming. And completely evasive. She warmly welcomed Maya into her elegant home, furnished with broad Turkish carpets, low-slung earth-toned leather couches, and hand-embroidered pillows.

Lena was a stunning woman of an undefined age. Her clothes were stylish yet modest. She wore her shining brown hair upswept in a chignon, accented with ivory combs. On her feet were gold lamé sandals. One ankle was circled with a thin gold chain. She wore too much makeup, especially around her eyes, which were heavily lined with kohl.

"How can I help you, Agent Rimon?"

The two women sat across from each other in gray loveseats. The midday sun flooded the room with golden light. A maid entered and set down a silver tray on the glass coffee table between them. Maya savored the sweet mint tea, served in delicate bone china cups. She helped herself to a pistachio pastry. Her host sipped her tea but took nothing from the tray.

"I'm investigating the murder of an American professor. Boaz Goldmayer. He was killed Sunday night at a West Jerusalem hotel. We're investigating everyone who registered to attend the scholarly conference being hosted there this week."

Lena al-Sayegh listened attentively, her attractive face a mask of aloof gentility. She took a sip of her tea, then patted her lips with a small white cloth napkin.

"What does any of this have to do with me?"

"One of the conference attendees is Habib Salameh. I'm sure you know him."

"Of course."

She pointed to a floor-to-ceiling wall of glass shelves, softly illuminated by recessed lights. Displayed on the shelves were glazed bowls and vases of various colors as well as a number of small clay figurines of ancient vintage.

"I've bought many beautiful things from Habib over the years. He has exquisite taste and a sharp eye for value."

Her English was impeccable. Maya detected traces of a French accent. Perhaps she and Salameh knew each other from his Paris days. Israeli Intelligence knew very little about Madame Lena al-Sayegh. Only that she was a social climber, who bred and raced champion Arabians in the Emirates. She had never been in trouble with the Jerusalem authorities.

"Mister Salameh was at your party Sunday night."

"Of course, he was. All evening. Habib is a popular guest at my parties. All the ladies vie for his attention."

Should she ask about security cameras? Photos taken by any of the guests?

She knew such questions would offend Lena. Levantine etiquette demanded that a guest take the host at her word. Maya would get nothing more from her.

They chatted pleasantly for a few more minutes. When Maya rose to leave, Lena insisted that she take a few pastries home with her. Had her hunger been that obvious?

She returned to her car and sat there quietly for a few minutes. The visit hadn't been a complete waste of time. She'd confirmed her suspicion that Salameh had lied about his whereabouts on Sunday night.

31

In the simmering heat of early afternoon, Maya turned her silver Corolla on to Betsalel Bazak Street, then drove on to the ramp leading to Begin North. The road soon merged into Route 50, then veered right onto Route 1, heading east from Jerusalem.

She flipped her visor forward to shield her eyes from the glaring sun. After several kilometers, she passed the sprawling West Bank community of Ma'ale Adumim. Its sparkling white houses and modern shopping malls stood in sharp contrast to the humble Arab villages surrounding it.

Once past Ma'ale Adumim, Maya shifted into fourth gear and settled back against the seat. She unwrapped the pistachio pastries she'd accepted from Lena al-Sayegh and popped them in her mouth, one after the other, washing down the sticky sweetness with lukewarm water. Then, she turned on the radio and spun the dial until she found a classical station. Mahler wasn't one of her favorites, but it beat the alternatives. Relaxing into the andante tempo, she stared at the road ahead. There wouldn't be much to see until she reached Qumran National Park.

The heat mounted steadily as she drove further into the desert. The air conditioning was too feeble to combat it. Floating above the macadam surface, molten air rippled in the bright sun. The low scrub vegetation bordering both sides of the road was brown and desiccated. Nothing moved over the bleak landscape.

Her thoughts drifted, then zeroed in on the investigation.

Stanley Lowenthal remained the only credible suspect among the scholars. By all accounts, he was a vindictive man, merciless in his public take-downs of rivals. And his son was fiercely protective of his father's scholarly reputation. Both men were tall, Adam especially. Stanley wore silver rings on his right hand.

But was either capable of murder?

And then there was Habib Salameh. Ever since interviewing him at the LTM Center months ago, Maya had suspected him of having ties to fanatic religious groups, perhaps laundering illicit cash through his antiquities business. Salameh lived high on the food chain, collecting vintage cars, French mistresses, and pricey wines. Would he risk murder to satisfy his prodigal appetite?

Suddenly, she saw rising ahead of her the limestone cliffs and stone ruins of Qumran National Park. The birthplace of the Dead Sea Scrolls.

She pulled the silver Corolla into the half-filled parking lot and turned off the engine. The cooled air inside the car evaporated rapidly, effervescing into hot steam. She would have preferred to interview the Lowenthals back at the air-conditioned hotel, but the professor had insisted that this was his only available time this week. He and Adam were doing a photo shoot this afternoon in Cave 3 for Stanley's forthcoming book on the Copper Scroll.

As soon as Maya opened the car door, she felt like she'd stepped into a white-hot kiln. The air was aboil, shivering like ruffled silk. She glanced toward the main grounds of the park, impressed as always by the stark setting of this ancient desert enclave. She noted that the red metal arch spanning the park entrance had recently been repainted. Through the arch, she could see the jigsaw of uneven, low stone walls arranged in various rectangular configurations. Among them were the remains of an ancient guard tower, several one- and two-story buildings, storehouses, ritual baths, and cisterns.

Seated in the ticket booth near the entrance was a large, bearded man, wearing a Bukharan kippah. Maya flashed her Service credentials at him. He smiled and waved her in. She smiled back at him, then shook her head. Today, she was not here as a tourist. Her meeting with the Lowenthals would be taking place outside the park, in an off-site cave within walking distance.

She turned and headed away from the entrance.

32

CAVE 3 WAS ONLY A two-kilometer walk from the parking lot. The hard, cracked marlstone surface was full of dips and crevices; boulders strewn everywhere. Cave 3 was among the most northern of the Qumran caves, located between a broad wadi and the Rijm al-Asbah, "the Rock of the Thumb," about one kilometer further north. By the time Maya reached the cave entrance, her white blouse was plastered against her back, soaked with sweat.

As she approached the limestone cliffs, she noticed a slanting outcrop of brown rock topped with scrub grass. Several meters below the grass was an irregular opening, partially blocked by a large boulder. She peered into the inky mouth of the cave. The entrance appeared too small to admit an adult.

Posted a few yards away was a dented metal sign that read: "Danger. Unstable ground. No admittance except by permit." The sign was written in Hebrew, English, and Arabic.

Bending low, Maya stepped carefully over piles of rubble and entered the darkness. She shone her Maglite toward the back of the cave. The bright beam was quickly swallowed up by the gloom.

"Stanley! Stanley Lowenthal!"

Her cries echoed off the pitted walls.

"Who's there?" The reply was faint, the last syllable echoing before dying.

"Agent Maya Rimon! Israeli Intelligence!"

"Be careful as you approach the entrance," the disembodied voice called out from the darkness. "Most of the ceiling there has collapsed."

Carefully, Maya stepped inside the cave. She found herself standing in a large open space with a low ceiling. She waited patiently until a figure emerged from one of the dark recesses in the back wall. In the beam of her flashlight, Stanley Lowenthal's shock of white hair gleamed like bone under fluorescent light. Maya noted that today, he wore only a single scarab ring. In contrast to the natty suit and bowtie he'd sported at the conference reception, he now wore the standard archaeologist's outfit—khaki shorts and a khaki shirt with many pockets, ribbed white socks, and laced boots. Around his neck dangled an expensive Nikon with a zoom lens. On the narrow bridge of his nose perched horn-rimmed glasses, which glinted in the flashlight's glare.

"Cave 3," he said, delivering the words as though addressing a large audience. He swept a wrinkled hand across the cavernous space. "Where the Copper Scroll was first discovered in 1952. Unlike the other caves, they found nothing here dating before the first century of the Common Era. No sectarian scrolls. Only a rusted javelin. Some think this cave might have been a hideout for the Zealots fleeing the Romans."

Adam Lowenthal now stepped out of the shadows, stooping to avoid hitting his head on the low ceiling of the branch tunnel. He wore denim cut-offs, stained around the groin. Emblazoned in large black type across the front of his frayed tee shirt were the words: "Beware Geeks Bearing Gifts!" On his feet were dusty sandals. In place of the brown fedora, he wore a black baseball cap.

"Just getting some last pictures for my book," said the older Lowenthal. "My definitive work on the Copper Scroll."

He removed a small square of light blue flannel from his back pocket and wiped off the lenses of his glasses. Then, he carefully set them back on his nose and looped the thick brown plastic temples behind his ears. He folded up the square of cloth and returned it to his pocket.

"As I told you on the phone, Miss Rimon, I have no information regarding Boaz Goldmayer's murder. I told the Jerusalem police everything I know. This conversation is a waste of time."

"Let me be the judge of that, professor."

Stanley sighed, then shook his head.

"My son and I have nothing to hide." The professor's speech revealed the hint of an Oxbridge accent. "What is it you wish to know?"

From her shoulder bag, Maya withdrew a sleek silver object, which she placed on a flat stone outcrop to her left.

"With your permission," she said, flicking a switch on the mini-recorder. "It's too dark in here for me to take notes."

"And here I thought you had unlimited talents, Miss Rimon."

Lowenthal's bright teeth, mostly his own even at eighty-five, sparkled in the artificial light. He tipped his head waggishly at Maya, animating the white curl in the center of his forehead. Then, he winked at her.

"So, shall we begin?"

Although Maya had not been looking forward to this interview, she nonetheless found herself captivated by the elder Lowenthal's charm. Not that she was taken in. From her online research, she'd learned that Stanley had been born to poor Russian Jewish immigrants in Detroit. His accent was all affectation. Yet the old professor drew her under his spell. His blue eyes were clear and penetrating. He was rumored to have been quite a Lothario in his younger days. Some said he was still chasing skirts.

"Boaz Goldmayer didn't think much of your theories, did he, professor?"

"I'm not the only scholar who challenged Goldmayer!" The old man's British accent now collapsed into a broad Midwestern twang. "I still don't understand why so many respectable journals published his articles—but rejected mine. And why was he invited to deliver this year's conference keynote? The man needed to be put in his place!"

"Dad!"

Adam suddenly snapped out of his fixation with the cave's pitted walls. He flicked his head toward Maya.

"The truth is," said the senior Lowenthal, his voice moderating. The toothy grin was back. "I didn't take Boaz's scholarship seriously enough to consider sabotaging his work. If I were even capable of doing such a thing."

"*You* may not be capable," said Maya, pivoting now to face Adam, "but what about your son? I hear he's quite gifted. Yale Law, isn't it? A Ph.D. in philosophy. And an IT genius."

"What is your point, young lady?" Stanley's voice regained its earlier tartness. "What are you accusing us of?"

Maya picked up the mini-recorder and clicked it off.

"We're done here." She dropped the mini-recorder into her shoulder bag. "Please don't make any plans to leave Jerusalem over the next few days. I may have more questions."

Abruptly, she spun around and began picking her way out of the narrow mouth of the cave.

"Mind where you step!" Stanley yelled from inside the cave. "There's wild hemlock growing near the entrance. The leaves with the purple speckles. Toxic to the skin. I told Adam to rope off that area. I guess he forgot."

Once outside, Maya quickly located the deadly plants and made sure to steer clear of them. When she glanced up, the searing mid-afternoon light momentarily blinded her. She fumbled in her bag for her sunglasses. Through the filtered lenses, the landscape looked like photos she'd seen of Mars. Desiccated plains and rubble.

Suddenly, she noticed a second cave close by. Though she knew most scholars disputed the presence of copper oxide around Qumran, why not take a look? If the ancient Jews, who'd lived in the Dead Sea settlement, had hidden the Copper Scroll in Cave 3, wouldn't they have fabricated the copper sheets there, using a local source?

She knew it was a long shot.

She began walking toward the cave.

33

MOMENTS BEFORE MAYA EXITED CAVE 3, a tall man arrived at the entrance to this second cave, sweating from his arduous climb. The brim of his dark baseball cap partially shielded his face from the brutal sun. He looked down at the small piece of crumpled paper in his palm and re-read the cryptic words:

> *In the underground passage that is in Sehab north of*
> *Kochalit, with its opening to the north, and which has*
> *tombs at its entrance.*

He'd come here because his partner had suggested that he search near the place where the Copper Scroll had first been found. There was an ancient cemetery nearby. And this particular cave faced north.

But what about the specific places named in the decrypted file—Sehab, Kochalit? None of these places appeared on any modern map. Were they here or someplace else?

O Lord, the tall man prayed, *let this be where the Treasure Scroll lies!*

He stared into the small, dark cavity yawning in front of him. He took a step inside. The cavernous space was cool. But it smelled funny. Like ancient mold and decay. He stepped back into the bright sunshine.

Of course, that young coding geek had no clue about the real secrets hidden in Goldmayer's files. Neither did his own partner, who had insisted on managing the decryption operation alone. The tall man knew that the man was only in it for the money. What a fool he'd been to put his fate in that ungodly man's hands! But what choice did he have? His partner was an expert on antique scrolls and claimed to know about ancient codes. And his insatiable greed certainly kept him motivated and focused. But what was that man's aspiration compared to his own! Well, he would make good use of this heathen Midas until he no longer needed him. Then, he'd throw him to the Israeli wolves. Kill two birds with one stone.

A cascade of falling pebbles drew the tall man back to the present. He looked up to see an ibex perched on a rocky ledge just over his head. The animal looked at him quizzically, then shook its curved horns and scampered up over the top of the escarpment. More rock debris spilled down in its wake, littering the cave entrance with dark scree.

Suddenly, he heard loud voices coming from Cave 3. It was too far away to make out the words. He poked his head out and squinted in that direction. He saw a petite young woman emerging from the cliffside cave a short distance off. She began walking at a brisk trot. Heading directly toward him!

He quickly ducked back into the cave and was instantly swallowed up by darkness.

When he stuck his head out moments later, he saw her standing about a hundred meters off. In one hand, she held a Maglite; in the other, a small black notebook. She faced away from him, staring back at Cave 3.

He needed to act quickly. If she caught sight of him, it would ruin everything!

While the woman was busy scribbling in her notebook, he pulled his baseball cap low over his enormous brow, slipped out of the cave, and edged along the cliff ridge until he found a rock large enough for his purpose. He dragged the heavy rock back to the cave. The shelf over the entrance was narrow, but it would have to do. Carefully, he positioned the rock so that it balanced precariously over the opening. From his backpack, he withdrew a length of thin nylon rope. Then, he searched until he found a small oblong stone. He wrapped the rope several times around it, then wedged the stone behind the larger rock. He threaded the blue rope along the outside perimeter of the cave entrance, obscuring its presence with crumbled stone and dirt. Hastily, he laid down a trip-wire of rope, brushing sand over it. Then, walking backwards, he carefully let out the rope until he found an outcropping that he could hide behind. Gently, he drew the rope taut. Then, he crouched down to wait.

The woman approached the cave but stopped a short distance from the entrance. She shone her bright light into the darkness and peered inside. But she did not enter the cave. What was holding her back?

Suddenly, he heard a scratching sound.

It was the ibex, coming toward the cave from the opposite direction. It deftly maneuvered along a knife-edge of rock. Its graceful body, blocking the setting sun, was outlined in an aura of white light.

The woman laughed out loud.

The sudden sound startled the ibex. It leapt forward. Its bony hoof caught on the hidden rope, bringing the animal to its knees in the sandy shingle. Shoved by the stone wedge, the large rock tumbled down, landing on the ibex and crushing it. Blood spurted from several wounds in the animal's soft brown hide. One of its horns broke off and rolled, coming to rest near the woman's feet.

She knelt down beside the bleeding ibex, but there was nothing she could do. The creature's black eyes quickly clouded over and stared up at her. The skin above one of its hoofs was lacerated by a tight coil of nylon rope. Flies began gathering around the torn hide.

She stood up. Her face turned toward him.

He was out of time. He could not risk discovery.

He dashed out from behind his hiding place and began to run. A fusillade of pebbles shot out behind him. He fought hard to keep his balance as he slid and stumbled down the steep slope. His lungs screamed for air. He did not stop until he reached the parking lot at the front gate.

And never once did he look back.

34

It was close to 5:00 p.m. by the time Maya returned to Jerusalem from Qumran. She fought her way through the clogged city streets. Traffic crawled at a snail's pace along Emek Refa'im. In the space of four short blocks, she witnessed two fender benders. In neither case did any of the drivers stop to assess the damage to their vehicles or call the police. Instead, they cursed at each other through open windows, then tore away with a screech of tires.

When traffic ground to a halt, her mind flashed back for a moment to the caves at Qumran. That poor ibex felled by a falling stone. The tall man with the dark baseball cap running away across the rubbled plain. Who was he? A treasure-hunter raiding the caves for souvenirs? Someone hiding from the law or from some enemy? He had moved too fast for her to get a bead on him.

At last she arrived at the underground garage near her office. She walked to the small hole-in-the-wall restaurant around the corner and bolted down a falafel, washing it down with bitter coffee. She walked through the front door of Service Headquarters just as Roni Qattawi and Arik Ophir, the Minister of Internal Security, were on their way out for dinner.

Roni eyed Maya's sweat-soaked blouse and dusty sandals.

"Been out catching desperados, I see."

Maya grunted, then grinned sheepishly. "You've been watching too much American TV, Roni."

Roni chuckled.

As always, Maya tried to keep her gaze trained on the top of her boss's head, above the unnerving port-wine birthmark that stained his left cheek. She now noticed that Roni's forehead was rapidly gaining ground on his receding hairline. He'd be completely bald in a few years.

"So, any promising leads?"

"Not yet. Still following up on some hunches."

Roni snorted and jabbed his forefinger at her.

"You and your damn hunches! I've warned you, Maya! Stop chasing after wild conspiracy theories. They're a waste of resources. Keep it simple. Just follow the evidence. Like I always tell new recruits—Occam's Razor."

Arik Ophir chortled. The minister was a large, fleshy man, with bloodshot eyes and a bulbous cauliflower nose. He and Maya's father, Moti, had crossed swords for years. That was probably why Ophir had promoted Roni to head the agency over his more senior colleague. After all the years Moti had given his beloved Service, they'd unceremoniously stabbed him in the back and sent him packing into forced retirement.

"You know, you look very sexy, drenched in sweat." Roni ran his eyes up and down Maya's trim frame. "A regular Amazon."

Ophir guffawed and punched Roni in the shoulder. The latter raised his thick eyebrows and ogled Maya down his sharp wedge of a nose.

Maya smiled at the two men, refusing to snap up the bait. Suddenly, she slapped her thigh in mock dismay and shot a trigger finger at her boss.

"I almost forgot! I have a new riddle for you, Roni. I know how much you like to show off that sharp wit of yours."

Maya winked at the minister and turned to face her boss.

"What does a male secret agent use for birth control?"

Roni eyed her suspiciously, his right brow cocked over one dark eye. The burly minister shrugged, his grin drooping, provisional.

"His personality!"

Roni guffawed. He raised his cigarette, vised between two fingers, to his receding hairline and saluted.

"*Touché*, Rimon! But watch the mouth. There are limits to my patience."

Roni's thin lips curled into a disdainful smile.

She bowed her head in mock deference. "Sir."

Chuckling, Maya swept past the two men, heading toward her office. As she brushed by Roni, he patted her buttocks with his open palm. She brusquely slapped his hand away. Ophir laughed. He gave Roni a soft punch to the shoulder.

Both men raised their hands in a mock salute, then exited the building.

Cursing under her breath, Maya entered her eight by eight office and slammed the door. She quickly changed out of her sweaty clothes into a fresh set she kept hanging on pegs attached to one wall. She kept her back to the closed door, not bothering to lower the white mini-blinds.

How tired she'd grown of Roni! It hadn't always been this way. When she'd first started at the Service, she had found him attractive and clever. When he'd come on to her after a few weeks, she was thrilled by his deep, gravelly voice, which purred like a stalking cat's. His dark Egyptian features and sinewy muscles were so different from Rafi's soft, pale body. But she soon came to find his sexual attentions boorish, even somewhat menacing. The more she fended him off, the more aggressive he became. She finally had no choice but to tell him to fuck off and leave her alone.

That's when the unrelenting teasing had begun. The sexist jokes, the sly insults, the sexual innuendos. It had gotten worse over the past year. She noticed that he'd also begun drinking late in the day. His voice slurred over the intercom. But she wouldn't probe. Unless he crossed the line. Every one of them carried *pekels* on their back.

Still buttoning up her blouse, Maya eyed the stack of manila folders piling up in her inbox. She expelled a loud gust of breath, then breathed in slowly. She flopped into her swivel chair and stared for a few moments at the black screen of her monitor. Then, she pressed "escape" to wake up the computer and logged on. Dozens of new emails crammed her inbox, most of them cc's from colleagues here or at other government agencies. She quickly scrolled through the news feeds to see if any crises were brewing. Only the usual: Several Hamas rockets had been launched this morning from Gaza toward Ashkelon, but had been successfully intercepted by Iron Dome. A Palestinian had stabbed a Jewish settler in the Territories. The suspect was still at large. An anti-Israel vote had taken place in the UN Security Council, sponsored jointly by Syria and Russia. New security measures were being proposed in the Knesset to crack down on suspected Arab terrorists inside the Green Line. A typical day in the Arab world's crosshairs.

Next, she opened up her browser and typed in: "decryption algorithms." As she scrolled through the dozens of articles that popped up on the screen, she realized that she was rapidly falling behind in the field. It was almost impossible for her to follow some of the recent academic articles on digital forensics and cryptography. She should be taking refresher courses to keep up. But that would cut even more into her time with Vered. If she really wanted to do a good job as both a mother and an intelligence agent, she probably should give up the cryptography piece of her portfolio and rely on outside experts. Stick to spycraft. No denying that she was completely maxed out.

Feeling depressed and frustrated, she logged into the Agency's database and did a search for "Adam Lowenthal."

She wasn't surprised to discover that Adam had been on the FBI's radar for some time. He'd been accused of harassing his father's academic rivals over the internet. So far, he'd evaded punishment for his cyber-mischief. He'd also been accused of mailing threatening letters to a few of his father's most vocal adversaries, but the charges hadn't stuck. The FBI continued to monitor him closely.

She recalled the elder Lowenthal's menacing sneers and vindictive grievances. His ominous outbursts about Goldmayer.

Both Lowenthals were definitely staying on her suspect list.

She fished her cell phone out of her purse and called Masha, who was sitting only a few meters away at her desk on the other side of Maya's glass door. She knew Masha considered Maya paranoid for not using her office landline, but you never knew with Roni.

"Busy? I could use your help."

Moments later, Masha stepped into Maya's glassed-in cubicle, closing the door behind her. Like Maya, she was dressed in her Service "uniform"—white button-down blouse, dark blue pencil skirt, dark sandals. Due to the stifling heat on this floor, she wore no stockings or jacket. Their offices were supposed to be air-conditioned, but the system never worked at full strength, especially when the mercury climbed over thirty.

Although both women were petite, Masha's physique was the opposite of Maya's. In contrast to the latter's willowy form, Masha was chunky and square-shouldered. Maya almost never wore lipstick or mascara, whereas Masha's subtle makeup flattered her ruddy face, whose flat cheeks and slightly tilted eyes suggested Tatar origins. Masha's honey-blonde hair was coiffed in an attractive short cut that framed her full face. The slender lady's watch that she wore on her wrist, with diamond chips in place of numbers, offset her big-boned arms. The two women certainly made an odd couple. But they shared the same wicked sense of humor and passionate temperament, which is what had initially drawn them together and quickly made them best friends.

Masha hopped up onto the edge of Maya's gray steel desk, her stubby legs dangling midway to the floor. The steel desk wobbled, upending several small objects perched in the center. Looking sternly down her arched nose at her friend, Maya carefully re-assembled the array of wooden puzzles, fidget spinners, puzzle rings, and miniature Rubik's Cubes she kept neatly arranged in the middle of her desk.

"Sorry, *chooki*."

Masha thrust out her lower lip in an exaggerated pout and fluttered her eyelids. Maya smiled.

"*Nu?* So how's it going with your favorite nemesis?"

"How d'ya think?" Maya spit out a puff of air between compressed lips. "Roni probably pulled strings to get Sarit assigned to this case. Just to watch the sparks fly."

Masha raised her sandy eyebrows and grinned.

"So Luke Skywalker and Darth Vader meet again."

Maya grabbed a fidget spinner and began to twirl it between her fingers. With her other hand, she pushed back an auburn curl from her forehead.

"I definitely won't get any help from Sarit. But she won't get anywhere, either. As usual, she'll drill down on the forensics and miss the big picture. This particular murderer was very careful. Left behind no hairs, DNA, fingerprints, or trace evidence."

"So what's *your* strategy?"

"Track Goldmayer's stolen laptop and files. Given how top secret the professor considered his research, he must have encrypted his files. Whoever stole them needs to get them decrypted." Maya set the fidget spinner down on the desk's steel surface and pointed a slender finger at Masha. "Get me a list of hackers and programmers currently active in Jerusalem. One of them might lead us to our killer."

"And maybe to lost treasure!"

"One puzzle at a time, Masha."

The two women laughed. Masha pointed her square chin at the wood and metal objects lined up neatly once again on the desk. Maya grinned.

"So what's your next move?" Masha asked.

"I'm going to pay a visit to the LTM Center. I'm still looking for a link between Christian extremists and Habib Salameh. Something I missed in the previous investigation."

"Didn't Roni warn you...."

"Damn Roni's warnings! I know I'm right."

She was feeling that familiar itch in the center of her palm. The same itch she'd felt the first time she'd met Reverend Kirby Sechrist, LTM's sanctimonious former director. And when she'd discovered their secret lab hidden behind that false wall. This time, she was going to prove....

Be careful, Maya! Don't become like your father. Look how he ended up.

Maya took a deep breath and let it out slowly. Then, she sank back in her chair.

Masha suddenly hopped off the broad metal desk and walked toward the office door. It was then that Maya noticed her friend's new footwear—high red platform sandals with silver sequins studding the thin ankle straps.

"Are those new, Masha? Must have set you back plenty!"

Masha blushed. "I simply couldn't resist! I saw them in an online ad and just had to have them."

"You'll soon need a bigger apartment. Just for your shoes."

The two women laughed. Masha tipped an imaginary cap toward her friend. Then, she left Maya's office and returned to her work.

Moments later, Maya left her office and headed toward the front door. Her service weapon nestled at the bottom of her shoulder bag.

Masha didn't look up from her screen. Under her breath, she whispered a prayer: *Keep her safe. Keep her sane.*

Maya would kill her if she knew that Masha whispered this prayer every time Maya went out on her own.

Especially when she was intent on proving Roni wrong.

35

It was just after 5:00 p.m. when Sarit Levine arrived at Habib Salameh's antiquities shop on Salah e-Din Street in East Jerusalem. Contrary to departmental protocol, she was conducting this interview solo. She'd asked two uniforms to stand by. Just in case.

From the outside, the building that housed Salameh's shop on its ground floor was rather unassuming. Two-stories high and constructed of rose-colored stone blocks, it most likely dated back to Ottoman times. Tall mullioned windows, many of which opened onto small wrought-iron balconies, latticed the façade. The heavy red curtains that darkened the antique shop's plateglass windows at street level were clearly meant to discourage casual browsers.

Next to the dark entryway hung several polished rectangular brass plates. The top one read: "Habib Salameh, Dealer in Rare Antiquities." The other nameplates identified the offices of a lawyer, an endodonist, a psychiatrist, and an acupuncturist.

The entryway led to an ascending staircase on the right and a glass door on the left. The glass door was criss-crossed by a grid of iron bars. Attached to the stone wall next to the door was another rectangular plate engraved with Salameh's name. The shiny brass glowed even in the entryway's dim light.

Sarit rang the buzzer and waited in the semi-dark.

While she waited, she peered through the bars. Inside was a narrow room lined from floor to ceiling with horizontal glass cases mounted one above the other on the wall. The cases were filled with museum-quality antiquities, softly illumined by invisible light sources. Clay oil lamps, figurines, bowls, pitchers, and cups. Silver coins. Gold headbands, earrings, and hair pins. Glass perfume vials of every color. Knives and spear points. Stone and bronze tools. Several cases displayed rows of yellowed parchment scrolls, lined up side by side like fallen and wounded soldiers awaiting transport home.

When Salameh finally came to the door, she was surprised to find him dressed in evening clothes. She noticed that his nails were manicured. The clear polish glinted in the soft light.

"To what do I owe the pleasure, Detective Levine? I was about to close up. I can only spare a few minutes." He smiled at her, exuding charm. "Are you perhaps in the market for some rare object of antique beauty?"

Sarit smiled but said nothing in reply.

Salameh ushered her inside and waved her over to a small desk in the center of the room. He turned on a small antique lamp that sat on one corner of the desk. The light cast a honeyed glow over the glossy surface. Sarit sat down in an uncomfortable chair directly across from the antique dealer. For all its elegance and charm, the chair failed to fulfill its main function: providing comfort to its occupant. Sarit could feel the curved wooden slats digging into her back. The chair Salameh occupied was more hospitable, with embroidered padded back and arms.

"I'm investigating the murder of Professor Boaz Goldmayer."

"*Ey*, I heard about his tragic death at the scrolls conference. *Allah yerhamo*. A great loss to Qumran scholarship."

If the Lebanese dealer felt genuine grief at Goldmayer's death, his face hid it well. It had become a dark mask, inscrutable.

"Good fortune seems to favor you often, doesn't it, Mister Salameh?"

The dealer grinned, courteousness oozing out of his tawny skin.

"Indeed, I am very fortunate in my business, Detective Levine. People bring me the most remarkable things to buy and sell. Including information."

"My sources tell me that before his death, Boaz Goldmayer may have pinpointed the location of a lost Dead Sea Scroll. A document that scholars call the Treasure Scroll. What do you think of such rumors?"

Salameh's thick black eyebrows leapt up in surprise. He smiled, then nodded, signaling his respect.

"I have learned to pay close attention to rumors," he said. "They sometimes carry profitable truths. But in this case, I am deeply skeptical. I have yet to encounter any evidence supporting these claims."

The dealer's unctuous smile remained stamped on his leathery face. His voice was like fine silk, matching the Christian Lacroix tie he wore. But his broad smile quickly vanished, replaced by a beetled brow and a smirk, which pulled at the corners of his mouth like a drawstring. His thick bottlebrush eyebrows met over his angular nose. His breathing, too, had quickened.

Sarit recognized the signs: fear of exposure. It confirmed her suspicions.

"You must be aware, *ya Habib*, that my colleagues and I have followed your business career for years with considerable interest."

The dealer showed no offense at her use of his first name. His dark eyes did not blink. His smile slowly regained its purchase on his fleshy lips.

"Indeed, we are well known to each other."

Though Sarit wouldn't admit it publicly, she didn't much like Arabs. Partly, it was her upbringing. Her mother's Syrian Jewish family eagerly engaged in Arab-bashing whenever they got together. Policing the minefields of East Jerusalem had only deepened her antipathy. Yet despite these negative stereotypes, she couldn't help admiring this Lebanese businessman. He was resourceful and shrewd.

Salameh looked down at his watch.

"I believe I've told you everything I know, Detective." His voice rasped with irritation. "Now, if you'll excuse me, I have a party to attend."

Sarit stood up and walked to the door. Placing her hand on the ivory knob, she twisted around to look back at him.

"I'm not done with you, Mister Salameh. You remain a person of interest in this case. A person of considerable interest."

She opened the door and let it close behind her. The barred frame rattled as the door clicked shut.

36

It had taken Cassandra a while to figure out how to engineer her escape. Without access to the internet, she'd had no way to research how to cut through iron bars or how to jimmy a rotating cylinder lock. It was like being deaf and blind.

So she'd no choice but to improvise. Under the kitchen sink, she found a large plastic container of chlorine bleach. In a cupboard, she found bottles of ammonia and vinegar. In the bathroom, rat poison and roach killer. Although chemistry had never been her best subject, she was sure that a mixture of all these poisons would make a toxic brew.

She mixed the chemicals in the bathroom sink, grateful that the stopper was made of stainless steel, not rubber. The stink was awful. Reeking vapors of gas soon filled the small room, making Cassandra's eyes water. Lacking rubber gloves, she could only protect her skin by wrapping plastic garbage bags around her hands. But her face and hands were itching like crazy.

Using a small dust mop as her brush, she covered the six vertical iron bars on the small bathroom window with the viscous solution, then added a second coat. As she watched, dark bubbles formed on the iron, fizzing and popping like boiling tar.

When the air became too noxious to breathe, Cassandra closed the bathroom door and padded back into the main room. She tore the plastic sheeting off her hands and washed her face and arms in soap and cold water at the kitchen sink. Then, she padded over to the desk and sank down into the chair. She sat, staring at the screen, her eyes too irritated to focus. She blinked hard, trying to wash away the fumes. Her vision refused to clear. Still, she could tell from her reflection in the dark screen that her purple mascara was smudged. Some of it ran in uneven rivulets down her pale cheeks. She closed her eyes to let her tears wash out what was left of the poison.

How long would it take for the chemicals to eat through the bars? Would there be enough of an opening for her to squeeze through? How far was it to the ground? How far was it to safety?

She didn't hear him come in. Suddenly, he was standing next to her. His hot breath smelled of garlic and lemons.

"So have you found it? The secret hiding place of the Treasure Scroll?"

His voice was mocking. He grasped her head on either side and pulled her face close to his. Her silver nose ring quivered as she struggled to speak.

"I decrypted two more files since you were here! I'm working as fast as I can!"

He laughed. The sound resembled a donkey's harsh bray. Abruptly, he unfurled his fingers and released her head, which dropped forward, stopping just shy of the desk's hard surface. She slowly sat up. She tilted her thin neck first to one side, heard a soft crack, then tilted the other way. She didn't look him in the eye.

"I applaud your dedication, my dear, but I am only interested in results, not effort. I fear you have become too attached to this Mariamne and her maudlin soap opera. Perhaps your daydreaming has caused you to miss what you are supposed to be looking for."

Then, he smelled the chemicals. He ran over to the closed door of the bathroom, yanked it open, went inside.

She held her breath, hoping, hopeless.

When he came back into the room, his face was dark and menacing. The smile on his lips chilled her to the bone. His eyes were opaque, like dark wells.

She wasn't expecting the sharp smack to the side of her head. But she wasn't surprised. The man was clearly on edge. She pitied any woman who shared his bed.

"I warned you that there would be consequences for failure. And there are also consequences for defiance."

"I'm so sorry!"

She knew that whining would only make him angrier. Men like him hated whiners and crybabies. She fought back tears, but her eyes were so irritated from the chemicals that briny mucous seeped out onto her cheeks. She squeezed her sticky lids shut and rubbed her lashes.

"I'm so close. Just give me one more chance...!"

When she opened her eyes, he was gone.

37

WHEN MAYA ENTERED THE GRAND reception hall of the LTM Center—*much closer to a corporate lobby than an apse*, she thought—she was immediately aware of the tension. A sense of expectancy. The quiet murmur of sound, which had greeted her on previous visits—whispered voices, solemn church music, the occasional jingle of wind chimes that dangled near the ductless air conditioning units positioned high up on the walls—was now replaced by a frenzied din. Hurried footsteps. Loud electronic music. LTM staffers rushed in and out of the high-ceilinged room, suddenly appearing, then vanishing down side corridors.

The giant flat screen that now took up most of the lobby's rear wall displayed dazzling images of the heavens: exploding supernovas, rainbow-colored gas nebulae, asteroids blazing through Earth's upper atmosphere. Maya stood transfixed in front of the screen. The pictures reminded her of the colorful images she sometimes saw on Facebook, broadcast back to Earth by the Hubble Telescope. But why were such images being shown at the headquarters of the Liberators of the Temple Mount, an apocalyptic Christian sect?

As though divining her question, Tim Hargreaves, LTM's young Community Outreach Director, quietly approached and stood beside her.

During her last investigation at the Center a few months back, Maya had spent a fair amount of time with Tim, a nervous young man, tall and thin as a beanpole. His close-cropped tawny hair reminded her of the boy pictured on the cover of her Hebrew translation of *Huckleberry Finn*. Except Huck hadn't had a bald spot growing in the middle of his head. Tim often wore a dark baseball cap to cover it.

"You can feel it soon as you come in, cain't you?"

Tim's boyish face, pitted from terrible acne, beamed at her. He had a toothy smile that gleamed like a solar corona.

"What's going on, Tim?"

"We're gittin' close! *Real* close."

In his enthusiasm, Tim let fly a few drops of spittle, which sprinkled Maya's chin. She wiped the moisture off with the back of her hand. Tim appeared not to notice.

"Keep yer eyes on the screen."

As they stared up at the giant screen, a deep red sphere materialized out of the blackness. Maya recognized the sphere as Earth's moon. But this was unlike any image of the moon she'd ever seen. Although the bright surface displayed the well-known lunar dry seas and cratered plains, its red color seemed completely unnatural. This was not the primary red of children's crayons but a bright crimson. The warm, wet color of blood.

"Awesome, isn't it? Even if it's not part of a Tetrad."

"Tetrad?"

Tim grinned. His fingers fidgeted with a large wooden cross dangling around his sinewy neck on a heavy gold-linked chain. He lowered his voice and leaned in closer.

"It's kinda like a secret code. The sun, moon, comets, and stars—they're like God's secret alphabet. He uses 'em to tell us what's gonna happen in the future. A blood moon's one of His special signs. When four of 'em bunch together, it's a Tetrad. That's a *real* special sign."

Tim's glassy pupils stared off into space like pale fish eyes. Had this gawky young man succumbed to Jerusalem Syndrome since she'd last seen him? She was relieved when the pallid lids shuttered his eyes.

Maya felt shivers prickling her skin. The cooled air inside the LTM Center had turned to ice.

"So when's the next Tetrad?"

She had to ask twice before Tim opened his eyes.

"Not 'til 2032."

His voice conveyed a deep sadness.

Maya felt some of the tension drain from her shoulders and lower back.

"But there's a blood moon the night after tomorra!" Tim's voice brightened; his blue eyes glittered. "A one-off. Even one blood moon's enough to bring on the Cataclysm."

Maya's shoulders edged back up toward her ears, the muscles tightening. "Is the Center planning anything special to...mark this event?"

Tim shook his head.

"Nah, they kinda lost interest in the blood moon thang after the Tetrad in 2014-15 turned out to be such a bust. And our new director says that blood moons and Tetrads is un-Christian superstition."

Maya listened to Tim's speech as if it were a communiqué from outer space. Is this what these fanatic *goyim* believed? Not once during her previous investigation of LTM had she ever bothered to pick up one of the beautifully designed, glossy LTM brochures displayed prominently in waist-high Lucite holders throughout the Center's reception area. She had no interest in finding out what American Christian evangelists were selling. At that time, she'd been solely focused on preventing them from blowing up themselves or anyone else. Israel didn't need its own Waco or Ruby Ridge. But maybe that had been a mistake. These fanatics seemed eager to share their destructive visions with anyone who cared to listen.

Tim was on a roll, showing no signs of wrapping up his fervent spiel. Maya let him prattle on, hoping he'd give her a valuable new thread to tug on.

"So, ya might ask, why's the Center still displayin' pi'chers of blood moons if our director don't believe in 'em? 'Cause Reverend Puckett—that's our new director's name—thinks that usin' photos from NASA is good PR. Shows that LTM's on the cuttin' edge. Always lookin' toward the future. Proves that we're expectin' the Second Comin'—jes' not right away."

Tim's voice dropped to a stage whisper. Maya had to lean in to hear his words over the loud soundtrack accompanying the galactic video onscreen.

"Truth to tell, Miss Rye-mahn,"—Tim had never learned to pronounce her name correctly, and Maya had given up correcting him—"I still believe the Lord's cosmic code prognosticates the future. That's why I decided to change churches after Reverend Puckett arrived. I've joined a brand-new church with an amazin' preacher. He says the End 'a Days is comin' real soon. It's what I believe too. Jes' don't tell Rev'rend Puckett, okay? Everyone who works here is s'posed to belong to the LTM Church."

So someone was poaching from other evangelical churches. Whoever this upstart was, he was probably ruffling plenty of feathers. He should watch his back.

"Speaking of your director, any chance I could talk to him?"

"Lemme check."

Tim reached down and pulled his mobile phone from the black plastic holder clipped to his belt. He thumbed a brief text message, then waited for an answer.

"He says c'mon back. You remember where the director's office is?"

Maya nodded. She thanked Tim for his help, then headed toward the rear of the Center to have a conversation with the Reverend Zephaniah T. Puckett.

38

Maya walked quickly through the center's permanent exhibits.

In the first gallery, desktop monitors ran short video clips, demonstrating some of the ritual activities that would take place in the future Third Temple. White-robed priests offered bloody animal sacrifices on stone altars. Gray-robed women wove priests' linen garments on sewing machines. Balanced on high aluminum ladders, white-clad Levites lit a giant seven-branched candelabrum. Others prepared holy incense on long stainless steel tables.

At the far end of the room, Maya stopped to read a placard. It described LTM's new cooperative project with a group of American cattle ranchers in Wyoming. The ranchers were applying the latest selective breeding methods to produce a pure red heifer.

In the second gallery, her pace slowed a bit.

This room was lined with glass cases, skillfully designed so that the displayed objects were bathed in buttery pools of light. The cases were filled with shining silver, gold, copper, and bronze vessels, exact replicas of those formerly used in the priestly services in the Second Temple.

The third gallery contained a scale model of the future Third Temple. The gates, windows, walls, and towers were painted in pure gold leaf, burnished to a blinding sheen.

She rushed through the fourth gallery. She had no interest in watching a video of priests-in-training practicing their butchering skills on live goats, lambs, and pigeons. But her hurried pace didn't completely shield her from the animals' pathetic cries.

She finally reached Reverend Puckett's office, tucked away in a corner of the first floor. He was waiting for her in his open doorway, a pudgy hand extended in greeting. His slicked-down dandelion-yellow hair glistened in the corridor's bright light.

"How nice to meet you, Miss Rye-mahn." His Tennessee accent was broad, his gap-toothed grin even broader. "Now what c'n I do you for?"

She looked at him, baffled. Maya prided herself on her conversational English. But hadn't the American minister just made a grammatical error? She didn't dare correct him.

"I'm investigating a case for Israeli Intelligence, Reverend Puckett."

The short, burly man's grin broadened. Maya let out a quiet sigh of relief. After her botched investigation a few months ago, she was afraid she'd be unwelcome here. But the powers-that-be seemed to have turned the other cheek. Or else the new director of the LTM Center hadn't yet been brought up to speed.

"I'd like to ask you a few questions about Habib Salameh."

The man's fulsome smile instantly vanished.

"The Liberators of the Temple Mount no longer has any association with Mister Salameh."

"And why is that?"

Puckett ushered Maya into his office and closed the door. He waved her into an ornately upholstered armchair and sat down in its twin directly across from her.

"Tea? Coffee? Cold water? Reg'lar or Diet Coke?"

"I'm fine, Reverend." Maya's right foot began tapping the plush carpet. "I'm eager to hear what you have to say about Salameh."

"We cain't prove none of this, y'understand, but we've recently learned that Mister Salameh may be involved in certain...unlawful activities. Obviously, my predecessor wasn't payin' enough attention to the situation." He cleared his throat a few times. His eyes, limpid and droopy like a hound's, veered away from hers. "I been meanin' to give your office a call about it. But I been so incredibly busy of late."

Maya leaned forward in her chair, barely able to contain her irritation.

"What exactly have you learned about Mister Salameh?" Maya spoke through gritted teeth.

"'Fraid I don't have no specific details." Reverend Puckett kneaded his beefy hands together. Sweat beaded on his shiny brow. "But we don' want no part of anythin' on the wrong side of the law."

"What's the source of your information?"

Maya knew that it was pointless to ask. In this contentious city, trading in secrets was even more lucrative than trading in antiquities. She had nothing to offer in exchange for such information.

Puckett shook his head and extended his empty palms toward her. Maya noticed that his nails were neatly clipped, the cuticles rounded into pale half-moons.

Maya placed both her hands on the brocaded arms of the chair.

"That's it, then," she said. *And don't count on cooperation from us, either.* "Anything else you'd like to share with us?"

He smiled coyly at Maya.

"I'm sure Israeli Intelligence monitors all the Temple Mount Movement groups." His voice was seductive, almost conspiratorial.

Of course, the Service was aware of them, all those Jewish and Christian fanatics, who believed that the Messiah was about to appear—or reappear, summoning all the Jews home to Zion. With resolute faith, they envisioned the Third Temple rising on the Mount, built upon the smoking ruins of the two great mosques that currently occupied that sacred space. But before this Age of Universal Peace could dawn, an all-out war would erupt, pitting the forces of Light against those of Darkness. Armageddon. The Apocalypse. And if the Messiah procrastinated in showing up, well, one of these groups might just have to hasten His coming.

Puckett grinned. He ran a fleshy finger over his bottom lip. Maya resented the cat-and-mouse game he was playing with her. Her face remained blank, revealing nothing.

"I wanna assure you, Miss Rimon, that LTM rejects all forms of violence and extremism. We are purely an educational institution."

They shook hands. Puckett promised to keep Maya apprised of any new developments relevant to her investigation. She promised him nothing.

She hurried through the exhibition rooms to the central lobby, her mind whirring. Here was another piece of the puzzle. As she'd suspected, Habib Salameh was connected in some way with religious extremists. But how? And how did the Treasure Scroll fit in?

39

As an undergraduate at Hebrew University, Hillel Stone had seldom gone to bars. Drinking was not a big part of student life in Israel. After their stint in the army, most Israelis were generally focused on getting on with their careers and starting a family. As Hillel's own *frumkeit* had steadily increased after finishing college and graduate school, bars were the last place he'd go to relax.

Yet here he was tonight, standing at the entrance to the Twelve Tribes Pub, the Zion Gate Hotel's new upscale bar. It felt strange. And exciting. Hillel realized that he hadn't set foot inside a bar in over a decade. He'd agreed to meet Maya Rimon at the bar only because he thought there was little chance of running into one of his Orthodox colleagues here. He could also use a little liquid courage.

He now stood at the cash register, waiting for the hostess to finish ringing up a couple of very drunk young American women. Their loud, high-pitched laughter made him step back as if physically assaulted. He looked away, affronted by the women's immodestly short skirts, plunging décolletage, and cloying perfume.

"We won' bite, ya know."

The blonde's slurred voice carried the drawn-out vowels of Long Island. Before looking away, Hillel noted that she had a silver tongue piercing, which jiggled as she spoke. He also noticed a bright blue streak running through her hair like a lane divider.

Her taller, dark-haired companion giggled. "Maybe's playin' hard to get." Her accent matched her friend's. "*Hawd* to get." She eyed Hillel's dark knit kippah, barely visible against his jet-black hair. "Y'know how hypocritical these *frummies* c'n be. Pretend to be so pious when they're secretly lookin' for it."

They doubled over in laughter. Hillel resisted the temptation to cover his ears. He was more embarrassed for them than for himself. In his ear, he heard his mother: *a shanda far di goyim*. She would have been mortified by the girls' shameless behavior in front of the non-Jews here.

With a swoop of her hand, the blonde snatched the paper receipt held out to her by the hostess. Then, the two women wobbled off down the corridor toward the lobby. Their bare arms grasped each other's waists as though clinging to life preservers.

"May I help you?" the hostess asked. She was slim and dark, with heavily made-up eyes and lips.

"I'm meeting someone." He paused. "A woman."

The cashier answered him without looking up, her hands busy shuffling receipts.

"You can either wait at the bar or take a seat at a table. Unless you prefer to wait here."

Why was she giving him so many choices? It was hard enough for him to figure out what he was going to order to drink, let alone what he would say to Maya. He didn't need to make any extra decisions.

Hillel walked over to the bar, a long elbow of shining dark wood, lined with high barstools set atop swiveling chrome posts. The wall behind the bar was all mirror, parts of its surface intersected by horizontal glass shelves displaying a colorful array of bottles. The bartender was a middle-aged Israeli wearing a black shirt and dark pants. His shaved head gleamed as brightly as the dark wood he was wiping with a damp cloth. Hillel sat down, hiking up one leg, then the other onto the high bar stool. The bartender slapped down a round cardboard coaster in front of him.

"What'll you have?"

He was not surprised the bartender addressed him in English. Hillel was dressed like an American academic. Dark suit jacket and pants, wrinkled after sitting all day in conference sessions. His white shirt was unbuttoned at the collar, his tie balled up in a pocket. He'd slipped his conference badge into his pocket, but he must have looked the part of a visiting foreign scholar.

"White wine," said Hillel. "No, on second thought, give me a beer, something not too hoppy. No, make that a whiskey. Neat."

The bald man grinned at Hillel, raising his eyebrows at the sight of the knit kippah. He then nodded and pivoted around to grab a bottle of Seagrams. He poured a finger of the amber liquid into a shot glass and set it down in front of Hillel.

"Meeting someone?"

Hillel didn't feel like talking, especially to an anonymous bartender. But he didn't want to violate bar etiquette. The expectation of a certain friendliness among strangers. So he lifted his glass in a mock salute and took a sip.

"A woman. Someone I just met."

"Good for you! Got to live a little, right? Even religious people need to have fun!"

The bartender chuckled. He now switched his attention to a middle-aged couple, who had just sat down a few stools away. Hillel let out his breath and took another sip of his drink. He resented the man's intrusion into his private life. His presumption of intimacy.

Now that the bartender had left him alone, Hillel gazed into the mirror, studying his portrait in the glass. He was still young, his dark hair not yet showing a hint of gray. But his bushy beard was beginning to resemble the groomed salt-and-pepper beard his father had worn when Hillel was a child. His clear blue eyes stared back at him, curious. No, perplexed. He studied his nose, the most prominent feature on his otherwise unremarkable face. The distinctive curve, which began a little below the bridge, was sharp and pugnacious, like a hawk's beak.

He wondered whether he should have worn a beret or a fedora instead of a kippah, but he would have felt pretentious wearing a hat indoors. Still, the knit kippah was such an unequivocal declaration of Hillel's position on the Israeli religious spectrum: Modern Orthodox.

What did Maya think the kippah meant? She must have noticed it. But she had still agreed to meet him.

"Is this seat taken?"

He hadn't seen this woman approach the bar. She was a striking slender brunette, wearing a form-fitting dove-gray dress and a strand of pearls with matching pearl drops in her delicate ears. She smiled warmly at him, her eyes asking to become better acquainted. He guessed she was from the American Midwest. She had that corn-fed look: pink complexion, glowing skin, and chicory eyes.

"Uh, I'm waiting for someone," said Hillel. "She should be here any minute."

The woman frowned. It was a good-natured frown. The corners of her lips immediately curled back up into a grin. She gave him a mock salute, then ambled down to the end of the bar, where another man sat alone, studying his beer mug. This time, she had better luck.

Nervous that Maya wouldn't show up, Hillel set his mind to working the puzzle of Boaz Goldmayer's murder. It was what he always did when he was bored or anxious. Or alone. Since childhood, he'd been obsessed with puzzles of all kinds—codes, cryptograms, wooden spheres and cubes constructed of interlocking pieces, riddles, logical paradoxes. His mother told him that this passion for solving puzzles ran in her family. Two of her great-uncles had been chess grandmasters back in Russia. How he would have loved to play with them!

According to the Israeli press, Goldmayer had been poisoned with hemlock. From his brief stint in the Israeli Scouts, Hillel knew that this plant grew wild all over Israel at this time of year. As for access to his victim, it would have been easy for the killer. Security was lax at academic conferences. And scholars were so distracted, their heads lost in their laptops and smartphones.

As for the killer's motive, Hillel didn't know what to think. Boaz Goldmayer was such a mensch, well-liked and respected by everyone. Why would anyone want to kill him? Hillel had never personally known anyone who'd been murdered. Such things didn't happen to scholars. The usual risks in their profession were disgrace and obscurity.

He didn't envy Maya her assignment. A scholar's murder was an uncommon puzzle. As baffling as the Greek letters in the Copper Scroll.

40

HILLEL'S THOUGHTS WERE INTERRUPTED BY Maya's arrival.

Tonight, she wore a light spring dress of a lemony color, which was accented by swirls of orange, brown, and forest green. Her lips showed only the barest trace of lipstick, a shade of ruddy copper that matched her hair. She wore a thin copper bangle on one wrist. From her ears dangled shimmery copper coils, reminding him of maple seeds twirling to the ground during New England autumns. She put one sandaled foot on the silver hoop at the base of the barstool next to him and hoisted herself up onto the black leather seat.

"Sorry I'm late," she said. "Vered didn't want to go to bed tonight. She's not always comfortable sleeping at my parents.'"

"Vered?"

"My three-year-old daughter."

He hadn't noticed a wedding ring on her hand. He didn't see one now. So she was either a divorcée or a widow. In Israel, either was just as likely.

"Been waiting long?"

"Just a few minutes. I snuck out of the final conference session before it ended. The last speaker was making the Dead Sea Scrolls deader by the minute."

She smiled. Something stirred in Hillel's chest. An electric charge rushed through his veins as if he'd been chilled by a sudden breeze. He gulped down the remainder of his whiskey and signaled the bartender for another.

He turned his head toward Maya, his palm extended.

"What will you have?"

"I'm not much of a drinker," Maya said. "The house wine is fine. A glass of Pinot Grigio, if they have it."

When the wine arrived, they sat in silence for a few moments. Maya twisted the stem of her wine glass. Hillel stared into his whiskey.

"So," Hillel said, pivoting on his stool to face Maya, "tell me about yourself."

"I thought we were meeting to discuss my case. The scrolls."

"That's all I've talked about all day. I'd love a little distraction."

"Not much to tell," Maya said. She took a sip of the wine, then twisted her stool to face him squarely. "My story's an Israeli cliché. My mother's family fled Marrakesh after the Arab riots in '48. My father's father came to Israel from Belarus during the British Mandate. Changed his name from Milgrom to Rimon and never spoke a word of Yiddish again. He and Bubbe Nadia had three children. My father's the oldest. My uncle Gadi was killed in the Yom Kippur War. My Aunt Ilana and her second husband live on a hilltop in the Territories with their seven children. There you have it—the story of modern Israel in a nutshell."

Hillel heard behind Maya's flippant tone the familiar undercurrent of sorrow and bitterness, so deeply rooted in the Israeli psyche.

She took another sip of her wine and smiled, her shoulders relaxing. He nodded for her to continue.

"After the army, my father joined the Intelligence Service. He was one of the agents who recovered the Temple Scroll from Kando."

"So you already know some of the history of the Dead Sea Scrolls."

"I wasn't even born when that operation took place." Maya paused, sipped some Pinot, then wiped her lips with a napkin. When she set the napkin back on the bar, Hillel noticed a ghost of lipstick on the white paper. "My father likes to joke that the Service is our 'family business.'"

"Is he still active?"

"Just retired. Doesn't know what to do with himself. The Service was his life."

A cell phone jangled in Maya's shoulder bag. She fished around for it, glanced at the screen, frowned, then disconnected the caller.

"I'm not sure how long I'll stay at the Service. I'm a single mother with a small child. My work often takes me away from home overnight. I have to leave Vered with my parents." He could hear the sharp, bitter edge to her voice. "And it's dangerous work. I don't want to leave my daughter an orphan."

"What about Vered's father?"

Maya's face changed abruptly, losing its softness. Her green eyes narrowed. Her angular chin thrust forward.

"He hardly deserves the title! He's a real shit, my ex, a drunk and a gambler. And now, he's threatening to take Vered away from me! I'll quit my job if that's the only way I can keep her."

Hillel felt assaulted, even though he knew Maya's anger was not directed at him. He felt an urge to protect her. But—he quickly chided himself—she could probably do that a lot better than he could.

Maya quickly downed the rest of her wine. She pivoted away from Hillel. Her face slackened into an impassive mask.

"What about you, Hillel? I don't hear an accent in English or Hebrew. So where are you from?"

"My story's not quite as typical as yours. My mother comes from a prominent rabbinic family in Lithuania. They came to America in the '30s. Mom received more education than most ultra-Orthodox girls. Went to Princeton, got a Masters in Biblical Studies. During her last year there, she met Christopher Stone III, a descendant of Boston bluebloods. He was a grad student at the Princeton Theological Seminary, on his way to becoming an Episcopalian minister. They met in a seminar on Second Temple Judaism. And now comes the 'only in America' part. They fell in love, and Chris asked Haya to marry him. She told him it was impossible. So he offered to convert. My mother signed on, even though she knew it was crazy."

Hillel stared at the mirrored wall. His light blue eyes glazed over, as if blinded by the glare from the track lights overhead.

"When my mother told her parents, they disowned her and sat *shiva*. She never spoke to them again. When my grandparents died, she wasn't allowed to attend their funerals or sit *shiva* with her siblings."

The bartender turned up the music. Cool jazz. A saxophone wailed plaintively, joined by a double bass, its cadenced thrumming low and mournful.

"In 1991, my parents brought me to Israel for my bar mitzvah. We stayed for the summer. While we were here, they applied for research fellowships at a few places. Eventually, they found permanent teaching jobs—Mom in a women's yeshivah, Dad at Hebrew University. Dad died a few years ago. Mom now lives on her own in Emek Refa'im. But she suffers from atrial fibrillation. Needs constant monitoring. It only takes me a half hour to get to her place from my apartment."

Hillel realized he'd gone on too long, probably boring Maya. He had that tendency, to talk too much.

"Sorry. Once a teacher, always a teacher."

"And once a detective...." Maya grinned, her gold-flecked green eyes sparkling in the soft light. "I make it a habit to say little, listen much. We make a good pair."

Hillel shifted uncomfortably on his stool. His sit bones were hurting from the hard seat. This was all moving too fast. Or maybe it was normal for first conversations. He had so little experience by which to judge.

Hillel noticed that Maya's wine glass was empty. He gestured to the bartender to refill it. She held up one hand to protest, then let the hand flutter down when the bartender appeared with the bottle of Pinot.

Hillel debated whether to ask for another shot. How was it possible that he was feeling giddy? He'd always prided himself on his high tolerance for alcohol. On Simchat Torah and Purim, he typically consumed multiple glasses of slivovitz, which only sharpened his fervor and lightened his steps as he danced and sang with the other men. He never became sick or unruly. It was another legacy from his Russian Jewish ancestors. With maybe a little Cossack thrown in.

He ordered another whiskey, a double. The golden liquid got smoother with each sip.

He glanced over at Maya. Her smile lit up her lovely face like a polished bronze medallion. There was an impish gleam in her shimmering green eyes. She was so lovely, this secret agent.

He ran his hand through his hair, ruffled his tangled beard with his fingers. The alcohol coursed through him, making his head throb and tingle. His feelings tumbled in his chest like clothes in a dryer. He hoped his dreams tonight would be filled with Maya's silky hair and skin.

And he didn't care if he tumbled headlong into sin.

41

Maya was feeling pleasantly lightheaded. It felt good to relax after being so intensely focused these past two days. She let her exhausted body slump against the padded back of the stool. Her short legs dangled weightlessly, her sandals banging softly against the chrome post. Vered was staying at her parents' overnight. She was a free woman. At least for tonight.

Hillel interrupted her drifting thoughts.

"So, how can I help you with your investigation? What do you want to know?"

"I have to confess that I'm pretty much a virgin on this whole subject," said Maya. She looked away when Hillel blushed, then brushed an invisible speck of dirt from the gauzy bodice of her dress. "So much for Israeli Intelligence!"

They both laughed, Maya's voice rich and sonorous, his taut like a stretched bow.

"Tell me more about the Copper Scroll."

Hillel laughed, then waggled his forefinger at Maya. "Be careful what you wish for, Agent Rimon. Once you get me started, it's hard to stop me."

Maya cocked her head to one side, then raised an eyebrow. She reached into her purse and withdrew a ballpoint pen and a small black notebook. She straightened her spine and sat erect.

"Okay, professor, fire away!"

The bar had become crowded. The noise of conversation, clattering silverware, and the *whoosh* of beer taps forced Maya and Hillel to lean in toward each other.

Maya took a sip of her wine. The room began to swim in front of her. Not an unpleasant feeling. Like leaning on the rail of a boat on a calm sea, watching the waves shimmer and curl. She could smell the sharp, smoky tang of whiskey on Hillel's breath. She nodded toward him to encourage him. *Tell me more.*

"So here's the standing-on-one-foot version," said Hillel. He swallowed. His throat was dry as sand.

He lifted his eyes and looked at Maya. She was aiming her pen at him, playing the investigative journalist, a smile warming her full lips. Playing along, he pulled himself upright on the high stool and tugged down on his jacket lapels. Then, he leaned forward on the bar, his hands gripping an imaginary lectern.

"As I already told you, the Copper Scroll is unlike any of the other Dead Sea Scrolls that have been found in and around Qumran. *Everything* about it is unique. It was composed later than the other scrolls. Its Hebrew is more modern than theirs. The spelling and shapes of the Hebrew letters are different from the script used at that time. And perhaps most significantly, it's the only scroll written not on parchment or papyrus—but on metal. Almost pure copper. It's also the only inventory that's been found among the scrolls. That's what's really captured the popular imagination. The Copper Scroll is an inventory of lost treasure!"

Maya listened, a child spellbound before a magician. She drained the rest of her wine. Then, she signaled the bartender to refill her empty glass. While she waited, she dipped a finger in the shallow puddle that had formed under her wineglass and drew a series of radiating lines on the shiny surface of the bar.

Hillel watched her. When the circle of spiky lines was complete, she lifted the wet finger to her lips and sucked it dry.

The skin of Hillel's face flushed bright red. His eyes fixed on the floor. His heart pounded in his chest like a steam-drill. He was trying his best to keep his voice conversational, slow and measured. It was so easy for him to become pedantic.

He almost giggled with relief when he saw Maya's face light up with a smile. He sucked in his breath, then cleared his throat. His shoulders collapsed in relief. He grinned, somewhat embarrassed by his enthusiasm.

"Unfortunately, this treasure map is indecipherable. The scroll is written in some kind of code. Boaz was particularly interested in the fourteen Greek letters scattered throughout the Hebrew text, sometimes in pairs, sometimes in groups of three. No one's ever been able to figure out what they mean. Boaz assumed it was some kind of cipher, put there to keep the Romans from finding the Temple treasures. He wondered whether the lost duplicate scroll might contain the key to unlock the code."

Maya nodded in rhythm with Hillel's words. The movement made her dizzy. She swayed on her stool. Hillel reached out his right hand to steady her. His hand closed gently around her bare upper arm.

She began to giggle. Heat flushed her cheeks. She placed her right hand on Hillel's left, which rested on the bar. She pressed down. She was surprised that he didn't move his hand away. And was it her imagination, or had he tightened his grip on her left arm? Then, her bladder began demanding attention.

"Time f'me to pay a vis't to th' Ladies Room!"

She lifted her hand from the bar and twisted around to grab the back of her stool. She missed her target and almost fell. Hillel steadied her, his hand gently pushing back on her bare shoulder.

He held out his hand to her. She waved him away.

Walking with as much dignity as she could muster, she made an uneven beeline toward the bathroom. Even after she was out of sight, her sandals continued to slap the tile floor like a military tattoo.

The whiskey was making him woozy. The room spun when he closed his eyes. He signaled the bartender and ordered black coffee.

Maya returned to the bar and resumed her seat. This time, he didn't offer to help.

He looked at his watch. "It's late. We should go."

Maya nodded, then began fishing in her purse.

"I'll take care of it," he said.

Maya vehemently shook her head.

"Oh, no, you don', professor! I pay my own way, thank you very *mush*." Her words were slurred.

She grabbed a fistful of paper shekel notes and slapped them down on the bar. The bartender came over and riffled among the notes, taking what they owed. Hillel reached into his pocket, scooped up some coins, and handed them to the bartender. The man grinned from ear to ear and nodded. Had he given the man too big a tip? He hadn't even seen the tab.

"It's *sush* a nice night," said Maya. "I think I'll walk home."

She slid off her stool and staggered toward the door. Hillel ran after her, grasping her gently by the elbow.

"I don't think you should walk by yourself. I'll get you a cab."

She shook herself free and waved a dismissive hand back toward him as she continued toward the exit.

"I c'n take care of myself, Prof'ssor. I'm a trained profesh'nal!" She hesitated before exiting the bar. "I'll be in *toush*."

And then she was gone.

Hillel stared at himself in the wall mirror. He noted the two empty glasses on the gleaming bar. The small puddles at the base of each glass. He could still smell her. Traces of pungent aloe and Dead Sea salts.

42

HOLDING HIS KIPPAH DOWN WITH one hand, Hillel ran out of the Twelve Tribes Pub. How could he have let her go off by herself? No matter what she said.

When he reached the main lobby, he caught sight of her just as the glass doors whooshed closed behind her. He waited impatiently for the doors to re-open, then burst out into the warm, dark night.

"Maya! Let me walk you home. Please!"

Leaning against the cool white stone of the hotel's facade, a young security guard took a drag on his cigarette and chuckled to himself.

Even frummies fall in love. And act like fools.

Hillel and Maya walked side by side at a comfortable pace on the uneven paving stones, heading south. Occasionally they accelerated their steps to pass by an elderly couple or a dawdling group of teens. Despite the late hour and the fact that it was a Monday night, the sidewalks were bustling with people. Unlike many urban capitals, Jerusalem was still a pedestrian city. And a safe one, despite what the headlines said.

Neither of them had spoken since leaving the hotel. Hillel found himself caught in a welter of emotions—exhilaration, bewilderment, embarrassment. For the past two days, he'd been on an adrenaline high. As always, he'd thrown himself headlong into the giddy ferment of an academic conference. And now, he was playing Watson to a stunningly beautiful Holmes. The combination might prove too potent for his bookish temperament.

Yet he had never felt so alive. So *virile*. At thirty-five, Hillel had almost given up hope of ever marrying. Despite intense pressure from friends, his rabbi, and his family, he remained single. Not that he hadn't tried. Dutifully, he'd met his share of "nice Orthodox girls," but none had seemed right for him. He suspected that they kept the most eligible ones away from him because his father was a convert to Judaism. He'd finally concluded that he was just not meant to marry. Not that he had any inclinations the other way. He had never felt drawn to men, even in the intense intimacy of the yeshivah. No, he just seemed destined to be a lifelong bachelor. To live out his life as a Jewish monk.

But then he'd met Maya Rimon. Something about this beautiful, gutsy, bright young Sabra had broken through his shell. Surprisingly, they had been drawn to each other, despite the vast chasm separating them. She was secular; he was religious. He was an intellectual; she, a woman of action. He was thinking about taking a job in America. She would never leave Israel. No wonder they said that love was blind.

Maya suddenly stopped walking.

"It's late, Hillel. I've had too much to drink. I'll take a cab the rest of the way."

"I'd rather walk you home. I could use the fresh air. And I have more to tell you."

She turned to look at him, her eyes narrowed under a furrowed brow.

"I don't feel like talking any more tonight. And it's too far to walk. Over an hour. I'll just take a cab."

"I would really like to walk you home."

He took her hand, gave it a gentle squeeze, and let it drop to her side.

She nodded, then led them toward Derech Beit Lechem, the main road south to Bethlehem.

"Don't say I didn't warn you." She led them off Keren HaYesod onto a quiet street. "It's quite a shlep."

But her tone was light-hearted, teasing. She seemed pleased to have his company.

The crisp air was clearing his head, the effects of the whiskey wearing off. His speech had shed its sloppiness. He noticed that Maya, too, was walking more surely, her head erect, shoulders squared.

Even at this late hour, the Bethlehem Road buzzed with car and truck traffic. Whenever possible, the two of them detoured into neighborhood streets, following a route parallel to the main road.

"Wait!" Maya's voice was sharp. "You're walking too fast. We've still got a long way to go."

Hillel halted, turned, and took a few steps back to stand beside Maya. He hadn't realized he'd gotten so far ahead of her. He often lost track of how fast he walked. His mother was forever lecturing him about this. *Nu, bubbeleh, so where's the fire?*

"Sorry."

He reached into his knapsack and took out a half-full bottle of water. They each took a few sips. He returned the bottle to his bag.

They reached a curved metal gate, which cordoned off an intersection. Maya grasped the top of the gate, thrust one leg back, and stretched her hamstrings. She then switched to the other leg. The traffic light turned green, and they crossed the street.

For the next fifteen minutes, they walked without speaking, lost in their own thoughts.

The early summer night was warm and clear. It was the end of the spring holiday of Lag Baomer. The air was perfumed with the pungent aroma of barbecuing meat, seasoned with za'atar, s'chug, baharat, and cumin. Smells of wood smoke and burnt tar. Many people were still barbecuing; others, visiting with neighbors or strolling. Children chased each other with sticks and toy bows and arrows. Dogs yapped excitedly at their heels.

Even though it was almost midnight, pedestrians still filled the streets. Many were religious Jews in long, black gabardine coats, with oversized brimmed hats and heavy black shoes, their corked ear curls bouncing like springs. Maya and Hillel brushed past two young female soldiers on patrol, their assault rifles slung over their shoulders, giggling and whispering to each other. On a bench, a wizened old grandmother comforted a crying child, whose fingers had been burned by stray embers. Some people sat out on their apartment balconies, watching. In the entryway to a building, a young Filipino helped an old man with a cane make his way up steep stone stairs.

Jerusalem is a living, breathing organism, thought Hillel, not just a picture postcard of gleaming domes surrounded by stone walls. Or photographs of gruesome carnage, scenes of blood and the conflict of incompatible gods. It's full of real people, raising children and working and getting sick and quarreling over trivialities. It's full of music and memory and dog-eared photographs and love letters. And yet it was like no other place on Earth. Every stone was contested territory. Every street a border.

"Hillel? Are you listening? I asked if you had a tissue?"

"Huh? Sorry. I drifted off."

Hillel reached inside his pants pocket and pulled out a clean, white handkerchief. He handed it to Maya. She shook it open, blew her nose, then folded it back carefully along the creases, handing the small, white square back to him. He shoved it back into his pocket, then looked at her, still lost in the fog of his thoughts.

"How much further?"

"About ten more minutes. I told you it was far."

They continued on in silence.

"So, what do you know about kohl?" asked Maya.

Maya's question came at Hillel like a sudden slap on the cheek. "What?"

"Kohl," she repeated. "The dark blue eye makeup women wore in ancient times."

"Does it have something to do with your investigation?"

"It might."

Maya paused and held up a finger, signaling Hillel to stop. Balancing herself with one hand gripping his shoulder, she shook out a small pebble from her left sandal. Then, she slipped the sandal back on and turned to face Hillel.

"At the crime scene, I found traces of blue powder on Goldmayer's backpack. Could be copper oxide. I'm wondering whether he searched for the duplicate scroll near an ancient copper mine."

Hillel felt a prickle of excitement.

"According to the Copper Scroll," he said, "the duplicate was hidden in a place called 'Kochalit.' The name might refer to a manufactory, where kohl was refined from copper ore."

Hillel blushed when he saw Maya smile. His enthusiasm sometimes made him sound like a child. He was grateful that his flushed skin was hard to see in the jaundiced light of the streetlamps. They were relying mostly on their voices to read each other's moods.

"So where is this place, Kochalit?" asked Maya. "Why hasn't anybody gone there to look for the duplicate scroll?"

"Because we don't know exactly where it is. Some scholars think the name refers to Mount Gerizim or Mount Zion. Others have suggested a site east of the Jordan River or near the Yarmuk River south of Damascus. Even Qumran's been mentioned as a possible location. But nobody's found the duplicate scroll or the Temple treasures in any of these places."

Hillel was again a few paces ahead of Maya. He stopped and waited for her to catch up.

"That's probably what got Boaz killed," said Hillel. "He claimed to have found Kochalit. But he didn't tell anyone where it was. Only the murderer knows."

Suddenly, Hillel grabbed hold of Maya's arm and yanked her toward him. A dark blue compact jumped the curb, missing her by inches.

"*Meshugeneh!*"

Hillel shouted and flapped the back of his hand at the speeding car.

"It's crazy the way some people drive in this country. I'm surprised there aren't twice as many accidents!"

He strained to make out the car's license plate, but it was too dark. The only thing he caught sight of before the blue car vanished into the night was the light-colored back door on the passenger side. No doubt replaced after an accident. The man was clearly a menace on the road.

He relaxed his grip on Maya's bare arm, then let go. Even in the faint light, he could see the spectral outline of his fingers on her flesh.

43

MAYA BEGAN TO TREMBLE. THE air had chilled considerably during their walk. She sniffled but didn't ask him for his handkerchief. He didn't offer it. The sidewalk had disappeared, giving way to gravel.

"I just have one more question," said Maya. "Does the phrase, 'De Vaux's field notes,' mean anything to you?"

Hillel froze in his tracks.

"*Roland* De Vaux? How in the world did you hear about *him*?"

She unzipped her shoulder bag and rummaged around with her hand. She withdrew the paper cocktail napkin and handed it to Hillel.

"I meant to show this to you earlier at the bar. Guess I got distracted." He smiled. She didn't. "The light there would have been better."

Hurrying over to a streetlamp, Hillel held up the napkin, pinched between the thumb and index finger of each hand, then unfolded it to reveal the spidery writing on the inside fold. He squinted through his glasses, then looked over at Maya. In the yellow glow of the sodium light, the skin of her face looked ghostly, her teeth almost metallic.

"Where did you get this?"

"On the floor of Goldmayer's hotel room. Under the bed. The crime scene techs missed it."

She offered no excuses for removing evidence from a crime scene. Hillel didn't challenge her. He brought the napkin closer to his glasses and squinted again. Then, he handed it back to her.

"De Vaux was a French Dominican priest, who excavated around Qumran in the 1950s. A number of his archaeological field notes have never been published or translated. Some scholars think there are still secrets buried in them. Apparently, Goldmayer thought so, too."

"What about this Wolters that Goldmayer mentions? And the *protokollon*?"

Although Maya had already looked all this up, she knew it wouldn't hurt to hear it all again. The arcane world of the Dead Sea Scrolls still remained foreign territory to her.

Hillel felt the pedant in him stirring. He knew he should chase it back into its dark, musty burrow. But he was too fond of this familiar to banish it too quickly. He looked down his angular nose at Maya.

"Okay, I'll fill you in. But *al regel achat*, I promise." Hillel balanced awkwardly on one leg to make his point.

Maya grinned. Hillel felt his spirits rise.

"Knock yourself out," she said. "We still have well over a kilometer to go."

They resumed walking, their pace slowed by fatigue and the prolonged darkness between streetlights.

"A *protokollon* was like an ancient table of contents. It generally appeared on the first leaf of a scroll. The last line of the Copper Scroll mentions a *protokollon*. It claims it was hidden in Kochalit along with a duplicate copy of the Copper Scroll."

Hillel cited the final line from memory: "'In the underground passage that is in Sehab north of Kochalit, with its opening to the north, and which has tombs at its entrance: a duplicate of this document, and the interpretation, and 'their portions,' and the *protokollon* of the one and the other.'"

Hillel paused and looked at Maya. Her face was a mask. Or maybe it was just the play of shadows on her skin.

"The last line doesn't seem to make sense, does it?"

No response from Maya. Was he boring her? Had he lost her in the weeds?

"At least, it didn't seem to make sense, until Professor Albert Wolters came along. He claimed to have deciphered its meaning."

Maya raised her eyebrows and blew out a frustrated sigh. Hillel pushed on.

"Professor Wolters proposed a radical new interpretation of the Copper Scroll's final line. He pointed out that a detailed inventory like this would normally have included a *protokollon*. But the Copper Scroll doesn't have one. Wolters seized on the *absence* of the *protokollon* as proof that whoever wrote the Copper Scroll deliberately left out the *protokollon*. He argued that this omission was part of a secret code."

Hillel clapped his hands together, then thrust his index finger toward Maya. She tramped steadily forward, a few steps behind him, unresponsive to his relentless monologue. He found himself too keyed up to stop.

"He claimed that the author of the Copper Scroll was using what cryptographers call a 'dual cipher.' Two halves of a puzzle that depend on each other for the solution. In this kind of code, you need both halves to decipher the code. It's like fitting a key into a lock. According to Wolters' theory, the pairs and triplets of Greek letters scattered throughout the Copper Scroll constitute the first half of the puzzle. The second half of the puzzle is located in the *protokollon* of the duplicate copy. You have to admit it's an ingenious theory. In order to find the hidden Temple treasures, you have to get hold of *both* scrolls. It's a great script for a detective novel, eh?"

"What do other scholars think about Wolters' theory?"

Hillel sighed, then threw up his hands.

"Most dismiss it as too speculative, based on almost no evidence. Without having the duplicate scroll in our hands, there's no way we can test his theory."

"What do *you* think?"

Hillel stopped walking and turned to face Maya.

"For years, I was skeptical just like everyone else. But now, I wonder whether Wolters might have been on to something. The Copper Scroll's final line has to refer to a *protokollon* found only in the duplicate scroll. Something must be written there that was left out of the Copper Scroll."

"Such as?"

"I don't know. The decryption key to the Greek letters. A secret password. Maybe some kind of authorization code needed by whoever finds the duplicate scroll, proving that he has a legitimate claim to the Temple treasures. Maybe the duplicate scroll is also missing something, a key that's included only in the Copper Scroll. We won't know until we find it."

"So Goldmayer must have believed Wolters' theory."

"Probably. But even if he did, we still don't know whether he actually *found* the duplicate scroll. All your note confirms is that he was convinced he knew where it was."

Although he had stopped walking, Hillel suddenly felt short of breath. His pulse was racing. It was almost as if he were now standing next to his old mentor at the threshold of a newly discovered ancient site. If only Boaz had been more wary!

Hillel looked over at Maya. Her forehead was knotted, her narrow jaw set. But in the shadowy light, her green eyes sparkled. His pulse raced faster.

"We may find answers in De Vaux's unpublished field notes. Hidden in plain sight for sixty years. First thing tomorrow, I'm going over to the Qumran Archives. See what I can dig up."

Maya nodded, then let out a soft sigh. He could sense her exhaustion. He felt it, too. The two walked on together in silence.

44

Near the intersection of the Bethlehem and Hebron Roads, they came to a small plaza set back from the main road. In the stuttering light of two streetlamps stood a gas station and a run-down snack bar and grill. Maya noticed a couple clinging to each other in an alley between the two buildings. In the glow of the waxing moon, their skin shone like black pearls. Probably Ethiopian Jews from her neighborhood.

The couple continued to grope each other in the dark. Maya knew she should look away, give them privacy, even though they were unaware of her presence. But she couldn't tear her eyes away from them. The man was extraordinarily tall and slender, almost a head taller than the woman. Her long hair reached below her waist as she tilted backwards. Maya was too far away to hear the couple's voices or the sounds of their kisses. Her imagination filled in the silence. She imagined the girl protesting, the boy insisting. Kisses interrupted their debate, which was only half-hearted, anyway. Blood rushed to the surface of their skin. Their hearts beat faster as they struggled to loosen their clothing. They were oblivious to the chilling air, to the cars whizzing past, to the two strangers walking by. They were aware of nothing except their rushing blood and beating hearts and fumbling hands and burning lips.

And then the two disappeared from view.

Hillel kept striding into the night, his pace matched by the rushing traffic on the broad Hebron Road. The air smelled of gas fumes from cars and trucks. Hillel's hurried pace was no doubt fueled by the presence of the many Arab villages nearby. Maya wished she could have lingered to watch the lovers, but she felt embarrassed by her voyeurism. It had been so long since she'd had a man in her bed.

Would Hillel be the one to end her long dry spell? So far, the signs hadn't been encouraging. She had to admit that she was attracted to him. Drawn by his jet-black hair; his slender, lanky form; his quiet hands, and his intense cornflower-blue eyes. But he was so bottled up inside that she wasn't sure about his sexual appetite. Was he just a shy man, perhaps stung by a bad experience? Or had he been utterly screwed up by his religious upbringing? Or was it something more essential—a natural coldness? She'd find out soon enough. Tonight, she would force him to decide. What did he want? No sense letting her fantasies get too far ahead of reality. That would only hurt them both.

Feeling self-conscious, she turned away from the alley and glanced down the road. About a hundred meters ahead stood a huge billboard, brightly lit from below. The bottom left corner of the billboard was defaced with angry gashes of black spray paint. Maya thought the Hebrew graffiti spelled, "Idol Worship!" but the thick black scrawl was hard to decipher.

A single familiar image filled most of the surface area of the billboard: the face of Rabbi Menachem Mendel Schneerson, the Rebbe, as he was popularly known, the last world leader of Lubavitch Hasidism. The rabbi's pallid face was framed by a squared-off gossamer beard and a black fedora. Like a wizened cherub, his piercing blue eyes and cryptic smile blessed the cars and battered pick-up trucks speeding south. The words beside the giant image read: "Mashiach Now!" To his thousands of followers, the Rebbe had assumed a new status since his death in 1994. Many of his followers now embraced him as the incarnation of the Jewish Messiah. Why else had his Hasidim named no successor after his death?

Although Maya had passed by this billboard countless times on her bus ride home, she'd never before thought of linking the Chabad Rebbe to the Christian fanatics whose ambitions had consumed her these past two days. *So we're not so different from them, are we? All of us longing for someone to come save us from ourselves before it's too late.* Chuckling, she saluted the old rabbi as she passed by.

What did Hillel think of the Rebbe? she wondered. *How far did his Orthodoxy extend?*

But before she could ask him, Hillel spoke.

"Don't we turn off here?"

"Sorry?"

"The sign says, 'Givat HaMatos.' Isn't this where you live?"

Embarrassed by her self-absorption, Maya overtook Hillel and strode quickly down the macadam pedestrian strip parallel to the road's exit ramp. He had to run to keep up with her. In a few hundred meters, they reached the first buildings of her neighborhood.

Givat HaMatos, literally, "Airplane Hill," had been established where a small Israeli Air Force plane had crashed on the second day of the Six-Day War after being hit by Jordanian anti-aircraft artillery. The Israeli government had built a settlement here in 1991 for the many Ethiopian Jews who had been airlifted to Israel during Operation Solomon that year. Until then, the site had been an empty, windswept hillside on the southern edge of Jerusalem's municipal limits. The cluster of trailers brought in for the first residents was located close to the Arab communities of Bethlehem and Beit Jallah. The area included a minefield left over from the War of Independence. The settlement quickly became a dumping ground for new immigrants. Russian and homeless families soon joined the Ethiopians. Plans were put in place to build new housing for the residents or move them elsewhere. But so far, nothing had come of these plans. The trailers remained, along with a few hastily-erected apartment buildings. Everything was already run-down, in desperate need of repair. But the rent was dirt-cheap. And since Givat HaMatos was on the bus line to central Jerusalem, only a twenty-minute ride to Maya's office, she was content to stay.

"My building's just around the corner."

Maya headed down a rutted two-lane street with no sidewalks. She turned at the end of the road and was immediately lost from view.

Hillel scurried after her. There were only a few streetlights in the development, most of them missing bulbs or flickering with weak light. The trailers and low apartment buildings were mostly dark. Near the end of the street, the last embers of a trashcan fire sparked and sputtered. A stray yellow dog loped behind Hillel, its ribs outlined against its mangy fur. Nearby, a few other dogs picked through the scraps of a meal, snapping at each other over the bones. The yellow dog ran over to join them, provoking a chorus of howls and yips.

When Hillel turned the corner, he found himself facing a four-story apartment house constructed of poor-quality Jerusalem stone. The exterior surface had eroded in places to reveal the concrete shell and I-beams underneath. The building was square, consisting of sixteen identical block units. The windows, too, were square, divided into two panes bisected by a vertical frame. There was nothing architecturally noteworthy about the construction. It was simple, cheap, and utterly without character.

Hillel caught sight of Maya bent down in a half-crouch under a bare yellow bulb near the front entrance to her building. Her head swiveled nervously from side to side. In her hand, she held a snub-nosed handgun. It too swung slowly back and forth in a half-arc.

She beckoned him toward her, then tugged on his sleeve to make him crouch down beside her.

"I think we've been followed."

With her free hand, she pointed to one corner of her building, its stone edge blurred by dark shadows.

"Dark cap, dark clothes. Tall and thin. That's all I could make out. He's no longer there."

She paused, inhaled sharply, then spit out a breath.

"I could swear I heard a camera click. I think I also saw him near the Hebron intersection, but I can't be sure."

"Should we call the police?" Hillel laughed uneasily. "Oops, I forgot. You *are* the police."

Maya's face was a stony mask. She stood up and shook out her legs. "Whoever he is," she said, "he's long gone."

She forced herself to put the stalker out of mind. Probably some snoop Rafi hired to document her questionable morals and negligent parenting. No sense worrying about it now. She had a different agenda tonight.

Taking a slow, deep breath, she stepped into the dark doorway of her building. The yellow light of the bare bulb now revealed only the toes of her right sandal.

"Hillel." Maya's voice was soft and sensual, lacking its customary edge. "Come here."

Hillel walked slowly toward the dark entryway. His gait seemed somewhat unsteady, but it could no longer be the whiskey. Maya eyed him keenly, like a stalking cat.

She felt a tingling on the surface of her skin. Her heart pounded in her chest. Her palms were moist. It had been quite a long time since she'd felt this way in the presence of a man. Her body was already far ahead of her brain. Her slender arms reached out. She longed to hold him—in her arms, between her legs. To taste his lips and tongue. To drown in his unfathomable blue eyes.

Maya held out her hand and drew Hillel close. Tangled together, they staggered deeper into the dark hallway, beyond the reach of the yellow bulb. She reached up to cradle his soft, dark curls in her hand. She gently pulled his head toward her until their lips met. They kissed tentatively. Maya placed her hand behind his head and pressed his face into hers. She pushed their lips together until his opened. She thrust her tongue between his lips. He pushed back with his. She ran her tongue against his teeth, sliding over the smooth enamel.

By now, she'd lost all orientation in space and time. No inner voice told her to stop. Nothing cautioned her to think about what she was doing. Her will had been hijacked.

And so had his. Desire now had Hillel completely in thrall. His soft hands glided eagerly from Maya's hair down to her shoulders. Then, they slid down to her full breasts, which were straining against the light material of her dress.

"Let's go inside." Maya's breath exploded in quick puffs. "My daughter's with my parents for the night."

Whether it was the mention of her daughter or her parents or just the sound of her voice after so much silence, something made Hillel pull away. He stepped back into the harsh light of the bare yellow bulb.

"I should be getting back," he said. He turned his face away. "It's late."

Maya remained in the shadows. Her breath slowed, then became inaudible.

"If that's what you want."

Her voice revealed nothing.

For an incalculable period of time, neither spoke. A dog barked. An ambulance or police siren wailed in the distance. Maya listened to her breathing, steady and calm.

"I'll call a cab for you," she said. "Might be a long wait this time of night."

And then she was gone.

She didn't bother to press down the timer in the first-floor hallway to illuminate the dark stairwell. She hurried up to the fourth floor in the darkness, her sandals slapping the stone stairs. When she got to her landing, she fumbled for her key. She unlocked the door, pushed it open, and slammed it shut behind her. Then, she leaned back against the wall, her chest heaving.

In her bones and muscles and nerves, she felt the fatigue of the long walk. It was exacerbated by the tension she'd been carrying for the past few days. Apprehensiveness about the case. Fear of failure and humiliation. And on top of this, her anxiety about what was going to happen with Hillel. She felt as if she'd been transported to some giant planet, its unbearable gravity weighing her down. Her shoulders sagged. She slumped to the hard, stone floor.

She retrieved her mobile phone from her purse and called the local taxi service. The dispatcher told her he couldn't guarantee a pick-up time this late at night. She opened the bedroom window and leaned out.

"They said ten minutes, which probably means a half hour. But they're dependable. I use them all the time." She paused and swallowed. Her throat was raw. "If you don't mind, I'd rather not come down to wait with you. I'm exhausted."

Hillel waved up at her but said nothing.

She closed the window without saying goodnight. There was a faint squeak and thud as she pulled the metal frame tight and bolted it.

DAY 3

Wednesday

45

THE NEXT MORNING, MAYA ARRIVED at Service Headquarters shortly after 8:00 a.m., her auburn curls still kinked and damp from the shower. Several of her colleagues glanced down at their watches or phones, eyebrows raised. A few clapped or gave her a thumbs up. She ignored them.

As soon as she sat down at her desk, her cell phone chimed.

"About last night...."

"I don't want to talk about it, Hillel. I'm busy. I have an investigation to run."

She wanted to add: "Without you!" But she didn't. She had promised herself last night that she was through with him—both as a consultant and a would-be lover. But when the phone rang, she found herself hoping it was him calling to apologize. Would she never learn?

He took her silence as encouragement.

"I can understand why you're upset. We need to talk."

"What's there to talk about? You've made your feelings quite clear."

"That's just it! I haven't!" His voice was loud, almost a whine. "Look, I'll be the first to admit that I'm an idiot when it comes to women. I spend too much time in my head. And I don't have much practice."

"Nice speech, professor." She tried to keep the hurt out of her voice but didn't try hard enough.

Come on. Break it off. Now. But then she pictured his gentle hands. His intense, cornflower-blue eyes. And her resolve faltered.

"Look, Hillel. The truth is that we have nothing in common."

"Opposites attract. Excuse the cliché."

She needed to get mad at him, override her own neediness. How did Roni put it? *Man up*! So she pushed harder, hoping to provoke him.

"You've got too much damn luggage!"

"I think you mean 'baggage.'" She heard him chuckling. Despite herself, she blushed. At least over the phone he couldn't see the roses coloring her cheeks.

"You know what I mean. I appreciate all the help you've given me up to now. I'll take it from here."

"I think you could still use my help."

She finally felt the gorge rising in her throat. Her fingers clenched around the phone. She needed to end it now—before it became too hard.

She pressed the red hang-up icon. Then, she tossed the cell phone into her large shoulder bag. Her held breath whooshed out of her like a deflating balloon.

For the next few minutes, she sat at her desk, drumming the gray metal surface with her fingers. Her unfocused eyes stared at the drawn mini-blinds covering the glass door. Then, her hand floated up to her chin. Her forefinger stroked the roughened skin. Her fingertip encountered a stiff bristle, and she began pulling at it with her clipped fingernails, trying to pluck it out. Her therapist called it self-soothing. Only it didn't always work. It certainly didn't now.

She forced her hand away from her chin. Then, she picked up the black desk phone and called Ziggy Dweck.

46

"WHAT DID YOU LEARN FROM the hotel's phone logs?"

"You were right," Ziggy said. "Turns out the Lowenthals"... *mumbling*..."a lot more than just eating dinner and watching"...*mumbling*..."night. You'll never guess"...*mumbling*..."were up to!"

No doubt Ziggy's mouth was full of food. Her fellow agent was forever noshing, mostly on his mother's sticky Syrian pastries. She heard him swallow hard, gulp water from a plastic bottle, then twist the cap back on.

"Just spit it out, Ziggy! I don't have all day."

"The old professor was on a phone sex hotline. For three hours!"

Maya gasped. That pretentious old peacock!

"And his son, Adam?"

Ziggy bit down on something crunchy. His chewing was like wax paper crackling in her ear.

"Even more unbelievable. One of our IT guys hacked into his computer. Turns out Junior spent all night sockpuppeting. Posing as one of his father's arch-rivals, Professor Geoffrey Cox."

"Sending bogus emails."

"*B'diyuk*. The phony emails made it look like Cox was confessing to having committed scholarly fraud."

There was a pause. Maya heard Ziggy guzzling water, then fussing with a paper bag.

"So, both Lowenthals were 'otherwise engaged' when Boaz Goldmayer was breathing his last?"

Maya didn't tell Ziggy that she'd already eliminated the senior Lowenthal. This new information only deepened her scorn for the old man. But now, she had to exclude the son as well. No way Adam could have poisoned Goldmayer and stolen his data while he was busy sending out sock puppets on his laptop. Even a mad genius wasn't that clever. That left only Habib Salameh as a credible suspect.

But something didn't make sense. Why had the antiquities dealer felt compelled to kill the American professor? All he had needed from Goldmayer was the location of the duplicate scroll so that he could track down the Temple treasures. Adding murder to the crime of theft significantly upped the risk for him. And Habib Salameh was nothing if not cautious. Some might even say paranoid. He would have resorted to murder only if he felt he had no choice.

What was she missing?

47

Maya stared vacantly at her office's mottled green walls. She recalled the disturbing conversation she'd had with Tim Hargreaves at the LTM Center. About blood moons as apocalyptic omens. Something about this information still gnawed at her.

And the next blood moon was going to occur tomorrow night.

Bending over her keyboard, she logged into her secure account.

Eagerly, she typed in the keywords, "blood moon." Clicking through various scientific sites, she learned that during certain lunar eclipses, the Earth's moon turns blood-red, due to a light effect called Rayleigh scattering. It had something to do with shortened wave lengths and air pollution.

But the Christian websites she clicked on offered a very different spin on this common astronomical phenomenon. According to them, blood moons were messianic signs. All the sites quoted the same two verses from the Bible:

From the Book of Joel 2:31: "And the sun shall be turned into darkness, and the moon into blood, before the great and terrible day of the Lord."

And from the New Testament, the Book of Revelation 6:12: "I watched as he opened the sixth seal. There was a great earthquake. The sun turned black like sackcloth made of goat hair. The whole moon turned blood red."

She probed deeper. It turned out that an American televangelist from Texas, John Hagee, had first coined the term, "blood moon," to suggest its prophetic significance. "The blood moon is a warning sign to humankind that darkness will overcome the Earth; the Lord will come during these dark times." According to Hagee, there was a special connection between blood moons and Israel. Many significant events in Jewish history had coincided with blood moons, including the fall of the Babylonian Empire and the Spanish Inquisition in 1492.

Maya shook her head and sighed. Why did so many Israelis applaud the pro-Zionism of Christian evangelicals? Didn't they realize how crazy these people were? Didn't they understand that these Christians only supported Israel because they needed the Jews to come home to Zion and convert in order to pave the way for the second coming of Christ? She chuckled to herself. Religion certainly made strange bedfellows!

Maya also learned more about what a Tetrad was. The term referred to a sequence of four blood moons, that is, lunar eclipses, occurring close together, with six full moons in between. Such occurrences were very rare. During the past two thousand years, Tetrads had only happened sixty-two times.

But even rarer were the Tetrads that coincided with Jewish holidays. Such sequences had only occurred eight times in twenty-one centuries. There had been a Tetrad during Israel's War of Independence and another coinciding with the Six-Day War. Their infrequency made these particular Tetrads especially significant to those eagerly awaiting the End Times.

The most recent Jewish Festival Tetrad had occurred in 2014–15. During both these years, there had been total lunar eclipses on Passover and Sukkot. Hagee and another American minister, Mark Blitz, announced that the world would end after the fourth blood moon in fall 2015. Following that final eclipse, the Middle East would be wholly transformed. Jews and Arabs would sign a peace treaty, agreeing to share control of the Temple Mount. Jews would then erect the Third Temple on the Mount, without destroying the two Arab shrines currently standing there. And then the Antichrist would come, setting off the Abomination of Desolation, which would result in a second Jewish Holocaust, this time in Israel. But before this catastrophe happened, Christians would rush to the aid of the Jews, persuading them to embrace Jesus and be saved.

Of course, the world had not come to an end in the fall of 2015. But the Christian prognosticators weren't discouraged. There was always the next Tetrad, due to occur in 2032–33.

Maya stood up from her chair and threw back her shoulders. She felt a satisfying pop as her bones and muscles realigned themselves. How could Habib Salameh get involved in this nonsense? He was a Muslim, even if a lapsed one. Muslims didn't go in for such outlandish ideas, did they? They were carrying out scientific astronomy when Christians were still burning witches in Europe. But he'd be happy to make a profit from anyone's beliefs, no matter how wild. Religious chicanery was fungible.

She logged into the agency's archives, hunting for any Christian groups in Jerusalem that had any known connections to "blood moons" or "Tetrads." The keyword search identified several such groups, including the "New Children of Light," Tim Hargreaves' new church. Their website announced that there would be an event marking the blood moon tomorrow night on the Tayelet. It would definitely be worth checking out.

On a hunch, she pulled up her old case file on the LTM Center investigation from several months ago. That case continued to niggle at her, despite Roni's repeated warnings to let it go. She wasn't even sure what she was looking for. Rapidly, she skimmed through her old notes. One name popped out. Pinkas Mashiak. She wasn't sure why it flagged her attention. She must have questioned him during the course of her investigation, but she couldn't put a face to the name.

She entered the name in the Service database. The search turned up nothing. She started combing through online newspapers, websites, and blogs. Bit by bit, a profile of Pinkas Mashiak began to emerge.

He had been born Tyrell Quimby in Davis Creek, West Virginia. Known to his family and friends as Troy. Raised by his mother and grandparents on their family farm. Dropped out of high school at sixteen. Several years later, he'd founded the Good News Gospel Church in nearby Yawkey, West Virginia. A year ago, he had immigrated to Israel and legally changed his name to Pinkas Mashiak. The New Children of Light, the name he'd chosen for his new church in Jerusalem, was inspired by the ancient Qumran community, who'd composed the Dead Sea Scrolls. Mashiak's was a small congregation, claiming fewer than two hundred members. They held Sunday services in a rented room inside a large evangelical church in East Jerusalem.

There was much more she wanted to know, but there was only so far you could go on the internet.

It would help if she could get access to the police databases. But what were the chances that Sarit would give her that access? The woman guarded her turf like a Canaan dog. Well, she should at least give it a shot. Maybe the bad blood between the two of them was beginning to leach away. Their last conversation had given Maya some hope. Given the trouble they might all soon be facing, it was clear that Israel's guardians couldn't afford the luxury of domestic squabbles.

48

Bent over her desk, Cassandra slept fitfully until dawn. Then, she stumbled into the bathroom to pee. Sitting on the wobbly plastic toilet seat, she gagged from the nasty fumes still lingering in the tiny room. As soon as she was back at the desk, she laid her head down on the hard, smooth surface and returned to her troubled dreams.

She wasn't aware that someone had entered the apartment until steely fingers grabbed a fistful of her hair and jerked her head back. She yelped in pain.

She looked up. Her captor smiled down at her, but his dark eyes were not happy. They glinted with rage.

Suddenly, he grasped her slender neck with both his hands. His powerful thumbs pressed against her windpipe, lifting her out of the chair. As she struggled for breath, he released her neck and dragged her by one arm over to the single bed at the other end of the room. The Indian print bedspread lay unwrinkled on the narrow mattress, the soft pillow uncreased.

He pushed her down backwards onto the bed. His face was blank like wet clay. Quickly he undid his belt, wrenched it free of its loops, and held it up by the metal buckle.

Howling and flailing her hands, Cassandra rose up from the bed and tried to push him away. But her strength was no match for his. With a triumphant grin, he pinned down her wrists with his free hand, feeling the fight suddenly go out of her.

Slowly, he stood up and raised up the hand grasping the belt buckle. The leather strap swayed back and forth a few times, then halted its movement. Like a stopped clock.

Sucking in a deep breath, he bent back his arm.

Cassandra's eyes widened. Under her buttocks, she felt the warm seep of urine, smelled the sour stink of fear. She tried to scream, but her airways had turned to stone. She closed her eyes and waited for the pain.

But it didn't come.

When she opened her eyes, he stood as before, his arm once again raised high, the leather belt dangling in front of him. But his face was no longer blank. It was twisted like highway wreckage.

"I am not a violent man," he said. His words were clipped and without inflection, as though spoken by a robot. "I have devoted my life to beauty. I never meant.... But this is what comes from selling your soul to the devil."

Turning his face away from her, he opened his raised hand. The belt buckle fell behind him, jangling when it hit the cement floor. He then walked rapidly toward the door and slipped outside. The door shut behind him.

She heard the familiar rattle, the sharp click of the lock. Then silence.

49

CASSANDRA HAD NO IDEA HOW long she remained on the bed. Unmoving, eyes closed, barely breathing. She remembered hearing the soft thud of the door, the snap of the lock, his receding footsteps. But was that ten minutes ago? Or ten hours?

She looked out the window. The diffuse chalky light suggested it was mid-morning.

Slowly, she sat up. Then, she dragged herself into the shower.

The plumbing in the apartment was old. The small showerhead, attached to a black hose, hung from an iron bracket on the wall. When she turned the handle all the way to the left, lukewarm water mixed with rust particles trickled on to her head, then down her back and legs. The brittle plastic curtain reached only halfway across the wooden bar. She could see a blurred image of herself in the misted mirror above the sink.

With a sliver of crusted soap, she scrubbed her body until the skin was raw. Trying to wash off the humiliation and fear. She was glad to replace one pain with another.

After she shut off the water, she glanced up at the small window. The iron bars were stained brown and pitted in many places. But her chemical cocktail had failed. The bars of her prison were still very much intact.

Wrapped in the threadbare towel, she walked into the kitchen area. She threw her panties into the trash can. From her backpack, she took out a clean pair of underwear, a pair of cargo shorts, and a loose white blouse with peasant sleeves and delicate lace bordering the scoop-necked collar. Then, she went back into the bathroom and combed her wet hair, happy to see that the purple dye was beginning to wash out. She longed to return to her former dirty-blonde self.

She took out a bottle of cold water from the refrigerator and drained it in a few gulps. She felt ravenously hungry but feared she would retch if she ate anything. She contented herself with a couple of dry crackers. It was barely enough to still her hunger.

Leaning against the wooden counter, she looked over at the desk. Goldmayer's laptop sat there, waiting for her. Its dark screen reminded her of a cave. A black mouth ready to devour her. To swallow her alive. But she had no choice. She had to face that ravening maw. She had to keep hoping that she would come out of this alive.

As soon as she sat down in the chair, her thin body started shuddering, as though suddenly plunged into ice-cold water. Her hands trembled on the keyboard. Her eyes lost their focus. Icy fingers crawled all over her skin. Her head was wrapped in suffocating wool. Her nostrils twitched with the stench of poison. The floor beneath her bare feet tilted so that she had to hold tight to the arms of the black chair to keep from falling. She screamed, but no sound came out. And then came a hot wind, full of sand that stung her flesh like a thousand flies. She was lost in a thick fog.

Suddenly, something materialized out of the fog. It was the figure of a young woman, slender and very tall. She approached. It was Mariamne! Her skin was the color of honey; her hair, the ruddy color of wild dates. Her eyes were green, flecked with gold. Her generous mouth was creased in a smile. A dimple puckered her right cheek.

Cassandra reached out her arms. The phantom paused. Cassandra froze in place. Try as she might, she was unable to advance a single step.

"I'm so glad you're here, Mariamne! I feel so alone. So afraid!"

The stationary figure continued to smile but did not answer. Cassandra divined deep sympathy in the young woman's emerald-gold eyes.

"We understand each other, don't we? Like sisters."

Still not a whisper from the silent figure in the mist.

"We're seekers, you and me. Looking for answers. What terrible dangers we've faced alone! With you, it was thieves and assassins, Roman soldiers and mad zealots. And with me, it's been grifters and psychos and desperate men. But I'm still alive. We're both survivors!"

The ghostly figure glistened as if showered in bright light. Then, it began to thin. Pieces evaporated into the silvery fog. Soon, only a glittering sheen of vapor remained. Then, that, too, vanished.

Cassandra blinked. What had just happened? Was this the aftershock of his abortive assault? Some kind of PTSD? But the apparition had seemed so real! She closed her eyes again, hoping to bring the figure back...but she couldn't. Mariamne's avatar refused to re-appear on the dark screen of Cassandra's underlids. But she could still feel the other woman's comforting presence in the room. Recall her guileless smile.

The shrill, nasal cry of a muezzin coming from outside the kitchen window startled Cassandra. Time for the Muslims' morning prayers. She flailed her arms, shook her head. She gazed toward the door. Had he returned to finish what he'd begun? She looked around in panic. The room was empty. She was alone.

She looked down at her watch. 9:45. Still five more files to decrypt. Maybe she would discover where the Treasure Scroll was hidden before she reached the last file. But would he then let her go? In her mind's eye, she envisioned his triumphant smile. Heard his cold-hearted laugh.

She had to believe that she could bargain her way to freedom. Like the Pharisees with their copper scroll. There always had to be a way out. She was a survivor. She was still alive. And she aimed to stay that way.

50

LIKE A GIANT SWIRL OF whipped cream bobbing on a sea of cocoa, the aboveground portion of the Shrine of the Book Museum floats in the center of a reflecting pool. The architects designed this white-tiled capstone to resemble the lids that covered the large clay jars in which the first Dead Sea Scrolls were discovered.

On the south side of the plaza is an imposing rectangular wall made of black basalt. According to the architects, the black and white contrast is meant to symbolize the apocalyptic vision expressed in the Dead Sea Scrolls—the final battle between the Children of Light and the Children of Darkness at the End of Days. Others have discerned in the white dome and black wall a physical allegory of the Holocaust. Still others, the emergence of the Jewish State out of the ashes of catastrophe and exile.

The architects, who were commissioned to build a museum to exhibit the Dead Sea Scrolls, Israel's most precious ancient documents, went out of their way to load the building with symbolism. To reach the exhibit halls buried deep underground, visitors first have to walk through a long, dark passageway resembling the caves where the ancient Qumran scrolls were first found in 1947. In the middle of the circular central exhibition hall, located directly beneath the white dome overhead, stands a giant wooden knobbed cylinder shaped like one of the rollers of a Torah scroll. The cylinder is illumined in a bright shaft of golden light. Concentric circles reverberate out from this light source like ripples in a pond. If the architects' aim was to inspire awe, they certainly succeeded. No one who visits this place leaves unmoved.

It was close to noon when Hillel Stone arrived at the entrance to the Israel Museum in the Givat Ram section of West Jerusalem. The only way to reach the Shrine of the Book was to pass through this museum. Hillel showed his Bar Ilan Faculty ID to the museum security guard, then headed toward the underground tunnel leading to the Shrine of the Book.

Hillel was relieved to find the Shrine of the Book almost empty at this hour. The connecting tunnel was lined on both sides with lighted glass boxes containing artifacts from Qumran. The display cases jutted out from the walls like skeletons in a funhouse. He passed by them without a glance. He'd been here too many times to count.

He soon reached the main exhibition hall, bathed dramatically in golden light. Its conical, striated ceiling loomed overhead like an artificial sun. In the center of the room stood a circular glass case, which displayed sheets of yellowed parchment, illuminated by a hidden light source from within the pedestal. This was a replica of the famous Isaiah Scroll, one of the first seven scrolls found in Qumran in 1947. It was one of the oldest Dead Sea Scrolls, copied in the settlement's scriptorium around 125 BCE.

Ringing the outer circular walls of the large chamber were more illuminated glass cases, displaying other Dead Sea Scrolls. Only a few were on public display here at any one time. The rest were housed in a climate-controlled storage facility at Har Hotzvim, in northwest Jerusalem. That's where they had been transferred after 1967, when Israel had gained control of the Palestine Archaeological Museum in East Jerusalem, now known as the Rockefeller Museum.

But the Copper Scroll was not in any of these places.

By an accident of history, it had ended up in Jordan. When the Six-Day War had erupted in 1967, the Copper Scroll had been on exhibit at the Amman Archaeological Museum. And there it had remained. Hillel had never gone to Amman to see it. But he had promised himself that someday, he would.

Stop daydreaming, Stone! Focus on De Vaux's notes. Find the location of Kochalit.

Hillel swiftly made his way through the cavernous room to a small wooden door that stood opposite the main entrance to the exhibit hall. This door led to the Qumran Archives, located in a restricted area. The archives were open to scholars but closed to the public. Hillel had spent many hours there, hunched over ancient manuscripts and yellowing articles, searching for obscure references for his scholarly papers, hoping to find a juicy footnote or an overlooked detail.

Over the years, he had become friendly with one of the archives' curators, Hakob Eskandarian, a myopic old scholar from Armenia. Eskandarian was reluctant to let Hillel stay in the archives alone, while the archivist took his lunch break. But Hillel finally persuaded the old man that he was working to safeguard the Dead Sea Scrolls from an imminent threat.

"We're trying to keep certain scoundrels from getting their hands on them!" he explained. Because Eskandarian was almost completely deaf, Hillel had to lean down, only inches away from the old man's ear, and yell. "As they have so many times before!"

The archivist grunted and muttered something to himself. Then, he hawked up some phlegm and spewed a viscous gob into a dented copper spittoon sitting on the floor. For a few moments, he sat lost in thought, his milky eyes fixed on the teetering piles of papers completely covering his desk. Then, he turned toward Hillel and grumbled his assent.

"What documents I can get for you?"

"Roland De Vaux's unpublished field notes. From his excavations in the Judean Desert in the fifties."

"Why so much interest all of sudden in De Vaux's notes? You are second one to look at notes in two days."

Hillel's lower jaw dropped open. He stared at Eskandarian. "Who else asked for them?"

The old Armenian scholar poked among his papers, muttering under his breath. Finally, he pulled out a black-and-white speckled school notebook. As Eskandarian flipped through the blue-lined pages, Hillel gazed at the old man's hands. The gnarled fingers with their corrugated, yellowed nails seemed to reflect the old man's close contact with artifacts of antiquity.

"Ah, here is it! A Mister Habib Salameh. Antiquities Consultant. No one I meet before. To me, this one not look like Qumran scholar."

How had Salameh found out about De Vaux's notes? Maya had not told anybody but Hillel about the note she'd found in Goldmayer's hotel room. Had Boaz written about De Vaux's notes somewhere, perhaps in a private communication? Or were they mentioned in a file on his stolen laptop? If so, Salameh had just shown his hand.

"What did he look like, this Mister Salameh?"

"A giant. Big bald head." The archivist raised his skinny arms toward the hang-drop ceiling. "Ugly red bump grow out of back of head. American, I think. Not Arab scholar."

Definitely not the Lebanese antiquities dealer. Then, who was he?

Hillel waited impatiently, while Eskandarian shuffled back and forth among the poorly lighted stacks. He returned in a few minutes, carrying three thick black binders. He led Hillel to a narrow carrel and clicked on the small light clamped to a steel shelf above a small desk.

"These what I give Mister Salameh. I hope he not scoundrel you worry about."

The old man laid the binders down on the small steel desk and left Hillel alone.

51

ROLAND DE VAUX'S NOTES WERE hand-written in an elegant script. His French was pedantic and somewhat antiquated. Fortunately, Hillel had taken classes in French literature as an undergraduate, so he was able to translate the monk's words without too much difficulty. It was obvious that the French Dominican monk would have been right at home in the 19th century.

The first binder yielded nothing of interest. It contained detailed notes about one of the Qumran caves, where De Vaux had found a few scroll fragments and some potsherds. The second binder was likewise unrelated either to the Copper Scroll or to the duplicate scroll.

But when he looked in the third and last binder, Hillel hit pay dirt.

The black ink had faded over sixty years, but De Vaux's words were still easily legible:

> *Ibrahim El-Assouli and I have encountered considerable difficulties excavating this area, now known as Khirbet al-Tajmil. It is the site of several ancient mines and a manufactory in the upper Negev Desert, near the Biblical city of Tekoa. At several points, we were forced to search out alternate paths, because the original paths were obliterated or impeded by landslides, sinkholes, earthquakes, or flash floods. Quite an unstable landscape. It is a miracle that the caves are still accessible at all.*
>
> *The Arabic name for this place, "al-Tajmil," connotes "cosmetics." I am assuming it refers to kohl, the*

*eye makeup that was once mined and fabricated here.
I believe that Khirbet al-Tajmil is the site of ancient
Kochalit, the place referenced at the end of the recently
unveiled Copper Scroll.*

*For the first phase of our operation, I have chosen
to focus on two caves situated near a small group of
ancient burial mounds, as described in line sixty of
the Copper Scroll: 'U-k'varin al pi-ha'['and tombs are
at its opening']. One cave's entrance is small and low
and shaped like a dog's head. The other cave's opening is large enough to admit a full-grown man. Two
meters from the second cave's entrance, we discovered
a rusted iron spade. Judging by its shape and size, I
would speculate that it dates from 1st century AD,
but we will have to wait for the results from the laboratory to determine a precise date. El-Assouli and I
have spent two days exploring the larger cave but so
far have not uncovered any scrolls or other artifacts.*

*We need to return to Jerusalem tomorrow for
discussions with other members of the Scrolls Team.
We plan to return as soon as possible to explore the
smaller cave. I am filled with optimism that we will
soon unearth priceless treasures in the Judean Desert.*

That was the end of the entry.

Hillel's hands trembled with excitement. So that young scholar
whose name he couldn't remember had been right about Kochalit.
And Roland De Vaux had pinpointed its precise location! But it
appeared that he hadn't found the duplicate scroll. There was no
more mention of Kochalit in the binder.

So it had taken sixty years for someone—his ill-fated mentor,
Boaz Goldmayer—to stumble upon De Vaux's discovery and continue where the French Dominican monk had left off. Had Boaz

finally laid his hands on the scroll? Or had he, too, been stymied like De Vaux? Unfortunately, he'd been killed before he'd been able to share his findings with the world.

Hillel's hands shook as he closed the third binder. He had to share this news with Maya. Ignoring the small hand-written sign above the desk, "No cell phones," he fished his mobile out of his pocket and tapped in Maya's phone number, already listed in his "Favorites." It rang six times before his call went to voicemail. He tried again. Same result. The third time, he left a message.

"Maya, I'm at the Qumran Archives. I found a vital piece of information in De Vaux's notes. I think I know where the duplicate scroll is. We need to get there before Boaz's killer does. Please call me ASAP."

He disconnected. He waited another ten minutes and called her again. He let it ring four times before hanging up. It was obvious that she didn't want to talk to him. Not after what happened last night. She'd probably delete his voicemail message without even listening to it. And he couldn't text her, because he'd maxed out his data plan for the month. Not that she would have paid attention to his text, either.

He stood up, clicked off the light, and carried the three binders back to Eskandarian's desk.

"Thank you, Hakob."

"You find what you want?"

"Yes, I did."

Hillel reached out his hand to shake the old man's hand but halted in mid-air when he saw that the Armenian's twisted fingers would not fit into his own. His arm glided up to the old man's stooped shoulder and patted it gently. Eskandarian closed his eyes and nodded.

"You call me when you catch scoundrel, Professor Stone."

Hillel grinned, tipped an imaginary cap toward the old archivist, and headed down the corridor toward the main exhibit hall.

He had to get to Khirbet al-Tajmil straightaway and find the scroll. For the past several years, there had been an American university dig there, but they only worked during the summer months. This year's dig season had not yet resumed. The site would be empty.

As much as he disliked hitchhiking, especially in the West Bank, it was the only way he could get there quickly. It was less than an hour away by car. He would just have to take his chances.

52

THE MAN WOKE EARLY, SO tired he thought he was coming down with something. But his forehead felt cool. Maybe it was all the anxiety he'd been carrying. Now that the plan was in motion, all that worrying and guilt had finally caught up with him. His long limbs felt like concrete. His eyes teared, blurring his vision.

He forced himself to stand up. In the cracked mirror above the bathroom sink, his face, seamed with dark lines, belied his youth. His eyes were red and rheumy. He rinsed out his mouth, tasting chlorine and rust. The public water here, like so much else in this Arab half of the city, was inferior to that supplied to the Jews in West Jerusalem. He spat out the foul-tasting liquid and wiped his mouth with the back of his hand.

Stumbling into the small kitchen area, he filled a small tin pot from the tap and lit the gas on one of the two burner rings. While he waited for the water to boil, he spooned some soupy yogurt into a bowl, added brown sugar and honey, and shoveled the sweet goop into his mouth. He wished that American cereals weren't so expensive here in Israel. He'd never get used to the raw vegetables and garlicky paste they ate for breakfast here.

The water boiled in the small pot. He poured it into a cracked white teacup. Then, he carefully measured out a teaspoon of Folgers. American coffee was an indulgence on his budget, but he couldn't stomach the mud that passed for coffee in the local café down the street. He added milk and sugar and stirred. Then, he leaned over the rising steam and breathed in, savoring the familiar fragrance.

But before he allowed himself a sip of the coffee, he knelt down on the hard stone floor and clasped his large hands together. And prayed for a sign. To calm himself, he repeated several times: *I am being guided from above.* But deep down, he knew that he was flying blind. For days, he'd been looking for signs. He'd scoured the clouds for hidden messages. Had looked for portents in the murmur of doves flying above minarets and church towers. All in vain. The Voice wasn't speaking to him.

He looked down at his long, slender fingers, with their groomed, pearly nails. Unconsciously, he used his thumb to rotate the thick silver ring he wore on his right hand. He recited from memory the words from Psalm 2 that he'd had etched on the ring in microcalligraphy: "He Who is enthroned in heaven laughs; the Lord scoffs at them. Then, in anger, He rebukes them, terrifying them with his fierce fury." Yes, the nations of the world would soon be terrified. And God would have the last laugh.

Still unconscious of his body's movements, he began to spin the slim silver ring on his other hand with the opposite thumb, feeling with the soft skin of his sensitive finger pad the embossed forms of a menorah, a Jewish star, and a Jesus fish. The seal of Saint James. His hands now moved down to the heavy silver breastplate hanging on his chest. He caressed the twelve semi-precious stones arrayed in three rows, their convex surfaces smooth as silk. On his head, he felt the comforting weight of the white flower-like turban of the High Priest. His entire body felt embraced by the flowing white robes of Aaron. Yes, he was every inch a prophet. And soon to be much more.

He carried his coffee over to a small wooden table and sat down. He stirred the coffee a few times and took a sip. His mouth tingled with pleasure. Then, he fished a business card out of his pocket and punched in the numbers on his mobile.

"I was expecting you'd call by now," he said, when the other man picked up.

"The girl's talented, but she's not superhuman. It's only been three days. She's already cracked six of the ten encrypted files."

"The blood moon is tomorrow night!"

"Quit worrying! You're worse than an old lady."

Oh, how this man exasperated him! To him, this operation was just one more lucrative deal. Not a holy mission.

What if I were to tell him about the divine plan? What if I revealed all that was at stake? But what do I know about this man's faith? Why risk his ridicule—or his blasphemy?

No, it was better to tell him only what he needed to know. To accept him for what he was. Just another instrument in the Lord's plan. His avarice had been enlisted to serve a higher purpose.

"What if I offered you a bigger share of the treasure? Would that guarantee I get what I need in time?"

"What exactly did you have in mind?"

"Say, a thirty percent share?"

"Ah, *mon cher*, simply by doing business with you, I risk so much. I have my professional reputation to think of. How do I know that I will not be implicated in your crimes? Such a scandal would ruin me."

The man's voice had an edge, like a sharp, tempered blade.

"But I'm not a greedy man. Shall we say...one-half?"

"Fifty percent! Do you realize how much money we're talking about?"

He was wasting too much time negotiating with this snake. Didn't trust him, but still needed his help. Needed to know where that Treasure Scroll was. He was running out of time.

"Fine. We'll split things fifty-fifty. But only if I get the information I need by tomorrow."

The other man attempted a laugh, but his throat was so tight that the sound came out as a stutter.

"But if you fail, your share goes back down to twenty percent. Is that clear?"

Silence on the other end. The other man had hung up.

53

THE TOWERING AMERICAN ARRIVED FIRST; the other man, wiry and unshaven, a few minutes later. The American was dressed in black pants and a short-sleeved black shirt. He wore a large black watch cap to hide his bald skull. The other man, half the American's height, also wore black, but his head was bare. His curly mat of dark hair blanketed his head like lichen. They spoke in whispers, even though they were at least twenty meters from the main tunnel shaft. The shorter man spoke with a heavy Eastern European accent and a slight lisp.

As arranged, they met in a narrow passage off an underground drainage tunnel. At the end of the passage was a small chamber, constructed of pitted stone blocks, only partially cleared of debris. The British archaeologist, who'd been in charge of this phase of the tunnel excavations back in the 1940s, had abandoned the site, when his team had discovered coins and other artifacts dating to the late nineteenth century. This room had probably served as a storage area during that earlier excavation. They'd never bothered sealing it up.

"Thirty-five years ago, when Etzion plan his attack," the shorter man began, "he calculate it take twenty-eight charges. But we not need so many now. Python anti-mine system big improvement over Viper. Will destroy much bigger area. We can do job with fifteen charges. Max."

"How will you get in to plant the charges?" the tall man asked. "Security's been really tightened."

The shorter man snorted impatiently. He scratched the rough stubble shading his cheeks, then ran his fingers through his welter of dark hair.

"Not to worry! Israelis not look for repeat of 1980s. They expect more high tech. We attach explosives to places that bear most weight. You smart to pick Friday as day to strike. Will be big crowds."

The American shivered. It was dank and cold in the subterranean tunnels. He also recognized that he was afraid. Not only was he terrified that he might be caught, but he feared for his mortal soul. He already had the blood of one man on his hands. And he was about to murder a second. But these two deaths were nothing compared to what was about to occur. Carrying out the next phase of the plan would result in the massacre of men, women, and children at prayer. But they were praying to a false god! Was Allah any different from Mastema and Belial and Samael, the demons worshipped by the Children of the Kittim? Had it not been foretold that at the End of Days there would be a great battle, which would destroy the Children of Darkness? These were not innocents he would be killing. They were the Children of Satan!

"You done good, Imri," said the tall man. "Real good."

He stifled the urge to pat the small, dark man on the head like one of his old hounds.

"As agreed, yer gettin' one and a half million for yer services. Here's a down payment."

He handed Imri a thick bundle of Euros, encircled with a rubber band. Imri pocketed the wad of bills and smiled up at the giant man.

"The men I hire meet me tomorrow night. All is ready by Friday."

They did not shake hands when they parted. Imri left first, the tread of his sandals so light that the American heard no more than four footsteps before the room fell silent. He waited a few moments, then headed down the dark passageway.

Rounding his broad shoulders and slouching down to mask his large frame, the American slipped in among a dense cluster of Scandinavian tourists. When the group emerged from the dark mouth of the tunnel a few minutes later, he was grateful that the sun had not yet crested the ancient stone walls. In the shaded plaza, the air was still cool.

He made his way quickly to a taxi stand. He had a lot to do before tomorrow night.

54

DESPITE HER RESOLVE TO RESUME work immediately, Cassandra found that she could only move at a snail's pace. It was as if she were swimming through thick sludge. When she tried to crack the next encrypted file, her natural talents failed her. She felt like a pathetic muggle. Hopelessly flummoxed, all thumbs.

She tinkered with the file for another few minutes. Then, she gently lowered the silver lid of the laptop. She stood up and stretched her thin arms toward the knobby white ceiling. Then, she reached down to touch her toes. Her body felt stiff, foreign. She walked over to the bed. She shuddered when her legs brushed against the thin Indian spread.

She grabbed the pillow at one end of the bed and pulled it free from under the cotton bedspread. She walked into the center of the room and dropped the pillow to the floor. Then, she sank down on it, cross-legged, feeling her bony buttocks rocking from side to side on the hard cement surface. She longed for her comfy Zafu. Sitting on a soft pillow like this gave her too little back support. She placed both her hands, palms up, on her bent knees, joining her thumbs and index fingers to form lotus flowers. She closed her eyes and began to breathe slowly. In and out. Emptying her mind.

But it was impossible to meditate. Her mind flooded with distressing images and sensations. She felt the man's thumbs pressing on her windpipe, choking her. She heard his metal belt buckle jangle as it hit the stone floor. Hard as she tried, she could not hollow out a peaceful space. She felt like she was drowning. Out of breath. Sinking into quicksand.

She finally gave up. She stood up and padded over to the refrigerator. She gulped down icy water from the plastic bottle. Then, she took another shower. She put on a clean pair of underpants, khaki shorts, and a simple white t-shirt silkscreened with a picture of a crested hoopoe, Israel's national bird. Then, she walked back to her desk to try again.

Whether it was the meditation, the shower, or simply the passage of a little time, she could now focus on decrypting the files. In half an hour, she was back with Mariamne, who had fled south into the desert, finding refuge in Secacah, a Jewish sectarian settlement near the Salt Sea.

The garrulous young diarist was back in travelogue mode, rambling on in infuriating detail about what these Jewish ascetics ate, the kind of work they did, and how they kept themselves pure from ritual defilement. Growing increasingly impatient, Cassandra began to skim, desperate to discover the fate of the two scrolls that Mariamne had smuggled out of Jerusalem.

She finally found what she was seeking a few pages later.

> *During my first night here, I debated what to do with the two precious scrolls I kept huddled in the folds of my woolen cloak. How could I make sure that the Temple treasures would forever elude Roman hands?*
>
> *I thought of hiding the scrolls in my family's mineral works at Kochalit, which is not far away. But I quickly dismissed the idea as too risky. They would be much safer hidden here in Secacah.*
>
> *I slept poorly that first night. Perhaps it was....*
> [text corrupted]

That was the end of the file. It contained less information than any so far.

Cassandra's temples were throbbing. She recognized the familiar symptoms of an impending stress headache. She should take a break, turn off the lights, rest. But she couldn't afford the time.

What would she find when she finally decrypted the most important file, the one that identified precisely where Mariamne had hidden her precious scrolls? What if the words were illegible? Over two thousand years, Mariamne's parchment scroll had fallen prey to so many assaults—dust, fungus, insects, pollution, and the corrosive chemicals in the ancient ink. What if the name of the scrolls' hiding place had been nibbled away to end up as "*text corrupted*"?

Cassandra's slender body began to tremble. She felt light-headed. Her mouth and lips were dry. When was the last time she'd had anything to eat or drink?

She didn't feel much like eating, but she forced herself to get up and walk over to the fridge, to gulp down half a liter of cold water. Then, she lay down on the narrow bed, intending to rest for only a few minutes. She was soon asleep. As she slept, the day's heat steadily rose, finally knocking out the window air conditioner. The air soon became stale and heavy.

When she awoke an hour later, she felt drained. Her short purple hair clung to her skull like seaweed, the strands shiny with sweat. But she had no choice other than to keep going. She had to find out where the Treasure Scroll was before her captor returned.

"Help me, Mariamne! Where exactly did you hide it?"

She felt foolish speaking out loud to a woman who'd been dead for two thousand years. But she'd come to regard her as a sister. A soulmate. Both desperate to survive.

55

MAYA RETURNED TO SERVICE HEADQUARTERS, still gnawing on the schnitzel sandwich she'd picked up for lunch at the hole-in-the-wall around the corner. The breaded chicken patty was cold and rubbery, but it would quiet her hunger pangs for the time being. She was counting on her mother to have leftovers to warm up when she went to pick up Vered.

She sat down at her desk and inhaled deeply. She felt a brief spasm at the base of her spine. She wasn't used to spending so much time in front of a computer screen. But she knew she was getting closer to finding the answers she sought.

In her browser's search box, she typed in the phrase, "Temple Mount Conflicts." The screen instantly filled with links, mostly to news reports, posted in reverse chronological order. The most recent entry was from July 2017:

> *In response to the killing of two Israeli soldiers outside Al-Aqsa Mosque yesterday, Israeli Security installed metal detectors at the mosque's entrance. Protesting these "Gates of Shame," hundreds of Palestinians rioted on the Temple Mount today....*
>
> *September 29, 2000. Ariel Sharon, the right-wing Israeli opposition leader, led a group of Israeli legislators onto the bitterly contested Temple Mount today to assert Jewish claims there, setting off a stone-throwing clash that left several Palestinians....*
>
> *In early 1996, Israeli antiquity authorities began excavating beneath the Temple Mount, setting off*

> *what became known as the "Tunnel Riots." Hundreds*
> *of Palestinian protestors....*
>
> *July 23, 1985. An Israeli court today convicted*
> *Yehuda Etzion, founder of Hai Vekayam, a group*
> *dedicated to allowing Jewish prayer on the Temple*
> *Mount, of a plot to blow up the Dome of the Rock....*
>
> *On 21 August 1969, Denis Michael Rohan, an*
> *Australian citizen, set fire to the pulpit of the Al-Aqsa*
> *mosque, in Jerusalem....*

The list went on for pages.

Maya knew about all these attacks. Every member of Israel's Intelligence Service was trained to view the Temple Mount as the flashpoint for the next Intifada. Or the next Arab-Israeli war. Maybe the final war. The public only heard about the attacks that made the headlines. For every one of these, Israeli security foiled ten.

She closed her eyes and took a few deep breaths. As the case picked up speed, so did her hyperactive imagination. She needed to slow herself down. Moderating her breathing, she retrieved her cell phone from her bag and texted Masha.

Seconds later, Masha trotted into her office and hopped onto the corner of Maya's broad metal desk. Leaning toward Maya, she arched her thick eyebrows and smiled.

"*Nu*, so how did it go last night with your *frummie*?"

Masha let out a spirited guffaw. Normally, her friend's uninhibited laughter delighted Maya. Though Masha was a petite woman, her laugh was oversized. But today, Maya found her buoyant humor annoying.

"I don't want to talk about it."

Masha didn't press her. Maya's gruff bark warned her to stick to business.

"What did you find out about the hackers we currently have under surveillance?" asked Maya.

Masha handed her a hand-written column of names.

It was a short list. The Service's Cybercrime Unit was notoriously effective at shutting down online pranksters and black hat hackers as quickly as they popped up. Maya was surprised to see Cassandra Sucher's name on the list. She'd considered the young American drifter harmless, strictly a geek-for-hire. Too flaky to warrant scrutiny.

Maya had met her a few months ago at the LTM Center during her ill-fated investigation. Cassandra had been freelancing there. With her spiky purple hair, pierced eyebrows, lips, and nasal septum, her purple eye makeup and lipstick smeared on like war paint, the young woman had stood out among her co-workers like a flamingo among crows. Whenever Maya had visited the Center, Cassandra had been glued to her screen, her forehead deeply furrowed like a shar pei's.

It wasn't surprising that Cassandra had since ventured into cyber-crime. With her exceptional computer skills, she could command top dollar from any number of unprincipled clients. Like Habib Salameh.

Maya held up one hand as she rifled through her top right drawer with the other, pushing aside thumb drives, SIM cards, pads of sticky notes, and loose keys. She finally found what she was looking for: a wad of paper scraps clamped together by a large clip. One of the scraps listed Cassandra's cell phone number. It took Maya fifteen minutes to put everything back into the drawer in its proper place.

When she looked up, her fellow agent was texting on her mobile. Masha noticed Maya staring at her. She grinned sheepishly.

"Sorry, *chooki*. Got distracted."

"Makes two of us." They both laughed. "And now, I need you to go on one more errand for me."

Maya peeled a small yellow sticky note from the pad on her desk and wrote down Cassandra's name and address. She handed the note to Masha.

"Bring her in for questioning. She may be mixed up in the Goldmayer case. But be careful. She's skittish. She might bolt."

Without knocking, Ziggy now trotted into Maya's office, chewing on something sweet-smelling and crunchy. Slumping down into the brown plastic chair, he wiped off his sugar-coated hands with a paper napkin. Then, he carefully plucked a few shreds of wax paper from his sticky fingers, rolled them into a tiny ball, and tossed it into the metal basket next to Maya's desk.

"So, girls, what's new in the spy biz?"

Maya quickly glanced over at Masha, whose face had flushed beet-red as soon as Ziggy had entered. Now, she realized what she'd sniffed when Masha had come into her office. Perfume! Something French or Italian. As usual, Ziggy was oblivious.

Roni's dark face suddenly appeared in the glass window of Maya's office door. He marched in and stood, arms crossed, glowering at Maya.

"I need to speak to Rimon. Alone."

When her two colleagues were gone, Maya motioned Roni toward the empty plastic chair across from her. He remained standing. Then, he shuffled sideways and leaned his back against one of the green walls.

"*Nu*, so what's with the case?" he asked.

"I'm following up on a new lead. It's connected to the stolen laptop files. I'll let you know if it goes anywhere."

"Don't let this drag on too long."

"Just doing my job, Roni."

Roni aimed two splayed fingers toward his eyes, then reversed the "v" and jabbed his fingers at Maya. Without a word, he strutted out of the office, slamming the door behind him. Maya's puzzles tumbled helter-skelter over the broad metal desk.

Her forefinger now floated up to her chin and began stroking the roughened skin. She pulled off a crust of dried concealer and stared at it for a few seconds, disturbed to find a fresh spot of blood showing through the flesh-colored makeup. Reaching into her bag, she retrieved the tube of concealer and dabbed the bloody spot until it blended into her skin.

Then, she reached across the desk for a Rubik's Cube.

56

The old IDF ammunition depot was located about twenty kilometers west of Ashkelon, less than thirty kilometers from the northern border of Gaza. It was not far from the Reches Gvar'am Nature Reserve. The army had chosen an especially desolate spot for its supply station, an undeveloped region of scrub forest, ragged hills, and stony ground, reachable only by four-wheel drive. The depot was one of the oldest still in service, dating back to the early '50s, when Ashkelon was little more than an immigrant outpost named Migdal. The depot was a relic of old wars, badly in need of paint and more efficient air conditioning. And an updated security system.

A foreign worker named Imri had been hired to upgrade the depot's aging electrical wiring and panels. For the past week, he and his two assistants, all three Eastern European migrant workers in Israel on temporary visas, had reported each morning to the soldier on duty. They'd spent each day fiddling with cables and circuit breakers to bring the station up to code. Knowing no Hebrew and little English, the three had kept to themselves, stepping outside several times a day to smoke their foul-smelling unfiltered cigarettes.

Yesterday had been the final day of their contract. Because Imri had called in sick, it had fallen to his senior assistant to sign off on the work order. As soon as he and his companion had cleaned up and packed up their tools, they'd piled into their rented jeep and driven off without saying goodbye. The commanding officer hadn't been sorry to see them go. His uniform stank of their cheap cigarettes.

This morning a soldier had discovered that some C-4 explosives were missing from the supply room, enough to make up at least two dozen charges. The plastique had been left unguarded, along with dozens of semi-automatic rifles, crates of bullets, and miscellaneous small weapons.

Suspicion immediately fell upon the three foreign workers. The commanding officer wasn't surprised to learn that the men's contact information and work visas were phony. It was unlikely that Israeli Intelligence would be able to track them or recover the stolen explosives. With almost a twenty-four-hour headstart, they were now in the wind.

Being a yeshivah-educated Jew, the commanding officer knew that he wasn't supposed to wish harm on others simply in order to protect his own family. But today he found himself praying that the thieves' target lay outside of Israel's borders.

The theft did have one positive consequence, however. Later that day, the Technology and Logistics Directorate of the Israeli Defense Forces informed the commanding officer that the depot would soon be outfitted with the latest security system, including an Iron Dome anti-rocket battery.

Better late than never, thought the officer. And would it be too much to ask for new air-conditioning and a satellite dish as well?

57

CASSANDRA GLANCED OUT OF THE only window in the room, framed on the outside by a cage of iron bars. The setting sun was nearing the city skyline, an uneven landscape of flat-topped stone roofs punctuated by solar-water heaters, minarets, church towers, flapping laundry, and patches of azure sky.

It had been hours since she had looked outside. That's what happened whenever she was absorbed in a project. She stopped paying attention to what was going on in the real world. The only reality resided in the mind of the Machine. The virtual world often seemed so much safer than that other world, where so much was out of her control. Inside her imaginary reality, she was master. Outside, she was a hapless prisoner—or a victim.

She glanced at the upper right-hand corner of the computer screen. 4:10 p.m. He would be here in less than an hour. And there were still two more files to go.

It was beyond her talents to unlock both files in under an hour. Should she jump ahead to the last file, the climax to Mariamne's tale? But what if she had hidden the scrolls earlier, mentioning the hiding place in the previous file?

What should I do? If I guess wrong, he'll definitely hurt me. Or worse.
She pushed back from the desk and rotated her stiff shoulders.

She decided to flip a coin. She fetched a shiny New Israeli Shekel from the front pocket of her backpack. She examined the silver coin closely. On one side was the number "1," the words, "New Shekel" and "Israel," in English, and some Hebrew and Arabic writing. On the other side was an image of a lily, a tiny menorah, and some strange writing she couldn't identify. Despite all those years of religious school, she couldn't understand any of the Hebrew.

If it landed on the side with the pictures, she'd tackle the penultimate file next. But if it landed on the side with the number "1," she'd skip to the last file.

She rested the coin on the flat side of her forefinger and flipped it up with her thumbnail. It twirled in the air and landed in her palm. Without looking, she slapped the coin down on the back of her opposite hand. And then she looked. The coin had landed with the flower and menorah facing up. For some inexplicable reason, she took that as a good omen. She'd accompany Mariamne on the next leg of her journey.

The next-to-last file yielded to her efforts in less than half an hour. Maybe she would still get out of this nightmare alive.

I lifted up the copper scroll and extended it to the examiner. He held it with a tenderness usually reserved for delicate glassware or a newborn child. Slowly, he unrolled the thin hammered foil. His jaw fell open as he pored over the first leaf.

"What is this? Where did you get it?"

I told him that the Temple priests, fearing the imminent sack of Jerusalem, had concealed the Temple treasures and recorded their hiding places in this scroll.

I made no mention of the Pharisees' conspiracy, nor did I reveal that this copper scroll was a duplicate of the parchment original.

"And they entrusted this precious jewel to.... [text corrupted]....

"Be assured that I will safeguard this scroll with my life. I will reveal its existence to no one. It will be a secret between us."

> *My original intention had been to hand over*
> *both scrolls to the Examiner. But in the end, I did not*
> *tell him about the other scroll still concealed in my*
> *palla. I am not sure why I kept this secret to myself. I*
> *suppose that once one gets used to keeping secrets, it is*
> *difficult to give up the habit.*

Cassandra coughed, stood up, and walked over to get another water bottle from the refrigerator. She carried it back to her desk and sat down. Without the air conditioner, the heat had continued to rise. Sweat soaked the back and underarms of her tee shirt.

Would her captor be satisfied with this information? Or would he demand to know where the other scroll was as well? If so, the coin toss had turned out to be an evil omen.

With a loud whoosh of breath, Cassandra struck the desk with her open palm. She had made the wrong choice. She should have opted for the final file. That had to be where Mariamne revealed her last secret: where she'd hidden the parchment scroll.

She reached out her hand and gently lowered the laptop's lid. Then, she sat back in the comfortable desk chair, closed her eyes, placed both hands on her knees, her fingers upturned like lotus flowers, and began to breathe slowly. She surrendered her will and emptied her mind.

58

A FEW MINUTES AFTER FOUR, Sarit Levine left police headquarters and flagged down a cab. It dropped her in front of Habib Salameh's shop on Salah e-Din Street.

Sarit smiled when the Lebanese antiquities dealer appeared on the other side of the barred glass door. Despite the man's flawed complexion, Sarit had to admit that his face—with its broad-planed cheeks, prominent nose, and bright, dark eyes—was rather hand-some. He would probably look good on television.

She walked in and sat down in the wooden chair across from Salameh's small antique desk.

"So, Detective Levine, to what do I owe the pleasure this time?" Salameh's voice was smooth like limpid oil. "Ah, but I am forgetting my manners. Can I bring you tea or a coffee?"

Sarit shook her head.

Throwing up his hands, Salameh stood and walked to the back of the room. He opened the closed door in the middle of the rear wall. Just before the door shut behind him, a large black cat dashed out between his legs and raced toward a corner of the room. Sarit caught a glimpse of golden eyes before the cat disappeared behind a pile of cardboard boxes.

While Salameh was gone, Sarit rummaged through her small black leather purse. She withdrew a ballpoint pen and a small pad, which she rested on her lap.

A few minutes later, Salameh returned, carrying a cup filled with steaming liquid. He set the cup down carefully on the black leather blotter that covered most of the desk's surface and sat down. Then, he picked up the cup, blew gently over its dark surface, and took a sip. Sarit noted that the cup and saucer were made of fine porcelain, decorated with tiny roses. She smelled mint, lemon, and a trace of cardamom.

Salameh now gazed at her across the desk, his bushy eyebrows slightly arched.

"I have a few more questions relating to the murder of Professor Goldmayer."

Salameh inclined his head but said nothing.

"Can you explain, Mister Salameh, why you visited Vladislaw Cywiński in Vilnius three times over the past six months?"

"Who?"

"Don't play games with me!"

Salameh bristled at her badgering tone. He took another sip of his tea.

"It so happens that Vladislaw and I share a common interest in the ancient Near East."

"He a good customer of yours?"

"More of an intermediary, I would say."

Salameh seemed to be enjoying himself, grooming his caterpillar eyebrows with one sleek finger, while he taunted Sarit with dark, furtive eyes.

"I assume you know that Professor Cywiński is suspected of laundering money made on the black market. Rumor has it he sells Middle Eastern antiquities to Russian oligarchs."

In response to her accusation, Salameh raised his bushy eyebrows and opened his mouth wide, disclosing a few gold teeth.

"All news to me, detective."

Sarit couldn't hold back her laughter. What hutzpah this man had! Even after she showed Salameh a photograph of himself drinking vodka with Cywiński and several Russian billionaires on the balcony of a dacha on the Black Sea, he persisted in his denials. He swore it was someone else in the picture.

"What about your recent visits to...," she named a few notorious fences operating in Slovakia, Albania, and the Canary Islands. "Do they also share with you an interest in the ancient Near East?"

His dark skin flushed. Then, his eyes lost their amused twinkle, becoming beacons of malice.

"I am not familiar with any of these names, I assure you."

Sarit knew she was on precarious ground with this line of questioning. She'd called in a few favors in Intelligence to get her hands on this information. If anyone found out....

She shook her head vigorously to dispel the disquieting whispers. In her experience, the ends usually justified the means. They indisputably did in this case. She squared her shoulders and resumed her interrogation.

"My sources tell me that these men have been tipped off about some unusual merchandise coming their way in the near future. Could it be a newly discovered Dead Sea Scroll?"

Salameh gazed at her through opaque eyes. Their dark color was accentuated by the blue-black lines of eye makeup drawn above and below his luxuriant lashes.

"If you were to lay your hands on such a treasure," continued Sarit, "I imagine you might want to use some of your profits to benefit your people. Maybe stir things up a bit in Jerusalem, eh, *ya Habib*?"

As Sarit had hoped, her comment caught Salameh completely off-guard. His dark eyes opened wide, then quickly narrowed.

"What are you implying?"

"I'm thinking you might want to donate some of your windfall gains to Hezbollah or some of its allies inside Israel's borders. Surely, you still retain some loyalty to your homeland?"

Sarit stared at Salameh's face, watching closely for any of the Lebanese dealer's well-known "tells." He revealed them all. He emitted a few raspy grunts, as though clearing his throat. His broad shoulders arched up toward his ears. He shot his cuffs, revealing diamond-studded cufflinks at the ends of crisp white sleeves. For the first time, she noticed that Salameh wore two large silver rings on one hand. One ring displayed a dark polished stone, onyx or dark jade. The other bore a serpent's head.

Salameh shook his head. Not a single strand of his Brilliantined black hair moved out of place.

"I don't know what you're getting at, detective! I am a businessman, plain and simple. I trade in beauty, not violence or death. And as for my loyalty, I'm afraid it's woefully limited. My sole allegiance is to myself."

Sarit fought back a grin. She'd touched a nerve. She was closing in on the truth.

When she exited the antiquities shop moments later, she failed to notice a dark figure, tall and thin as a beanpole, loitering across the street. As soon as her small, trim figure disappeared around the corner, the man withdrew his mobile phone from his pocket and tapped in a number on speed-dial.

He had some intriguing new information to report to the preacher.

59

IT WAS AFTER SIX WHEN Maya left her office. The air was much cooler. The late afternoon sun had softened the day's bright colors to muted grays and browns. Even the sounds of traffic seemed muffled by the waning light.

As she descended the stone front steps of her building, she caught sight of a tall, thin figure skulking in the shadows across the street. In the uncertain light, she couldn't clearly make out the man's face. Fortunately, he was turned away at the moment. His head was mostly concealed under a dark baseball cap. It had to be Rafi's PI, still sniffing at her trail. Looking for evidence of maternal delinquency, no doubt. She was almost certain he hadn't seen her leave the building.

While the man's head was still turned away, she ducked into the shallow doorway of a three-story apartment building that abutted Service Headquarters. For a few minutes, she stood watching the tall figure, making sure she remained concealed in shadow. After a few moments, the stalker turned, fixing his eyes on HQ's front door.

She waited patiently. Shadows lengthened along the street, throwing most of the building facades into semi-darkness. The largely residential neighborhood was beginning to fill with people returning from work, walking dogs, shopping for dinner.

To avoid suspicion, the stalker pretended to be shopping for groceries in a small shop just behind him, tucked in between two small apartment buildings. Periodically, he turned around, one hand shading his eyes, and peered into the grimy window. Then, like a government inspector, he ran his eyes over the oranges, melons, and bananas displayed in wooden crates on an outside table. After each of these feints, he spun around and returned to his rapt surveillance of the Service's front door.

But such obvious ruses only work for so long. Maya grinned as the old Arab grocer finally burst out of his shop, waving his hairy arms, his leathery face flushed. He was a small, dark man, wearing a dirty apron and a large white *taqiyah* that covered most of his head. The two men talked animatedly for a few minutes, the grocer flapping his hands, the tall man offering his palms. Then, the grocer threw up his hands and scowled. He swept one hand vigorously toward the right, shooing the loiterer away like a stray cat.

The tall man shrugged and took off in the direction of the grocer's wave. He crossed the street, then picked up speed as he neared the nondescript stone building that housed Service Headquarters. When he walked past the front entrance, he stooped over, as if trying to hide his conspicuous height.

As he neared the shallow entryway where Maya was hiding, she pressed herself against the back wall until she was completely swallowed up by shadow. The stalker walked right by her, head bowed, muttering to himself, his pace accelerating. He never once looked in her direction.

She waited another minute, then stepped out into the fading light. She glanced down at her old Poljot, strapped to her wrist with its frayed leather band. It was already 6:15 p.m. She was due at her parents' apartment in fifteen minutes to have dinner with her daughter.

Poor Vered!

She'd started wetting her bed again. And having nightmares. Damn that Rafi! Feeding their daughter horror stories about Maya's being constantly in danger, certain to get killed in action. Prepping the little girl for the custody trial, no doubt. Providing convincing proof that she was being traumatized by an unfit mother.

Maya felt a sob catch in her dry throat.

As much as she hated to admit it, her recent conversation with their social worker, Penina Yarom, had unnerved her. For the second time that day, Maya promised herself to spend more time with Vered from now on. Re-order her priorities.

But first, she would strike back at that son-of-a-bitch Rafi! How dare he hire a private investigator to intimidate her! If she exposed Rafi's underhanded tactics to the family court judge, it would definitely improve her chances of sharing custody. She'd show the judge that Mr. Father-of-the-Year was nothing but a blackmailer and a bully. If she had to miss her dinner tonight with Vered, it was only so she could ensure that the two of them would have many more shared dinners together in the future. One day, Vered would understand: everything Maya was doing was for her sake. She was a mother leopard protecting her defenseless cub.

Maya had had lots of practice tailing marks, especially in large cities. It was one of her best skills in tradecraft. It wasn't difficult to follow the tall man through the crowded streets of West Jerusalem. He towered over most of the other pedestrians. The jostling crowds gave her plenty of cover. But she didn't need it. Her quarry never once looked back. His stride was determined and hurried. She soon found herself at the northwest corner of the Old City. At Jaffa Gate.

It was too bad that the only camera she had on her was her smartphone. In this light, the photos wouldn't be very sharp. But they'd be clear enough to identify the man. The Service had files on all the snoops in the city. It would be easy for her to obtain the PI's name through facial recognition software.

Careful to keep her distance in the narrow alleys of the Old City, she followed her target into the heart of the Christian Quarter. The tall man stopped in front of Third Temple Artifacts, a small shop tucked away on a narrow lane off Saint Francis Street. Maya recalled the name from the exhibit booth she'd stopped at during the conference reception at the hotel. It was where she'd learned about kohl.

Everything about this shop shouted "kitsch!"—from the Gothic lettering of its gold sign to the ersatz Second Temple reproductions crammed into its front window. The overstuffed display featured chrome censers and incense pans. Miniature red heifers cast in iron and glazed ceramic. Chess sets peopled with Biblical figures. Board games titled "Sacrifices" and "Prophets and Kings." Sets of tin priests and rubber animals. In one corner, a doll-size wax figure of Aaron shuttled back and forth on a track between altar and ark. On the large plastic altar lay the charred remnants of a sacrificed calf. Small satin satchels lay scattered among these objects, labeled "Frankincense" and "Myrrh."

For the next few minutes, the tall man stood motionless in front of the dusty store window, staring at the display. Maya stayed back, although the plateglass was too smudged to reflect her presence. Visualizing the map of the Old City in her mind, she realized that this spot was only a short walk from L'Académie biblique, where she'd interviewed Father De Plessy. Had it only been the day before?

What had drawn this man here? Obviously nothing to do with her custody battle with her ex. He was probably doing surveillance for a different client. Working multiple cases at once. He'd return to spying on Maya later.

Or maybe the man had caught her watching him back at Headquarters. And then led her on a wild goose chase to throw her off. Any minute he'd turn around and mock her: *Think you're so clever, eh? Gotcha!*

Maya dug her nails into her palms to shut down the nattering in her head. She focused her attention on the store window, which the tall man continued to study with intense concentration. She'd give it a few more minutes, then catch a cab to Rehavia.

Suddenly, Maya heard a scuffle behind her. She whipped around. Three young Arab boys were fighting over some dropped coins. When she turned back, the stalker had disappeared.

60

ANNOYED AT HERSELF FOR HAVING taken her eyes off her target, Maya shoved open the grime-streaked glass door and entered the shop. Her entry was announced by the loud clanging of cowbells attached to the other side of the door.

Inside, the narrow shop was stuffed with merchandise like the display window. Behind the front counter in locked glass cases were breastplates made of silver-plate, encrusted with semi-precious stones; miniature bronze seven-branched menorahs, and brass implements that looked like they belonged next to a fireplace. Along another wall were shelves stacked high with clothing—gray, brown, and white robes made of rough cloth, white undergarments, sandals, and oracle pockets. Against the back wall were shelves of books, rolled up maps and charts, DVDs and CDs, including screen savers and choral music.

The whispering in her head now resumed, even louder.

What are you doing? This has nothing to do with your case! You're wasting precious time and accomplishing nothing. Better you should keep your date with Vered. Stop chasing phantoms!

Maya begun to hum to herself under her breath, drowning out the chiding voice. Her palm itched and prickled. She stopped humming and took a deep breath.

Behind the counter stood a buxom young woman, dressed like a well-off matron from ancient times. She wore a beige sack-like dress, whose blue-edged hem reached down to the floor. Her dyed blonde hair was almost completely covered by a blue and black kerchief, tied at the nape of her neck. She was counting money, New Israeli Shekels in coins and bills. She muttered to herself, appearing bewildered.

When she heard the bells chime, she looked up and smiled warmly at her new customer. Her broad, pale face expressed relief.

There was no sign of the tall stalker. He'd probably slipped out a back door or had gone up to the roof. Little chance she could catch him in the dense warren of narrow lanes threading through the Old City. She turned to leave.

But before she reached the door, the woman behind the counter addressed her.

"Can I help you? Lookin' for somethin' in pa'tic'lar?"

Maya pegged the accent as coming from the American Deep South. The woman's pasty complexion, watery blue eyes, and slightly porcine nose reinforced the stereotype.

"I'm looking for the tall man who just came in here. He was wearing a black baseball cap. I need to talk to him."

The woman shook her kerchiefed head.

"No one fittin' that description here."

It was a young man who responded to Maya's query. He now rose up from his crouch behind the wooden counter. His Southern accent was even thicker than the woman's. A heavy wooden cross dangled from a braided rope around his neck. From his thin neck protruded a pointy Adam's apple, which wobbled up and down like a fisherman's float in a stiff breeze. Maya recognized in the young man's intense dark blue eyes the shining zeal of the new convert. He shot a dark look at the woman, who blushed and quickly ducked down behind the counter.

"But I just saw...."

"You must be mistook. We ain't had no customers for at least an hour."

Maya again berated herself for letting the stalker get away. Perhaps he hadn't entered the shop but had slipped into a nearby alley. Maybe she was misreading the young man's unease. But maybe she wasn't.

"Uh...I'm looking for something special," she said, improvising. "A gift for a friend."

"You come to the right place! We got all sorts of special things"—*thangs*—"for those anticipatin' the comin' Glory. All robes are now on sale, half off. Machine-washable. But let me show you our 'Blood Moon Special.'"

The young man hurried out from behind the counter and drew Maya over to a display stand near the front of the shop. On the low table sat a white plastic bust of an ancient Temple priest. His head was crowned by a broad, flat-topped turban, resembling the blossom of a flower. Stretching across the front of the turban was a rectangular plate, made of thin copper, engraved with two Hebrew words: "Holy to the Lord." He explained to Maya that this was the miter of the ancient High Priest. The bust was draped with white linen covering the priest's shoulders and upper torso. Around his neck was a square silver plate, studded with twelve colored stones.

"How's this fer somethin' unusual"—*unyoo-zhuhl*—"something you won't find nowheres else. The breastplate of the High Priest."

The young man lifted the breastplate off the bust and brought it closer for Maya to inspect. Two of the stones—one, golden yellow; the other, deep purple—fell to the floor and rolled toward the counter.

"Jesus Christ, Honey! I told you to make sure they was glued in properly!"

"Cal! I mean, Caleb," whimpered the woman behind the counter, rising into view. She stood frozen, a deer in the headlights. "Watch yer tongue. You done blasphemed!"

The young man coughed. His Adam's apple shuddered in the loose skin of his neck, then subsided into stillness.

"Beg yer pardon, ma'am," he said to Maya.

Then, he turned toward the woman. "And beggin' yer pardon, too, Devash."

Devash. The Hebrew word for "honey." Cal pronounced it like something likely to be found in an Indian restaurant.

He turned back to face Maya.

"All this here's pretty new to me. Gotta learn to guard my tongue better." He thrust out his hand. "Caleb Wattle. And this here's my wife, Devash."

Maya suppressed a grin. Many new immigrants who came to Israel took new names for themselves. Cal and Honey had probably been assigned their Hebrew names by their church.

Maya shook Cal's hand, then quickly released it. She offered nothing else, though Cal seemed to expect more. He let his hand drop to his side, disappointed. Maya stared at him, unblinking, until he looked away.

Looking past Cal, Maya's eyes narrowed when she noted an array of oversized books lined up in a bookcase on the wall across from her. Among the tall volumes on the top shelf, she recognized the volume about ancient gemstones and minerals from the conference booth. A few other titles caught her eye: *An End of Days Handbook. Preparing for Armageddon. Ten Prophecies of the End. The Satanic Conspiracy to Foil the Apocalypse. Who reads such books?* she asked herself. *And who writes them?*

"It sounds like you've recently come here from the States."

Did her voice sound patronizing, too earnest? Cal's toothy grin widened. Maya pressed on.

"Did you have a store like this back there?"

"Oh, goodness, no!" said Honey/Devash. Her broad features relaxed into a smile. "We was just poor folk back home. Me, I worked the deli counter at the Winn-Dixie. Cal, he worked graveyard shift at KFC. But we was laid off. And then we heard 'bout this amazin' preacher in the Holy Land. Our friends Beau and Mary Grace came here a year ago to join his church. So we jes' up 'n followed 'em. And here we are!"

She stopped and took a deep breath, her cheeks flushed from the exertion of so much speech, her large breasts heaving. She looked over at Cal, who nodded. Her smile broadened.

Cal picked up where Honey had left off.

"We was lucky to get set up almost soon as we got here. The New Children of Light sure take care 'a their own."

61

Maya felt sharp needles pricking the soft skin of her palm.

"The New Children of Light?"

"Our church."

Honey walked out from behind the counter and stood next to Cal, tentatively reaching for his fist, which he unfurled to admit her stubby fingers.

"Our preacher's received word direc'ly from God that the End is near," said Honey. "We're preparin' ourselves for the Last Days."

"And how exactly are you doing that?"

Maya's voice was brittle, but neither of the young Americans seemed to notice. They were caught up in their fervor, their voices infused with ecstasy.

"Accordin' to our preacher," said Cal, "the Apocalypse is right close. That's why we're sellin' this merchandise. We gotta be ready for the comin' of His Kingdom."

Cal walked over to the bookshelf and pulled out an oversized coffee table volume entitled *The Oracle of Judgment: the Christian Meaning of the Priestly Breastplate*. "You should read what it says in here 'bout the End 'a Days. It's jes' like our preacher says. Won't be long 'fore the Third Temple rises on God's Holy Mountain. Praise the Lord!"

"Praise the Lord!" echoed Honey, clasping her hands together in a gesture of reverent prayer.

Cal forged ahead.

"Lots of folks reco'nize that our preacher's the real deal. The true Messiah. But he ain't officially declared hisself yet. Even though he was born in America, he c'n prove that he's descended from the Tribe of Judah. Jes' like King David. Like Jesus Hisself. He named his church after the first Children of Light, who used to live down by the Dead Sea in the olden days. Like them folks, we're waitin' on the End Times. Which we know is comin', 'cause of all the wars and terrorism and nat'ral disasters."

Honey was staring at Maya, delighted by how keenly the Israeli woman was listening to her husband's fevered words.

"Maybe you'd like to join our church? Come to the Lookout tomorra night."

"The Lookout?"

"In East Talpiot."

"Oh, you mean the Tayelet. The Promenade."

Honey ignored Maya's correction. She bent down and reached into a cardboard box under the display table. When she straightened up, she held a white flyer in her hand, which she handed to Maya.

The flyer announced a "Gathering of Witnesses for the Blood Moon" tomorrow night at the East Talpiot Promenade. Preacher Pinkas Mashiak, spiritual leader of the New Children of Light Church, would be speaking on "The End of Days and the Coming Kingdom of Glory."

Maya stared at the grainy black-and-white photograph that took up the left half of the flyer. Even out-of-focus, Pinkas Mashiak cut an arresting figure. He looked to be in his 40s, but she suspected that his boyish features belied his true age. She noted the broad, billowing turban crowning his large, shaved head. The miter of the High Priest, identical to the one displayed in this shop. The headdress's extra twenty centimeters of height would no doubt make this already giant man appear like a colossus to his worshipful followers. In the photograph, Mashiak's radiant smile revealed a generous mouth, full of brilliant white teeth. His massive body was cut off mid-chest in the photo. Yet the large head and broad shoulders did not convey an impression of fleshiness or brute strength. Rather, he appeared noble—like a conquering hero or an emperor.

"That's our Preacher!" declared Honey, almost breathless. "We're hopin' he'll be makin' the announcement tomorra night. Revealin' hisself."

Cal stared at Honey, who shrank beneath his sharp gaze.

"How many times have I done told ya, woman? This gatherin's only fer members of our church." He tossed his head dismissively in Maya's direction. "Not people like *her*. Dammit, Honey! You c'n be so goddam stupid!"

Head bent, Honey shuffled back to the wooden counter, the hem of her robe dragging on the dusty floor. The spark had gone out of her. Her shoulders slumped as she leaned over the messy pile of bills and silver coins.

Cal turned to face Maya.

"Why're you askin' all these questions?"

His tone had changed. The initial edginess was back. His missionary zeal was gone, replaced by suspicion. He reached for the large volume in Maya's hand, grabbed it, and slipped it back among the other tall volumes on the top shelf.

Maya was tired of playing games, listening to all this pious blather. She was fed up with the thousands of fanatics who clogged Jerusalem's arteries.

An image suddenly sprang to mind. A fragment of a dream she'd had last night but had forgotten until this moment.

Like a balloon, she floated near the ceiling of the LTM Center's vast main lobby, looking down at two men. One wore a finely tailored dark suit. His black, wavy hair glistened with hair gel. His bony nose appeared sharp and curved, like a raptor's beak or a scimitar. She recognized the man as Habib Salameh.

The other man was a giant, well over two meters tall. He was dressed simply. Chinos, a dark shirt, and flashy designer sneakers. Definitely American. His head was bald or shaved. Bulging from the back of his skull was a peculiar wine-colored growth. His shoulders were broad, his neck thick. Bushy black eyebrows arched high over dark eyes. The man radiated incontestable authority and fanatic zeal.

The two were haggling over a small metal object. Somehow, Maya knew it was ancient. She floated down until she hovered just above their heads. At this point in the dream, the tall man looked up and noticed Maya. He glared at her with such menace that she woke up.

She now knew the identity of the tall man in the dream. It was Pinkas Mashiak. From the moment she'd begun investigating Goldmayer's murder, she'd been convinced that Habib Salameh had not acted alone. But why had the Lebanese dealer teamed up with this Christian fanatic? What did they want with the Treasure Scroll? Were they partners—or rivals?

She suspected that she would learn many of the answers tomorrow night. At the gathering under the blood moon.

62

WHEN MAYA REACHED HER PARENTS' apartment in the upscale West Jerusalem neighborhood of Rehavia, it was after seven. Vered had long since finished her simple dinner of chicken cutlets and peas and was dressed in her pajamas, watching television with Saba Moti. Maya's father did not look away from the TV when Maya came in. Vered blew her mother a kiss but kept her eyes fixed on the cartoon she was watching.

Maya found Camille in the kitchen, washing the dinner dishes. Even though the Rimons had owned a dishwasher for years, her mother insisted on doing the dishes by hand, except when they had a large company meal. Having grown up in Marrakesh, where drought was a constant threat, Camille was convinced that dishwashers and washing machines used too much of Israel's precious fresh water. No matter how much Maya's father teased her about this, she refused to change her mind. That was her mother. Opinions set in concrete.

Camille walked over to her daughter, bent down, brushed aside a tuft of auburn curls, and planted a kiss on Maya's upturned brow. Then, she straightened her back and flattened her apron with the palm of her hand.

"So, *ya binti*," Camille said, "I'm glad you remember you have a daughter."

"Don't start, Ima! I've had a rough day. I just came by to pick up Vered. Did she eat her dinner?"

"She eats like a mouse, your daughter." Reaching up with her hand, her mother steadied her wobbling tower of frost-blonde hair.

Then she drew in a sharp breath and launched into one of her familiar diatribes. "She's much too skinny. If you were a proper moth...."

Maya quickly cut her off. She slammed her open palms on the glass table, making the crystal salt and pepper shakers rattle. Her mother glared at her. Maya stood up, scraping the wrought iron chair over the ceramic tile floor. She walked into the living room and plopped down next to Vered on the white leather couch. She sank into the cushion, which exhaled softly under her weight.

Without taking her eyes away from the large flat screen TV on the opposite wall, Vered extended her small hand toward Maya, letting it rest on her mother's bare knee. Maya covered her daughter's hand with her own, curling her hand around Vered's tiny fingers. She caressed the small, silky palm with her thumb. With her other hand, she smoothed down Vered's wild tangle of Orphan Annie curls. They sat together, not speaking, in companionable silence.

At the other end of the couch, Moti sat stolid and slumped. Every so often, he reached into his shirt pocket for a cigarette. Then, his empty hand reached for a handful of dark green olives in the ceramic bowl on the glass coffee table. He began popping them into his mouth, spitting out the pits into his other hand. He stared at the large television screen without seeing, his dark brown eyes like frosted glass.

Camille came into the room, drying her arms with a towel. She still wore her frilly flowered apron.

"Come, *arnouba*, time for bed."

"No, Jedda!" Vered's shrill voice pierced the air like a siren. "My *favorite* cartoon is on next! 'Shafan and Shafani.'"

Camille raised her eyebrows and beckoned to her granddaughter with a crooked finger.

Vered's lower lip quivered. But she bravely held back the meniscus of tears threatening to spill down her silky cheeks. Solemnly, she shook her head up and down. Then, she slid off the couch. On bare feet, she padded over to her grandmother, who reached down to enfold Vered's tiny fingers in her plump, moist hand.

They disappeared into what they now referred to as "Vered's room." Within moments, Camille's deep, soothing voice drifted into the living room, carrying Vered away to some Moroccan fairyland of djinns and flying carpets.

After her mother had left the room, Maya tiptoed in. She paused at the threshold. The single bed was empty. Vered was on the carpeted floor, kneeling over the doll cradle her grandparents had bought her for her birthday. She was tucking in her new doll under her ratty old baby blanket, humming Jedda's lullaby. Chuckling to herself, Maya walked over to her daughter and bent down to stroke her daughter's hair.

"Go 'way, Ima! Can't you see I'm putting Merida to bed."

With a flick of her hand, Vered waved her mother away. In Vered's sharp bark, Maya recognized her own impatient voice, eager to escape her parenting duties. Without a word, she closed the bedroom door and left.

63

Becoming aware of the silence that had replaced the non-stop babble of children's cartoons, Moti suddenly came out of his reverie. He noticed Maya sitting near him on the couch. She stared off into space, lost in her own nightmares of abandonment.

"Didn't hear you come in."

Maya started at the sound of her father's raspy voice.

"I came to pick up Vered. But Ima's already put her to bed."

Moti looked at his watch.

"It's almost 8 o'clock, Maya! She's only three years old. If you want to take her home for the night, you have to get here earlier."

"I meant to, Abba. But something came up at the last minute. It's the case I'm working on. Things have begun to move fast. You know how it is."

Moti nodded and rubbed his chin. He had begun letting his beard grow after years of being clean-shaven. He was letting his hair grow longer too. He no longer wore it close-cropped like a soldier.

"Unfortunately, I do." He sighed. "The unpredictable schedule comes with the job. But it's hell on your family."

He released a wheezy breath. Then, he sank back against the yielding flank of the couch.

"I really want to succeed in this job, Abba! I want to make you proud."

As usual, no response from her father, not even a nod. His eyes were closed, his breathing labored.

"I'm trying to be both a good mother *and* a good agent. But I'm afraid I'm failing at both."

Moti reached over and patted his daughter lightly on the back of her hand. She flipped over her hand and grasped her father's hand in hers. She squeezed three times—their old private code for "I love you." She noticed how wrinkled her father's hand was. The leathery skin was covered with liver spots and herringboned with blue veins.

"Can I ask you something, Abba? About Livni and Etzion's plot to blow up the Dome of the Rock back in '84. Must have been during your first years in the Service."

Moti nodded. He began reaching toward his pocket but promptly redirected his hand toward the bowl of olives.

"It was my first big case," Moti said. "We were watching Gush Emunim closely after the bomb attacks on the Palestinian mayors. We knew the attacks were revenge killings for the yeshivah students, who had been gunned down at the Tomb of the Patriarchs in Hebron. Of course, we didn't know at the time that Gush's bomb attacks were only a sideshow. Their real target was the Temple Mount. It was only due to Livni's bad luck that the Dome of the Rock was spared. Livni caught hepatitis. The others couldn't pull off the attack without him. And by the time he recovered, it was too late. Political realities had changed. Imagine what would have happened had they succeeded!"

"And after that?"

"The Service became much more vigilant. So did the Waqf. Luckily, we managed to foil a number of later plots targeting the Mount. Not that we've managed to head off all the violence. The Intifadas. The Tunnel Riots. Yehuda Glick and his *meshuggeneh* idea that Jews should be able to pray on the Temple Mount. That place is a ticking bomb!"

"What about Christian extremists?" asked Maya. "Don't they also want to destroy the mosques on the Mount and build a new Temple on top of their ruins? Kick off the End of Days?"

Moti reached forward and scooped up another handful of olives. He stuffed several into his mouth, spit out the pits, then picked up the glass of water on the table and washed them down.

Retirement is not treating you well, thought Maya. *Stuck home all day with Camille. And in the evenings, at the mercy of a chattering three-year-old.*

"The Christians were never my bailiwick," said Moti. "My job was to keep an eye on the *yid'n*. Roni was in charge of watching the *goyim*. They've certainly kept him plenty busy."

Camille came out of the kitchen, fanning herself with one hand.

"*Ya lahwy*! Even with the fan on, it's like an oven in there. We absolutely have to put in central air." She glared at her husband, her dark eyes smoldering. "No matter what it costs."

Moti stood up and walked past his wife, heading toward the master bedroom. They soon heard the sound of loud male voices. Moti spent most evenings watching news shows until he fell asleep.

Camille sank down in the white leather recliner and pushed back. Her feet, shoehorned into spiked heels with open toes, were swollen and veiny, the toes bloodless.

"We didn't finish our conversation about Vered."

Maya sighed. She didn't have the energy to fight with her mother tonight. It was like trying to drain the sea.

"Look, Ima, as soon as this case is over, I'm cutting back on my hours so I can spend more time with Vered. How many times do I have to say it?"

"Oh, please, Maya! You know you'll do no such thing. The Service runs in your blood, just like in your father's. You're completely blind to what you're doing to that child! You think your nights away don't affect her? You think she doesn't worry that something might happen to you? *Dai k'var!*"

Maya recoiled as if she'd been slapped. Why was everyone accusing her of being such a bad mother? First, it was that meddling caseworker, and now her own mother. No one was telling Rafi to quit his job and stay home with his daughter.

Camille huffed out a noisy sigh.

"Oh, why do I waste my breath! It's like pouring water on a bottle."

Maya looked at her mother. What an unhappy woman! Despite all their money, their big apartment in Rehavia, and their vacations in Europe and the States, Camille was never satisfied with what she had. She always felt short-changed.

"I'd better get going, Ima. The bus schedule gets sketchy this time of night."

"I hope you haven't forgotten about Vered's school play tomorrow night? She has the starring role. Queen of the Butterflies! She's crazy about her costume. And all that makeup she gets to wear! Glitter on her face and hair!"

Tomorrow night! In fact, Maya had forgotten. She had so much else on her mind. Vered would just have to understand that her mother couldn't always attend her school performances. What kind of play could three-year-olds put on, anyway? It would probably only run twenty minutes, followed by an hour of schmoozing and noshing with the other parents. The children would get all hyped-up on sweets, right before bed. Vered would just have to forgive her...again. What choice did Maya have? She had to go to the Tayelet tomorrow night. Something dreadful was about to go down.

"The play starts at seven," said Camille. "You need to pick her up early so she can get dressed and made up."

"I can't guarantee I can get her there in time."

Her mother scowled. She muttered something in Arabic under her breath.

"Of course, you can't." Camille snorted. "So call Rafi and tell him to pick her up a little before five. I'll feed her before he gets here." Camille paused, then eased the recliner back into its upright position. "Don't disappoint her, Maya. These things mean a lot to a child."

Maya stood up and threw back her shoulders. Then, she rolled them forward, feeling the knotted muscles ripple over her bony shoulder blades.

She walked over to her mother and leaned down, brushing the stiff tussock of blonde curls with her lips. Then, she strode quickly toward the front door.

"And wear something nice!" Her mother's voice sounded desperate. "Ask your friend Masha to help you with makeup and accessories. You may be on the wrong side of thirty, but you're still an attractive woman."

As she closed the heavy door behind her, Maya heard her mother call out:

"We'll save you a seat near the front! Don't be late! Vered's counting on you!"

DAY 4

Thursday

64

"THE TWO SCROLLS WEREN'T HIDDEN together," said Cassandra. "They're not in the same place."

It was early morning, but the heat was already defeating the air conditioner. The heavy air shivered as bright sunlight blazed through the barred windows.

Cassandra sat at her desk, facing her captor, who had just walked in the door. Her back was ramrod straight, her purple-maned head calm and steady. She was pretending to be strong. But her gut twisted in agony.

He smiled at her in that fake-friendly way of his and nodded his pomaded head like a wigged aristocrat in some old-fashioned play. Then, he walked over to the kitchen counter and set down the string-net bag of groceries he was carrying. Oranges, bananas, mangoes, broccoli, and tomatoes. A box of tropical fruit juice. A small sack of brown rice. Enough to keep her alive for another day.

"Not in the same place, you say?"

Cassandra nodded. She felt her shoulders tensing. Quickly, she eased them down. By the end of each day, her back had been twisted in spasms.

"Mariamne gave only the copper scroll to those religious fanatics down by the Dead Sea. She didn't tell them about the other scroll, the parchment one. I don't know what she did with it. Yet."

"Ah."

He walked over to the narrow bed, covered with the thin Indian spread. The bed was still neatly made, except where the weight of two bodies had left a rumpled hollow. He sat down at the end of the bed and smiled at her.

Cassandra shuddered. She felt the man's thickset body pushing her wrists down on the flimsy mattress. Saw him raising his hairy arm, gripping the metal buckle. Watched the leather strap writhing behind him. She wiped her mind clean. Then, she filled the blank screen with a shimmering ghost. With skin the color of honey; hair, the ruddy hue of wild dates; green eyes flecked with gold. The spectral image quickly thinned into vapor, then vanished, leaving only a white void.

"So where is it, then, the missing Treasure Scroll?"

"I just need one more day! Half a day. A few more hours!"

He grinned, obviously enjoying her panic. Her small breasts heaved as she hyperventilated.

"I'm afraid you leave me no choice, my dear. I must find someone else to finish the job."

"The answer's gotta be in the last file! Please!"

She tried to calm herself. He'd just brought her food. Why would he do that if he planned to kill her?

She swiveled her head toward the front door. Had he locked it when he came in? Maybe she could reach it before he could stop her. She looked over at him. He was leaning back on his elbows, relaxed on the narrow bed. His eyes were half-closed.

Suddenly, she leapt up, sending the desk chair crashing to the floor. She dashed toward the front door, her bare feet slapping the stone surface. He was on her instantly. As her hand touched the doorknob, his large hands gripped her skinny forearms. Like hot steam, his breath scalded the skin of her neck. One of his knees pressed into the small of her back. He pulled her toward him, bending her backwards until she thought she would break in two.

"Let me go! I can decrypt the last file right now." She gasped for air. "Then, I'll...go away. I promise...I won't ever...tell a soul what I know!"

He chuckled. Then splayed open his hands.

She pitched forward. Just before she hit the floor, she reached out her hands to break her fall. Her palms stung as they slapped the stone surface. She dropped to her knees. Her kneecaps slammed the floor with a bone-cracking thud. She cried out. Then, she placed her forehead on the cold stone and sobbed.

She heard him walk toward the desk, then stop. A few moments later, he resumed walking. When she looked up, his hand was grasping the doorknob. Under his free arm he carried Goldmayer's laptop. In the v-shaped gap between the keyboard and the lid, the power cord nestled like a coiled snake.

"I will leave you now." He turned back toward her and smiled. It was a smile that could petrify flowing lava. "Urgent business awaits."

"But what about the last file? Don't you want me to find out where the other scroll is hidden?"

He set down the laptop on the floor and walked over to her. His dark lips still gelled in that evil smile. With one finger, he lifted her up gently by the chin. He peered down into her terrified eyes. Then, he clucked his tongue.

"I am afraid it is too late for that."

Cassandra shook her head free of the man's clammy finger. Then, she pushed herself up by her arms, stood up, and marched over to the refrigerator. Leaning in, she grabbed a bottle of water from the top shelf and twisted off the plastic cap. She dribbled some of the cold liquid on her bloody knees. Then, she gulped down the icy liquid until it was all gone. She flung the empty plastic bottle into the sink. She leaned back against the wooden counter and faced him. Her lips were taut in defiance. But her breath was caught in her throat.

He raised his dark eyebrows. Then, he shook his head, feigning sorrow.

"You see, my dear, I am but a pawn in this game. I answer to a more powerful player. The Chess Master, let's call him. This man has grand designs and a rather exacting timetable. I fear that his grandiose schemes will only succeed in setting off another pointless bloodbath in an already-traumatized city. Not that I care. My sole interest in this matter is, I must confess, strictly mercenary."

What were these monsters up to? If her captor was only a pawn, how terrible his master must be!

"The endgame commences tonight. That is when the Chess Master will proclaim to his followers who he truly is." He laughed, his tone mocking and sour. A sound completely devoid of mirth. "He will certainly make headlines when he announces that he has recovered the long-lost treasures of the Second Temple."

"But he hasn't! I still haven't found out where that other scroll ended up!"

Cassandra tittered nervously. The man glared at her. The blood drained from her face.

"A failure for which you will pay an even steeper price than you've paid already."

He walked back to the door, cracked it open, and peered outside. Then, he turned back to Cassandra. His thick, black eyebrows angled sharply over his hawklike nose.

"Someone else will return this evening to deal with you."

Her entire body trembled when she heard the brassy rattle of the shackle and hasp. When the lock clicked into place, she cried out loud.

65

WITH GOLDMAYER'S LAPTOP TUCKED SECURELY under one arm, Habib Salameh hurried toward his shop on Salah e-Din Street. At this early hour, the sidewalks were empty, the shops and cafés still shuttered. Most of the street was still in shadow. The sun wouldn't reach his draped storefront until mid-morning.

Damn that harebrained hippie, Salameh thought to himself as he dug in his pocket for his keys, *with her purple hair and perforated face!* How could he have ever trusted someone like that to finish such a difficult assignment on time? It was not like him to show such poor judgment. He'd probably lose everything because of her incompetence. But he would make her pay!

He considered his options. At this moment, he was, as they would say in America, between a rock and a hard place.

If he told Mashiak that the girl hadn't finished decrypting all the files, hadn't yet discovered the location of the Treasure Scroll, the American preacher would be furious. Of course, he would blame Salameh, who had foolishly insisted on handling the decryption of the files himself. He'd demand that Salameh immediately hand over the last file to him, so he could find someone else to decrypt it. Salameh didn't understand why Mashiak needed this information by tonight, but the American preacher had made it clear from the outset that failing to meet this deadline was a deal-breaker. And Salameh had failed to meet it.

So Mashiak would now cut Salameh out of the deal. The American could easily find another unscrupulous dealer who could fence the Temple treasures once he recovered them. Habib Salameh was certainly not the only antiquities merchant in this part of the world who traded in contraband. All that crazy preacher cared about was getting his hands on enough funds to carry out his mad vision.

Salameh felt needles of panic piercing the tender skin of his chest. His breathing hollowed out, making him gasp. Why should Mashiak let him live? He knew far too much. As soon as he told Mashiak that the girl hadn't finished the job, he'd be a dead man. He wouldn't even have time to take care of that damn girl, whose fault this all was.

And then it came to him. How he could solve his problem. He would strike first.

Salameh looked down at his watch. It was a few minutes after 8:00 a.m. Mashiak was due to arrive at his shop in an hour. He'd have to stall for time, tell the Preacher that they needed to reschedule their meeting for later in the day. He'd explain that the girl just needed a few more hours.

Buoyed by a renewed feeling of optimism, Salameh quickened his pace. He soon reached the front of his building and stepped into its cool, shady entryway.

"*Ya Habib.*"

Salameh jumped, then whipped around, seeking the source of the whisper.

A thin young man stepped out of the shadows. He wore dark clothing and a dark visored cap on his head. His black eyes were furtive, darting nervously from side to side. His small mustache wriggled restlessly under his crooked nose.

"I told you never to come here!"

"I need money, *ya Habib*. My wife, she needs an operation. Right away."

"You want more money? I pay you very well."

"It is very expensive, this operation. If she don't get it soon, she dies."

What was it with these young Palestinians? He was already paying this man through the nose.

"What about the Israeli agent?" asked Salameh. "Who's keeping tabs on her while you're here talking to me? If you let her slip away...!"

"Not to worry, *ya Habib*. My friend, Tayeb, he keeps an eye on her 'til I get back."

The thin man smiled weakly, revealing several large gaps between his yellow teeth. He fired a gob of spit at the sidewalk. It landed near the toes of Salameh's shiny black shoes.

"Then, who's keeping an eye on the American preacher?"

"Also Tayeb. He has a new phone app. It links to a camera that watches the apartment of the American. So he keeps his eyes on both."

Salameh grunted irritably. He inched away from the gob of spittle.

"You've come at a most inconvenient time. We'll talk about this later."

The thin young man turned to leave.

"Wait!"

He halted, then pivoted around to face Salameh.

"You say you need money for your wife's operation?"

The young man's dark eyes shone with hope.

"Step into the entryway. And keep out of sight. I'll be right back."

Silently, the man slipped into the shadows and disappeared from view.

Salameh unlocked the two bolts securing his front door and entered his shop. He quickly navigated the familiar darkness until he reached the antique desk in the center of the room. He switched on the lamp. From the slim center drawer, he withdrew a small pad, a pen, and a small, square envelope. He tore the top sheet from the pad and placed it on the blotter. Writing quickly, he penned a few lines, then folded the paper in half and stuffed it into the envelope. He licked the seal and pressed the diagonal edges firmly. Then, he scribbled a few words on the front of the envelope. Leaving the desk lamp on, he hurried back to the entryway.

The thin man took a step forward and re-emerged into the pallid light.

Salameh handed him the sealed envelope.

"Deliver this *in person*. Put it into her hands yourself. Then go straight home. I'll see that you get the money you need."

The young man looked at the address. He swallowed hard.

"How much money you giving me, *ya Habib*? What you ask is very dangerous for me!"

Salameh looked up at the spindly young man and frowned. Why did they always insist on upping the ante? No wonder the Israelis wouldn't negotiate with them.

"Enough. Now, leave."

Without another word, the thin man sped away and disappeared around the corner.

Salameh re-entered his shop and walked back to the small desk. The soft light of the desk lamp fell on a small terracotta figurine that Salameh had acquired a few days ago. It was an almost perfect Judahite pillar figurine: a full-breasted woman, with finely shaped facial features and an Egyptian hairstyle, cornrows of tight curls. Her curved arms cradled pendulous breasts. Below the waist, her body formed a cylindrical pillar. Early Iron Age Israel, he guessed, though he'd have to bring it to an expert for precise dating. He'd already had several inquiries about the figure and one very tempting offer. But he was loath to give her up so soon. She was one of the most exquisite figurines that had ever come into his possession.

He carefully picked up the clay figure and rotated her in his hand. He caressed the sleek flanks of her lower half. With his index finger, he delicately stroked her smooth breasts, which reminded him of ripe melons. Had she been a fertility goddess in a barren Israelite family's home? A good luck charm? Or had she been an Asherah, the banished consort of ancient Israel's God? He brought the figure close to his face and planted a soft kiss on the cool, clay ringlets crowning her head. Gently, he set her back down near the corner of his desk. He would wait for a better offer before letting her go.

He folded his hands and calmly placed them in the center of the soft leather blotter. Then, he took a deep breath and waited for the American preacher to arrive.

66

BALANCING A HALF-EATEN BAGEL, A banana, and a hot cup of coffee, Maya pushed through the front doors of Service Headquarters shortly before 9:00 a.m. She hadn't slept well. She was too keyed up about going to the Tayelet tonight. All night, her mind had tossed like a shuttlecock in a strong wind, buffeted between scenarios of catastrophe. She'd finally given up, gotten out of bed, showered, dressed, and left for work, grabbing a bite to eat on the way in.

When she walked into the wide open space of the first floor offices and cubicles, she refused to look toward Roni's office at the other end of the long room. No doubt he was watching her, wrinkling up his dark eyes and sharp nose, thinking: *What's this? Rimon showing up two days in a row before eleven?* She spun on her heels and headed toward her office.

As usual, she first scanned the headlines. No major crises or scandals. But it was still early. Then, she scrolled through the agency ListServ, skimming through the comments posted earlier that day by some of her colleagues.

One brief item caught her eye. It had been posted at 7:10 that morning:

> "A package of C-4 explosives was reported missing this morning from the IDF supply depot near the Reches Gvar'am Nature Reserve outside Ashkelon. The chief suspects are three foreign contract workers. The incident is currently under investigation."

There it was again. That familiar frisson chafing her skin. She made a mental note to talk as soon as possible to the colleague who posted it.

Her black desk phone started to ring. She picked it up without taking her eyes off her screen.

"Maya? Didn't expect to find you in so early. I was going to leave a voice mail."

This was a first: Sarit calling *her*. Maya was surprised at how satisfying it felt.

"I'm very busy, Sarit."

"Just wanted to bring you up to speed on where things stand with the Goldmayer case. We've narrowed down our suspect list."

Had the police gotten ahead of her? If Sarit scooped her, Roni's teasing would be insufferable.

"Who're you looking at as prime?"

"Habib Salameh."

Maya let out a deep breath and smiled. So they were still one step behind her. She was now convinced that Salameh was only a supporting actor in a much larger plot.

Should she share what she knew with Sarit? Could she trust her? Was Sarit's call an olive branch—or a baited hook?

"What about Goldmayer's scholarly rivals?" Maya asked. "Any of them still on your radar?"

"Quite a shifty lot, aren't they?"

Both women laughed. Maya envisioned Sarit's mouth, her glossy lips slightly parted, revealing small perfect teeth. Maya licked her own bare lips. Once again, she'd forgotten to put on Chapstik.

"We've ruled them all out," Sarit said. "The only credible suspect we're looking at is Salameh. His motive? Old-fashioned greed."

Maya glanced down at her watch. Precious minutes were ticking away while she and Sarit jockeyed with each other. Maybe it was best that she keep her cards close to the vest. The more people Maya told, the greater the chance of leaks, tipping off the conspirators. If they suspected the Israelis were on to them, they might even alter their timetable or target.

"So what's your next move?" Maya asked.

"That's why I'm calling. As a professional courtesy. I wanted to let you know that we're about to pick up Habib Salameh and charge him with murder."

"No, it's too soon! You have to wait!"

If the police arrested the Lebanese dealer now, they'd lose any chance of netting the rest of his crew. And the operation would go on without him. But how could Maya convince Sarit that there was a greater conspiracy in play? Sarit would most likely interpret Maya's request to delay Salameh's arrest as a tactic in their ongoing turf battle. She'd accuse Maya of wanting to make the collar herself in order to claim all the glory. Sarit would laugh in her face if she started talking about Pinkas Mashiak and his messianic delusions.

"Are you sure you have enough to make the murder charge stick? I thought you found no forensics at the crime scene."

"There's been a new development. Salameh's asked us for a deal. If we grant him immunity from prosecution, he'll tell us everything he knows—about Goldmayer's murder, the lost scroll, and a lot more. He's even promised to send us a piece of his intel before we agree to his terms. As a 'gesture of good faith.'" She laughed. "As if we're going to negotiate with that schmuck! He'll tell us what he knows. Without any deal."

Maya's mind was racing. What should she do? Without any hard evidence, she'd never convince Sarit—or Roni, for that matter—to take seriously her fears about an impending terrorist attack. And if she told them about the blood moon, the lost Temple treasures, and the End of Days, they'd lock her up. Diagnose her as hopelessly stricken with Jerusalem Syndrome.

But if they took Salameh into custody now, it would send them back to square one. The conspirators would disappear, regroup, and probably try again later. That's what must have happened in the LTM case a few months back. Maya's discovery of the underground incense lab had come close enough to the truth to make them postpone their plot. But not cancel it. They had patiently waited for the next opportunity. Tonight's blood moon.

In the end, she said nothing to Sarit, except: "Keep me posted."

After she disconnected, Maya sat at her desk, her slim hands folded on the gray metal surface. She unlocked her fingers and reached for a pair of interlinked steel rings.

As she worked the puzzle, she considered her next move. If she told Roni about her conversation with Sarit, he'd tell her to back off, let Sarit arrest Salameh, and close the case. But that would be a colossal mistake. Salameh was not the master strategist here.

But Salameh knew enough to help her stop Pinkas Mashiak. It was time for the two of them to talk. Before Sarit showed up with handcuffs.

67

A LOUD KNOCK INTERRUPTED HER thoughts. A moment later, Roni marched in. His dark pants and short-sleeved black shirt reeked of cigarette smoke. The tight line of his mouth warned Maya to be on her guard.

"When were you going to tell me that Sarit's about to arrest Salameh?"

"But she only called me a few minutes ago!"

Roni reached into his pants pocket, wriggled out a crushed pack of cigarettes, and shook out the last one. Maya jabbed her thumb toward the "No Smoking" sign taped to the wall behind her. Roni grinned and lit up.

"Looks like you fucked up again, Rimon." He took a long drag on his cigarette. Then, he blew out a sinuous ring of smoke. "While you were out chasing your phantom bogeymen, the police closed the case."

Still puffing on his cigarette, he turned and headed for the door.

"Roni...." Maya's voice was steely. Anger tightened the muscles of her jaw.

He froze with his hand on the brass knob. He didn't turn around. Maya waited for him to speak. He didn't oblige her.

"You probably don't want to hear this," she said, "but I'm now totally convinced that Goldmayer's murder is part of a much larger plot."

Roni spun around. The dark features of his face were drawn taut like a cinched pouch. His narrow forehead was creased into a dozen slashed lines. His black bead eyes glared at Maya.

"You're damn right I don't want to hear it!"

Roni flung the smoking stub of his cigarette onto the cement floor and smashed it with the heel of his sandal. Then, he dug out the empty pack from his pocket, crumpled it in his fist, and threw the wadded paper against the wall. It bounced once and landed near the gray metal trash can next to Maya's desk.

Maya kept her gaze fixed on Roni's smoldering eyes. She refused to be bullied by his trantrums.

"The plan has something to do with the scroll Goldmayer was looking for." She spoke fast, slamming her words together like cars skidding into each other on an icy road. "And the lost Treasures from the Second Temple. And Christian extremists. I'm pretty sure the plotters' target is the Temple Mount."

Maya realized how crazy this all sounded. She had no proof to back up any of it. Just some fragmentary clues. And her own intuition, which had previously proved so disastrously wrong.

"You're grandstanding again, Maya! Just like your old man. It won't make up for your failures."

Roni was almost choking in his rage. She lifted up her thermos to offer him water, then set it back down. He'd probably throw it at her.

"Enough with the Indiana Jones scripts! Just stick to the facts and do your job."

Maya's shoulders sagged. She collapsed against the hard back of her chair. Then, she straightened her spine and stood up. From the top drawer of her desk, she took out her SIG Sauer pistol and shoved it into her shoulder bag.

"Where're you going?"

"To catch the bad guy."

She pushed past Roni and walked out of her office.

As she exited the building, she scrolled through the contacts on her mobile until she found Salameh's phone numbers. His home. His cell phone. His antiquities shop. She left voicemails at all three numbers, telling him she needed to speak with him as soon as possible.

As she listened to the last series of stuttering trills, followed by a rapid-fire voicemail message in Arabic, she thought about what she'd say to the antiquities dealer when she confronted him. *Tell me precisely what the Preacher is planning: when, where, and how.* A man like Salameh would show little loyalty to his partner if it meant his going to prison. Especially if that partner happened to be an infidel.

68

PINKAS MASHIAK STEPPED OUT OF the dark alley into the pastel glow of early morning. Across the street, the rose-colored façade of Habib Salameh's antiquities shop was still cloaked by night. A shadowy line bisected Salah e-Din Street into parallel lanes, light and dark. Like the two sides of an empty chessboard.

Mashiak had arrived almost two hours early for his scheduled appointment with Salameh. Hidden in the dark alley across from the antiquities shop, he'd watched the Lebanese dealer arrive and exchange a few words with a tall, mustachioed young Arab, who was waiting for him. The young man then receded into the shadows. Salameh disappeared into the shadowy entryway, carrying a silver laptop tucked under one arm. Moments later, a light had flickered on inside the shop, turning the heavy front drapes blood-red.

When Salameh had re-emerged minutes later, he held a small white envelope, which he'd handed over to the young man. After the man scurried off, the dealer returned to his shop, where he now awaited Mashiak's arrival.

What was that shifty Arab up to?

Mashiak took out his phone and tapped a number on speed dial.

"Tim, you were right. Salameh's double-crossin' us. He jes' sent off a courier."

"Describe him."

"Tall, skinny Ay-rab. Thin mustache. In his twenties."

"I seen 'im before. Hangin' 'round the shop."

"I wanna know what's in that message, and where it's goin."

"And if he don' wanna tell me?"

"Offer to buy it."

"And if the price is too high?"

"I leave it to yer discretion. Use whatever means necessary to stop that message from gettin' through."

Tim broke off the connection without saying goodbye.

Mashiak continued to hold the phone against his bald skull until the dial tone hummed in his ear. He silenced the phone and slid it into his pocket. Then, he reached his right hand behind his neck and rubbed his lucky bump. The scaly flesh made his soft fingertips tingle.

Clenching his teeth and sucking in a deep breath through his nose, he spun around and smacked his open palm hard against the rough stone of the building that stood behind him.

The Arab was no doubt betraying him!

But before he took his revenge, he needed Salameh's help one last time. He needed the Arab to tell him where that parchment scroll was.

When Mashiak had visited the Qumran Archives yesterday, masquerading as Salameh, he'd scanned Roland De Vaux's French notes into his phone and then brought them to a French-speaking member of his flock to translate. But even in English, the notes made no sense. Where were these places—Tekoa, Khirbet al-Tajmil, Kochalit? According to Goldmayer's journal entry, the professor believed that De Vaux had located the duplicate scroll during his explorations in the Judean Desert in the 1950s. But now that Mashiak had read De Vaux's notes himself, he wasn't so sure. The information in the French monk's notes seemed pretty imprecise. He needed Salameh to pinpoint the exact location on a map.

Mashiak grinned. With one giant foot, he pushed off from the wall and drew himself up to his full height. Then, he crossed to the other side of Salah e-Din Street and entered the dark entryway at the base of the rose-colored building.

It was time to have one last conversation with Habib Salameh.

69

As soon as Pinkas Mashiak returned to his small two-room apartment, he rushed over to the kitchen sink to wash his hands. He scrubbed his palms and fingers vigorously with coarse green detergent until the flesh was raw. Then, he went into his tiny bathroom and splashed cologne on his neck, face, and hands. But the fetid smell from Salameh's shop still lingered like a bad dream.

He walked into the living room and knelt down in one corner. The hard floor hurt his bony knees. He clasped his large hands together and fixed his gaze on the wooden altar. Within moments, he felt a calm descend upon him like a warm spring shower.

It wasn't much of an altar, he had to admit. Just a simple table made of West Virginia red cedar. Standing behind it, mounted on a square base, was a six-foot cross made out of the same wood. Mashiak had made everything with his own hands, although he wasn't very skilled as a carpenter. He'd polished all the wood until it glowed. These two homemade pieces—the table and cross—were the only things he'd shipped over from the States. They were precious souvenirs of the church he'd built in West Virginia and then abandoned to come here to found a new church. He had done this because the Voice had commanded him.

Ignoring the intensifying pain in his kneecaps, Mashiak prayed for the Voice to speak to him one last time. But his prayers failed. As they had ever since he'd set the plan into motion.

Had the Lord abandoned him because of his mortal sins?

But he'd only done what had been demanded of him!

Since coming to Jerusalem six months ago, Mashiak's days had been filled with visions, his nights with fevered dreams. They had revealed to him that his final instructions, concealed in an ancient parchment scroll, awaited him inside a cave. The same cave that had appeared to him in a vision when he was a young child.

It was all part of the divine plan.

When Habib Salameh had first informed him two months ago that an American professor, Boaz Goldmayer, was dropping hints that he'd zeroed in on the lost Treasure Scroll, Mashiak had known right away that this was the sign he'd been waiting for his whole life. He had come to the Holy Land to wait for just such a sign to appear.

Although Goldmayer had not revealed the scroll's precise location before the conference, Salameh had mapped out a few likely sites in the Judean Desert near Qumran. Over the past few months, Mashiak had explored all of these places: an ancient cistern, a burial tomb, a number of caves in Qumran. He'd moved furtively, keeping out of sight. But he'd found nothing.

As the night of the blood moon neared, he had begun to panic. His destined moment would soon be at hand. Goldmayer's announcement about the Treasure Scroll had been an unmistakable sign. But Mashiak needed to be the first to locate the scroll. Only he could decipher the divine message placed there specifically for him. He'd had no choice but to stop the professor and confiscate his notes.

It was all part of the divine plan.

But Habib Salameh had proven unworthy of the vital role assigned him in that plan. He had shown himself to be greedy and treacherous. All he wanted was his thirty pieces of silver. What did he care that another blood moon was about to set upon a still-unredeemed world? And now, another murder weighed on Mashiak's conscience. How sorely the Lord was testing him!

With an impatient shake of his head, Mashiak pulled himself out of his musings. His knees were screaming with pain. He placed both his hands on the floor and slid forward on his belly until his large frame stretched out flat, like a Muslim on his prayer rug. With the blood pounding in his ears, he beseeched the Voice to speak to him:

O Lord, You guide my every step. Please speak! Show me the way!

Suddenly, he felt electric pulses surging through his long bones.

The room filled with blinding light. Mashiak squeezed his eyes shut but quickly opened them again. He must show no fear. He must prove himself worthy. He bowed his head and listened, hardly breathing.

The Voice reverberated in every fiber of his being. It was like a surge of high voltage, making his whole body quiver.

Hearken to Me, My beloved son! Go to the place that I have shown you. There, you will find an ancient scroll, holding a message meant for your eyes alone. Hearken to My words and obey them. This is My final command to you. For behold, the blood moon will soon rise over My Holy Mountain!

When silence returned to the small apartment, Mashiak continued to hear a sonorous ringing in his ears. He felt loved as never before. Soon, he would be anointed King Messiah, God's special messenger on earth. The Holy Spirit was commanding him to herald the coming of the Divine Kingdom. He would build a new Temple on the Holy Mount to celebrate God's triumphant return. He would fill it with the Temple treasures lost for two thousand years.

It was all written in an ancient scroll, meant for his eyes alone.

70

THE CAB DROPPED MAYA OFF in front of Salameh's East Jerusalem shop a little after 10:30 a.m. The morning shadows had already receded from that side of the street as the sun climbed higher into a brilliant blue sky. At this hour, only a few pedestrians strolled the weathered pavestones in the quiet neighborhood.

The heavy red curtains covering the front plateglass window were still drawn. Maya did not find this unusual. As a dealer in high-end antiquities, Salameh deliberately discouraged passersby from peering in.

She ducked into the dark entryway of the building and pressed the buzzer. No answer. She pressed again, holding the buzzer down for a few seconds. She shaded her eyes and peered through the bars into the dark shop. The glass cases filled with antiquities were not illuminated. The only light came from the open door at the back of the gallery. She rattled the iron grillwork, then stuck her small hand through the bars and rapped on the glass door with her knuckle. Still no response.

As her eyes adjusted to the poor light, she noticed a broken table lamp lying on the floor. A headless woman with an upraised arm. All that remained of the bulb was a bare filament. A short distance away lay the lamp's ripped satin shade. Maya squinted, trying to make out more details. She noted that many of the unlit horizontal glass cases on the opposite wall were smashed, emptied of their treasures. Loose papers lay scattered on the floor. There was no sign of the shop's owner.

A robbery? Or something more sinister? Maybe she should call it in before investigating further. But why bother? The break-in had happened during the night. The thieves were long gone. It didn't look like Salameh had arrived yet.

Maya twisted the glass knob. The door swung open. She inspected the double bolts. No sign of forced entry.

She stepped into the shop, careful not to disturb any evidence. Feeling around in her shoulderbag, she pulled out her smartphone and turned on the flashlight. Then, she poked around in one of the bag's inner pockets for rubberbands. As a courtesy to the crime scene techs, who would arrive later, she slipped a rubber band over each sandal to distinguish her footprints from the intruder's. She leaned down to examine the papers on the floor. Sales receipts and routine correspondence.

She walked over to the small antique desk in the center of the room.

Most of the polished wood surface was covered by a black blotter, edged in brown leather. In its center sat a Macbook Pro, its silver lid closed. Goldmayer's missing laptop? Had she been wrong about Salameh? Was he Goldmayer's killer?

Maya lifted up the laptop's cover and stared at the dark screen. She pushed down the power button. The screen remained black. The laptop's battery was completely drained. She looked around for the power cord and found it on the floor, snaking back to an outlet in the wall. She picked up the magnetic end of the white cord and connected it to the port. Then, she pushed down on the power button and waited. The white Apple icon appeared. When the icon vanished moments later, the screen filled with a crazy quilt of yellowed parchment. Maya recognized the Greek letters of the Copper Scroll. Definitely the screensaver of a Qumran scholar. But when she clicked on the Finder icon, she discovered that the hard drive held no data. Just standard applications. No folders or documents. The computer had been wiped clean. If this was Goldmayer's computer, all his research was gone.

At opposite corners of the small desk sat two ancient artifacts: a bronze inkwell and the small clay figure of a woman, whose lower body tapered into a slim cylinder. Between the two objects was a dark brown circle, ringed by a thin line of dust, where the lamp had stood.

If this was a robbery, why hadn't the thieves taken the expensive laptop and the two valuable antiquities perched on the desk? Maya glanced over at the floor-to-ceiling glass cases. Most of the contents had been left behind. What had the thieves been after?

She tried pulling open the thin center drawer of the antique desk, then the four narrow side drawers. They were all locked. She decided against prying them open. It was doubtful she'd find anything of value. Salameh was too careful. She would leave the drawers for Sarit.

Taking her service weapon out of her shoulder bag, Maya set the bulky bag down on the floor next to the desk. Then, she turned and headed toward the open door at the back of the long, narrow room. She moved cautiously, making no sound. In one hand, she held the SIG Sauer, its snub barrel pointed forward; in the other, her phone, the focused beam of its flashlight trained on the floor.

A clattering noise suddenly broke the tomb-like silence. It was the sound of breaking glass or pottery. Maya froze in her tracks. Cold sweat beaded on her neck, despite the stifling air inside the shop. Quickly, she switched off the flashlight. Were the thieves still here? Roni was instantly in her ear: *Why don't you ever call for backup?*

She knelt down and slipped off her sandals. Barefoot, she approached the doorway and peered in. The darkness was so thick, she could feel it pressing against her eyes and skin. Carefully, she bent her knees, set her phone on the ground, and straightened up. Then, she reached through the doorway and patted the wall to her right until she located the light switch. *Breathe, deep and slow, breathe. Focus. Now!*

She flipped the switch and dropped down into a crouch, grasping the stock of the SIG Sauer with both hands. Rapidly, she swiveled the pistol back and forth across the brightly-lit room. Looking for the slightest movement, listening hard.

"Israeli Intelligence! Nobody move!"

She heard the creature before she saw it.

In the middle of a small round table sat a large black cat, mewling softly. On the embroidered tablecloth sat tea service for two, but the cat must have knocked the second cup and saucer to the floor. The animal now stared at her with golden eyes, its sinuous tail whipping back and forth. The animal blinked twice and leapt off the table. Then, it scurried into the shadows with a peevish yowl.

Maya giggled nervously and lowered her arms. With a swift glance, she looked over the cat's meal, which she had just interrupted. A plate of crescent-shaped cookies. A creamer of milk. A small bowl of pink and yellow candies. She noted the dainty porcelain teapot, decorated with delicate roses, a crystal sugar bowl, and a half-filled cup of tea on a saucer. She smelled mint and lemon and some exotic spice she didn't recognize.

Her eyes continued to survey the small back room, which was filled from floor to ceiling with metal shelving. Most of the shelves held clay artifacts, some of them broken in pieces. Against the rear wall stood a rectangular wooden table, bordered at one end by an industrial sink. A few pottery shards lay on the table's dust-covered surface.

It was only when her eyes returned to the small round table, then slid down to the floor that she saw the body.

Habib Salameh lay sprawled on his back on the stone floor. His handsome face was relaxed, his eyes closed. In death as in life, the impeccably dressed businessman seemed completely at ease, as though napping. Near the round table lay the shattered saucer. Beside Salameh's right hand lay the second teacup. The thin porcelain, decorated with tiny roses like the teapot, was broken into several pieces.

A few wet spots on the floor glistened in the gray light that filtered in from the room's only window.

She turned her attention to Salameh's lifeless body.

His white shirt had been sliced from collar to mid-chest. The ragged edges of the tear suggested some sort of serrated blade. With the barrel of her gun, she carefully pushed aside the jacket lapel and found two similar vertical rips. She poked the shirt open at a buttonhole and found deep slashes in the olive-toned skin underneath the shirt.

She straightened up and continued to stare down at the body, bothered by something she couldn't quite put her finger on. Then, she figured it out. There wasn't enough blood. With thrusts this deep, the shirt should have been soaked with Salameh's blood. But there were only some reddish stains near the path of the blade.

The scant amount of blood only made sense if the stabbing had been done post-mortem, after the victim was already dead and the blood had stopped circulating.

Her nose wrinkled as she caught a whiff of an unpleasant odor. She crouched down and bent her face toward the floor. The smell was coming from the liquid spilled from the broken teacup. She lifted one of the thin porcelain shards to her nose. She immediately recognized the smell. The fusty odor of mouse droppings. Wild hemlock.

Salameh had been poisoned.

Maya reconstructed the scene in her mind:

The killer arrives at the antiquities shop. It's someone Salameh knows well. He lets the visitor in and offers him tea. The killer slips a lethal dose of hemlock into Salameh's cup. The two men talk, go over the final details of their plan. The killer leaves, letting the poison begin its deadly work. He returns later to stage the scene as a robbery and impulsive stabbing to throw the police off the scent.

Maya could think of only one person who'd carry out such a diabolical scheme.

She walked back to the doorway, retrieved her mobile, and called Roni.

"Salameh's dead. I found his body in the back of his shop. Poisoned and stabbed. Shop's been ransacked. I also found Goldmayer's laptop."

"Call Sarit. Tell her to send a team ASAP to process the scene. She's gonna be pissed that you got there first." Maya heard Roni chuckle, then the scrape of a match. "Then, come back to the office and write up your report. Case closed."

"No, it's not."

"Excuse me?"

"We haven't solved the case yet."

Maya heard a sharp intake of breath. Then a loud whoosh of smoke.

"Look, Rimon, as far as I'm concerned, we're done. Salameh killed Goldmayer to get his hands on some valuable merchandise, then some *gonifs* killed him. Call it 'poetic justice.' If Sarit Levine wants to keep on investigating, let her knock herself out. But you're finished with this case. Take your victory lap and move on."

Maya hung up without responding to Roni's remarks. She had no intention of ending her investigation. After what she'd seen today, she was more convinced than ever that Pinkas Mashiak was getting ready to make his big move.

71

CURSING RONI UNDER HER BREATH, Maya returned to headquarters, making sure that her boss saw her come in. For almost an hour, she tried to write up her report, so he'd stop breathing down her neck. But she was too wound up to focus.

Instead, she spent the rest of the afternoon skimming online articles about Evangelical Christianity, messianism, premillennialism, the Rapture, and the apocalypse. After a few hours, she'd had enough. She just would never comprehend Christianity's implausible beliefs any more than she would ever understand the mumbo-jumbo of rabbinic law or the hocus-pocus of Kabbalah. Living in the real world was complicated enough.

Late in the afternoon, she called Vered at her parents' apartment to wish her luck in the school play that evening. She was glad to hear her daughter so happy, prattling on about her butterfly costume and her glittery makeup. Maya reassured her daughter that she would make it to the play on time, though she now doubted she would get there at all. She told Vered to look for her in the front row, sitting right next to Jeddah Camille and Saba Moti. She also promised Vered that Ima and Abba would be on their best behavior in front of her new friends.

Maya felt guilty lying to her daughter. But she didn't want to upset her before the performance. And if Maya missed the play, she'd make it up to Vered by taking her out for chocolate ice cream the next day.

She didn't feel so guilty lying to Masha. She'd decided not to tell her that Roni had shut down the Goldmayer case. That he'd ordered Maya to stop investigating. Maya needed Masha to ride shotgun beside her tonight at the Tayelet. If things went sideways, the less Masha knew, the better. Maya was prepared to take the fall alone.

The two women left Service Headquarters a little after six. Although Maya generally preferred driving with the windows open, she had no choice but to turn on the air conditioning as soon as they got into the stifling car. Though it was almost evening, the air still smoldered. It didn't help that both of them wore light jackets, as much to conceal their holstered weapons as to warm them later on. Because the Tayelet looked down on Jerusalem from six hundred meters above sea level, there was usually a stiff breeze up there.

As they crawled along General Pierre Koenig, then Rivka Street, neither woman spoke. Out of the corner of her eye, Maya saw Masha glancing over at her, her thick eyebrows furrowed. She recognized that look and steeled herself.

"*Nu*, so how are things at home?" asked Masha. She chuckled. "Is Vered still jabbering about the leopard cubs?"

"It's not funny, Masha! I almost lost her the other day. I just don't think I'm cut out to be a mother."

"You're doing the best you can. Vered feels loved and protected. That's all that matters."

"What if my best's not good enough?" Maya bit down on her upper lip. "I'm always working, leaving her with my folks. Then, in swoops her Abba with presents and special outings. Rafi's always the hero, and I'm the big, bad villain."

Masha looked over at her friend, rolled her full lips into a mock pout, then smiled. Her light hazel eyes softened.

"If Vered doesn't see through that *mamzer* yet, she will soon enough. Forget all this nonsense about being a bad mother. You're the best she's got. And it's better than most, believe me."

Maya heard the bitterness in Masha's words. As a young girl, Masha had been sexually abused by an older brother. Her parents, traumatized from their experiences in the Soviet Union, hadn't believed Masha when she'd told them. She hadn't spoken to any of them in years.

Suddenly, the traffic came to a standstill. Maya stared ahead at the battered pick-up truck in front of them. The back of the truck was stacked high with wooden crates packed with agitated chickens. Even through closed windows, she could hear the terrified squabbling as the birds strained against their prison bars.

She looked over at Masha. Her friend was checking her makeup in the visor mirror. Masha's face was always perfectly put on. Every honey-blonde hair in place. Maya couldn't remember the last time she'd flipped down her own visor.

In a few moments, the flow of traffic resumed. Maya turned her attention back to the road. They crawled along Avraham Shalom Yehuda Street. Then, they turned off to follow the access road leading up to the Promenade.

Without warning, a motorcycle zipped around from behind their car and tried to cut off the cab in front of them, which was about to make a left turn. But the rider had miscalculated the angle of his turn and skidded off the road. Luckily, he managed to jump free of his bike just before it slammed into a streetlamp.

The taxi driver, a wiry young man with a thick mustache and a gold earring in one ear, flung open his door and leapt out of his cab. He shook his fist and cursed the cyclist, who yelled back at him.

The shouting match went on for two or three minutes. Several other drivers leapt out their cars and joined in, although it was hard to tell whose side they were on. And then, abruptly, it was over. The cab driver ducked back into his cab, slammed the door, and made his left turn. The motorcyclist, now helmetless, mounted his dented bike and sped off. The traffic returned to its slow crawl up the hill toward the Promenade.

Maya looked over at Masha and shrugged. Masha threw up her hands.

"Only in Israel," they said at the same time.

They laughed and smacked their palms together in mid-air.

Maya gunned the engine, switched lanes, and sped past two cars. When the burly driver in the second car gave them the finger, Masha waved and made the sign of the cross.

72

Bordered by low white walls and iron railings, the Haas Promenade now rose into view. Among the most popular tourist sites in Jerusalem, the Promenade curved along the contours of the Armon HaNatziv Ridge for more than a kilometer. As the day slipped toward dusk, the tree-lined paths filled with walkers eager to glimpse the Old City lit up against the night sky.

"So what exactly d'you think he's up to, this Pinkhas Mashiakh?"

"*Pinkas Mashiak*," Maya corrected Masha, emphasizing the hard "k" in both names. Like most English-speakers who hadn't learned Hebrew as children, the American preacher wasn't able to pronounce Hebrew's guttural *khet* or *khaf*, so he'd transliterated his new Israeli name improperly. Why in the world had he chosen a name that he couldn't even pronounce?

"Not that these *goyim* would know the difference," said Masha.

She chuckled, but Maya's mouth was clenched into a grim line.

"That's what makes them such easy targets for a God-crazed lunatic like Mashiak," said Maya. "They're so desperate to be lifted up to Heaven that they're willing to follow any pied piper who comes along. Then again, they're no different from the Ultra-Orthodox, who want 'Mashiak now,' or the Jihadists, who can't wait to blast themselves into the arms of heavenly virgins. When has the human race ever stopped hankering for redemption?"

Maya gazed out of the window, somewhat embarrassed by her pontificating.

"Why do you think Mashiak's so interested in finding the Temple treasures?" Masha's grin had disappeared, curdled into a scowl. "Is it simple greed or grandiose dreams of power? You think he really believes his own PR? That he's the Messiah, come to rebuild the Temple. You think he really believes the world's about to come to an end?"

"He's probably too crazy to care. Zealots like him tend to blur the line between reality and delusion. It's almost as if they've entered an altered state. They might start out as charlatans, but along the way, they become true believers, duped by their own fantasies. Maybe we should stop seeing them as con artists and start thinking of them as not guilty by reason of insanity."

"Oh, give me a break!" Masha slammed both her hands on the dashboard and exhaled a loud whoosh of breath. "Jerusalem Syndrome's no excuse for terrorism!"

Maya placed her right hand gently on her friend's shoulder.

"Easy, *havivi*. I was just yanking your chain."

They reached the end of the drive. Maya pulled the silver Corolla into the visitors' parking lot, which was almost full. Lined up along one edge of the lot were several large tour buses, emblazoned on their sides with "New Children of Light." She noticed that many of the parked cars were rentals. Near the entrance, taxis drove up in a continuous stream, discharging passengers.

As she and Masha headed toward the Promenade, Maya slowed her pace to admire the magnificent view. From this vantage point, one could see the entire city of Jerusalem. The white stone buildings glittered in the last bright embers of sun. Far to the south lay the bright blue oval of the Dead Sea. To the north, the green hills of the Galilee. And directly below them lay the walled ramparts of the Old City. In its heart on the Temple Mount shone the gold and silver moons of Al-Aqsa and the Dome of the Rock. *Al Haram Esh Sharif.* The navel of the world.

The crowd grew denser as they approached the designated spot for tonight's gathering. Most of them seemed young. Many held small children by the hand or carried babies on their backs or chests. But as she drew nearer, Maya saw that her first impressions were mistaken. Older people were here as well, some leaning on walkers or canes. The babble of voices included many languages. English predominated, in a wide range of accents. Maya recognized Deep South, Midwest; even Brooklyn.

When they reached the Geoffrey and Rhoda Goldman Promenade, the two agents found themselves in a beautifully landscaped park, bounded on three sides by stately cedar trees. The ambience here was festive, similar to what one might find at a rock concert or a political rally. Or after a victorious battle.

In front of a border of trees and flower beds, enterprising vendors had set up tables. There were silk-screened tee shirts and handmade jewelry, posters, paintings, and hanging ornaments. Most of the items were branded with Messianic symbols: fish; six-pointed stars; the joined menorah-hexagram-fish seal of the ancient Jerusalem Church, attributed to James, brother of Jesus; the runes and planetary icons favored by the ancient Essenes. Contemporary variations included peace signs and Eastern mandalas. There were also elixirs and oils to renew the soul. One table offered CDs of chants and songs produced by New Children of Light Music, Ltd. as well as DVDs of Pinkas Mashiak's speeches. There were free pamphlets about the New Children of Light Church and inspirational books, including signed copies of Mashiak's newly published autobiography, *Visions of Apocalypse: The True Story of a Modern Prophet.*

Many in the crowd wore long white, gray, or brown robes of rough cloth, cinched with braided rope belts. A few wore colorful dashikis or tie-dyed shirts and sundresses. Despite the cooling air, almost all were barefoot. Most of the men covered their heads with *kippot* or colored cloth caps. The women covered their heads with scarves, woven snoods, or modest hats. A number of people wore large wooden crosses around their necks, hanging from silver, gold, rope, or beaded chains. Most faces displayed an eager expectancy. Their eyes shone.

No sign yet of the American preacher. But everything was ready for his arrival.

At one end of the park stood a high wooden platform, bordered on two sides by gigantic speakers the size of refrigerators and wide flat-screens. Alongside the stage were high-intensity halide lights perched atop tall poles, waiting to be turned on. The crowd was fidgety, excited, tense with anticipation. Every once in a while, someone would start up a song, and others quickly joined in. The playlist ranged from black gospel to country western to congregational hymns.

Circulating around the edges of the crowd were about a dozen tough-looking men dressed in black, pistols on their hips, corked wires in their ears. Journalists with boom mics and video cameras tried to push their way forward, but the black-clad sentinels wouldn't let them get close to the stage. Maya picked out a number of plainclothes Israeli policemen. They were keeping their distance, but their eyes never rested. The crowd was a coiled spring.

"So where should we position ourselves?" Masha asked.

"Definitely not in front. Too easy to get crushed if things get out of hand. Best to stay off to one side." She pointed to the left of the stage. "From here, we can keep an eye on the preacher as well as their security people. We can also try to sneak a few photos."

Maya suddenly realized that she was afraid. Her hands were clammy. Goosebumps pricked her skin. Her heart was racing. And she was chilled to the bone. She feared being caught in a stampede. It would only take a random spark.

She was eleven years old. Standing with her father in Kings of Israel Square in Tel Aviv, waiting for Prime Minister Yitzhak Rabin to speak. Although everyone seemed happy, she felt scared. Never in her life had she been surrounded by so many people. She couldn't breathe. She was too short to see a way out. She grasped her father's hand tightly. Suddenly, BANG, BANG, BANG! Three claps of thunder. And then chaos. Feet running in all directions. She was torn from her father's grasp and knocked to the pavement. Shoes pounded on her chest. It was dark, loud, and hot. Someone yanked her to her feet. She was dragged along the rough ground until she was blinded by light. For many nights afterwards, she went back to that place in her dreams. Bang, bang, bang. Shoes pounding on her chest. Her skin scraped on rough stone. And always the hot, pulsing crowd, crushing her, stealing her air and light.

She would never subject herself to that again.

Aware of her friend's unease, Masha hooked her arm through Maya's and led her through the bustling crowd. They were careful not to jostle anyone, not to attract attention. For the most part, the crowd was friendly. People talked excitedly among themselves. Most were talking about Mashiak, their words almost idolatrous. Many eyes glanced up frequently to see if their leader had yet taken the stage.

Maya and Masha reached the front of the crowd and took up their positions off to one side. Maya was impressed by all the sophisticated technology—the elaborate sound system; special stage and perimeter lights; huge plasma screens; microphones suspended from trees. Security was heavier here. Uniformed guards carried semi-automatic weapons. Either they expected trouble or were just not taking any chances.

Maya glanced down at the old Poljot on her wrist.

"It's already 7:25." Her eyes skimmed over the dense sea of humanity. "Crowd's getting restless. Mashiak better show soon, or there'll be a riot."

Someone shouted: "We want Mashiak now!"

From the crowd came an echoing chant, swelling quickly into a roar: "Mashiak! Mashiak! Mashiak!"

As if directed by an invisible choreographer, all heads craned toward the stage.

73

PINKAS MASHIAK FLUNG OPEN THE door of the white stretch limousine, which was parked behind the stage. The sounds of the exuberant crowd rushed in. The cooling air pulsated with the whine and buzz of excited conversation. He heard the shrill cries of bored, hungry children, the distorted garble of songs broadcast from giant loudspeakers. These sounds were soon drowned out by hundreds of voices shouting, "Mashiak! Mashiak! We want Mashiak now!" The shouts surged and ebbed like breakers.

He leapt out of the back seat of the limousine and sprinted toward the empty stage. His long legs bounded up the stairs. Suddenly, he appeared in a bright cone of light illuminating the center of the stage. He was a white-robed and white-mitered giant, glowing like an incandescent flame. The crowd went wild. They punched their fists into the air, screaming, their clenched fingers reaching up toward the sky. Captured in the giant plasma screens flanking the stage, Mashiak's magnified image beamed out to the adoring crowd. His dark, lustrous eyes seemed about to pop out of his skull. Like a skilled maestro, he quieted the crowd, then revved them up again, waving his long arms. Once, twice, a third time. Then, he silenced them with upraised hands.

From their spot near the front of the stage, Maya and Masha were swept forward by the rushing crowd. The two women pushed back with sharp elbows until they managed to break free. They now took up new positions in the shadows behind the stage, just beyond the floodlights, careful to keep themselves hidden from the private security guards that patrolled the perimeter. In the distance, the gleaming gold and silver domes on the Temple Mount sparkled under a blood-red moon.

"Buckle your seatbelt," Maya hissed into Masha's ear. "Here we go!"

Mashiak no longer stood in the center of the stage. He moved rapidly across the wooden boards, expertly pursued by the spotlight. Then, suddenly, the entire stage blazed with light, bright as day.

"Blessed Brothers 'n Sisters! New Children of Light! Hearken to my wonderful news!"

"Tell us, Preacher! Tell us!"

Mashiak pointed a long, slender finger toward the horizon.

"Behold, the blood moon! The End is nigh!"

The rising full moon glowed red like an inflamed wound. Due to the glare of the bright halide lights, only a few stars could be seen in the dark sky.

"I'm here tonight to inform you of what is to come! Great suffering and travail. But in the end, the Lord of Hosts will triumph over His enemies."

The crowd cheered. Mashiak waited until they settled down.

"The Lord has done revealed to me the secret hidin' place of the lost Temple treasures. Long ago, the Temple priests hid 'em away to keep 'em safe from unclean Roman hands. They stayed hid for two thousand years. Waitin' for this moment."

A hush fell over the crowd. They became silent as the grave. Even the children hushed, sensing the gravity of the Preacher's words.

"With this treasure—sacred vessels of silver 'n gold, a fortune in tithes 'n taxes brought by the faithful with glad hearts—we c'n restore the Temple to its former glory."

Mashiak paused and looked over the vast multitude. Then, he strode up to the front lip of the stage. His white miter, encircled by a shiny gold frontlet, gleamed in the artificial light. The tall, pointed headdress was like a guided missile, poised for flight.

"But first, we gotta remove the abominations pollutin' the sacred ground."

Scores of clenched fists shot up. A deafening roar rose up from the crowd.

"Remove the abominations!"

Masha thrust her hand into her pocket and pulled out her cell phone. Maya grabbed her wrist. Masha's throat discharged a sharp, low growl.

"What? You don't think we should call this in? He's just called for an attack on the Temple Mount!"

Masha struggled to free herself from Maya's grip. But her colleague refused to let go.

"We don't know yet if he's acting alone." Maya kept her voice down. Mashiak's security guards were close by. "If we pick him up too soon, we'll lose our chance to stop the others."

On stage, Mashiak was in continuous motion. His arms gyrated. His thick neck swiveled left and right. His long legs scissored back and forth across the stage. His thunderous voice was alternately commanding, seductive, threatening. He was a one-man band, trumpets and drums thundering through his windpipe. Back and forth, he strode, a flying shuttle of zeal. The crowd followed his movements as if watching a breakneck tennis match. "Beware the deceits of Belial, the Angel of Wickedness! The torrents of Satan shall break into Abaddon! The deeps of the Abyss shall groan amid the roar of heavin' mud!"

Sweat poured down Mashiak's flushed face. His high-pitched voice strained at its breaking point. The crowd moaned and swayed.

"Amen!" roared a thousand throats.

Maya marveled at Mashiak's strange words. *Abaddon? Belial? Roar of heaving mud?* How bizarre these oracular words sounded, coming out of the mouth of a backwater preacher from America's Deep South. No doubt Hillel would have been able to tell her the Scriptural sources of Mashiak's words. If she were still talking to him.

Suddenly, a loud explosion went off. People started to scream. But they were too packed together to move. They jostled for space and stamped their feet. Several private security guards, guns drawn, ran toward the source of the noise. Fortunately, it turned out to be only pranksters setting off firecrackers.

The guards soon hustled the two young men, dressed in jeans and dark hoodies, toward a black SUV. The young men shouted obscenities in English until the closing car doors abruptly cut them off.

Around the edges of the crowd, several plainclothes Israeli police patrolled in the shadows. They watched unobtrusively, whispering into their ear comms.

On stage, Mashiak continued his apocalyptic rant.

"Listen up, New Children of Light! God has heard your prayers! He done sent you the Branch of David, the Prince of the Congregation, the Scepter of Israel." He paused, then flung his arms out to the side as if embracing them all. "King Messiah!"

From the crowd came thunderous shouts: "Mashiak! Mashiak! Mashiak!"

A group of young people, wearing long brown robes and sandals, pushed quietly past Maya and Masha, carrying straw baskets. They began circulating among the crowd. The baskets filled up rapidly with American dollars and Israeli shekels.

"Brothers and Sisters, we'll soon have in our possession the priceless treasures of the Holy Temple. Are you ready to restore 'em to their proper place?"

A deafening roar rose from the crowd.

"Behold!" With a long, trembling finger, Mashiak pointed up into the sky.

The full moon had risen over Jerusalem. Around it shimmered a corona of pearly clouds. The bright lunar disk glowed red like a burning coal.

"Let's build a new House for the Lord on His Holy Mountain! He's sent us a sign! The End is near!"

The crowd stilled. They held their breath.

"As it is written: 'And I beheld when he had opened the Sixth Seal, 'n, lo, there was a great earthquake; 'n the sun became black as sackcloth of hair, 'n the moon became as blood.'"

The crowd erupted. Loudspeakers blasted the opening strains of "The Battle Hymn of the Republic." A thousand voices rose in joyous song.

Waving to the singing multitude, Pinkas Mashiak bounded off the back of the stage and raced toward his white stretch limousine.

Hemmed in by the screaming mob, Maya and Masha pushed forward, shoving and kicking when they met resistance. Maya was the first to break free. Masha reached out her hand to hold her back, but she twisted free and ran toward Mashiak.

"No, Maya! Wait for backup!"

"No time! Can't let him get away!"

Maya accelerated her pace, straining to overtake the long-limbed preacher.

"Pinkas Mashiak!" Her heaving breath burst forth like backfire. "Stop! Israeli Intelligence!"

Mashiak hesitated, scanning for the source of the unfamiliar voice. When he realized it was coming from his left, he abruptly changed direction and sprinted toward a cluster of cars parked behind the stage. He zigzagged around a tangle of video equipment and cables, then knocked over a pile of cardboard boxes to block his pursuer. Cursing herself for wearing sandals instead of running shoes, Maya tore after him.

Two burly bodyguards were quickly on her heels. One of them knocked Maya down in a flying tackle. She cried out in pain as her shoulder hit the hard ground. When the guard climbed off her, Maya saw that the man's partner had his Glock pointed at the center of her forehead. She heard the click as he released the safety.

Seconds later, Masha burst out of the churning crowd and ran toward them.

"Hey!" she shouted at the two beefy guards. "Pick on someone your own size!"

Still running, she pulled her SIG Sauer out of her underarm holster. Then, she skidded to a stop and took aim. Holding the stock with both hands, she fired a single shot high over the guard whose Glock was trained on Maya. Both guards whipped around, aiming their pistols at Masha. She grinned and pointed her gun at them, swinging it slowly back and forth from one to the other. The guards glowered at her. Masha shrugged, then broadened her grin.

"You're on your own, *chooki*! I'll handle these two goons," she shouted to Maya. "Go after him! I'll call for backup."

Forcing herself not to look back, Maya levered herself up from the ground and ran toward the parked cars behind the stage. The area was unlit, except for the ruddy glow cast by the moon. She heard a car door open, then slam shut. Squinting, she spotted Mashiak behind the wheel of a small, dark blue Fiat. The engine turned. Then, the car sped off with a screech of tires, racing along a paved stone walkway. Its headlights remained dark. It headed down the hill, away from the Promenade.

Her lungs raw and wheezing, Maya ran to the visitors parking lot and yanked open the door of her silver Corolla. She gunned the Corolla's engine and raced after the fleeing Fiat.

Under the parking lot's bright lights, she noted the Fiat's mismatched rear door, the light metallic surface stark against the dark blue paint. A memory flashed to mind. A dark car with a light-colored rear door nearly hitting her on the Bethlehem Road the other night. Her hands shook on the steering wheel.

At the bottom of the hill the Fiat made a sharp left turn. Mashiak was heading south toward Hebron.

At this speed, they would be in the desert very soon, their way lit by a blood-red moon.

74

THEY RACED SOUTH THROUGH THE night, the darkness thick as paste. Heavy clouds blanketed the sky, covering the moon. Near Rachel's Tomb, the blue Fiat swerved off Highway 60 and headed southeast on Route 398. As they ascended into the Judean Hills, dense fog forced both cars to drop their speed. Maya made no effort to avoid being spotted by Mashiak. There were very few cars on the road. No way to take evasive action. She kept at a safe distance, in case he tried something desperate.

Several times during the long drive, Maya pulled out her cell phone and let her index finger hover over Roni's number.

What the hell do you think you're doing? You need to call this in, let Roni know what's going on. Promise not to approach Mashiak until the rest of the team arrives. If you don't, Roni'll have your head!

But she kept putting off the call. The truth was that she wanted to bring in Mashiak on her own. Wanted to close this case by herself. But she was also being held back by self-doubt. What if Mashiak was bluffing? What if he hadn't actually located the Treasure Scroll and the Temple treasures? What if he was simply psychotic, claiming to have found a lost treasure, when all he was doing was chasing phantoms? If it turned out that the preacher was just a harmless lunatic, she'd never live it down. It would be the end of her career.

Her thoughts turned to Masha. How could she have left her alone with Mashiak's thugs? Israeli soldiers never left comrades behind. She kept telling herself that she didn't have to worry about Masha. She was tough, one of their best agents. And the plainclothes cops would have quickly come to her aid. But what if they hadn't heard the gunshot over the raucous crowd?

She bit down hard on her lower lip. The blood tasted bittersweet.

A little north of Tekoa, the two cars exited the main route. The local roads were in a bad state of disrepair, potholed and littered with loose gravel. The macadam was pocked with cracks and hard blisters of baked sand. They drove past a number of dark Arab villages and a small Bedouin encampment.

Several kilometers on, the road narrowed even further, becoming a one-lane gravel track barely wide enough for a single car. Maya was forced to slow down as the Corolla began to rumble over large rocks, some sharp enough to blow out a tire or rupture the chassis. A few car lengths ahead, Mashiak hit something that almost tipped over his car. He slowed his speed to a crawl. For what seemed like hours, they rumbled along in a slow-motion game of cat and mouse, until the Fiat suddenly disappeared from view.

Maya leaned forward and peered through her dust-covered windshield. She saw nothing but vague outlines of large, dark shapes looming in the heavy mist. She braked and yanked open her door. Then, she stepped outside into the night.

She was in some sort of narrow wadi. The ground under her feet was hard and rutted, strewn with pebbles. Cratered walls of packed sand rose up on either side. Although it had been warm when she'd left the Tayelet, the air temperature had quickly plummeted out here in the desert. In short sleeves, light slacks, and sandals, Maya shivered.

She drew her gun and began walking. Her ears strained to pick up any sound, the crack of a twig, a dislodged stone.

Then, she spotted an opening in the sandstone bank. Erosion had carved a space just wide enough for a small car. She ran back to her Corolla and floored the gas pedal. The Corolla leapt forward. In the rear lights, a shower of pebbles sprayed into the air. She drove about fifty meters until she spotted Mashiak's car. Its dark blue surface was coated with sand, which sparkled in the Corolla's headlights. The car was empty.

Maya walked back to her own car and turned off the headlights. From the trunk, she retrieved two bottles of water and some protein bars and dried dates that she always carried with her. She slammed down the lid and clicked the locks. Clasping her gun tightly in her right hand, she walked past the Fiat until she saw a dirt path heading off into the darkness.

It was a goat path, probably used by the wild ibex that lived here. Maya was surprised that Mashiak was willing to risk such a treacherous path at night. He could break his neck. But desperate men did desperate things. So did desperate women.

It was slow going along the trail, which was not much more than a narrow, V-shaped furrow scratched into the hard soil by thousands of hooves over the centuries. She stumbled frequently. The sharp rocks and brambles bruised her hands. She wiped the blood off on her pants and continued. She heard nothing but her footsteps and labored breathing as she made her way in the dark. There was no sign of Mashiak. No sign of life at all.

And then, suddenly, the path ended at the edge of a cliff. She stopped herself just before plunging over the edge. She heard pebbles cascading down the cliffside, rattling like dead leaves in the wind. She imagined herself tumbling down after them.

Maya fought the urge to head down the cliff in the dark. The odds were not in her favor. There were too many places for Mashiak to hide in ambush. And there was too great a chance that she would trip and plummet to her death.

She would just have to wait until sunrise.

75

THE NIGHT PASSED SLOWLY.

An hour before dawn, Maya pulled out her mobile and tapped Roni's number on speed dial. She knew she'd wake him, probably get her head bitten off. But it couldn't be helped. He'd be mad enough that she'd waited so long to call.

He picked up after four rings. Still half-asleep, he mumbled his name, sounding as though he'd just been waterboarded.

"It's Maya."

Roni grunted something unintelligible. He cleared this throat and coughed.

"Where the hell are you, Rimon?" A pause. "Do you know what time it is?"

"You hear what happened at the Tayelet tonight?"

"Sarit called me. At least her people report in to her."

"Is Masha okay?"

Maya heard the flick of a lighter, then a sharp intake of breath. Roni exhaled the smoke slowly before answering.

"Not to worry. Masha knows how to take care of herself. She knows better than to count on her partner."

Roni took another long drag on his cigarette.

"You gonna tell me where you are, or do I have to send out a search party?"

"Not far from Tekoa. GPS is kind of sketchy out here. Have to wait 'til daylight to get my bearings."

"And Mashiak?"

"He's close by. Terrain's too rough for me to go after him in the dark."

"Don't make a move 'til we...."

Maya wasn't sure why she decided to end the call just then. As if possessing a will of their own, her words came tumbling out like spilled grain: *You're...breaking...up, Roni....Too far...from...cell towers.* Then, she abruptly hung up.

Afterwards, she sat alone in the dark, letting her phone ring over and over until Roni finally let his call go to voicemail. She deleted his message without listening to it. She noticed Hillel's old voice-mail—*Was it only yesterday he'd called?*—and deleted it without listening to it.

She was on her own.

She thought about Vered. She was putting more than her career at risk by going after Mashiak alone. What would the custody judge think if he found out she'd gone after a dangerous suspect on her own? Rafi, of course, would rub it in her face. More evidence of her dereliction of maternal duty.

She quickly shut down these thoughts. She needed to focus on staying awake. She'd been up for almost twenty-four hours straight. She needed to stay sharp if she was going to get the jump on the American preacher.

The sky began to lighten. Off to the east, the clouds pinked, then whitened. She still couldn't see beyond the cliff's edge, but she knew that Mashiak was down there. She just hoped she could stop him in time.

DAY 5

Friday

76

From his hiding place behind a boulder, Pinkas Mashiak watched the light creep across the broad plain until it reached the eastern slopes of the surrounding hills. The warming sun slowly drew the chill out of his bones. It had been a long, anxious night, crouching here in the dark. His long limbs ached. His cramped muscles craved movement.

And then he spotted the caves.

Cut into the base of a low, barren mountainside were two stone cavities. One was quite large, its entrance almost completely blocked by rubble. The mouth of the other cave was low and shaped like a dog's head. Had he not been looking for this second cave, he might have missed it, mistaking it for a shadow. But it was this smaller cave that he'd been seeking. It was this cave that had appeared to him long ago in a childhood vision.

A grouping of vertical boulders stood near the mouth of the small cave. On one of them perched a large bird with a white head, a sharp gray beak, and golden feathers. Nearby grew a plant shaped like a seven-boughed menorah, its branches flanking the stem on both sides. The branches looked two-dimensional as if steam-pressed by an invisible hand.

It was exactly as it had appeared to him when he was a boy. Exactly as described in the final line of the Copper Scroll: "*In the pit, which is to the north of Kochalit, its entrance hidden, and tombs are at its opening.*"

He had found ancient Kochalit.

He'd learned since coming to Israel that this white-headed, golden-feathered bird was a griffon vulture, a raptor still commonly seen in deserts in this part of the world. And the menorah plant was *salvia palaestina*, whose multiple branches often grew in laddered arcs like this. But how was it possible that young Troy Quimby, a boy living in rural West Virginia, could have known about such things—unless they'd been expressly communicated to him by the Voice of God?

When he had first heard the Voice speak, he'd been only three years old, too young to understand what he was hearing. His Mama and Grandmom had called it his "imaginary friend." Many children had them, they told him, nothing to be ashamed of. But even then, he'd known it was more than that. Even at that tender age he'd known that he was special. He had been chosen. Still, he hadn't argued with them. They always looked so worried when he described his visions to them, when he shared the holy mysteries the Voice revealed to him. When he told them after some years that the Voice hardly spoke to him anymore, they were relieved. He was lying, of course, but they left him alone after that.

The teasing at school also eased up when he stopped revealing these fantastical conversations to the other boys and his teachers. But the bullying didn't stop. Many days, he came home covered in blood. The Voice told him not to mind; assured him that he was destined for great things. Such trials happened to all who had been chosen. He needed to have faith and be patient.

It was only much later that he'd come to understand who he'd been talking to all these years. None other than the Holy Ghost! This bolt of recognition had jolted him like a second baptism. That was the moment he'd truly come of age as God's chosen prophet. From that moment on, his conversations with the Voice had become more give and take, like with Abraham and Moses in the Bible. He'd done some talking as well as listening. Sometimes, he'd even challenged the Voice, wrestling like Jacob with the angel. Eagerly, he'd waited for another sign, instructing him how he could serve his Master. But nothing had appeared. So he'd continued to wait.

Then, one day in church, he'd been seized by the Holy Spirit. Leaping up from the pew, he'd begun to preach, sweat pouring down his face, his lungs heaving. And soon, he had his own church, The Good News Gospel Church, which grew and grew, until they had to put up a new building to accommodate his burgeoning flock.

Then, the Voice had revealed to him the next step of his journey: he needed to move to the Holy Land. Leave everything behind. *Go forth to a land that I will show you.* It was another test. He was to start a new church in Jerusalem and assemble a flock there. Then, he was to wait for another sign. The final one.

So he'd sold his double wide, said goodbye to his tearful congregation, and boarded a plane for Israel. And here he was, six months later, almost at the end of his astonishing journey. He was about to fulfill his special destiny as God's Messiah. In a matter of hours, he would herald the End of Days!

77

In the pale light of dawn, Maya began to make out details in the surrounding terrain. Near her lay a tumble of rust-colored boulders and scrub vegetation. Here and there, desert blooms sprouted out of cracked ochre soil. To her right stood a lone tamarisk, its trunk gnarled and leaning toward the ground, its gray-green needles moist with dew that would soon evaporate in the sun. Behind her, the zigzag goat path disappeared behind a heap of rocks carpeted with yellow lichen.

A scratching sound now caught her attention. Instinctively, she crouched down, her eyes searching for danger. She drew her gun from its holster and pointed it at the edge of the cliff. Had Mashiak already found the scroll and was now headed back to his car? She had no place to hide. She cocked the gun and placed her index finger lightly on the trigger. Her heart thundered in her chest. She pictured the dew beading on the tamarisk needles and licked her parched lips.

A pair of curved horns now rose from below the edge of the cliff, followed by a tawny bearded head. It was followed by the large body of an adult male ibex. The animal froze when it caught sight of her. Maya, too, froze. Slowly, the ibex lowered its head and angled its sharp horns in her direction, preparing to charge. She held her breath, her finger tensing on the trigger. Time slowed, then stopped.

Suddenly, the ibex raised its head, shook its coiled horns, and scampered up and over the cliff's edge. Its horned head erect, it bounded past Maya and headed toward the tamarisk tree. In seconds, it was lost from view.

Maya laughed and rose from her tight crouch. Her shoulders collapsed. Her sweaty hand clutching the pistol relaxed its tight grip. With her thumb, she relocked the safety on her gun. Then, she stretched both arms into the air and bent over to reach down toward her toes.

She took several sips from the half-empty water bottle. The water was warm but quenched her intense thirst. She ate her second protein bar. There was no telling how long she would be out here. Her training had prepared her to ration everything. Even adrenalin.

A rind of sun peeked over the hills toward the east. A few dark-winged birds circled in the thermals overhead. Several hundred feet below stretched an empty desert landscape of sand and stone, cradled between a semi-circle of craggy hills. Maya imagined that this was what the moon looked like up close. There was no sign of human habitation. The only things moving were dust devils. The shadowed eastern slope, ringed by low mountains, was pocked with crevices and piles of dark slag.

Maya reproached herself for leaving her small field binoculars behind in the car. Fortunately, her natural vision was excellent. She squinted to shut out some of the glaring sunlight and examined the desolate landscape below. She discerned traces of human presence.

The broad plain seemed to be the site of an abandoned or suspended archaeological dig. Layers of loose dirt covered brown plastic sheeting. Sections of ancient walls protruded between the plastic sheets, piled with sandbags to prevent water from eroding mud bricks and loosening stones. A barbed wire fence protected the antiquities from theft. It also prevented people and animals from falling into the covered trenches. Off to one side sat a dark shipping container, concealed by shadow, for storing tools and unprocessed artifacts. She strained to locate the placards usually posted by the Israel Antiquities Authority, forbidding entry to archaeological excavation areas. She couldn't see any from this far away.

Her eyes scanned the dark perimeter of the dig, where the mountains met the flat plain. The sun had not yet lit up the western flank of the mountains, but the north, east, and south edges of the semi-circular plain revealed several low caves. Mashiak could be hiding in any one of these, searching for the Treasure Scroll. And lying in wait for her.

Maya looked down at the steep cliffside. The surface was uneven, a hardened scree of rock and clay, affording plenty of foot and handholds for experienced climbers. Broken zigzagging lines of packed clay indicated where a footpath had once snaked from the top of the cliff to the plain below. Centuries of erosion had sliced away so much of the path that it was no longer a safe way down.

Too bad she was not an ibex or mountain goat, so she could scramble down to the bottom, surefooted and unafraid. Too bad she was so afraid of heights. She wished Masha was with her now to talk her through her fear. Maybe she should just wait for the rest of her team to arrive. But it was too risky to wait. Once Mashiak got hold of the scroll, he would proceed straightaway with his plans.

Then again, maybe she didn't have to climb down to the bottom to catch Mashiak. She could just wait for him to emerge from his hiding place, then pick him off as he made his way across the open plain toward the cliff. She was an excellent marksman. She'd just have to wait until he got close enough. But if she missed, he'd retreat back into the caves and escape after dark. No, her best option was to surprise him while he was busy looking for his precious scroll. That's when he'd be most off-guard.

Drawing in her breath, her pulse racing, she headed over the edge of the cliff. Carefully, she retraced the ibex's steep climb. She inched her way down, finding scant purchase among the rocks jutting out from the cliff. Often, her sandaled foot slipped from its toehold, forcing her to cling to the rock face like an insect pinned against a windshield. Several times, she thought about climbing back up, waiting for the others. But she pushed on. She willed herself not to look down.

She had no idea how long it took her to descend to the plain below. When she finally touched flat ground, she let out a loud breath. She sank to her knees and sobbed with relief. Then, she swiftly made her way to a nearby boulder and took shelter in its shade. The sun was now fully visible above the mountains. Its incandescent rays blasted the air with blinding light and heat.

Looking around her, Maya noticed a small puddle of fine sand lying in a crater-like depression between several ridges of baked clay. Perhaps it had been deposited by a recent sandstorm. In the middle of the sandy patch was a large footprint, pointing south. When she looked in that direction, she noted a small cluster of stone mounds. Squinting, she could just make out two caves behind the mounds: one blocked by rubble, the other much smaller, its low entrance shaped like a dog's head. Perched on one of the stone pillars was a large griffon vulture, surveying the broad plain with its obsidian eyes. Scouting for prey.

Before heading toward the cave, she decided to call Roni. To bring him up to speed, just in case. She wasn't quite sure where she was. The last road sign she'd seen had been the turn-off to Tekoa. If Mashiak killed her, they could ping her phone to find her body. It was a good thing she'd fully charged her cell phone during the drive south. She grinned at her dark humor. She had no intention of letting the American preacher get the better of her.

She tapped Roni's number on speed-dial. Her screen immediately flashed back: "No Service." Although Maya was generally not superstitious, she couldn't help interpreting this state of affairs as karmic payback. The Evil Eye was punishing her for lying to Roni about the unreliable cell service out here. Now, her words had come true. She was truly cut off from the rest of the world.

Cautiously, she headed in the direction indicated by the giant footprint. Disturbed by her approach, the griffon vulture took flight, its long golden wings casting a giant shadow on the ground. It was soon soaring with the other dark birds in the thermals high above.

Every few meters, she paused. When she reached the first stone mound, she crouched down and listened, stilling her breath. No sounds came from either cave. Pulling her service pistol from its holster, she edged closer.

Now, she heard metal scraping rock. The sound came from the smaller cave. A man's shrill voice muttered angrily. More scraping, this time softer. A shovel scuffed against coarse sand. More muttering. A shoe stomped on the ground, kicking free loose stones.

Then, a high-pitched voice cried out jubilantly: "Thank you, Jesus!"

Her pistol cocked, Maya crept up to the low, dark mouth of the smaller cave. She hoped that Mashiak was too distracted to look out toward the light. And she hoped that both his hands grasped a shovel, not a gun.

78

WITHOUT MAKING A SOUND MAYA ducked down and stepped into the cave.

Mashiak stood with his back toward her, his hands raised. His thick knuckles almost scraped the cave's serrated roof. In one hand, he clutched a small steel spade; in the other, a dark oblong pouch. As her eyes adjusted to the dark, Maya saw that the pouch was made of leather, cracked and spidered with age. It was cinched at the top by a frayed cord.

"Mashiak!"

The tall man spun around. In the gritty light, his dark eyes glittered. Was it with malice or madness?

Mashiak immediately assumed a defensive stance, one long leg thrust forward, the sharp point of his spade leveled at Maya. He shielded the leather pouch behind his back.

"You ain't gonna stop me now, you whorin' daughter of Belial!"

"It's over, Mashiak. Give it to me."

She aimed the SIG Sauer at the center of Mashiak's broad chest, clutching the grip with both hands. She kept her face expressionless, but her heart pounded inside her chest.

She needed him alive to discover the details of his plot. But how would she control him until the others arrived? She had left her cuffs behind in the car. And even though she was armed, Mashiak had the greater advantage in height and weight.

She didn't like her odds.

Nobody knows where I am.

She was on her own. Just as she had foolishly wanted to be.

Mashiak began rocking back and forth on his heels, staring up at the cave's pitted roof. Then, he looked down at the floor and started muttering to himself. Maya couldn't make out his words. He waved the small spade like a snake charmer's flute. His dark eyes were glazed, unseeing.

"At the time of Judgment, the Sword of God shall hasten. All the sons of iniquity shall be no more. For the battle shall be to the Most High God!"

His Southern accent was so thick that Maya could barely understand him.

"Save the hellfire speeches for your fans, preacher."

Her grip tightened on the gun. She fixed her aim on an invisible spot in the center of Mashiak's barrel chest.

"To me, you're just an ordinary terrorist. Not the Messiah."

Mashiak raised his large bald head and stared at Maya. His gawping eyes looked past her, gazing into the stippled light streaming into the cave.

"The heavenly warriors shall scourge the Earth. It shall not end a'fore the appointed destruction, which shall be forever 'n without compare!"

She needed to stop him before he completely spun out of control. She knew from experience that it was especially difficult to subdue agitated suspects. Like comic book superheroes, their natural powers increased when fueled by madness.

"I've heard enough from you, Mashiak! Now, shut up!"

Maya's voice ricocheted off the cave walls. Some bats sleeping in a dark corner roused and flew out of the cave, with high-pitched squeals and a loud flapping of leathery wings. The noise startled Mashiak out of his trance.

"You'll never git yer hands on this scroll! The treasure's mine!"

Waving her gun sideways, Maya steered Mashiak toward the mouth of the cave. She'd have to improvise, figure out how to control him until she could get him back to her car and into cuffs. If she had to, she'd put a bullet in his arm or leg to show him she meant business.

"Let's go, preacher! I don't have all day."

Mashiak didn't move.

"You have five seconds."

Maya pulled back the pistol's firing pin.

79

"Maya!"

The thunderous shout came from outside. It echoed in the resounding hollow of the cave, then swiftly died away. Maya recognized the voice immediately. Hillel Stone! What was he doing here?

Squinting, Hillel stepped under the cave's low-slung opening, his eyes clouded by the muted light.

"I recognized your car at the top of the cliff. How did you find this place? And who does that blue Fiat...."

Thrown off-balance by Hillel's arrival, Maya momentarily took her eyes off her prisoner. She twisted her head toward Hillel and was immediately blinded by the sunlight flaming in.

Seeing his chance, Mashiak lunged at Maya. His right hand closed tightly around her gun. The cocked SIG discharged its bullet, which ricocheted off a wall and lodged somewhere in the roof of the cave. A few more bats swooped down in panic, shooting out of the cave, their wings chirring like swirling sand.

Maya leapt toward Mashiak, but it was too late. Her own gun now pointed at her head. Mashiak then swung the snub-nosed barrel toward Hillel, who had moved further inside. Then, back toward Maya. Nervously eyeing the seesawing gun, Hillel walked over to Maya and stood beside her.

"So, whadda we have here?" Mashiak giggled. But his eyes remained glazed. "Another spy?"

He continued to wag the gun back and forth between his two captives. His mouth was distended in a grotesque smile.

"So much for Israeli Intelligence!"

Mashiak guffawed. Though it was not yet the strident cackle of a man possessed, Maya knew it was only a matter of time. At this point, the man had only the barest grip on sanity.

"I'm most definitely not an intelligence agent," Hillel said. Maya detected a hint of umbrage in his tone. "I'm a Qumran scholar. I've come here to look for the duplicate of the Copper Scroll. I assume you're here for the same reason."

Hillel boldly looked his captor up and down, his eyes coming to rest on the giant's shiny bald head and the red, scaly lump at the nape of his thick neck. Then, he smiled.

"So you're the one who impersonated Habib Salameh at the Qumran Archives," Hillel said. "It's obvious that the only way you could've known about De Vaux's notes was from Boaz Goldmayer's computer. That makes you his killer."

"You don't know nothin' about any of this!" Mashiak laughed. His voice was like broken glass. "The scroll's got a secret message meant for my eyes alone. I been chosen to redeem the Temple treasures and bring 'em back to the Third Temple."

"Is that so?" Hillel snorted, making no effort to disguise his contempt. "Well, to me, you're just another greedy treasure hunter, looting antiquity."

"That's a lie! The treasure I seek is holiness! The Lord done chose me as His messenger. To herald the comin' of His glorious Kingdom!"

From behind his back, Mashiak retrieved the worn leather pouch, clasping it tightly in his left hand. He held it out toward Hillel.

"Here's the proof of my divine election!"

Hillel stared at the withered bag in Mashiak's hand, his blue eyes transfixed. His lips parted, revealing a slight gap between his upper teeth. His eyebrows arched together sharply like a dark seabird winging toward shore.

"It's jes' like the Voice promised! This scroll's been here, waitin' for cent'ries. Waitin' for me to come and git it. But before I c'n build a new Temple and put the treasures back where they belong, I first gotta purge the heathen abominations from the Lord's Holy Mountain!"

Maya eyed the small steel spade lying on the ground, where Mashiak had tossed it when he'd gone for her gun. It lay less than a meter away. Mashiak seemed to have forgotten about it. His eyes remained fixed on his two captives. He waved Maya's gun back and forth between them, mechanically, like a metronome.

Maya cleared her throat. Hillel turned his head toward her.

"Salameh's dead," she said. "Murdered by him."

She thrust her chin toward Mashiak.

Mashiak threw back his enormous head and laughed. His madness was now in full flower. His dark eyes glittered through his wire-rimmed glasses like shards of slate. His body twitched. But the SIG Sauer in his right hand kept a steady bead on his prisoners.

"Miss...Rye-mahn, i'n't it? Habib warned me 'bout you."

Maya's gold-green eyes bored into Mashiak's glassy pupils. She grimaced, her lips bloodless.

"That's right. Maya Rimon. Israeli Intelligence. Oh, but where are my manners?"

She swept her open palm from Hillel toward Mashiak.

"Professor Hillel Stone, allow me to introduce Preacher Pinkas Mashiak, a.k.a. Tyrell Quimby from Davis Creek, West Virginia. A.k.a. the Messiah."

Hillel tittered nervously. Mashiak glared at him through narrowed eyes. Then, he stomped on the cave floor with one giant foot. A small cloud of dust plumed into the air. A swarm of tiny motes danced in ribbons of light, then settled.

"Bet you find my beliefs ludicrous, don'cha, Professor? Well, I feel the same 'bout you scholars. Obsessed with dead history. Yer nothin' but vampires! Blasphemin' ghouls. I speak for the livin' God!"

While Mashiak ranted on, Maya wracked her brain for a plan of escape. Now that Hillel was here, it was two against one. Could he help her overpower this mad giant and disarm him? Chances were that Hillel would get himself shot in the attempt. But they had to do something—and soon. Mashiak was becoming more unstable by the minute.

And he had his own urgent timetable to follow.

80

"So what're you going to do, preacher?" said Maya. "Shoot us and leave us here for the jackals? You obviously have no qualms about murdering people."

"I'm only doin' what the Voice commands! The End is near!"

Mashiak was shouting, arguing with the stone walls. Spittle flew from his mouth. It speckled the dry ground with dark stains.

If Hillel could only distract him for a moment, she could go for the gun or spade. But how to signal Hillel without tipping off their captor? Then, she remembered what the wait-staff captain had told her, when she'd shown him Mashiak's photograph at the hotel.

"Yes, I recognize him. One of the fill-ins I hired for the conference banquet. I don't have enough of my own servers to cover such a crowd. That dumb golem *barely spoke a word of Hebrew. But I can't afford to be too choosy these days. Most of my overflow staff are African migrants. I can no longer depend on Palestinians like I used to. You never know when they'll get jammed up at a checkpoint and not show up."*

Maya cleared her throat. Then, she scuffed one sandal on the sandy ground.

"Tishma, haveri! Nedaber b-ivrit."

"Hey, none of that Israeli spy shit!" shouted Mashiak. "Speak English!"

The American preacher was again rocking back and forth again, heel to toe, muttering under his breath. Every few seconds, he glanced down at his watch.

"Aseh ma-shehu l'imshokh t'sumet lev mi-meni," said Maya. She barked out the words. Create a diversion! It was an order, not a request.

Hillel stared at her. Did she have to spell it out for him? Distract him, dammit!

Finally, Hillel started to shuffle sideways, slowly moving away from her, widening the gap between the two of them. Half a meter. A meter.

Mashiak noticed. He swung the gun toward Hillel, then toward Maya.

"Hey, back together, you two!"

Hillel ignored him. He continued to edge sideways. A meter and a half.

Mashiak stepped forward, touching the barrel of the gun to Hillel's head. The tall preacher's dark, burning eyes narrowed. His thick black brows almost met above his giant scythe of a nose.

"No way you c'n stop me now! Everythin's in place and ready to go!"

It was now or never.

"Shut your eyes, Hillel!"

Diving for the spade and grabbing its handle, Maya scooped up loose sediment from the cave floor and flung it up at Mashiak. The coarse grit flew into his face.

"Yeow!"

The giant man staggered back, dropping the gun and leather pouch as he clawed at his eyes.

Maya dropped the shovel and lunged for the gun, scraping her arms and upper body on the rough ground. Hillel dove to retrieve the dropped leather pouch, clutching it to his chest like a wounded child.

His sight cleared, Mashiak quickly sized up the situation. His only choice now was flight. With a rueful glance at the leather pouch gripped in Hillel's fingers, he ran toward the mouth of the cave. And he kept running into the searing light of the rising desert sun. A thick cloud of dust swirled in his wake.

Maya and Hillel raced after him. But they couldn't match the tall man's meter-long stride. The distance between them lengthened.

By the time Mashiak reached the base of the cliff, he had enough of a lead to scramble up the rutted sandstone wall and disappear from sight before Maya could get off a shot.

The two of them clambered up the cliff after him. Maya had to halt from time to time to reach down a hand to help Hillel, who kept losing his grip on the loose shingle.

By the time they reached the top of the cliff, Mashiak was gone.

81

On the way back to Jerusalem, Maya pushed the old Corolla hard, by turns praising and cursing Valdis, her cocky Latvian mechanic. By now, the morning sun had burned away the mist. The sky was a brilliant blue. High above, several vultures surfed invisible currents. Their dark wings flashed in the sun.

"Keep an eye out for Route 398," Maya told Hillel. "It's easy to miss."

Maya glanced over at him. Hillel was hunched over in the passenger seat. Because of her speed, Maya had to keep her eyes fixed on the road, but she could watch him out of the corner of her eye. On his lap was the Corolla's rubber floor mat. Lying on its dusty surface was the worn leather pouch. Gingerly, Hillel untied the frayed thong trussing the mouth of the pouch and eased the parchment scroll out of the bag. He held the furled scroll delicately between his fingers, as if it were made of glass. Or nitroglycerin.

With practiced patience, he unrolled the yellowed parchment, setting it down gently atop the weathered pouch. Then, he began to read. His index finger floated over the ancient Greek writing like a hydroplane, skimming over the parchment surface without touching it. *A scholar's soft hands.* An electric shock suddenly stung Maya's sweaty thighs. She forced her attention back to the pitted road.

She fished her cell phone out of her pocket and speed-dialed Roni. The call didn't go through. She must still be out of cell tower range, or maybe, he was avoiding her.

Suddenly, she spotted the sign for Route 398. It was almost completely obscured by a layer of sand. Grabbing the steering wheel with both hands, she wrenched it sharply to the right, then swerved onto the exit on two wheels. She had to brake hard to prevent the Corolla from rolling over. She gunned the engine and slammed down on the accelerator. She was soon traveling at ninety-five kilometers an hour, fifteen above the speed limit. She hoped no conscientious highway patrol officer tried to flag her down. She had no intention of pulling over.

"Listen to this!"

"We almost missed the turn-off, Hillel! Pay attention to the road, not to that stupid scroll."

Hillel opened his mouth to respond, then clamped it shut. "Sorry."

His voice was contrite. But he soon returned to his previous enthusiasm. Maya thought he sounded like a schoolboy, showing off his good report card to his parents.

"You have no idea how significant this is!"

The Corolla hit a pothole and leapt off the road. Hillel let out a cry, as if his skin had been pierced by a sharp blade.

"Sorry," said Maya. "I can't slow down. Once Mashiak reaches the city, it'll be almost impossible to track him." Maya's voice gentled. "Why don't you put that scroll away until we get there?"

"Not a chance! I've waited my whole life for something like this!"

It was useless to talk to him. He was as obsessed as the American preacher. If he ended up damaging the priceless scroll during this wild ride, that was on him. After a wait of two thousand years, what difference did an hour's delay make? But then she would never understand scholars. They lived on a different planet.

For the next ten minutes Hillel pored over the first lines of the ancient text, muttering excitedly to himself. Maya considered interrupting him but held back. He was deaf and blind to the real world.

"This isn't it! Oh, my God!"

Hillel's startled cry caused Maya to swerve out of her lane. For a few moments, the Corolla bounced along the gravel-strewn shoulder until she managed to wrestle it back onto the macadam.

"Don't yell like that, dammit! I almost lost control of the car."

Hillel paid no attention to her reproof. His eyes were locked on the wrinkled parchment like twin lasers.

"This isn't the duplicate scroll! It's in Greek. The Temple priests would never have written in Greek. And it's in the first person. Seems like some sort of chronicle. Written by a Jewish woman named Mariamne."

Hillel began reading the Greek words aloud. After a moment, he paused, took a deep breath, and looked over at Maya. She raised her ginger eyebrows, then giggled.

"It's all Greek to me."

Hillel didn't join in her laughter. His face was drained of color, his breathing shallow.

In a hushed voice, he painstakingly translated the first few lines into English:

> *My name is Mariamne, daughter of Jonathan and*
> *Livia, both of blessed memory. I was born when*
> *Claudius still sat upon the throne of Rome. I spent my*
> *youth in Tiberias, a beautiful city on the harp-shaped*
> *Sea of Kinneret.*

"Do you realize what this is?" Hillel's voice trembled with excitement. "It's the first Dead Sea Scroll ever found that was written by a woman! This could be the most significant find in seventy years!"

In his excitement, Hillel squeezed the rolled-up portion of the scroll with his left hand. Then, mortified by his recklessness, he loosened his fingers so that the scroll nestled lightly in his palm, like a fresh egg.

Maya burst out laughing.

"So it's not a treasure map? It's a goddam hoax!"

Hillel stared at her, his mouth agape. Then, his brow dipped and furrowed.

"No, it's not a hoax. It's just not the scroll we were looking for. It's something else entirely. Altogether unexpected. Of course, it'll have to be tested by experts to get an exact dating. But if it turns out to be authentic, this will be a ground-breaking find. Unique in Second Temple literature."

"But what about the Treasure Scroll? Wasn't that what got Goldmayer killed? And what about the Temple treasures? I thought you said that there's no way to find them without the duplicate scroll."

"Ah."

Hillel smiled, freeing the tight creases crinkling the corners of his cornflower-blue eyes. Maya thought he looked almost boyish. If he would only shave off that grizzled beard.

"You're right to be suspicious when it comes to stories of lost treasure. The field has seen its share of scam artists and hoaxes. But it's not *this* scroll that deserves our suspicion." He gently tapped the weathered parchment on his lap. "If there's any hoax here, we need to look for it within the Copper Scroll. The priestly authors of that scroll wanted to make sure that the Romans would never find the Temple treasures. They wanted them to believe they needed the duplicate scroll to lead them to the treasures."

"Are you saying that there never was a duplicate scroll?"

"Possibly. Or maybe the priests hid the parchment copy somewhere else. Not the site that De Vaux identified as ancient Kochalit. We'll probably never know."

"Then, if this scroll isn't a copy of the Copper Scroll, what is it? Who was Mariamne?"

"We'll only find that out after I translate the rest of this scroll."

Hillel fell silent. He stared out of the passenger window. There was not much to see. As they drew closer to Jerusalem, barren desert and scattered Arab villages gave way to tidy Jewish settlements and planted fields. At this early hour, massive, wheeled sprinklers were showering tender young crops. The crystalline spray sparkled in the bright sun.

Maya interrupted Hillel's musing. Her voice was gleeful.

"I can't wait to see that mad preacher's face when he discovers that he's bet on the wrong horse! His precious treasure map turns out to be nothing but an ancient lady's diary."

Hillel remained silent. His eyes vacantly scanned the passing landscape.

Suddenly, Maya pointed her right index finger at a large green sign on the side of the road. It was the turn-off for Jerusalem. She eased down on the brake, then swerved onto the ramp.

"We still might be able to catch him. Route 60's a faster road."

Maya pressed down hard on the gas pedal. The speedometer shot up to one hundred and twenty kilometers per hour. The old Corolla shuddered and rattled, then grumpily accommodated to its new speed.

82

CASSANDRA SAT UP ON THE blue yoga mat and wriggled her lower back. She had fallen asleep in child's pose last night: her calves resting on the floor, the rest of her body sloped forward, the thin arms lying, palms up, alongside her torso, her forehead resting on the padded mat. It was the most relaxing asana she knew.

She had expected her captor to send someone last night. To finish the job. But no one had come. More than twenty-four hours had gone by.

She knew she was of no more use to them. And she knew too much. They would see no alternative but to silence her. Why were they making her wait?

She stood up and padded over to the refrigerator. She'd been too depressed last night to eat anything. But now, she was ravenous. She cut up some vegetables, made a simple dressing of olive oil and lemon juice, and wolfed down the salad. Then, she drank almost a full bottle of water. All the time, her ear was cocked for the rattle of the hasp. The lock clicking open.

She left the dirty dishes in the sink and walked into the bathroom. Humming tunelessly to herself, she washed her face and brushed her teeth. Her mouth felt dry.

Gazing into the mirror, she ran her fingers through her spiky purple hair. The hair was growing out. The dirty blonde roots were showing. When had she last had it cut? She couldn't remember. She noted that her hazel eyes were bloodshot. Dark, droopy bags smudged the skin beneath the lower lids. Barely a trace remained of purple eyeshadow and black eyeliner. She stared at her pierced eyebrows, lips, and nasal septum. Her father was right. She did look grotesque with all that metal spearing her face. She hoped they removed all the piercings before they shipped her body home for burial. If they ever found it.

She walked out of the bathroom and padded over to the broad wooden desk. She sank down into the cushioned chair. Her lower spine hugged the chair's sleek, convex contours. She stared at the empty surface of the desk, where the laptop had once sat. She had no idea how long she remained there, staring into space. She felt paralyzed.

And then, from some unknown reservoir of inner strength, she felt the stirrings of hope. What if she could escape? After her last attempt, she'd been too afraid to try again. But maybe, this time, she'd succeed. Maybe he wasn't coming back. Maybe he'd left her here to starve or die of loneliness. She couldn't just give up!

She re-examined the two windows. No weak points in the iron bars. She rattled the front door knob. No give there. She tried to visualize the outside lock. When she had first been brought here, she'd caught a glimpse of it. The mechanism was made of a metallic alloy with four rotating disks. No way she could crack it from inside the apartment.

What about the neighbors? The apartment was located in an Arab section of East Jerusalem. Her captor had warned her not to make any noise, or there would be consequences. From him, not from them. What would these Arabs do to her if they found out she was being kept here, a prisoner? Could it be any worse than dying alone? Or waiting for her executioner to show up?

She began banging on the walls. The sound of her small fists hammering solid stone was barely audible. She looked around. She spotted a cast iron skillet lying on the wooden shelf under the sink. It was so heavy that she had to use both hands to lift it. The sound of cast iron hitting stone was oddly satisfying. She banged the skillet on each of the four walls, leaving deep gouges in the whitewashed plaster.

Then, she thwacked the skillet against the cement floor. She worried that the floor was too thick to carry sound to the apartment below.

She kept up the racket until her arms tired. She rested for a few minutes and drank more water. Then, she resumed her banging, yelling "Help!" as she swung the heavy pan. Since it was almost nine, she guessed that most people were already at work or at the market. But someone had to be home, caring for children or elderly parents.

And then she heard a voice outside. It was a young boy, shouting something in Arabic. She ran to the front door and pounded on the thick wood with both fists.

"Help me! I've been kidnapped!"

She heard more shouts in Arabic. Then silence.

She waited, not sure whether to resume banging on the door or just give up. That boy might have been her only hope. And now, he was gone.

Then, she heard him again. This time, he was accompanied by other boys. She also heard the voice of a grown man. Was it him? The voices were excited and eager. They began fidgeting with the outside lock.

"I'm an American! I'm being held hostage! Please help me!"

They began to repeat "Amrikiin" to each other. Now, they were laughing. Some kind of heavy tool rang out as it struck metal. She heard the clang of shattered steel. Daylight suddenly flooded into the room as the door burst open. She was immediately surrounded by several giggling boys with shiny, black hair and wide, dark eyes. Behind them stood a handsome young man holding a heavy wrench. He smiled shyly at her. He pointed at her purple hair and said something, which made the boys laugh.

"Thank you! Thank you so much!"

Cassandra threw her arms around the startled young man and kissed him on his cheek. He nodded, blushing, and laughed.

"You American?"

"Yes." Cassandra's eyes filled with tears. "I just want to go home."

He looked at her blankly.

"To America. Memphis, Tennessee."

"Ah, Memphees. Elvees. Grand Ole Opree."

They both laughed. Cassandra wanted to throw her arms around him again, but she restrained herself. She didn't want him to get the wrong idea.

They fell silent and just stood there, staring at each other. The young man wore faded blue jeans and a tee shirt displaying a scantily-clad Lady Gaga. His handsome face sported a day or two of dark stubble. He wore black high tops on his feet. Without laces or socks.

Cassandra ran over to the refrigerator and scooped up the remaining vegetables. She carried them back to the young man. He took them gratefully, bowing to her as if she had gifted him with treasure, then left. The boys ran after him, looking back over their shoulders and pointing at her, laughing. Then, they were gone.

Suddenly overcome by an overwhelming fatigue, Cassandra staggered back inside the apartment and collapsed onto the bed. Struggling to catch her breath, she stared up at the white ceiling, noticing for the first time a few mottled water stains and several patches of peeling plaster.

Now that she was free, she needed a plan. Out of the pocket of her shorts, she dug out the thumb drive she'd hidden away, containing the decrypted files downloaded from Goldmayer's laptop. She wasn't sure what to do with them. Maybe she could use the files as leverage if she was caught by the Israeli authorities, charged with aiding terrorists. Or they might work as bargaining chips to win her safe passage home.

But first, she needed to contact Maya Rimon. She remembered meeting the Israeli agent at the LTM Center when she'd worked there. The woman had seemed smart and honest. She needed to warn her about the Chess Master's plan, an imminent terrorist attack. It's what Mariamne would have done. She would have tried to save her people.

He had confiscated her cell phone. She thought about running after her young rescuer, but he'd disappeared. And it would be ridiculous to ask anybody in this neighborhood to contact Israeli Intelligence. She was on her own.

Where should she go? She had no money, no passport, no ID. For all she knew, she was wanted by the police.

She recalled her kidnapper's chilling words: *"This man has grand designs, and a rather exacting timetable. I fear that all he will succeed in doing is setting off another pointless bloodbath in an already-traumatized city."*

Cassandra knew where the Chess Master would strike. It was the only place that could trigger a bloodbath. Maybe she couldn't head off the attack, but she could alert the Israelis, so they could try to stop him before it was too late.

Taking a final look around her prison, Cassandra retrieved two plastic bottles of water from the refrigerator and strode out into the bright light of the Jerusalem morning. She didn't close the door behind her.

83

MAYA AND HILLEL WERE NOW only a few kilometers from the metropolitan outskirts of Jerusalem. They had to catch up with Mashiak before he entered the city, or he would quickly vanish into the tangled labyrinth of East Jerusalem.

Maya gripped the steering wheel with white knuckles. When she glanced over at Hillel, he was still staring out the window, transported to another world. With his left hand, he absentmindedly stroked his salt-and-pepper beard. Occasionally, he placed a hand on top of his small black kippah. His right hand rested lightly on the furled scroll. Sinking lower into the bucket seat, he expelled a loud sigh.

"These aren't the words of a privileged aristocrat or a crazed zealot. Mariamne was just an innocent young woman caught up in one of the greatest tragedies ever to befall the Jewish People. Until now, we've only had Josephus's account of what happened. But now, we have a second eyewitness account. Mariamne's narrative will provide an entirely different perspective. We may finally learn what really happened."

Maya turned to face him, her full lips rounded into an amused grin. Her gold-green eyes sparkled with amusement.

"You know, Hillel, you have the strangest priorities. As my mother would say: *W't n-n'ila herbo be-s-sofar*. 'During Ne'ilah, you run away with the shofar.'"

Hillel looked at her, lost.

"At a time when Israel's very survival hangs in the balance, all you can think about is translating a two-thousand-year-old 'tell-all.' We do live in different worlds, don't we?"

Hillel chuckled, then abruptly fell silent. His hands gently cradled the parchment scroll on his lap.

They drove on without speaking. Hillel soon returned to reading the scroll. Maya glanced down at her fuel gauge. She was just below half a tank.

Maybe Mashiak will run out of gas. I should be so lucky. She giggled to herself.

Suddenly Maya's mobile began to jangle. She grabbed it from the cupholder, tearing it free of the charging cable that was plugged into the Corolla's cigarette lighter. She pressed the phone to her right ear.

"What?"

"It's your mother, Maya. No need to bark at me."

"Can't talk now, Ima. I'm in the middle of something."

"When aren't you in the middle of something? Anything to avoid talking to your mother."

"*Nu*, what is it?"

"It's about Vered."

Maya's heart plummeted down a dark well.

"What's happened?"

"When you didn't show up for the play last night, Rafi offered to take Vered home for the night and bring her to *gan* this morning."

"You didn't let him, did you?"

"I didn't see any harm in it, *habibi*. He *is* the girl's father."

"Did something happen to Vered?"

"The school just phoned. Vered never arrived at *gan*."

Maya's blood turned to ice. Her breathing quickened. Her right hand tightened around her mobile phone. What was that bastard up to? Was he kidnapping his own child?

"Rafi called Rivka and told her he was keeping Vered out of *gan* today, so he could bring her to a friend's wedding."

"Where's the wedding?"

"Some fancy party place called 'Ahar Kotleinu Hall.'"

Maya had heard of it but had never been there. Once a medieval caravansary, the ancient underground vault was now available for bar mitzvah and wedding parties. It was located almost directly beneath the ancient Holy of Holies.

Suddenly, she caught sight of Mashiak's car. The dark blue Fiat with the mismatched door was several car lengths ahead in the left lane.

"Sorry, Ima. Gotta go. Bye!"

With her thumb, she cut off the connection and thrust her phone into the pocket of her slacks. She thought about calling Roni but decided to wait until she caught up with the American preacher. Gunning the accelerator, she pushed the Corolla to 130. She began to weave in and out of the clotted traffic, ignoring the signs telling her to slow down, deaf to the blaring horns and angry shouts of motorists as she tailgated and passed them.

The two cars raced through the fashionable neighborhoods of Baka, Talpiot, and Abu Tor. Then, they left Route 60 and proceeded east on Sultan Suleiman Street. They circled the walls of the Old City, passing Herod's Gate.

Maya felt the adrenalin surge under her skin. Mashiak was heading straight for the Temple Mount.

84

THE BLUE FIAT REACHED LIONS' Gate and entered the Old City. Maya followed close behind, driving under the ancient stone arch. She soon caught sight of Mashiak's car, parked illegally near an empty loading zone, just inside the gate. She parked right behind it and turned off the Corolla's gasping engine. Hurriedly, she rummaged through the glove compartment until she found her Service parking permit. She slapped it down on the dashboard and jumped out of the car. Hillel remained seated, hunched over the ancient scroll.

"Earth to Hillel!" Maya leaned into the passenger side and clapped her hands loudly. "We've got to move fast, or we'll lose him."

Hillel looked up from the yellowed parchment. He glanced around, disoriented. Maya pointed through the windshield at the tall arched gate flanked by a pair of stone lions in bas-relief. He now recognized where he was. The entrance to the Muslim Quarter. Their car was already surrounded by dark faces, many swathed in keffiyahs and head scarves.

Hillel carefully rolled up the scroll, slid it back into its weathered pouch, and cinched it loosely with the leather thong. Then, holding the pouch delicately in one hand, he got out of the car and kicked the door shut behind him. The crowd of dark faces scattered. Maya clicked the fob, and the Corolla's trunk popped open. Hillel slid the pouch into a back corner, covering it with some loose papers and clothing. Then, he slammed down the trunk lid.

Maya now rushed headlong down the high-walled cobbled street that led away from the Lions' Gate into the Muslim Quarter. At this hour, the street was dense with foot and motor traffic. She constantly had to dodge parked cars, motorbikes and bicycles, merchants with wheeled carts, shoppers, and beggars.

Hillel ran behind her, straining to keep up, holding on tightly to his kippah with one hand.

As they ran, their eyes searched for a tall figure, towering above the crowd, running desperately toward the Temple Mount.

85

CASSANDRA ENTERED THE OLD CITY through the Damascus Gate. Coming in through this crowded entrance gave her the best chance of escaping detection. Since it was a Friday morning, the market stalls were mobbed with shoppers. And now that tourist season had begun, busloads of foreigners crowded the narrow lanes. Many bargained earnestly with the fawning Arab vendors, only to be fleeced in the end. They didn't seem to mind. It was all part of the authentic shuk experience.

Cassandra pushed her way through the dense crowd, fighting the agoraphobia that usually kept her away from the Old City. When she'd first arrived in Jerusalem six months ago, she'd come to the shuk a few times to look for souvenirs. But she'd always had to cut short her visits when panic forced her to flee. She promised herself that this time, she wouldn't leave until she'd achieved her goal: warning the Israeli authorities about the Chess Master.

As she made her way through the congested market, she glanced down at her frayed shorts and bare legs, her calves crisscrossed by thin sandal straps. Her tight white tee shirt drew attention to her small, pointy breasts, especially when she was jostled, which made her nipples poke out against the thin cotton. And her Koosh ball of purple hair made her stand out like a peacock among pigeons. She was definitely not dressed appropriately for this mission.

She heard her therapist's calming voice whispering in her ear: *Center yourself. Breathe in, breathe out. You can do this!*

With great effort, she stilled the anxiety strafing her upper chest. Using both hands, she pushed her way through the crowd until she came to a wooden stand displaying colored headscarves. She deliberately chose the dullest one, a square of muddy brown cotton, speckled with small yellow polka dots. She gave the old woman a few of the shekel coins she'd squirreled away in the back pocket of her shorts. Then, she thrust her way out of the crush, gulping huge mouthfuls of air as soon as she found a wall to lean against without attracting notice.

But what about all her piercings? If she wanted to pass as a pious Muslim woman, she'd have to ditch all that metal in her face. Crouching down with her back turned to passersby, she methodically removed the many silver studs and small hoops perforating her ears, eyebrows, nose, and tongue. She hoped that the confetti of tiny holes pitting her skin wouldn't give her away. She thrust the handful of silver jewelry into a pocket of her shorts. Then, she covered her head with the scarf, carefully tucking in every purple strand of hair.

A few moments later, she pushed on through a narrow lane. At another stand, she bought a brown wrap-around skirt that reached almost to her ankles and a dark brown shawl that covered the entire upper half of her body. Passing a shadowed storefront, she caught sight of herself in the dusty glass. She looked like a monk, swaddled in brown cloth from head to toe. She smiled at the transformation. It felt good to be invisible.

She passed quickly through the broad white stone plaza in front of the Western Wall. She ignored the dense congregation of black-suited men, wrapped in fringed shawls, swaying back and forth in prayer. She hurried past the women on the other side of the high separation screen, many of them wearing white lace doilies draped over their hair. Pressing close to the Wall on either side of the barrier, men and women kissed the ancient white stones and shoved folded slips of paper into cracks already crammed with previous visitors' supplications.

She looked past the broad plaza, focusing her eyes on the far-right side of the Wall, where a dark vertical slit broke the white surface.

This was her destination: the Mughrabi Gate, the only entrance to the Temple Mount accessible to non-Muslims. No one gave her a second glance as she approached the gate. She was just another pilgrim on her sacred path.

The sign posted in front of the Mughrabi Gate, written in Hebrew and English, read:

"Announcement and Warning: According to Torah Law, entering the Temple Mount area is strictly forbidden due to the holiness of this site. The Chief Rabbinate of Israel."

How strange that religious Jews regarded the Temple Mount as *too* sacred for human contact. Did that mean that too much holiness might be as deadly as its opposite? She would find out soon enough.

When she approached the first security post at the Mughrabi Gate, the Arab guard eyed her suspiciously. Undoubtedly it was her ivory skin and hazel eyes that gave her away. She lowered her gaze, staring intently at the man's black military boots. He addressed her in heavily-accented English, his voice gruff and unwelcoming.

"This gate not open Friday."

Cassandra shook her head, pretending not to understand. She lowered her eyes and tucked her chin into her chest. She mumbled a few words in gibberish that she hoped sounded like Albanian or Serbo-Croatian.

"No tourists Friday," the guard repeated. He lifted up his arm and thrust out his flat palm toward her. "Only Muslims."

Cassandra continued to shake her head, muttering, "*Allahu Akhbar.*" She tried to sound fervent, like the terrorists on TV, who shouted these words before they blew themselves up.

The guard, a middle-aged Arab with garlicky breath and dirty fingernails, placed his forefinger under her chin and lifted up her face to study her. Cassandra smiled and bobbed her head, repeating the two Arabic words until he released her chin. She let her head fall heavily onto her upper chest like a puppet released from its strings.

Out of the corner of her eye, she saw the guard's uniformed arm point toward a wooden bridge. Without hesitation, she rushed forward. The bridge was enclosed on all sides by narrow slats of wood. It reminded her of a cattle chute, herding dumb beasts to slaughter.

When she emerged from the covered bridge, she found herself in a broad courtyard lined with leafy trees. In front of her rose a bowl-shaped marble fountain, completed encircled by a knee-high stone wall and surrounded by an ornate wrought-iron fence. The fountain was sunk into a round depression, which sloped upward to the courtyard plaza in a series of terraced stone stairs. Protruding from the fountain's knee wall was a series of silver spigots, each faced by a low marble chair. Many of the seats were occupied by Muslim men, washing their feet before prayer.

But her attention did not remain long on the Al Kas Fountain. Looking up, she gazed at the imposing structure that dominated the scene: the gold-crowned Dome of the Rock. Its high octagonal walls were decorated with a dazzling mosaic of blue, white, and golden tiles. She'd read in her guidebook that this mosque had been built directly over the Foundation Stone, a massive slab of rock, which, like a giant cork, held back all the subterranean waters flowing under the Earth's surface. Seeing this mosque for the first time and at such short range took Cassandra's breath away.

At this moment, the vast courtyard was mobbed with worshippers, mostly older Arab men dressed in white robes and white head coverings. Here and there gathered small clusters of women, their heads covered with scarves or hijabs, their bodies invisible beneath long, dark robes. Like a teeming hive, the courtyard buzzed with prayer.

Cassandra moved off to one side, concealing herself in the shadows of a small marble building. A flight of stairs led up to a balcony and, from there, continued up to a small dome resting on six pillars. The metal sign posted outside the building identified this building as *Minbar al-Sayf*, the Summer Pulpit. Although no one was currently preaching from the balcony, Cassandra worried that someone might mount the marble steps at any moment. She crouched down in the dark shadows beneath one of the arches, keeping her eyes riveted on the pillared façade of the Dome of the Rock.

Fortunately, no one was looking in her direction. Everyone was preparing for prayer. Many of the men and women carried copies of the Qu'ran. To Cassandra, the movements of the worshippers seemed random, like a crowd milling before a concert.

Suddenly, the courtyard resounded with the plangent cry of a muezzin, calling from a nearby minaret. *Allahu Akhbar!* His cry was echoed by another, and then a third. Soon, the entire plaza rang with a hundred identical cries. *Allahu Akhbar! God is great!* Drawn like tides summoned by the moon, the worshippers slowly made their way toward the Dome of the Rock. She could hear yearning in their low voices. Ardent expectation. Unassailable faith.

Cassandra felt none of these things. She considered going over to one of the armed Israeli guards posted at one of the entry gates and asking for Agent Rimon. Or going back down to the Wall, which was less than a hundred meters away. The broad plaza was crawling with Israel security. But she chose to do neither. Now that she was here on the Temple Mount, she was in a unique position to discover precisely what the Chess Master was planning. If she waited here, he was certain to show himself.

86

When Lions' Gate Street reaches the Convent of the Sisters of Zion, its name changes to Via Dolorosa. But Maya made no note of this change. For it was at this intersection that she finally caught sight of Mashiak's colossal frame and gleaming bald head, bobbing above a stream of blue-uniformed schoolchildren. Shouting to Hillel, who trailed less than half a block behind her, Maya thrust out her forefinger, pointing at the Umariya Madrassa, a Muslim elementary school that took up much of the street. In front of its white stone campus spread a broad plaza constructed of multi-colored paving stones. As she scanned the empty plaza, Mashiak suddenly dashed across it, ducking under a dark arch that disappeared beneath the school's entrance stairs.

"Where's he going?" asked Hillel when he caught up with Maya.

"The Western Wall Tunnel. North Exit. It runs underneath the Temple Mount."

Maya remembered when this northern access point to the Temple Mount Tunnels first opened in 1996. Despite vigorous protests from the Palestinian Authorities, the Israeli Prime Minister had authorized locating this new exit directly underneath a madrassa in the Muslim Quarter. His improvident decision had led to riots and the death of eighty people.

Not waiting for Hillel to catch his breath, Maya now crossed the plaza, dashed under the arch, and entered the dark tunnel. Seconds later, she froze. Mashiak stood only a few meters in front of her. Under the low-watt bulbs, his giant figure flickered like a phantasm in a magic lantern. Fortunately, he was facing away from her. She squinted as her eyes adjusted to the dim light.

Then, she noticed what Mashiak held in his hand.

The device was about the size of a compact walkie-talkie unit and resembled a mobile phone. At the top of the rectangular black box, a small green light blinked at a steady pulse. Years of training informed her unconscious mind what it was seconds before her conscious brain caught on. A remote detonator.

Mashiak was planning to blow up the Temple Mount!

In a split second, she made her decision.

Pivoting on her heels, she ran back out of the tunnel, stopping when she exited into the light. She scanned the plaza, looking for Hillel. She spotted him a few meters away, his hands in his pockets, looking lost. He was staring at the dark opening under the arch but didn't appear to see her.

Quickly, she dug her cell phone out of her pocket and speed-dialed Roni. He picked up after one ring.

"Where the hell have you...."

"Listen to me, Roni!" Despite her agitation, she kept her voice to a whisper. She knew that tunnels have ears. "I don't have time to explain. You've got to shut down all cell phone service under the Temple Mount. Right now. Mashiak's about to...."

"No, you listen to me, Rimon! I've had it with your bullshit! Where are you? Don't you dare make a move 'til I get there!"

"The North Exit of the Western Wall Tunnel. Look, there's no time...."

But Roni had already hung up.

Maya knew it would be useless to call him back. Once her boss had made up his mind, getting him to change it was like kneading stone.

Her only hope now was Sarit. Despite their troubled history, something had recently shifted between them. Maya sensed a renewal of the sympathy they'd once shared as young soldiers.

Sarit sounded distracted when she answered Maya's call.

"Levine."

"It's me. I need your help."

Never had Maya felt these words more genuinely. Ordinarily, these two headstrong women tried to use each other for their own ends, each wary of being outmaneuvered by the other. Neither liked to let down her guard or cede control to her rival. But at this moment, Maya truly did need Sarit's help, even if it made her look weak or incompetent. She had no choice but to stake her life on Sarit's sense of duty. And shared allegiance.

"The Goldmayer case?"

"I don't have time to explain. You're just going to have to trust me on this." Maya took a deep breath. "A Christian fanatic named Pinkas Mashiak is about to detonate a bomb under the Temple Mount. Blow up the mosques."

"Why're you calling me? Tell our security people there!"

"No time! Mashiak's got a remote detonator that's triggered by a cell phone signal. The only way to stop him is to cut off cell service in the tunnels. You've got to do it now!"

"What does Roni...?"

"Forget about Roni! Just do it, Sarit!"

"Okay, I'm on it. Keep me posted."

Just before Maya broke off the connection, Sarit added, "Be careful."

Maya shoved her phone back into her pocket and ran out onto the sunny plaza. Hillel hadn't moved, his hands still in his pockets. He stared at her, eyes blinking rapidly in the blinding sun.

"Stay here and wait for our team," Maya told him. "Tell them about Mashiak. The Temple Mount." She tossed him the fob to the Fiat's fob. "Then you can go back for the scroll."

"What are you going to do?"

"I'm going after him."

"By yourself? That's crazy, Maya! The man's dangerous. Insane! Wait here for...."

But she was already gone.

87

HEARING THE ISRAELI AGENT'S FOOTFALLS thudding on stone, gaining on him, Mashiak forced himself to run faster. Once in a while, he encountered narrow wooden catwalks arching over dark water or sudden steep drops into blackness. The stone surface beneath his feet was so uneven that he almost lost his balance several times.

The air in the tunnel was cool but smelled strange. He imagined it was the smell of moldering bones. He was treading in the footsteps of ancient Israelite kings, Muslim caliphs, and medieval Crusaders. The Temple Mount was the Grand Canyon of Israel's history. Each conqueror built upon the carcasses of his defeated foes. Layer upon layer of ruins, all now buried under dust.

Suddenly, the narrow tunnel opened up into a large cavern. The vaulted ceiling and square stone pillars reminded Mashiak of a grand cathedral. But there were no stained-glass windows here, no altar or pews. It was just a vast open space, bathed in soft light. As he burst into the room, he startled a number of black-uniformed waiters, who were scurrying around, setting tables for some kind of banquet.

In one corner were stacks of white plastic chairs, piled high on wheeled carts. Near a far wall stood an embroidered canopy held up by four wooden poles, each pole wreathed with flowering vines. Atop a high pedestal table in the middle of the room rose a multi-tiered wedding cake. The white cake was crowned with a miniature groom in top hat and tails and a bride in a flouncy white gown.

Ignoring the shouts of the waiters, Mashiak dashed across the polished stone floor and darted into another tunnel cut into the opposite wall. As he navigated this tunnel's tight walls, he was reminded of the slot canyons he had explored as a kid when his family had gone on their only road trip out west. Like those snaking canyons, these narrow passages forced him to contort his tall, bony body, twisting his torso and occasionally crouching down to squeeze under a low overhang.

And no matter how fast he ran, he continued to hear the Israeli agent in relentless pursuit.

Despite his mounting fatigue and labored breath, he found himself visualizing certain details about the Temple Mount that he'd spent hours studying. What a shame to destroy such beauty! But he had no choice. The Lord sometimes demanded great sacrifice in the service of His will.

He pictured the Foundation Stone, a huge honey-colored slab that jutted out of the sanctuary floor of the gold-domed mosque that perched atop the Mount. The Muslims called it simply *es sakhra*, "the Rock." Did it really reach all the way down to the center of the Earth, like the guidebooks said?

And then there was the Cave of the Prophets under the Foundation Stone, where according to Muslim legend, Abraham, Moses, Solomon, Elijah, Jesus, and the angel Gabriel had once prayed with Mohammad. And below this cave, a second cave, the Well of Souls, where ghosts of the dead came daily to pray. The ancient shaft connecting these two caves was now blocked off by a round marble lid, sealed for centuries. The Muslim authorities had declared the lower cave off-limits. It was said that nobody had ever emerged from there alive.

Mashiak had read that the Brits supposedly breached the Well of Souls during the Mandate Period and plundered the Temple treasures hidden there. Some even claimed that the Ark of the Covenant had been among these looted treasures. But no one had ever dared to raise the marble lid to find out if these rumors were true.

Suddenly, Mashiak stopped running. He cried out and dropped to his knees. He threw up his arms and turned his dark eyes toward Heaven.

"Lord, I humbly submit to Your will. Accept my sacrifice!"

The tunnel walls echoed with his exultant shout.

At last, he understood his true mission. How could he have been so blind? It had all been part of God's secret plan! He had not failed in Kochalit when he had surrendered the Treasure Scroll to his enemies. No! It had been another test of his readiness to serve.

He choked back the tears that suddenly threatened to overwhelm him. Only now did he realize what the Voice had been telling him all these years. He had never been destined to be the chosen one, King Messiah. No, he had been fated to die a holy martyr. Everything that had happened up until this moment—his quest for ancient Kochalit and the Temple treasures, the murders of the Jewish professor and the Lebanese antiquities dealer, his struggles in the cave over the ancient scroll—all of it had been a divine trial. And he had passed! His reward was to die as the first casualty in the war between the Children of Light and the Children of Darkness. He would be sacrificed on the altar of the apocalypse!

There was no time to lose! He needed to reach the Well of Souls. Once there, he would detonate the bombs that Imri's men had planted yesterday inside the mosque. The Well of Souls would be his tomb. A fitting resting place for a martyr of the true faith.

Mashiak began to laugh, a shrill chattering that ricocheted off the stone walls. It hurt his raw lungs, but he was powerless to stop himself. He was surprised when he felt hot tears streaming down his cheeks. He doubled over as pain overpowered him.

Now, he understood that God had other plans for him. From the very beginning of his life, his choices had been guided by an unseen hand. All along the Voice had been leading him to this ultimate consummation.

Suddenly, Mashiak was gripped by bone-chilling dread. What if this wasn't a test? What if it was a trick, a deception? What if the Voice he'd been listening to all this time was not that of the Holy Ghost, but of Mastema, the voice of Satan, sent to seduce him? If that was true, then he'd totally failed! He'd become an instrument of the Devil! If so, he should let the Israeli stop him before he brought disaster down upon all their heads.

Horrified by these blasphemous thoughts, Mashiak set about casting Satan out of his body and spirit. He uttered a soul-piercing scream. Then, he began to spew forth a stream of foul gibberish, guttural grunts, and barks. A spray of spittle spouted from his parched lips. He kept at it until his throat was too dry to produce any more sounds. Then, with his last reserves of strength, he rose to his feet and sprinted forward. As his sandaled feet smacked the rutted stone surface, he prayed that he would not fail this final test. That he would be guided faithfully by the true Voice and the unseen hand.

Lord, lead me straightway to the Well of Souls from which no one has ever emerged alive.

88

SLAP, SLAP, SLAP.

Mashiak's sandals propelled him through the endless tunnel, heading south. As he ran, he glanced more and more anxiously at the solid rock walls.

Where was the hidden entrance? Was he getting close? How would he know when he was directly beneath the mosque?

O Lord, show me a sign!

His eyes scoured the walls for the secret passageway. But the walls were featureless. How soon before he reached the other end of the tunnel? The last thing he wanted was to throw himself into the arms of Israeli Security at the Western Wall.

He couldn't go on much longer. His breath was spent, his body screaming out in pain. But at least he had put enough distance between himself and the Israeli agent so that he no longer heard her footsteps thumping behind him. He had bought himself a little time. He hoped it would be enough.

And then he saw it. The sign he'd been waiting for.

The plexiglass placard read: "Warren's Gate."

Standing in front of an illuminated section of layered stone blocks, a huddle of bearded Jews, holding small Hebrew prayer books in their hands, swayed in the semi-darkness. Some of the men sobbed or moaned. Off to one side, a tour guide with a British accent told a group of rapt tourists that this was "as close as observant Jews can come to the site of the ancient Temple."

Mashiak smacked his large right fist into his left palm, then hastily dropped both hands to his sides when the guide looked at him sternly and clucked his tongue. The man was soon droning on again about the two famous British archaeologists who had first excavated this site in the 19th century.

Mashiak knew he was very close. Somewhere behind this rock wall ran an ancient tunnel, leading to a staircase that climbed up into the Well of Souls. From there, a second staircase led up into the Dome of the Rock. When the Crusaders had conquered Jerusalem in 1099, they had blocked access to this staircase. But one of his guidebooks had mentioned an old Arab legend about a secret entrance, known only to a few, which granted secret access into the mosque.

Glancing around to make sure that no one was watching, Mashiak quietly shuffled his feet along the uneven ground, moving backward into the shadows. His back to the stone wall, his fingertips grazed the smooth surface of this former cistern, searching for a straight-edged fissure. It wasn't long before he found it. His hand detected a narrow slit between two mammoth rectangular stone blocks. The opening was just large enough for his fingers to probe inside. He slid his hand up the narrow slot until he felt rusty metal. Pushing up hard with the side of his hand, he felt the ancient latch yield. Slowly, a section of wall slid backward until a gap appeared between the huge stone slabs. The opening was just wide enough for him to squeeze through.

On the other side of the wall, the darkness was so thick, he couldn't even see his own hands when he held them up to his eyes. This had to be the Well of Souls!

He reached down into his pocket and wrapped his fingers gently around the hard case of the detonator. When he withdrew it from his pocket, the small green light flashed before his startled eyes like a blazing comet.

89

When Maya reached Warren's Gate, she saw no sign of Mashiak. A few of the Jewish worshippers, who huddled over their prayer books, looked up and saw the gun in her hand. They shook their heads reproachfully. She flashed her Service credentials at them. They quickly returned to their prayers.

Anxiously, she looked around. It was doubtful that Mashiak would have continued past this point. Fifty meters from here, this tunnel ended at the Western Wall plaza, which was crawling with Israeli guards. Mashiak wouldn't risk showing himself there. He must still be close by.

But where could such a giant hide himself?

She began inching back into the shadows, her SIG Sauer cocked. Her ears probed for any sound. Then, she saw a flash of green light, followed by another. They appeared to be coming from the other side of the tunnel wall. How was that possible? She edged toward the light. Then, she noticed a narrow vertical gap between two rows of stone blocks. Silently, she slipped between the stones.

In the faint light filtering through the gap, she could just make out Mashiak standing with his back to her. In his raised left hand was the detonator. Its small green light blinked steadily. On and off. On and off.

Time stopped.

In that infinitely long moment, Maya's mind raced at light speed.

Had Sarit Levine believed her story about a plot to blow up the Temple Mount? Had she acted immediately to cut off cell phone service under the Mount? Or would the mad preacher now blow them all to kingdom come?

Maya thought of her daughter. *Oh God, my darling Vered!* At this very moment, she was probably on her way with Rafi to the underground banquet hall that Maya had just raced through in pursuit of Mashiak. Why hadn't she stopped there to warn the set-up crew, to order them to call off the wedding and evacuate all the guests and staff? Save her daughter's life. But she hadn't stopped. She'd just kept on running. Maybe Rafi was right. She repeatedly fell short as a mother. Here, she'd chosen duty over family. Oh, why did she have to choose between them?

But she knew why she'd made her choice. It was not only Vered's life that was at stake here. She was responsible for all the Vereds in Israel.

"I'm so sorry, *havivati*!"

The words escaped Maya's lips before she could stop herself. She fell to her knees on the hard stone floor and wept.

Mashiak spun around. He looked down at the small, bent figure on the ground. Then, he raised his left arm high above his head, holding the detonator tightly in his hand.

"You cain't stop me, curséd daughter of Belial! O Lord, into Your hands, I commend my spirit!"

Maya raised her head and stared up at Mashiak. His broad mouth yawned open, as though in rictus. His dark eyes gaped wide, bulging out of their sockets. Time began to flow again but in slow motion, as though coursing through viscous liquid. She watched Mashiak's right hand float up toward the detonator. His long, bony forefinger slowly homed in on the blinking green light. The tiny light winked seductively, luring the finger closer. The white half-moon of his fingernail glistened in the emerald light. His fingertip pressed down gently on the button.

Instantly, the blinking green light turned red, a miniature rose glowing in the dark.

Maya held her breath. She saw Vered smiling at her, whispering her name: *Ima*.

She closed her eyes. And for the first time in her life, she prayed.

90

As Mashiak's finger pressed down on the detonator button, he closed his eyes, dropped to his knees, and prayed. And waited for hundreds of tons of limestone, marble, gold, cedarwood, and ceramic tile to crush him, entombing him forever in the Well of Souls.

But nothing happened.

Silence pervaded the darkness like a thick fog. He pushed the button again and then again. He rose to his feet and repeatedly jabbed his finger on the button. The red light shone steadfastly in the darkness. But nothing stirred above or below.

"My God! My God!" Mashiak cried out, his voice angry and desperate. "Why hast Thou forsaken me?"

Then, he heard a rustling nearby. A hunched figure rose up from the ground and took a step in his direction.

In the rosy glow of the detonator's light, the woman seemed insubstantial. Was she an apparition? Her curly hair framed her head like a halo of flickering embers. He thought he glimpsed the metallic glint of a pistol or maybe a knife. The woman's stance was bent forward, as if readied for attack.

"It's over, Mashiak."

He recognized that voice. It was that damn Israeli agent, Maya Rimon! She was surely one of the cursed spawn of Lilith, sent to torment him, to stop him from completing his sacred mission. He should have shut the entrance to this chamber behind him. But it was too late for that now.

His only choice was to move forward. He needed to finish what he'd been sent here to do. He didn't understand why Imri's detonator had failed. Now, he would have to get to the C-4 charges planted inside the mosque and trigger them manually. He knew the odds were against him. Perhaps this was yet another test.

Suddenly he remembered once hearing a preacher—he couldn't have been more than nine or ten at the time—describe how Jesus prayed to His Father in Heaven. The preacher explained that the words Jesus used had been remarkably simple, typical of those spoken by a child addressing a loving parent.

Mashiak sank to his knees and spoke those words aloud from memory: "I praise you, Father, Lord of Heaven and Earth, because you have hidden these things from the wise and learned and revealed them to little children."

If only the Voice would speak to him one last time!

He looked over at the Israeli agent. She was frozen like a statue. He could no longer see the silver glint of her weapon. Maybe he had imagined it.

Then, her sharp voice shattered the silence.

"I don't know what you're up to, Mashiak, but it won't work. Either put your hands up in the air right now, or we'll have to do this the hard way."

He could no longer wait for a sign from Heaven. He sucked in his breath, spun on his heels, and rushed away into the darkness.

He had no idea how large this dark space was. Nor did he know whether there was another way out besides the way he'd entered. For all he knew, he would soon run smack into a solid stone wall or plunge headlong down a bottomless well. Nonetheless, he ran forward at full speed. He trusted that God would show him the way.

91

WHEN HE RAMMED HIS LEFT toe into the lowest step of a stone staircase, Mashiak cried out in pain. But he didn't stop. Using both hands, he scrambled up the stairs, scraping his palms and knees on the rough-hewn stone. At the top of the steps, a round stone slab blocked his way. With his shoulder, he pushed hard against the heavy lid. It didn't budge. He was trapped.

Several shots now rang out from below. The Israeli woman was shooting blindly in the dark, using the sounds made by Mashiak's body to track him. He held his breath and again tried to lift the stone lid. It didn't move.

Frantically, he reached up and felt around the perimeter of the circular slab. It was smoother to the touch than the tunnel walls. Probably hadn't been touched for centuries. He wasn't sure what he was looking for, but he wasn't surprised when he felt the crusty bar of another rusted latch. With a strong shove, he thrust the bolt to one side. The lid creaked open.

Another shot rang out. Rock splinters sprayed his cheek and left arm.

"Wherever you are, Mashiak, I'm not letting you get away! Give yourself up before it's too late."

With his broad back and shoulders, Mashiak heaved the lid all the way open. Then, he squeezed through the round opening. As he emerged into the room above, he was temporarily blinded by bright electric light. After a few seconds, his eyes adjusted.

He found himself in the corner of a small, low-ceilinged cavern. The space was filled with Muslim worshippers, their foreheads pressed to the carpeted floor. They were thunderstruck by Mashiak's sudden appearance. Perhaps they took him for a ghost or djinn.

He quickly scanned the small room. The smooth stone floor was covered with thick oriental rugs. At one end, propped against a wall, stood some kind of stone hearth or carving, with a hole in its center.

Then, he noticed a second stone staircase, leading upwards.

He took the steps two at a time.

The staircase brought him up onto the surface of a huge yellow-ish-brown slab of rock. The Foundation Stone. Above him loomed the colossal curved dome of the mosque, webbed with gold and red filaments. He had arrived at his final destination.

Because it was Friday morning, the Muslim Sabbath, the mosque was crowded. Many of the worshippers lay flat on their faces in prayer. Those who remained erect or kneeling on carpets glared disapprovingly at the tall American, who now clambered over the sacred rock. His giant bald head was conspicuously bare. He was dressed in Western clothes, not the traditional long robes of the faithful. He clearly did not belong here.

When he reached the edge of the slab, Mashiak glanced back over his shoulder. No sign yet of his pursuer. But he didn't have much time. He had to locate and detonate one of Imri's explosive charges before she got here.

Smiling and bowing like a mock potentate, Mashiak straightened to his full height, raised both hands toward the great arabesque dome, and shouted: "Bomb!"

92

FROM HER HIDING PLACE BENEATH one of the arches of the *Minbar al-Sayf*, Cassandra noticed a sudden commotion near the main entrance to the great gold-domed mosque. Wave after wave of Muslim worshippers now spilled out of the arched doorway, scattering in all directions across the broad courtyard. Many were screaming, pulling at their hair, and wringing their hands.

Some of the panic-stricken worshippers were shouting in English. Cassandra strained to hear what they were saying. When they came closer, she could finally make out their words.

"Bomb!"

"Terrorists!"

"May Allah have mercy on us!"

Despite her natural instinct for self-preservation, Cassandra now found herself running *toward* the mosque. She pushed past the worshippers, who were desperately trying to get away, barreling through the heaving mob until she found herself entangled in a knot of bodies near the front entrance, a writhing octopus of arms and legs. The stench of fear was overwhelming. She felt her gorge rise to her throat, choking her. She opened up her mouth and retched, but her stomach was empty. All that came out were a few drops of rancid spittle. She gulped mouthfuls of hot air to calm herself.

As she struggled to break free, Cassandra caught sight of an old Arab woman, who had fallen to the ground. The old woman was being trampled by a hundred sandaled feet. The back of her head, which peeked out from under a dark head scarf, was bloody, the puckered flesh abraded and torn. Puddles of blood pooled under the old woman's neck. One of her sandals was missing. Her curled yellow toes bounced up and down as more people stepped on her scrawny buttocks and thighs.

Cassandra debated whether to try and help her. But she couldn't even tell if the old woman was still alive. And if she knelt down to help her, she too might fall victim to the frenzied mob and get trampled underfoot.

No, her top priority was stopping the Chess Master. It was obvious that his endgame was already in play.

Out of the corner of her eye, Cassandra sensed movement. She swiveled her head around. Approaching the mosque's front entrance were four Israeli guards, outfitted in riot gear and carrying semi-automatic weapons. It seemed to Cassandra that they were pointing their guns...*at her*! Summoning all her strength, she broke free of the tangle of bodies and stood up to face them.

Steadily they advanced toward her. Their black boots marched in lockstep. Their unblinking eyes accused her: *Why are you heading toward the mosque when everyone else is running away? Who else would do that but a terrorist!*

One of the guards, tall, with skin the color of fresh-brewed coffee, stopped abruptly and raised his hand. His three companions halted and waited for their leader's next order. Their weapons remained trained on Cassandra.

She took a step back toward the mosque's open doorway.

"Stop! Do not enter the mosque!"

Cassandra quickly considered her options. She could tell them about the Chess Master. But she had no way to back up her wild claim that an extremist plot was about to go down here. She carried no ID. It was more likely these men would regard her as some wack job and haul her away in handcuffs.

On the other hand, she could run.

She spun around and dove back into the middle of the dense crowd. The Israeli guards shouted for her to stop. One of them fired several warning shots into the air. The gunfire agitated the crowd even more. Like beans in a boiling pot, they began to thrash and jerk, many of them screaming loudly in Arabic. The Israeli guards yelled at them, ordering them to calm down.

Down on her hands and knees on the white stone pavement, Cassandra scrambled among the shuffling feet, doubling back toward the entrance to the mosque. Finally, she reached the open doors and tumbled in.

The vast prayer hall was empty. Silent as a tomb.

And then she noticed someone else inside.

She stared in wonder at the giant, who stood atop the huge rock slab that jutted up from the floor. His massive bald head swiveled restlessly from side to side. His dark eyes, bouncing in their sockets like pinballs, scanned the pillars that filled the prayer hall, as if searching for something.

It had to be him. The Chess Master.

93

WHERE HAD IMRI PLANTED THOSE charges?

Mashiak's dark eyes swept across the enormous sanctuary. Although he prided himself on being a God-fearing Christian, he had to admit that this Muslim church was awesome. The huge dome overhead was painted in dizzying swirls of red and gold. The inside was like a fairytale castle, decorated with dazzling mosaics and stained glass, colored marble columns, and luxurious oriental rugs. Although Mashiak had never been to Vegas, he imagined that this was what it must look like, only with neon lights and slot machines. Too bad he'd never get to see it.

Heathen pleasures, vanity of vanities!

Ashamed of his momentary lapse, Mashiak quickly turned his attention to the circle of round and square marble columns that supported the eight-sided sanctuary under the dome. Imri had told him he'd planted the explosive charges on six of the columns closest to the Foundation Stone. But which ones?

He leapt down to the sanctuary floor and strode up to one of the round pillars. The lustrous polished marble was crisscrossed with veins of gray, lavender, and pink. For the second time that day, he thought: *What a shame to destroy such beauty!* But he quickly reminded himself that this beauty was in service to a false god. *A Golden Calf!*

Carefully, his dark eyes explored the smooth, round column, beginning down at the square marble base, then climbing up to the gold Corinthian capitals at its crown. No sign of C-4 plastique. The same was true of the next three columns.

Guide my eyes, O Lord, to the instruments of Thy Vengeance!

As he searched, he kept telling himself that it didn't matter whether he lived or died. What mattered was that he was serving God's will. But the terrible truth was that he desperately wanted to live! He wanted to witness the final war between the Children of Light and the Children of Darkness. He wanted to celebrate the coming of the Kingdom.

He prayed for a miracle.

Let me survive the blast or be resurrected like Lazarus.

Suddenly, he heard the sharp report of a gunshot, then several others. The sounds came from outside the mosque. As he turned toward the source of the noise, he noticed a slight young woman with spiked purple hair standing a few feet inside the main entrance. She stood motionless as though made of stone.

She looked young, not much over twenty. Her brown head covering had slipped off and now circled her neck like a collar. Her fair skin and light eyes marked her as European or American. Definitely not Arab.

But what was she doing here? When he'd popped up from the surface of the Foundation Stone and shouted: "Bomb!" everyone had run away. They'd scattered like coons fleeing a hound. Then, where had she come from? And why hadn't she run away like the others?

Loud shouts interrupted his thoughts. Seconds later, a unit of Israeli security guards burst into the prayer hall, machine guns drawn. They paid no attention to the purple-haired girl, standing like a statue near the front doors. They were focused solely on him. They meant to stop him from fulfilling his holy mission.

Mashiak waited until they were close. Then, yelling at the top of his lungs, he ran at the nearest guard and grabbed the man's semi-automatic rifle. He dropped to the ground and rolled. He then took cover behind a nearby pillar seconds before a hail of bullets rocketed toward him, blistering the marble column with lead. Mashiak took a deep breath and sank down to the floor. Carefully, he inserted his right forefinger into the weapon's trigger guard.

He was so close!

In those first few seconds, he'd counted four guards. One was now unarmed. All he had to do was put a single bullet into one of Imri's C-4 packets before the Israelis took him down. If he blasted the plastique, it would detonate and trigger some of the other charges. The chain reaction would bring the mosque down on all their heads.

It would be the opening salvo of the apocalypse.

94

JUST AS THE FOUR ISRAELI guards burst into the mosque, Maya climbed up out of a corner of the Foundation Stone. Her thin white blouse now stuck to her skin like wet newspaper. Her auburn hair, matted with sweat, echoed the russet veins seaming the massive rock. In her right hand, she held a pistol. She moved cautiously, her eyes scanning the room. Seeking her prey.

She found him when he suddenly began shouting from behind one of the pillars. She knew that voice, deep and resonant, now laced with the stridency of desperation. Or madness. The American preacher's words were garbled, completely indecipherable. But uttered so loudly that they reverberated in the large empty space.

Maya soon realized that the two of them were not alone in the vast sanctuary. Several Israeli soldiers crouched behind other pillars, the metal barrels of their weapons poking out like the beaks of hungry birds. She counted at least three of them. She was tempted to shout out, to identify herself as friendly fire, but she didn't want to alert Mashiak to her presence.

Suddenly, a new figure appeared. Maya immediately recognized the purple hair. It was Cassandra Sucher. Masha had reported back to her that the young American computer whiz had vanished into thin air. Had disappeared, leaving rent and cell phone bills unpaid, no forwarding address. Poor lost soul. Somehow, she'd gotten swept up in Mashiak's web.

Crouched down on the great rock, Maya watched Cassandra dig into the back pocket of her jeans and retrieve a small black object. Pinching one end of the device between two trembling fingertips, the young woman held it up as high as she could. She tried to whistle to get attention, but all that came out was a rush of hot air.

"Hey!" she shouted. "Over here! Look what I have!"

Cassandra's reedy voice echoed through the vast chamber.

"A d-d-detonator! Anyone moves, I'll b-b-blow up this mosque!"

Everyone froze.

A second detonator? Maya judged the black object in Cassandra's hand to be too small for such a deadly purpose. It had to be a trick. But the stakes were too high to call her bluff.

From their hiding places behind the pillars, the Israeli guards slowly swiveled their weapons back toward the mosque entrance, their feet riveted to the floor. Atop the Foundation Stone, Maya lay stock-still, her body leaning forward, her eyes locked on Cassandra's upraised hand. No sound came from behind the pillar where Mashiak was hidden.

Cassandra took a deep breath and exhaled.

"You have five seconds to throw down your weapons."

The three armed Israeli guards emerged from behind their pillars, their guns held up in the air, their other hands empty, palms out. Carefully, they lowered their weapons to the floor and backed away. By now, they had caught sight of Maya up on the rock. But because she was dressed in plain clothes, they didn't recognize her as one of their own. They stared at her with nervous eyes, possibly taking her for another terrorist. She held up her SIG Sauer in her right hand and raised her left palm in a gesture of surrender. Then, she, too, laid her gun down on the ground.

Behind his pillar, the mad giant remained invisible and silent.

Keeping her upraised hand high in the air, Cassandra slowly walked toward the great slab of ochre rock until she stood a stone's throw from Mashiak's hiding place. Gingerly, she lowered her hand until it was about waist-high. She held out the small black device toward the pillar. Then, she rotated slightly, turning her back to the Foundation Stone.

"That goes for you, too, Chess Master! Throw down your weapon and come out! Hands up where I can see them!"

Now that the guards were disarmed, and the girl's back was toward her, Maya saw her chance. With barely perceptible movements, she bent down and retrieved her gun. Gently, she cocked it. Then, with both hands on the grip, she aimed the SIG Sauer at the spot where Mashiak was hiding. She began edging forward.

As she drew closer, she spotted the snub-nosed barrel of Mashiak's gun inching out from behind the pillar. The barrel slowly tilted up, aiming at the top of a neighboring pillar. Her eyes followed the gun's trajectory. Then, she saw it. A deadly packet of explosives. The charge was suspended near the top of the column, just below the gilded Corinthian capital. It was a clever hiding place. An unsuspecting eye would mistake the small gold-painted packet for part of the capital's baroque decoration.

She glanced nervously toward Mashiak. His gun was no longer visible from behind the pillar. Perhaps the target was too far away. She had to get to him before he found a better firing position.

But before she could edge closer, Mashiak suddenly stepped out from his hiding place. Maya flattened herself on the floor, raising her head only high enough to watch his movements. He raised both his arms. In his right hand, he grasped a semi-automatic rifle. As he stepped forward, he glanced up and to his right, calculating the distance, the correct angle, the time it would take him to aim and press the trigger. Maya crawled forward on her belly. Too slow, too far.

At that moment, a bright ray of morning sun broke through a cracked pane of red glass in the mosque's eastern wall. It glinted off the silver ring on Mashiak's right index finger and flashed like a dart into Cassandra's eye. She screamed.

The frozen tableau exploded into motion.

Mashiak took aim at the explosive charge and squeezed the trigger.

At that same moment, Maya fired several shots in quick succession. The bullets struck Mashiak in the temple, throat, and left chest, killing him instantly. His machine gun fell to the floor, its thud muffled by the thick carpet. A crimson jet spurted from his wounds, bleeding into the rug's soft fibers. The dark red stain rapidly merged into the swirling pattern of the carpet's rich hues.

Deflected by Maya's bullets, Mashiak's shot just missed its target. It ricocheted off the gold Corinthian capital just above the explosive charge. Its new trajectory carried it directly toward Cassandra. The bullet penetrated the soft white flesh of her right arm and exited without hitting bone. Stunned by the pain, Cassandra dropped the object in her hand. It bounced once on the carpeted floor and lay still. With glazed eyes, Cassandra stared down at it, as if it were a dead bird, dropped suddenly from the sky. Then, she crumpled to the floor, sobbing. Maya ran over to her and cradled her in her arms.

One of the Israeli guards ran over and began bombarding Cassandra with questions. *Who are you? What do you know about all this?*

Maya yelled at him: "Call an ambulance!"

They were still shouting at each other when Roni and his team arrived.

95

By THE TIME RONI QATTAWI and his agents rushed into the mosque, all was quiet. Roni's sharp eyes quickly took in the scene:

Two bodies lay on the carpeted floor. He immediately recognized the larger figure as Pinkas Mashiak. The American preacher lay sprawled on the ground, one long leg bent back unnaturally toward his head. In death, the gigantic man seemed much smaller than in his photographs. By now, the wounds to his head and throat had leached so much blood that Mashiak's already pale complexion looked ghostly. His face was frozen in a look of stunned surprise. His thick, black eyebrows arched high on his massive brow. The man's dark eyes, already filming over, gaped wide in astonishment. Roni noted that the weapon lying near Mashiak's head was a Jericho semi-automatic. One of their own.

The other body puzzled him. Who was this odd-looking girl with purple hair? And why was Maya Rimon holding her like some wounded stray? Then, he remembered seeing the girl's photograph in Maya's interim report. She was some lost flower child from the States, who had provided them with information about Habib Salameh. He couldn't remember her name.

Roni walked over to the two women entwined together on the floor. He nodded perfunctorily to Maya, but said nothing. Then, he looked at the wounded girl, quickly assessing her injuries. Maya had used the girl's head scarf as a tourniquet to stop the bleeding. She didn't seem in any immediate danger.

He squatted down on his haunches and peered intently at the girl. He noted the braille of tiny incisions stippling her ears and nose.

Why do they mutilate themselves like this? Such a pretty face. But with all that hardware—they're totally repulsive!

The girl's eyes, greenish-brown in the dappled light, were red-rimmed and bloodshot. Roni noted that she wore no makeup, which made her seem even younger than he'd first thought. Might even still be in her teens. He saw that her natural hair, dirty blonde at its roots, was overtaking the purple dye. She could really do with a makeover.

He straighted up, arched back his shoulders, then looked down at Maya. Despite how exasperated he was with her, his heart went out to her. This kind of operation was especially hard on women. Almost always, there was collateral damage. He couldn't help admiring her grit. Not many agents, men included, would have gone after Mashiak alone—and succeeded in taking him down.

He placed his hands on his slim hips and barked at her: "Rimon!"

Maya did not respond. She remained bent over the wounded girl, breathing rapidly.

"Enough! Get a grip!"

Maya raised her head. Roni stood over her, arms akimbo, his knobby muscles rippling under his shirtsleeves. His face softened.

"Okay, so tell me what happened here."

Maya gently eased Cassandra off her lap and laid her on the soft carpet. Then, she carefully undraped the brown cotton shawl from the young woman's upper torso, bunched it into a pillow, and placed it under her head. Sheathed in a thin white tee shirt, Cassandra looked young and vulnerable. Every now and then, she grimaced in pain.

Only then did Maya notice the small black object lying not far from Cassandra's right side. She leaned over and grasped the object carefully between her thumb and index finger. When she brought it close to her eyes, she realized what it was. A thumb drive. Cassandra had persuaded five armed shooters to surrender their weapons by threatening them with a thumb drive!

Maya slowly rose to her feet. She glanced over at Mashiak's blood-stained body lying still a few meters away. The fallen giant was now surrounded by crime scene personnel. The Medical Examiner, Avraham Selgundo, crouched over Mashiak's midsection, gently prodding at his wounds with a ballpoint pen.

Two orange-vested EMTs from Magen David Adom now entered the mosque and began attending to Cassandra. They placed an oxygen mask over her face, attached an IV to her arm, strapped her body to a portable stretcher, and secured her neck with a collar. Then, they carried her out to the waiting ambulance. Maya watched them until they disappeared into the bright sunlight.

She now took a deep breath, rubbed her eyes, and wiped her nose with the hem of her blouse. Then, she turned to face Roni.

Stripping her voice of all emotion, she quickly filled him in: the scene at the Tayelet, the car chase into the desert, her confrontation with Mashiak at Khirbet al-Tajmil, Hillel's unexpected arrival, the explosives planted in the mosque. Roni didn't give her a chance to finish her account.

"Ever hear of protocol, Rimon? You should've called for backup as soon as you realized what that maniac was up to. But no, you had to do it all yourself!"

Roni turned away from her and began to pace restlessly around the large prayer hall. His steps were quick, short, and erratic. He spotted the Israeli officer in charge of Temple Mount Security and marched over to him. He collared the man and instructed him to keep everyone out of the mosque, even the unarmed Muslim guards working for the Waqf. Next, he strode over to the team of Jerusalem District police, who'd just arrived on the scene. He chatted with them for a few minutes. Then, he called together his own team and ordered them to search for more C-4 packets.

When he returned to Maya, he found her seated in one of the white plastic chairs that were lined up against the mosque's back walls. Her head was down. Her chin rested on her chest. She didn't look up when he flopped down into the chair next to her and released a wheeze of air.

He dug a cigarette from his pocket. He lit up and sucked in a deep lungful of tobacco. Then, he slowly blew out the smoke, watching it spiral upward. The gray tendrils mirrored the red and gold arabesques swirling on the underside of the great dome. He took another drag and doubled over coughing. On the wall behind him hung a plastic sign written in Arabic, English, and Hebrew: "No Smoking."

"You know, Rimon, I've really had it with you!" he said. He spat out her name like a rotten sunflower seed. "You're just like your old man!"

96

MAYA OPENED HER MOUTH TO respond but clamped it shut when she spotted Arik Ophir, the Minister of Internal Security, striding briskly through the mosque's wide entryway. Maya's father was with him. Ophir was accompanied by a gaggle of reporters toting notebooks, electronic tablets, cameras, and video equipment. One of the reporters, shouldering a heavy videocam, thrust a microphone into the minister's face. With undisguised irritation, Ophir swatted the mic away. He glared at the short man, whose wire-rim glasses balanced precariously on the tip of his nose. The reporter quickly retreated behind his colleagues.

The minister saluted Maya with a chivalrous bow. Her father, one hand pressed over his heart, gave her a beaming smile.

"What an extraordinary thing you did for your country today, Agent Rimon!" Ophir said, addressing the cluster of reporters. "And at such great personal risk!"

Then, he turned to face Roni, who was mashing a cigarette butt into the thick carpet with his heel.

"Brilliant operation, Qattawi! Sarit Levine tells me that it was your idea to cut off cell service under the Mount. Quick thinking! It was lucky her people were able to get it done so quickly. If that *meshuggeneh's* bombs had gone off...." He shuddered. "The whole nation is in your debt."

So now we both owe you, Sarit, Maya thought to herself. *And I have no doubt that you'll collect on the debt.* She chuckled, feeling her spirits reviving.

Arik Ophir reached into his jacket pocket and retrieved a wooden pipe. With intense concentration, he filled the dark, shiny bowl with curly threads of tobacco, then tamped them down with a metal tool he fished out of the same pocket. Flicking his thumb across the tiny wheel of a blue plastic lighter, he shot a gold flame into the tobacco and puffed contentedly. Returning the lighter and tamping tool to his pocket, he took a few more puffs. The air began to smell of cherry, pine, and cloves.

Ophir leaned toward Roni and waggled a gnarled finger at him.

"Now, don't try to claim all the credit for yourself, Qattawi." He poked an elbow playfully into Roni's side. "Spread around the glory. I know for a fact that this pretty young lady," he pointed the stem of his pipe at Maya, who grinned uneasily, "played a crucial role in preventing this horrific attack. Isn't that right, Agent Rimon?"

Roni stared at Maya, his breath quickening. Maya noticed that his fists were balled up at his sides. She kept her eyes fixed on the Security Minister, who winked at her and smiled.

"Not to worry, sir," Maya said. "I'll make sure that I get proper recognition."

She relaxed her mouth into a restrained grin. For the first time that day, her breath traveled deep into her lungs and eased out slowly. A sense of wellbeing surged beneath the surface of her skin, warming her. She turned and stared into her boss's dark eyes until he looked away.

Ophir took a few more puffs on his pipe. He frowned when he realized the flame had gone out. He shook his head, grunted, then stuffed the cold pipe back into his pocket. He leaned forward and muttered a few words to Roni, who muttered something back in response. Then, the minister pivoted on his heels and marched briskly out of the mosque, trailed by the gaggle of reporters.

97

As MAYA AND HER FATHER stepped outside, their ears were assaulted by angry voices in Hebrew and Arabic. Israeli guards and Muslim worshippers shouted at one another, their words unintelligible.

The Temple Mount plaza swarmed with Israeli military personnel. Several Waqf officials, dressed in their usual floor-length gray cloaks and white tarbooshes, stood on the sidelines, observing their Israeli counterparts with suspicion and rancor. Although the Muslim and Jewish authorities had agreed to keep the press away from the Temple Mount, news of the attempted attack on the Dome of the Rock had already leaked out, sending shockwaves throughout the Palestinian community. Posts about the attack were flooding social media. Arik Ophir had already put the army on standby. The mood at the mosque was like a stewing geyser.

Maya heard someone call out her name. She recognized the voice immediately. *Hillel!* What an uncanny knack that man had for showing up at the wrong time.

She let go of her father's hand and pushed through the cordon of Israeli security. One of the guards grabbed her arm roughly, but dropped it like a hot coal when she flashed her Service credentials at him.

She pointed at the bearded man wearing a black knit kippah, being held back by another Israeli guard.

"He's with me. You can let him through."

The guard released his hostage, who nodded at him nervously. Hillel quickly walked over to join Maya, who'd found shade under the widespread limbs of a cedar.

Maya stared at him. "Why did you come here?"

"I was worried. You disappeared into that tunnel. I didn't know what happened to you. They told me you were here."

He reached out his hand toward her, then abruptly retracted it when he saw that her hands remained leaden at her sides. He stroked his grizzled beard, then cleared his throat. He reached up a hand to straighten his glasses, then removed them from his nose and wiped them clean with a handkerchief he fished out of his pocket. All the while his eyes remained fixed on the ground.

Maya's eyes intently scanned the courtyard. More Israeli soldiers continued to arrive, heavily armed, clad in helmets and protective vests. They began herding Muslim worshippers toward the four gates at the plaza's northern perimeter, as far away as possible from the Western Wall.

"What's going on?" asked Hillel. His cornflower-blue eyes met her gold-flecked green ones. Their gazes locked.

"I shot Mashiak. He was going to blow up the mosque."

"*Vey is mir*! That would have brought the entire Arab world down on our heads and launched World War Three!"

"Probably just what that religious fanatic wanted."

"Thank God he didn't succeed!" Hillel paused, then swallowed hard. "I'm glad you're safe."

Maya's eyes broke free of Hillel's stare and shifted to the soldiers. They had begun roughly prodding Muslim stragglers with the butts of their rifles, shouting,

"Move!"

"Hurry it up!"

"*Yallah*!"

A hornets' nest of rage now erupted from the crowd. Many of the young Arab men thrust clenched fists into the air. The soldiers tensed. Unconsciously, Maya's hand moved toward her SIG Sauer, which once again nestled against her side.

"You think we're safe now?" Maya's laugh was brittle. "We're standing on the launchpad of the apocalypse!"

Hillel took a step back and sucked in his breath.

"All I care about at the moment, Maya, is you. Not the entire state of Israel."

She turned to face him, her face impassive except for her gold-green eyes, which glistened in the mottled light.

Hillel now reached under his shirt and held up the weathered leather pouch he'd been concealing there.

"And this!" He grinned sheepishly. "You won't believe what I discovered in this scroll!"

98

"Not now, Hillel."

Maya felt an overwhelming fatigue crushing her like an oppressive weight. Her shoulders sagged. Her breath raked her throat like sandpaper. She needed to sleep.

"I guarantee you're going to want to hear this."

"Not now," Maya repeated. "I'm too tired to take anything in."

Hillel gently took hold of her elbow and led her to a smooth marble ledge near the Al Kas Fountain. She dropped ponderously onto the hard stone. Hillel remained standing. When he began speaking again, his voice was quieter, less fevered.

"After Mariamne gave the Copper Scroll to the Examiner in Qumran, she traveled north to Berytus, modern-day Beirut, where King Agrippa was holding her brother Alexander captive in his dungeon. He'd been accused of treason. Her idea was to trade the Treasure Scroll for her brother's freedom. But her plan failed. You know why?"

Maya stared off into space. Her mind was empty. She was deaf to the rising clamor of the Muslim protesters. She was oblivious to the beauty on display all around her. And she had absolutely no interest in hearing what Hillel had to tell her about that accursed scroll that had almost destroyed them all.

"Because the Temple treasures were gone!" Hillel was shouting. His bearded cheeks flushed pink. His chest heaved.

Maya stared at him.

"Gone?"

"Looted by the Romans, as most of us have always suspected. Carted off to Rome after Jerusalem was razed. When Mariamne offered King Agrippa the Treasure Scroll as ransom for Alexander, he laughed in her face. He told her that the conquering Romans had tortured the Temple priests until they confessed where they'd hidden all the Temple treasures. And then, just to pour salt on her wound, he burned her scroll right in front of her. So the duplicate scroll no longer exists."

Maya sighed. Her shoulders caved in, and her chin fell to her chest. Hillel took no notice. His eyes flashed with excitement. His hands swatted the heavy air.

"So if the duplicate scroll was destroyed, what's that in your hand?" Maya asked without raising her eyes from the ground. *If only she could close her eyes and sleep....*

"*Her* scroll! Mariamne's eye-witness testimony. Which will prove just as priceless as the Treasure Scroll. Mariamne saw it all first-hand—the Galilean Wars, the Roman military campaigns, the Destruction of Jerusalem, the beginning of Jewish Exile. This scroll will revolutionize the field!"

Maya raised her head and smiled absentmindedly. Hillel noted the weariness in her face. Dark smudges muddied the skin under her eyes. Fine creases laddered her wide brow. He sat down beside her on the stone bench.

They sat in silence for a few moments. Hillel thrust his hands into his pockets and waited. Giving her time to digest what he'd told her.

When Maya finally spoke, her voice was soft. Remote.

"So what happened to Alexander?"

"The king released him but condemned him to exile. Mariamne returned to what was left of her home in Tiberias and finished her chronicle. Then, she traveled to Kochalit and hid her scroll there."

Maya slowly breathed out and twisted an auburn curl around one finger. Hillel dropped both his hands to his lap. They lay there, palms up, like unfurled scrolls.

"I know this doesn't seem important to you at the moment, Maya. Not compared to the near catastrophe you just saved us from.

But mark my words. One day, this discovery will be viewed as one of the most significant archaeological finds of the twenty-first century!"

Maya placed her hand lightly on Hillel's wrist.

"I really need to sleep, Hillel. I can barely keep my eyes open."

Hillel turned and peered at her over his wire-rim glasses. Unconsciously, he placed his right hand on his kippah. Maya waggled a finger at him and grinned. Hillel's face flushed deep red.

"I would really like to see you again, Maya."

He reached out with both arms and pulled Maya close, holding her against his chest. She quickly broke free of his embrace. For a few moments, they sat there awkwardly, staring down at the ground. Maya finally ended the uncomfortable silence.

"I like you, Hillel. I really do." She smiled but the effort failed. Her full lips soon wilted into a sober line. "But the two of us would never work."

Hillel looked down at his hands. Then, he raised his head and looked at her.

"All I'm asking for is a second chance. And a little patience."

"I'm not a very patient woman." She smiled at him sadly. "And it would take a lot more than patience for us to click. As you yourself said, we live in very different worlds."

Hillel sighed. He opened his mouth to speak, then changed his mind. His head dropped to his chest. When he lifted it moments later, her heart ached to see those cornflower-blue eyes moist with tears.

Maya placed a hand gently on his shoulder, then gave him a quick peck on his bristled cheek.

"Don't take it so hard, Hillel. After all, it's not the end of the world."

THE END

Glossary

Abba: Father (Hebrew)

Al Haram Esh Sharif: the Temple Mount (Arabic)

Al regel achat: "on one foot," equivalent to the American idiom, "in a nutshell" (Hebrew, alluding to the Talmudic story in which the sage Hillel tells a would-be convert the essence of Judaism while standing on one foot)

Baharat: Middle Eastern condiment and sauce, a mixture of finely ground spices often used to season lamb, fish, chicken, beef, and soups (Arabic)

Balagan: mess (Hebrew; originally from Russian)

Bar/Bat Mitzvah: a religious ceremony at age thirteen, celebrating the coming of age of a Jewish child

B'diyuk: precisely (Hebrew)

Bezoona: cat (Judeo-Arabic; Iraqi Arabic)

Bubbeleh: "darling," "dear" (Yiddish)

Even shehorah: black stone (Hebrew), mentioned in Copper Scroll. See *pierre noir.*

Frum: religiously observant (Yiddish)

Frumkeit: Orthodox religious observance (Yiddish)

Frummie: Derogatory term for observant Jew (Yiddish slang)

Gan: literally, garden. In modern Israeli Hebrew, also refers to pre-school and/or kindergarten (Hebrew)

Goy/goyim: non-Jew (Hebrew/Yiddish; in Biblical Hebrew, the word means "nation" or "people")

Habibi: sweetie, darling (Hebrew, masc); the feminine is *havivati.* Among Arabic speakers, the feminine is *habibti.*

Hasid/Hasidim: followers of the ecstatic Jewish movement founded by the Baal Shem Tov in the 18th century and continuing to this day through dynasties associated with various rabbis

Haver: friend. *Haveri*, my friend. (Hebrew)

Hutzpah: audacity, nerve (Hebrew)

IAA: Israel Antiquities Authority

IDF: Israel Defense Forces, the Israel military

Ima: Mother (Hebrew)

Jeddah: Grandmother (Arabic)

Kabbalah: Jewish mysticism (Hebrew)

Khet: eighth letter of the Hebrew alphabet, pronounced like the "ch" in Bach

Khirbet: ruin (Arabic); often used to designate an archaeological site

Kibbutz: an Israeli cooperative community. (Hebrew)

Kippah: yarmulke, skullcap (Hebrew)

Kochalit: the place where the Treasure Scroll was supposedly buried

Kollel: Jewish study institute for adult men

Lag BaOmer: literally, the 33rd day of [counting] the Omer, the forty-nine day period between Passover and Shavuot

Mikveh: Jewish ritual bath (Hebrew)

Mitzvah/mitzvot: religious obligation, according to traditional Jewish law; in popular usage, a good deed (Hebrew)

Mizrachi: Jews who originate from North Africa and the Middle East (Hebrew)

Motek: sweetheart, sweetie (Hebrew)

Palla: Roman cloak worn by women, and also used as blanket; could also be made of silk, with gold thread, embroidery, and dyed various colors

Pierre noir: black stone (French); see *even shehorah*.

PI: private investigator

Protokollon: the first sheet of a papyrus roll bearing the date of its composition. In some instances, it consisted of a flyleaf that was glued to the outside of a manuscript's case and provided a description of its contents. From the Greek prefix *prōto* ("first") and the noun "kolla" ("glue"). Origin of English word, "protocol."

Qumran: modern name of Secacah

Rosh: wild hemlock (Hebrew); sometimes translated as "gall."

Saba: Grandfather (Hebrew)

Sabra: native-born Israeli, named after the prickly pear cactus, which is thorny on the outside but sweet on the inside. (Hebrew)

Salt Sea: ancient name for the Dead Sea (in Hebrew, *yam ha-melach*)

S'chug: hot sauce from Yemen, made of chilis and spices

Secacah: ancient name for Qumran

Shafan/Shafani: rabbit (Hebrew)

Shanda: shame (Yiddish); often shorthand for the phrase, "*a shanda far di goyim,*" literally, "a shame for the non-Jews," expressing the sense of being embarrassed about how Jews behave and are perceived by non-Jews

Shiva: the seven days of mourning following a Jewish funeral (Hebrew)

Shlumpy: sloppy or dowdy (Yiddish)

Shuk: open-air market (Arabic)

Sukkot: Jewish Festival of Tabernacles, celebrated in the fall

Yalla: onward; let's go! (Arabic)

Yeshivah: Jewish academy or school, traditionally for Jewish boys and men; in modern times, some of these are co-ed

Yeshivah bachur: literally, "study-house young man" (Hebrew and Yiddish); someone who spends most of his time studying in a Jewish religious institution

Za'atar: hyssop, used as spice in food

Postscript

THE EVENTS AND CHARACTERS IN *The Deadly Scrolls* are for the most part imagined. But many of the particulars animating its ancient and modern worlds are real. In this brief postscript, I will attempt to separate fact from fiction. But the reader should know that such a boundary is always permeable.

The first century of the Common Era, when most of the events recounted in Mariamne's scroll take place, was a particularly tumultuous period in Jewish history. The powerful Roman Empire ruled the land of Israel, forcing upon its people laws, taxes, and divergent cultural norms. Within the Jewish community itself, various interpretations and practices vied for dominance or mere legitimacy. Among these factions were the aristocratic Sadducees, the more plebian Pharisees (forerunners of the Rabbis of the Mishnah and Talmud), the militant Zealots, the cutthroat Sicarii, the ascetic Essenes, and the new sect of Jewish Christians. Rome itself fostered syncretism among its citizens, cross-fertilizing its widespread domains with seeds from many religions and cultures. Judaism was not impervious to such syncretic influences.

The time frame for Mariamne's account—the decade between 65 CE to 75 CE—was an especially significant moment in Israel's history. In 66, the Jews in the Galilee rose up in revolt against their Roman overseers, sparking a war that devastated most of Jewish Galilee. This was the beginning of the end of Jewish sovereignty in the land. In 68, the Roman army destroyed the settlement of Secacah/Qumran. By the year 70, Jerusalem and its Holy Temple lay in ruins, and most of the Jewish population was in exile. Jews took their final stand at Masada, where they reaped a pyrrhic victory in '73.

This historical period was significant in another way. This was the time when the official Jewish canon was winnowed from the vast Jewish library extant at that time. This sacred canon of twenty-four authorized Jewish books became known as the TaNaKh or the Hebrew Bible. Christians would rename this anthology of Jewish books the "Old Testament" and would add a "New Testament" as its purported successor. Many more ancient Jewish works remained *outside* the authorized canon than were ultimately included in it.

When some of these extra-canonical works were discovered in the Judean Desert in 1947, this lost Jewish library became known as the Dead Sea Scrolls. To date, almost 1,000 full and partial scrolls have been found in and around Qumran, including copies of almost all the books of the Hebrew Bible, many unknown extra-canonical works, and a collection of sectarian works unique to the Yachad, the community of Jewish ascetics, who lived at Qumran and scribed the Dead Sea Scrolls. The apocalyptic pronouncements uttered by the Examiner and Pinkas Mashiak in my novel are direct quotations from some of these sectarian works.

The Copper Scroll, which is at the center of *The Deadly Scrolls*, is a real document, discovered in 1952 in Cave 3 at Qumran. The details of its discovery, contents, and disposition recounted in my novel are historically accurate. The many theories about the meaning of the scroll's final line, the precise location of Kochalit, the existence and function of the Protokollon are also real, but I have taken considerable liberties in attributing certain theories to specific characters. Boaz Goldmayer, Stanley Lowenthal, Adam Lowenthal, and Father Antoine de Plessy are fictional composites of various scholars in the field. Father Roland De Vaux and Albert Wolters (Cf. "The Last Treasure of the Copper Scroll," *Journal of Biblical Literature* 107/3, 1988, 419-429) and their scholarship are real. However, De Vaux's notes are today archived at the École Biblique, not at the Shrine of the Book.

The Mariamne Scroll is entirely fabricated, although most of the historical events depicted in this scroll actually took place. The more intimate details of daily life in Second Temple Israel described in Mariamne's account are based on the extensive scholarship and archaeological discoveries available about this period. To date, no document written by a Jewish woman from this period has ever been found.

Even though two millennia separate them, first and twenty-first century Israel bear remarkable similarities. Then and now religious sectarianism, zealotry, and ferment rile Jerusalem. Then and now beliefs about an imminent apocalypse, the coming of the Messiah, and a doomsday war attract many adherents among both Christians and Jews. Although religious fanaticism wasn't called "Jerusalem Syndrome" in ancient times, something very much like it infected many Jews and non-Jews in ancient times, just as it does today.

Many Christian evangelical groups are active in Israel today. So are several Jewish groups who are preparing for the renewal of the ancient priestly cult in a future Third Temple. Although the Liberators of the Temple Mount (LTM) is a fictional group, it is based on similar millennialist organizations that are active in contemporary Israel, especially in Jerusalem. The Temple Mount Movement, driven by those who seek to disrupt the precarious status quo on the Temple Mount, still keeps Israeli and Muslim authorities awake at night.

It's sometimes difficult to invent plots more fantastic than what passes for reality in modern-day Israel. I often found myself ripping details for my story straight from the headlines. Although Mashiak's plot to bomb the Dome of the Rock is fictional, there have been other such plots, fortunately foiled by the Waqf and the Israelis. The plots that Maya discovers in her research all happened.

The Zion Gate Hotel and the Twelve Tribes Pub are fictional. I have taken great liberties depicting the Service, the Israeli Antiquities Authority, the Jerusalem District Police, and the Israeli Tourist Bureau, although I've based my portraits on real Israeli institutions and organizations. All mistakes and misrepresentations are mine. The Western Wall Tunnels and Ahar Kotleinu Hall exist.

Ever since they were discovered by Bedouin shepherd boys in 1947, the Dead Sea Scrolls have been a flashpoint of controversy. Their provenance, ownership, handling, and interpretation have roiled scholars, clergy, governments, and the media. The scrolls have frequently made headlines, giving rise to stories of cloak-and-dagger retrieval operations, alleged hoaxes, expensive litigation, and competing territorial claims. I've tried to capture this *balagan* (Yiddish: mess, chaos, circus) without risking a libel suit. (For readers interested in exploring the colorful politics of Dead Sea Scroll scholarship, I recommend reading *The Dead Sea Scrolls Deception* by Michael Baigent and Richard Leigh.)

The Copper Scroll today resides in the Jordan Museum in Amman. Despite continuing efforts by archaeologists and treasure hunters to find the missing Temple treasures and the lost duplicate scroll mentioned in the scroll's final line, they remain hidden. Both the ancient site of Kochalit and the archaeological dig known as Khirbet al-Tajmil are entirely figments of my imagination.

Most of the characters populating Mariamne's world are fictional, though based on historical prototypes. However, a number of ancient characters are real: King Agrippa II; the Caesars and Roman military commanders, and the Jewish historian Josephus.

All of the modern characters, with the exception of Roland De Vaux and Albert Wolters (mentioned above), are my own invention. Any resemblance to real people, living or dead, is purely coincidental.

A Note about Language and Terminology

I have chosen to include a number of untranslated foreign words from Hebrew, Yiddish, Russian, and Arabic. Almost from its beginning, Israel has been a multilingual society. In Mariamne's time, Jews in the north of Israel spoke Aramaic, the language spoken by Jesus. But Jews in the south, including Jerusalem, continued to speak Hebrew. Hellenized Jews spoke both the local vernacular and Greek. In Israel today, although Hebrew is the dominant language, significant minorities speak Yiddish as well as other Jewish dialects, English, Arabic, and Russian. My decision to include a few foreign words in my book honors this multilingual reality. I've included a Glossary of foreign words and expressions as well.

The Jewish community uses a different calendar than the Gregorian, dating back almost six thousand years. I have substituted the abbreviations BCE ("before the Common Era") and CE ("Common Era") for the more familiar BC ("before Christ") and AD (Anno Domini, "the year of our Lord").

Selected Bibliography

I consulted many books, articles, people, and online resources while writing this book. I'd like to single out a few that were particularly helpful.

I learned a great deal about the Jewish Wars in first century Israel from the writings of the Jewish historian Josephus. Shaye Cohen's *Josephus in Galilee and Rome* provided rich context about Roman Israel. Jodi Magness's superbly illustrated *The Archaeology of Qumran and the Dead Sea Scrolls* (Erdmann's, 2002) helped me find my way through Secacah and Qumran. I am indebted to the scholarship of Tal Ilan for insights about the role of women in Second Temple Judaism, especially in the Qumran community.

I learned an immense amount about the Dead Sea Scrolls from Lawrence Schiffman's book, *Reclaiming the Dead Sea Scrolls* (JPS, 1994). John Allegro's *The Treasure of the Copper Scroll* as well as books by Israel Knohl, Robert Feather, Neil Silberman, Kyle McCarter, and others gave me invaluable background on this fascinating Qumran document. I also benefited from working on a massive JPS project that I launched in 2000, finally published in 2013 as *Outside the Bible*. Edited by James Kugel, Louis Feldman z"l, and Larry Schiffman, this three-volume, three-thousand page collection represents the most complete collection of extra-canonical and Qumran texts written by Jews in the Second Temple period. It took twenty years and seventy-five scholars on five continents to prepare this extensively annotated lost library of Second Temple Judaism.

My ideas about Christian fundamentalism and Christian Zionism were greatly enriched by my reading of Vendyl Jones's *A Door of Hope: My Search for the Treasures of the Copper Scroll.* John Hagee's 2013 book, *Four Blood Moons: Something is About to Change*, taught me everything I wanted to know about blood moons. Gershom Gorenberg's *The End of Days: Fundamentalism and the Struggle for the Temple Mount* (2002) provided crucial background about Christian, Jewish, and Muslim struggles over this religious shrine. Motti Friedman's *The Aleppo Codex* served as a good model for blending spycraft and scholarship. Several novels focused on the Dead Sea Scrolls—Eliette Abécassis's *Qumran*, Joel Rosenberg's *The Copper Scroll*, and Nathaniel Weinreb's *The Copper Scrolls*—inspired me to try my own fictional version.

Acknowledgments

THIS BOOK BEGAN EIGHT YEARS ago on a rented pontoon boat on a quiet lake in Maine. While out cruising with my children and grandchildren, I received a call on my cell phone from Professor Lawrence Schiffman, a renowned Dead Sea Scrolls scholar, whose book, *Reclaiming the Dead Sea Scrolls*, I had edited and published twenty years before at The Jewish Publication Society when I was Editor-in-Chief.

After a brief exchange of small talk, Larry said to me: "There ought to be a novel about Qumran and the Dead Sea Scrolls, but I can't write fiction."

Despite this candid disclaimer, he then proceeded to outline the plot and subplots of the novel he couldn't write. Taking his comments as an invitation to work together, I suggested we try writing such a novel together. But after a few years of lively collaboration, we had to concede that our writing agendas were too different: disseminating research versus spinning a good yarn. So we amicably agreed to end our collaboration, and Larry gave me his blessing to continue spinning my yarn.

Many people helped teach me how to write a mystery.

I benefited greatly from Elizabeth George's *Write Away*, a detailed operating manual to her own craft. And I also owe a great debt to my writing coach, Greg Truman, who guided me through many drafts, schooling me in the strategic use of reveals, subplots, pacing, and suspense. I also owe thanks to Lois de la Haba, who referred me to Greg, and who encouraged me over the long haul.

This novel floats on an iceberg of research (most of which mercifully remains below the surface). My expert sources were Larry Schiffman, who pointed me toward other scholars as well as providing an extensive bibliography; Elizabeth Bloch-Smith, whose archaeological experience helped me imagine Kochalit and Khirbet al-Tajmil; Ilan Tal, Jodi Magness, James Vanderkamm, Hershel Shanks z"l, and the websites of Qumran National Park, the Temple Mount, and the Temple Institute.

Many friends contributed to this project. I'd like to thank my cousin Robert Kenyon, for suggesting the evocative title; David Brinn, for reading an early draft and providing details about life in contemporary Jerusalem; Ellen Steiker, for asking me to include food and restaurant fare whenever possible; the staff of the Trolley Car Diner, z"l, who didn't mind serving me breakfast for four to six hours every Wednesday for several years as I wrote this novel; and Helen Feinberg, Bob Hansen, Debbie Aron, Geanne Zelkowitz, Edna Berg, Rivkah Walton, Larry Hastings, Bob Stecker, and Herb Levine, who read and critiqued various drafts.

The folks at Wicked Son Press and its parent house, Post Hill Press, provided wonderful support, especially Wicked Son founders, Adam Bellow and David Bernstein, whose enthusiasm, trust, and collaborative style made preparing the novel such a joy. I'd also like to thank managing editor Aleigha Kely and publicists Devon Brown and Hannah Schaeffer for their professionalism, encouragement, and responsiveness. Thanks to Glen Pawelski, project manager at Mapping Specialists, Ltd, for the customized maps.

Thank you to my family—Les and Nicole, Sarah and Liz, and our three grandgirls, Riley, Teagan, and Finley—for their steadfast faith in me. I know that you never thought I'd finish, but as my friend Rachel always says: *Az men lebt, derlebt men.* "If you live long enough, you see surprising things."

Most of all, I want to acknowledge the unflagging support and generous counsel I received from my life partner and writing buddy, Herb Levine. Whenever I was ready to give up, he pushed me on. His insightful input on the manuscript, marketing plans, reader outreach, and book group questions have proved invaluable. He's been a boon companion on this long pilgrimage to publication.

Questions for Book Groups
Reading *The Deadly Scrolls*

IN PREPARING FOR YOUR BOOK group discussion on The Deadly Scrolls, we strongly suggest that all participants read the author's postscript.

1. Talk about Maya Rimon, the book's protagonist. What do you admire about her? What do you fault her for? Do you wish she had ended up with Hillel Stone? Would you like to read another book in which she appears?

2. During the course of the novel, Maya is informed about the historical background to this story by both Hillel and by her research on the internet. Did you enjoy learning about a different historical period as you read this mystery-thriller? Which part of that history remains most vivid to you?

3. One of the central themes in the book is messianism, the belief that an individual will appear to redeem the world and usher in a new phase of time. What does the author see as the danger of such beliefs?

4. A word that recurs throughout the book is "zealotry" and its complement, "zeal." How do you define zeal or zealotry? How does the book illustrate its dangers?

5. In her postscript, Frankel points out some parallels she finds between the first century CE, Mariamne's time, and the time of

the novel, Maya's time. Which of these parallels occurred to you while you were reading the novel?

6. This book has four "detectives": Maya, Sarit, Hillel, and Cassandra? What does it add to the book to have so many angles of approach to the mystery?

7. Reflect further on the character, Cassandra. Why does the author give her that name? Why do you think Mariamne inspires Cassandra so much?

8. Have you ever been to Jerusalem? Do you think that the experience of "Jerusalem Syndrome" portrayed in the novel is plausible? Talk about how the Jerusalem landscapes portrayed in the novel contributed to your enjoyment of the book.

9. Did you use the glossary of foreign words: a) while you were reading the novel? b) primarily after reading? c) not at all? Did this multilingual aspect of the book add to or detract from your appreciation of it?

10. Have you encountered the abbreviations BCE ("before the Common Era") and CE ("Common Era") before? Does it matter which ones you use?